P9-DHF-372

3 2503 13807 9012

PRAISE FOR

Modern Girls

"Brown pens the story of a Jewish immigrant mother and her unmarried daughter, both pregnant and neither planning on it, in 1930s New York City. The result is a thought-provoking tale of parents and children and the sacrifices they make for one another. Exploring our dreams and choices and the way they intersect to form our lives, *Modern Girls* is a heartwarming, haunting, and memorable debut."

—Pam Jenoff, international bestselling author of
The Last Summer at Chelsea Beach

"Be prepared to lose yourself in a mother-daughter tale unlike any other. With one generation entrenched in the Old World and the other struggling to make her way in the new, Brown expertly handles the complex nuances of family secrets guarded along with impossible choices made in the name of love and honor. Original and unique, you'll find yourself rooting for Dottie and Rose the whole way through."   —Renée Rosen, author of *White Collar Girl*

Modern Girls

JENNIFER S. BROWN

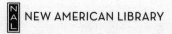 NEW AMERICAN LIBRARY

NEW AMERICAN LIBRARY
Published by New American Library,
an imprint of Penguin Random House LLC
375 Hudson Street, New York, New York 10014

This book is an original publication of New American Library.

First Printing, April 2016

Copyright © Jennifer S. Brown, 2016
Readers Guide copyright © Penguin Random House, 2016
The author is grateful for permission to quote from "As we understand it, Goering and Goebbels are Hitler's
G-Men. Their job is to stamp out the pernicious churchgoing element" from August 17, 1935, *The New
Yorker*, page 24, from "Of All Things" by Howard Brubaker/*The New Yorker*, copyright © Condé Nast.
Penguin Random House supports copyright. Copyright fuels creativity, encourages diverse voices,
promotes free speech, and creates a vibrant culture. Thank you for buying an authorized edition of this
book and for complying with copyright laws by not reproducing, scanning, or distributing any part of it
in any form without permission. You are supporting writers and allowing Penguin Random House to
continue to publish books for every reader.

New American Library and the New American Library colophon are registered trademarks
of Penguin Random House LLC.

For more information about Penguin Random House, visit penguin.com.

LIBRARY OF CONGRESS CATALOGING-IN-PUBLICATION DATA:
Names: Brown, Jennifer S. (Jennifer Sue), 1968–
Title: Modern girls/Jennifer S. Brown.
Description: New York, New York: New American Library, 2016.
Identifiers: LCCN 2015041939 (print) | LCCN 2015050012 (ebook) | ISBN
9780451477125 (paperback) | ISBN 9780698408524 (ebook)
Subjects: LCSH: Mothers and daughters—Fiction. | Jewish women—Fiction. | Life-change events—
Fiction. | Choice (Psychology)—Fiction. | Jewish fiction. | Psychological fiction. | BISAC: FICTION/
Historical. | FICTION/Jewish. | FICTION/Cultural Heritage.
Classification: LCC PS3602.R6987 M63 2016 (print) | LCC PS3602.R6987 (ebook) | DDC 813/.6—dc23
LC record available at http://lccn.loc.gov/2015041939

Printed in the United States of America
10 9 8 7 6 5 4 3 2 1

Designed by Tiffany Estreicher

PUBLISHER'S NOTE
This is a work of fiction. Names, characters, places, and incidents either are the product of the author's
imagination or are used fictitiously, and any resemblance to actual persons, living or dead, business
establishments, events, or locales is entirely coincidental.

Penguin
Random
House

In memory of my grandparents, Bessie and Nathan Brown,
who taught me that being a writer was a worthy aspiration,
and for my parents, Peter and Carol K. Brown,
who encouraged me to write even before I had anything to say

Modern Girls

Dottie

⚘

MY lower back ached as I sat, shoulders rounded, hunched over like a number 9, on the wooden stool at my desk at Dover Insurance. I shifted my bottom, unable to find a comfortable position, as I picked up the statement atop the stack. I didn't feel right: I had no fever, but my stomach sloshed and I needed another couple hours of sleep. The digits, though, drew me in, and I became absorbed in the dance of the numbers, the way they could come together and apart, making wonderful new combinations.

I didn't initially notice the new girl standing over my desk. "Dottie," she said, prompting me to look up. "Mr. Dover said to ask you if I had problems." She thrust her ledger under my nose. "The totals aren't matching up."

I scanned the column, my eye drawn instantly to the error. "Here," I said, pointing. "You've added the debits instead of subtracting." My eye ran up and down the page again, and, handing her back the book, I said, "The total should be $1,365.43."

She looked at the paper in her other hand, which listed the number she was supposed to match, and looked back at me wide-eyed. "How did you do that?"

I shrugged and she stared at me, bewildered, before walking away. I could calculate as fast as the tabulating machine. The skill was so natural that I was always surprised when others couldn't do it.

I turned back to my statement. The numbers were a relief because the rest of my brain was stuffed with cotton balls. *What was wrong with me?* Even before work, the morning had begun inauspiciously. When I attempted to fasten my brand-new dress—the dress that Ma had spent two evenings refashioning so it looked like it came from the pages of *McCall's* instead of the racks at Ohrbach's—the back zipper stuck. Pulling off the dress, I could slide the zipper up and down just fine, but when I glided the fabric over my head again, it bunched gracelessly at the waist, and I needed to suck in my stomach as far as it would go. I made Alfie tug the pull closed. "Lay off the egg creams," he'd said, unhappy at having to help his big sister get dressed. My body filled the fabric oddly, my bosom spilling out the top. Then, at breakfast, my bloated fingers were clumsy, and Ma scolded me when a glass slipped from my hand. I picked at the farina, which lay in a congealed blob in the bowl, then slid the dish over to my youngest brother, Eugene, who gobbled it down, but not before Ma spotted us. "My food isn't good enough for your Midtown ways?" Ma said, and yet, she hurried me to the door: "Don't be late for work."

Trying to shake the fog from my mind, I copied numbers from the statements to the ledger. Mr. Renke submitted a quarterly premium of $11.82 for his accident insurance policy, which guaranteed $100 a month for up to twenty-four months should he become disabled due to an automobile accident, a calamity in an elevator, a wall collapsing, or any of the other misfortunes that might befall him. The numbers shimmied in my head, and while I double-checked the totals on the machine as my job required, I had no doubt they were correct. Math is so simple: A plus B always equals C.

Numbers comforted me, soothed me. They were absolute, unequivocal, the opposite of what I was feeling at that moment. Taking a deep breath, I put down my pen and looked toward the high windows. The sliver of sky visible was devoid of clouds, just a wash of blue. A breeze from the fan in the corner ruffled my papers, and I put a hand atop them to keep them from flying away.

My dress constricted my stomach, making me squirm, which embarrassed me. I was no longer a schoolchild, but a mature woman of nineteen, and I certainly knew how to conduct myself in my place of work, which didn't entail flopping in my seat like a marionette. Would I have to start reducing? Zelda did the grapefruit diet after having her baby, but Ma would never let me get away with that. Ma always tried to fatten me up even though this wasn't the Old Country, where a woman was prized for a bit of flesh around the waist. This was New York City and all I wanted was to look like Claudette Colbert. My boyfriend, Abe, was dreamy—strong arms and devilishly handsome chocolate brown eyes—and while he thought I was beautiful no matter what, I didn't want to test that by plumping up like a matzo ball in broth.

The next statement: Mr. Norquist paid $12.65, the monthly premium on his $3,000 life insurance policy. I flipped to the correct page in my ledger, found the column, and entered it. Three thousand dollars. What couldn't I do if I had $3,000? Abe and I would be able to afford not only to marry and rent an apartment, but to furnish it with the finest trousseau out of *House & Garden*, and I would have no worries and a wardrobe from Saks.

My eyes skated over the room, watching the girls at work. Irene, as tiny as my seven-year-old brother, Eugene, typed letters to those delinquent on their payments. Florence dawdled, inputting numbers as I did, although three times more slowly, her pen looping in lazy circles. The other girls worked diligently, if not always precisely, only occasionally glancing at the clock or daydreaming while looking out the window. Our head bookkeeper, Mr. Herbert, had quit a week before, so an idle loll enveloped the room, and the tabulating machines weren't clacking as quickly as they normally did.

I picked up the next statement and tried to revel in the numbers, in the slippery feel of a *three*, the kiss of a *two*, the hiss of a *six*. But I was so aware of my body, of the way it filled my dress; I couldn't get comfortable.

Irene passed my desk as I pulled the fabric from my waist, trying to stretch it out a bit.

"Are you feeling all right?" she whispered. In the quiet room, though, her voice echoed. None of the other girls paid any mind.

"I'm just feeling out of sorts," I said, trying discreetly to pull up my stockings a bit. "I don't know why."

"Maybe it's your time," she whispered even lower.

"My what?" I asked, in a normal voice.

Irene's face washed in a warm blush. Leaning into me, she spoke into my ear. "You know. Your monthly."

I nodded. "Perhaps."

Irene set down the papers on Mr. Herbert's former desk and returned to her own.

That must be it, I thought. My monthly. I scooted the papers aside and looked at the calendar blotter on my desk. When was the last time I'd had my courses? Was I due?

My pen idly swirled in the air above the numbers. It was August 16. *Let's see. . . .* I didn't recall having it in July, but skipping a month wasn't unusual.

The pen froze.

But what about June? Did I have it in June?

Beads of perspiration formed on my forehead. I looked up and around the room to see if anyone noticed the consternation that must have shown on my face, but all the girls were involved in their own work, their own daydreams. What did I do in June? Abe and I went to the theater twice and the café once. We picnicked in the park with Linda and Ralph. We swam and played baseball at Camp Eden. *Think, Dottie, think!* No. Not once did I need to excuse myself to take care of things.

Returning to the calendar, I stared. June was clean.

I chewed on the end of the pen hard enough that I cracked the celluloid. My brain flew frantically back in time, back to

May, back to the one weekend I *hadn't* been with Abe. That was
May 24. I counted. May 24 to August 16. Eighty-four days. Twelve
weeks. The bloated fingers. The burgeoning bosom. My choking
waist. May 24. And since then, not a sign of my courses.

Act normal, I told myself, picking up the next form. If need
be, I could work by rote. Copy numbers from statement into ledger. Add the credits. Subtract the debits. My hands made the
motions while my mind desperately sought to make reason. One
night. That's all it had been: one night. A fight between me and
Abe. A night alone at Cold Spring. But then, I hadn't exactly been
alone, had I? If I had, I wouldn't be haunted by that night. I tried
to take breaths to calm myself. My hand was quivering, causing
droplets of ink to splatter on the desk. I set the pen in the inkwell
and placed my palms flat on the surface to steady them.

Slowly exhaling, I sat frozen, until my body settled. The most
important thing was to act normally. The stack of papers on my
desk was finished. My reputation as a worker meant standing up
and moving to Mr. Herbert's former desk to retrieve another stack.

After scooping up new papers, I turned to go back to my
desk, self-consciously placing my hand over my belly, as if to
shield it, even as I knew there was nothing to be seen. I caught
Florence's eye. She looked at the papers in my hands and rolled
her eyes. She used to tell me to slow down; my work was going
to make the rest of them look bad. I tried at first—I wanted Florence and her girls to like me—but I soon realized Florence was
never going to be friends with the Jew in the office, and to work
slowly was boring. My cheeks flushed, and I was sure Florence
could see behind the papers, could read my secret as easily as I
read the numbers. I felt exposed, humiliated.

My mind raced: Had it really been twelve weeks? I was careless in my counting of days, irregular in my time. Nothing unusual. *But twelve weeks?* Even I should have noticed that by now.
And what would I tell Abe?

Sitting back at my table, I vowed to get through as many

statements as I could before the lunch bell chimed. I needed the reliability, the honesty of the numbers.

I let myself drown in numbers—premiums for accident insurance, life insurance, fire insurance: $12.34, $7.56, $27.92. The minute my mind wandered from the ledgers, I forced it back: $34.23, $7.91, $43.34. So lost was I that I missed the ringing of the bell and didn't realize it was noon until the babble of the girls' chatter broke my concentration. They gathered their clutches and hats to go out for food as I sat dumbly at my desk. I never accompanied them, but I longed to today, anything to keep these thoughts from my mind. But going out to lunch with them was an impossibility. The girls thought me cheap, chalked it up to my being a Jew. I always said to them, if I had an extra forty cents, it would look so much nicer as a hat on my head than a meal I'd forget in an hour. The truth, though, was the food around the Midtown office was all *treif*, so Ma packed me a kosher lunch each morning. I was the only girl from the East Side working at Dover—the others were Italians, Irish, and Germans who commuted from Brooklyn and Queens.

I had no desire to eat, but I had to maintain appearances, so I made the motions of pulling out my lunch pail and unwrapping my sandwich. On her way to the door, Florence wrinkled her nose at the food on my desk. "What in heaven's name is that?"

The sandwich looked particularly unappetizing. But I coerced a smile and said, "Pickled calf's tongue."

"Ew. Is that Yid food?" The girls behind her giggled.

"It's scrumptious," I said, keeping the smile plastered on my face. With great show, I picked up the sandwich and took a large bite. "Mmmm," I murmured, trying to sound enthusiastic. Ma's doughy wheat bread stuck to my upper palate, but I managed to give Florence a full-mouthed grin while trying to dislodge the bread stuck on my teeth with my tongue. Normally Ma's sandwiches were delicious, but that day the tongue was slimy and the bread heavy and grainy. I swallowed, the food rebelling on its way down, and said nothing more.

Florence's eyes narrowed, and with a sniff, she turned on her little green ankle-strapped heel, straightened her hat, and left the office, her coterie of coiffed sheep trailing behind. I could hear them bleating down the hall as they headed to the Automat for lunch.

My stomach lurched, so I put down the sandwich, nauseated by the sight of it. I was about to toss it in the wastebasket when the front door of the office opened and Mr. Dover walked in. Florence would be annoyed to have missed him. She—and a number of the other girls—had a thing for the boss.

"Ah, Dorothea," Mr. Dover said, approaching my desk.

"Mr. Dover," I said, nodding my head. Did he notice how my leg trembled?

He spied the food on my desk and said, "Please, don't let me interrupt your lunch."

"No interruption, sir," I said.

"Please. Eat your sandwich. I want to chat, but I'd feel terrible if I disrupted your lunch break." Sitting on a stool, he gave me a paternal smile, as he removed his fedora and placed it on the table beside him.

Feeling trapped, I once again picked up the sandwich and choked down a bite. I gave Mr. Dover a wan grin. Making sure I swallowed completely before speaking, I said, "Delicious." My stomach roared its disapproval.

Mr. Dover chuckled. Perched as he was, he looked oversized. His body didn't fit at the desk that was the right size for the petite Irene. Row after row of tables and stools filled the room. At each table sat a tabulating machine or a typewriter and books with loose-leaf ledger sheets. I often thought we looked like overgrown schoolchildren at our desks, whispering, working, behaving impishly.

"So, Dorothea," Mr. Dover said. His face was handsome, even with the receding hairline. Those chiseled cheeks, deep-set blue eyes. No wonder the girls were mad about him. Of course, he didn't hold a candle to Abe. Besides, Mr. Dover was a *shaygetz*. I could no more fathom mooning over a non-Jew than I could imagine eating a ham sandwich. "You have a talent for numbers, don't you?"

"I do," I said.

Mr. Dover's laugh was deep and sincere. I didn't see the point in false modesty. Since grammar school, I've excelled in mathematics.

"You enjoy working with numbers?" he asked.

"Very much, sir," I said. "If you do the numbers properly, you'll always get the expected outcome." My mind alighted on *May 24* and the expected outcome, the horrific, dreaded outcome. "I find it much less complicated than—well, just about anything else."

"How refreshing to meet a girl who knows her strengths. So many girls try to hide behind ignorance."

I didn't want him to think me unkind, so I didn't point out that for many of these girls, the ignorance wasn't exactly feigned. Instead I said, "I find, sir, there is nothing to be gained from that."

Mr. Dover nodded sagely. He was old—probably a full ten years older than me, making him twenty-nine, maybe even thirty—and he projected an air of confidence that comes from privilege and age. "Are you planning on marrying anytime soon, Dorothea?"

A heat crawled into my cheeks as I considered how to answer him. I tried not to fidget, but I found myself tugging my dress, making sure my knees were more than well covered and my belly was hidden. Could others tell? I wasn't used to discussing such intimate matters with a man with whom I was not well acquainted. Mr. Dover must have sensed my discomfort, as he immediately corrected himself. "What I am given to say is that since Mr. Herbert left, I have been overwhelmed trying to perform the duties of head bookkeeper as well as manage the rest of the affairs of the office. I recognize the superiority of your work, and I would like to offer you the position of head bookkeeper, but I'm afraid you will leave us soon to start a family."

With a flinch, I wondered what he suspected. But no, I realized, he was speaking in generalities. A ray of hope rose through me, an honest smile that couldn't help but bubble to the surface. Was he promoting me?

"I have a beau," I said, "but we are not yet engaged. I would also hope, sir, you would perhaps consider keeping me on even if I do marry."

Getting married, which I had longed for during these past three years in which Abe and I dated, was fast becoming a necessity. May 24 to August 16. How much time did that give me? Could I convince Abe to marry me? Would he pretend the child was his? Even as the picture painted itself in my head, I knew the ridiculousness of it. Abe would no more marry me and have another man's child than he would run for president. He would be humiliated. Abe would despise me if he knew the truth. No, it was essential Abe never find out.

Mr. Dover said, "I'm afraid that would be up to your husband, now, wouldn't it? So how about it? Would you like to be the head bookkeeper? I've interviewed some men for the position, but I have decided you are significantly more qualified."

As he spoke, my mind did the math. How long did I have for Abe to reasonably think the baby was his, just early? A week? Two at the most. How long till my belly protruded, till my shame was declared to the world?

"I should add," Mr. Dover said, "that this comes with a raise. You'd be earning twenty-three dollars and fifty cents a week."

I perked up. Abe and I hadn't married before now because we couldn't afford it. More money meant we could afford a place to live that much sooner and perhaps this would convince him it was finally the time to marry. Trying to hide my excitement, I simply nodded at my boss. I knew I probably wasn't more qualified than the men, just cheaper. Yet this was a substantial raise, and I was pleased. This could be my salvation.

"That's a yes?" Mr. Dover said, a hint of tease in his voice.

"Yes, sir," I said. "Thank you, sir."

"Very good."

Right then the front door to the office opened again, and Florence bounded in, followed by her pals. "Irene, I can't believe you left my clutch behind. You took the lipstick from it and then didn't bother bringing it?"

"Sorry," Irene said.

Florence stopped abruptly when she saw Mr. Dover. "Well, well," she said, her voice suddenly overflowing with syrup. Looking suspiciously at me, she stepped closer to our handsome boss. "Mr. Dover! Fancy seeing you at the tabulation tables. Have you a sudden call to work the numbers yourself?" She tried to bat her eyes seductively, but she merely looked like she had an eyelash caught beneath her lid.

Mr. Dover spread his charm over the women. "As long as you're here, I have good news."

"Oh?" Florence said. She beamed at Mr. Dover, but as he stood and glanced around, she gave me a look full of arsenic.

"I've promoted Dorothea to head bookkeeper. She will take over for Mr. Herbert, so you will all now report directly to her. Dorothea, you may move your belongings to Mr. Herbert's table."

Under the watchful eye of the girls, I gathered my sweater, my purse, and the lunch—which was a little awkward, juggling the sandwich and napkin. Holding them all in front of my stomach, of which I was suddenly so aware, I moved to the head of the room. A single table faced the office, like the teacher's desk in grammar school. Nothing distinguished it except for its location and that it had a chair instead of a stool, and yet, a swell of pride rushed through me as I turned and faced the room, seated in my new location.

Mr. Dover said, "Congratulations, Dorothea, on work well-done. I'm confident we'll see more of the same in the future." He nodded at the girls, and then retreated to his office behind my new post.

The girls stood speechless, looking to Florence for cues on

how to react. Irene timidly said, "Congrats, Dottie. You deserve it," before Florence's narrowed eyes had her sputtering to silence.

With a self-satisfied smile, I ostentatiously glanced at the large ticking hands of the clock on the wall between the windows and said, "You girls better hurry along. Lunch ends in eighteen minutes."

"You haven't eaten much of your sandwich," Florence said. "I knew that Yid food tasted terrible."

With great show, I picked up the sandwich again and took a large bite, the meat flaccid in my mouth, as I pointed to the clock.

With a sharp intake of breath, Florence spun around and strode from the room, the other girls trotting to keep up. How long would it take Florence to realize she still didn't have her clutch?

I sat down, chewing slowly, hoping that would make the sandwich go down easier. I threw back my shoulders, feeling taller somehow from this vantage point. This was my solution. Abe would be proud of my promotion, proud of my raise. And perhaps we could marry—soon!—in time to solve the problem before anyone but me knew it existed.

Yet even the idea of a solution didn't stop my stomach from mutinying completely. Without even thinking, I grabbed the wastebasket next to my desk and crudely unswallowed the contents of my stomach. Tears threatened.

Two weeks. I had only two weeks.

Rose

I couldn't stop sweating. *How many* Shabbeses *have I made in August?* I wondered. If Dottie were here, she'd calculate, without even paper and pencil, the number of August *Shabbeses* I've had in my thirty-nine years. Except she'd be wrong. Because I've seen forty-two years of *Shabbeses*, not thirty-nine. Only Perle— the one who has been by my side since we were in the cradle back home—knows the truth of my age, but Perle can be trusted to take my secret to the grave. The point is that this was not my first August *Shabbes*, but still I suffered so.

The sweat rolled from me like water streaming from a pump. With the dishrag I wiped my forehead before holding the chicken over the gas flame of the stove, just long enough to singe the bird. The smell of the gas stung my nostrils. I leaned toward the window over the kitchen sink, but even the breeze up here on the fourth floor wasn't enough to cut the smothering closeness of the humid air.

With well-practiced hands, I pulled the pinfeathers from the carcass, but wooziness washed through me, so I moved to sit at the small kitchen table. *Kashering* a chicken was no difficult task, but it was important to be meticulous with the required steps; one small nick in the wrong place and the entire chicken would be rendered unkosher, inedible. Preparing chickens for *Shabbes* I've been doing since my hands were large enough to grasp the feathers, and of all the things that changed when I came to America, cooking chickens wasn't one of them. True, here I had a gas stove and a sink with a running tap, a vast improvement over a wood-burning stove and water retrieved from a well. And back home in Russia, there were *Shabbeses* when we had no chicken, but—thank God—they were few and far between.

Why was I so tired? I had my suspicions. Whispered among the women, referred to vaguely, was . . . What did they say? About how a woman's body changed. Her courses stopped coming. And it had been nearly three months since last I had my time. But wasn't forty-two too young for this? Of course that other possibility—the other reason a woman's courses stopped coming—had crossed my mind, but that was ridiculous. Forty-two was definitely too old for *that*.

My leg throbbed more than usual, the old injury flaring even though no cloud was in sight. My leg was as good a barometer as any on a ship at sea. I cut the fowl's nails, sliced off its head, and, turning back the skin at the nape, chopped the neck as close to the body as I could.

A commotion on the street distracted me for a moment, but who had time for such nonsense? I needed to focus on my task. I couldn't afford another chicken if this one wasn't *kashered* properly.

The sweat dripped down the back of my neck, into the collar of my dress. I attempted to wipe away the perspiration, but didn't want the chicken juice to drip into my hair. While bathing would be a proper way to usher in the day of rest, it was a luxury reserved for a less busy day.

My skin itched and the dampness not only cloaked me but seeped within. Trying to disregard my discomfort, I made an incision just below the bird's breastbone. Wrenching my hand inside the hole, I pulled at the fat and entrails until they yanked loose. Yet as my hand freed the greasy viscera, my stomach churned in a familiar way.

How could it be? I'd never heard of digestion troubles as a symptom of a woman's change. They were a symptom of . . . "No!"

I said out loud, before making sure the boys weren't there to hear me. Of course if they were there, they would merely assume I was speaking to them. It was the word I uttered most to my three sons.

Shaking my head to force out unpleasant thoughts, I waited for the feeling to pass. It subsided—a bit—and I fished out the entrails, placing them in a bowl. Deborah went to the new butcher the next block over, who *kashered* the chicken for her, but those chickens were three cents more a pound, and I had better things on which to spend my money. For nineteen years, I'd been keeping a secret stash, tucked in a tea tin at the bottom of my delicates drawer. Whenever I had spare change, it went into that tin. Just this morning, as I dropped a nickel in, I realized I had reached ninety dollars. If I had paid someone else to *kasher* my chickens, my tin would be empty. Besides, how could I trust someone else to *kasher* my meat properly? Some things must be done by oneself.

Looking back at the chicken, I removed the liver from the gall. This was the most delicate step; the gall is not kosher, and if it broke, I wouldn't be able to use the liver. This was one of the most important duties of being a wife, and I had no idea how Dottie was going to manage it when she made her own home with Abe. So many things Dottie never learned. Chasing her father around, looking after her brothers, daydreaming with her fashion magazines. Yet, lack of *kashering* skills aside, Dottie had done well for herself. Working in Midtown, with all those numbers. A bookkeeper was a respectable job. Dottie would do something with her life. It was for her I saved my pennies. But still. A woman also had to know how to keep a home. Although, at the pace Abe moved, there was time to teach her before he proposed.

I dumped the entrails in a pan and covered them with water. These would sit until after *Shabbes*, when I would use them to flavor the stew I would make on Sunday for the coming week. The head I would save to make a soup, but for now, I took the chicken and let it soak so I could sit and enjoy my cup of tea and the morning mail. I had a letter from my brother Yussel I was anxious to read.

This was my only moment to myself, when Ben was at work at the garage, Dottie at her office, and the boys had been shooed off to play. On most mornings, I'd sit at the table, spread open the *Forverts*, the daily Yiddish paper, and consume the news as if it were a morning snack. But when I had a letter from family, it was as if I had a feast.

Using a table knife, I gingerly slit open the envelope, not wanting to rip even a single word. Pulling out the thick sheet of paper, I smiled at the still-childish scrawl in which my baby brother wrote. The Yiddish lines slanted downward, as if trying to escape the page. No one would know, looking at this writing, that Yussel was a learned man of thirty-three years. A glance at the top told me the letter was written less than three weeks ago. The mail moved quickly these days.

"Dearest sister," the letter began. "At the outset I can write you that Gerda, the children, and I are healthy, and we are hoping to hear good things from you and to see each other in good health. I received your letter Friday morning and read with pleasure that you are well. I am pleased to hear of your work with the Women's Committee of the Socialist Party, a worthy cause to support. But I beg of you, please do not worry so for us."

Yussel wasted too much time on pleasantries. I brushed my hand across the creases of the paper, trying to make the words easier to read, but the sweat on my arm blurred the ink. Alarmed, I blotted the page and dried myself on the kitchen cloth. The letter continued: "Tensions are building between the Free City of Danzig and Poland over Danzig's seeming embrace of Germany, but so far it has no effect on us Jews. The Poles are only interested in the Poles. If anything, I'm profiting from the politics, as my business is flourishing with the new demand for photos for identity cards. My studio is so busy that I have taken on a second apprentice."

Was Yussel telling the truth? Or shielding me from his hardships? Even the American newspapers reported on the Poles' discrimination against the Jews. Frustratingly, though I am the elder, Yussel tries to protect me, and it was clear my brother needed to get out of Poland. It was no better than Russia, although at least in Poland no one was trying to conscript him. Warsaw had always been meant as a temporary stop, on the way to the port in Danzig. In 1924, Yussel had saved enough money to bribe Russian officials for a passport, yet he arrived in Poland only to discover that the United States had closed: No visas were being issued to Jews. So he settled in Warsaw. Married. Had a son and two daughters. And he waited.

"We hear alarming news from Gerda's relations in Munich, and they are working with the relief organizations to leave. Priority is being given to the Jews fleeing Germany. Perhaps if we had settled there instead of Warsaw, we would have better luck obtaining visas. I have been in contact with—" My attention was diverted by the pounding of feet on the stairs leading to the apartment. I recognized the lumbering footfalls of Alfie and the gentler ones of Eugene trailing behind. *Just ten minutes,* I pleaded to no one in particular. *Continue on up to the roof and give me ten minutes of peace.*

But who gives a mother peace? The steps stopped and the door opened so forcefully it banged against the wall behind it.

"You need to slam the door so?" I bellowed to Alfie in Yiddish.

"Ma," he called back.

"Wipe your feet. Don't go bringing the street into the house." The way we yelled at each other, you'd think we lived in a Park Avenue mansion, and not the two-bedroom apartment that was about as big as a streetcar. My eyes didn't leave the letter, though. I read, "I have been in contact with the HIAS representative and he believes a visa to Cuba is attainable. Luckily between the studio, the money from Gerda selling eggs, plus what the children bring in, we have plenty to soothe officials who may be less than eager to grant us papers."

Alfie came into the kitchen. "Ma, I need two cents to buy the paper," he said in English. Eugene trailed behind him, his eyes half-hidden by his cap, not that he ever looked folks in the eye. That boy. As shy as a bride on her wedding night.

"There's a paper on the dining table." It irritated me that my younger boys refused to speak in our own language. My English was fine—I understood everything said to me—but I preferred to use my mother tongue, and I wished my children had the courtesy to respond to me in Yiddish.

"Yitzak has gone to *yeshiva*," Yussel wrote, "fulfilling the dreams of Mama, may her memory be a blessing. God willing, we will be far from Hitler and the insanity of Poland soon. Write, dear sister, as soon as you can, if you haven't written until now. Be healthy, both you and yours. From me, your eternally devoted brother, Yussel."

Alfie hopped a few steps to the next room, before saying, "Not the *Yiddish* paper, Ma. I need the *Herald Tribune*." Coming back to the kitchen, he pulled at my sleeve and pointed to the kitchen window. "Don'tcha hear 'em?"

With an exasperated sigh, I set the letter down. I would reread it five more times today, trying to understand the meaning behind the words. But now, I gave my attention to my boys. Tilting my head slightly, I let myself tune in to the noise of the street, the noise I had been trying to ignore. It rang out clearly. The newsboy called, "Extra, extra! Will Rogers and Wiley Post killed at Point Barrow! Extra, extra!" His voice grew louder and softer as he walked closer to and then farther from the apartment on his march up and down the block. I groaned as I heaved myself from the table, my leg twitching in pain as I hobbled to the window. It wasn't easy to see through the blackened glass—how many times had I scrubbed the bottom clean only to have it clouded over with dust and ash before I'd finished the top pane?—but looking down, I couldn't miss the flood of children.

"Your father will have an English paper when he gets home," I said, distracted by the children who were pouring out of doors, tumbling down steps, and running through the streets to hear the news. All those children and my leg was throbbing and the chicken entrails, soaking beneath my nose, made my stomach seethe.

"Ma, I can't wait," Alfie said.

Eugene piped up behind him. "It's Will Rogers, Ma. Will Rogers! And he's dead."

Some actor who wouldn't have known these boys from Adam dies and they're all up in arms? Will Rogers. *Feh.*

But all those children. Swarming. Massing in the road. Children everywhere. Every apartment on Tenth Street housed throngs of children. In my own house, there were four. Seven-year-old Eugene. Nineteen-year-old Dottie. Izzy at seventeen. And ten-year-old Alfie. Oh, Alfie. Joey would have been ten as well but . . .

The sounds echoed through the street and the children scampered about. No doubt the children outnumbered the adults.

The roiling in my stomach threatened to erupt, and I was grateful I hadn't eaten yet, that there was nothing to return. That nausea that was so familiar and so unwelcome. Despair settled over me. *Please*, Hashem, *let this be my change.* Seeing all those children brought a deluge of unwelcome thoughts. Thoughts of Joey; thoughts of Yussel—who was a twelve-year-old boy last I saw him—trapped in Europe; thoughts of what this sickness I was experiencing might be.

The voice of the newsboy faded as he made his way down the street again, pausing at each newly outstretched hand.

All those children.

"Are you crying?" Alfie asked, his voice tinged more with fear than with concern.

Raising my hand to my cheek, I realized it was indeed wet.

"It's okay, Ma," Eugene said, always anxious at anyone's distress. "You won't be sad about Will Rogers forever. This too shall pass."

I wanted to smile, but I couldn't force my lips to move. My baby quoting back to me what I often said to the children. *This too shall pass.* It worked for scrapes and frights and playground injustices. It was a lie that was easy to believe when you were a child. But as an adult, I well knew some things hurt for a lifetime.

Pulling up my apron, I wiped my face. "Just some sweat dripping into my eye." I scuttled over to the kitchen cupboard and pulled out the tin with my grocery money, fishing out two copper coins for Alfie. "Here." I shoved them at him. "Go."

Alfie paused a moment, knowing that if I gave in so quickly, then surely something was wrong. But the boy had enough smarts to take the coins and leave before I could change my mind.

"Thanks," he said, as he bounded with Eugene out the front door, slamming it behind him.

"Don't slam the door," I yelled.

Back at the window, I stared out. Those children. Teasing and taunting one another. Children everywhere. So many children. Too many children.

Despite the emptiness of my stomach, another wave rose through my chest. Quickly reaching toward the sink, I vacated what little there was in my belly. I paused over the sink, afraid if I moved too quickly, more sickness would come.

Glancing back out the window, I saw Alfie running down the street, trailed by four other boys, waving a newspaper in his hand. Eugene could barely keep up.

I refused to allow the notion of babies to take root. This was old age. Pure and simple. *No more children*, I thought. *I am done with children.* But then, when did God ever listen to the plans of a *Yiddishe* mama?

Dottie

———— ⚜ ————

THAT night, walking home from work, I dawdled. I should have taken the elevated, or at least the streetcar, to make sure I arrived in plenty of time for *Shabbes*, but the idea of facing my mother was more than I could bear. I told myself I didn't want to end up sick on a crowded train, but it was simply an excuse. I shouldn't have been walking; my limbs were leaden, my feelings vacillating with each footfall between exhilaration at my new promotion and a growing fright at the way my body was betraying me.

With my mind distracted, I didn't notice where I stepped, and my heel caught in a crack in the sidewalk. As I lunged forward, my clutch flying from my hands, I let out an unladylike "Ow!" as I landed on my knee. A rip in my stocking. Just what I needed. A man passing by reached out and took my arm, helping me to my feet. He leaned down to pick up my purse and handed it to me. "Are you all right, miss?" he asked.

"I'm fine," I said, going for what I hoped was a smile. "Nothing bruised but my pride."

The man touched the brim of his hat and continued on his way, not a care in the world. Probably going home to his wife. And children. In a lovely uptown apartment with a new Kelvinator and a Westinghouse electric range, and a dinette set from Bloomingdale's and a powder room full of Helena Rubinstein cosmetics. To the life that should be *mine*. To the life I coveted more than anything. Me. Abe. Children of our own. A kitchen out of *House & Garden*. Abe would work at the store during the day, Ma would watch the kids for a few hours, and I'd continue at the insurance company. The picture was dreamy and I smiled before remembering I had botched it all up.

What if I told Abe I had been attacked? That a man forced himself on me?

No. That would never work. Then Abe would spend his life looking with abhorrence at the child, constantly searching her face, wondering to whom she belonged. And would Abe want to touch me, knowing I had been touched by another? How much worse would it be if he knew it *hadn't* been an attack, that I'd been merely drunk and foolish?

Leaning down, I brushed the dirt from my dress. The run in my stocking stretched down my leg, a train track scaling my thigh. The indignity was too much, so as tears threatened, I hobbled on my tender ankle and sat on a bench. Crossing my sore ankle over the other, I reached down and rubbed the bone. Nothing serious. But what if it had been serious? How easy it is to slip, on the stairs at home, perhaps a tumble down the front stoop. With my luck, though, I'd merely be in the same position, but with a broken arm or leg.

The men and women on their way home all looked so purposeful, so free. I tried to concentrate on them, conjuring their stories, but no matter how I tried to ignore my thoughts, they kept taunting me, like Izzy used to do with the mice he'd captured in the apartment when we were kids. I'd run and scream and close my eyes and try not to see the beady eyes of the rodents that Izzy swung in front of my face, as he laughed and called me a crybaby. The mice repulsed me, yet I had sympathy for them. It wasn't their fault; they were just trying to survive. If only they would do it elsewhere. At night I dreamed of those tiny wriggling creatures as they squealed to be free, only to be squashed by the hand of my younger brother. Right now I had about as much future as those mice. I suddenly wished Izzy had been kinder to them.

Glancing at the sky, I saw that the sun was starting its late summer descent, and I realized I'd need to dash to be on time even if home was the last place I wanted to be, with the boys arguing, my father proselytizing, my mother prying. My mother. I would have to tell my mother. The thought caught me short, made me gasp for breath as a sudden burst of sweat erupted across my brow.

I unclasped my purse and reached for a handkerchief to blot my forehead, and once again I saw the letters. The letters. My cheeks warmed and I looked around guiltily, as if caught in the act. Those letters confirmed my disgrace, held my shame in its entirety.

I had no need to pull out the papers, although my fingers moved of their own accord, caressing the thick, heavy cream card stock that bespoke wealth. The return address was engraved, and the raised type felt smooth and rich to my touch. Why had I kept them? With the thoughts of the day circling in my head, I determined to rid myself of this evidence once and for all. If the baby had been Abe's, well, there would have been a fuss, but with a quick wedding and an "early" delivery, it would be forgotten in a matter of months. But this? This pushed past the boundaries of decency.

I stood, and with just a ghost of an ache in my ankle, I walked toward the trash bin on the corner. Yet, when I reached it, I didn't stop, and the letters found their way back into my purse. When a droplet of sweat slid down my nose, I reached again for the handkerchief, dabbing my face as I hurried to Tenth Street.

The scenery changed dramatically as I left the sophistication of Midtown and sank back into the depths of the lower East Side, of home. Fedoras were traded for *yarmulkes*. Children walking hand in hand with mothers changed into ragamuffins darting through the streets. Storefronts gave way to peddlers hawking their wares. As much as I tried to retain the dignity of the highly proficient bookkeeper—make that highly proficient *head* bookkeeper—when

I descended into my own neighborhood, I reverted to the Dottie whose life revolved around doing the dishes, watching my brothers, and arguing with Ma about going to *shul*. I couldn't hold on to white silk when diving into a pit of mud, no matter how hard I tried.

I approached our building barely in time for the lighting of the *Shabbes* candles. As usual, Mr. Baum was sitting on the stoop with his newspaper.

"Good evening, Mr. Baum," I said.

"*Gut Shabbes*, Dottie," he said, licking his finger to turn the page.

I knew I was really late when Mrs. Baum stuck her head out the front window and yelled in broken English, "Mr. Baum! Upstairs, your *tuchus* you get." So I hurried past him into the building, where the smell of Mrs. Anscher's boiled cabbages nearly knocked me down. Our building was so claustrophobic it was as if we lived with our neighbors instead of beside them.

I rushed up the three flights of stairs, and stopped at the top, fighting for breath. My body wouldn't allow me to forget my troubles. In high school, I'd run track, and while it had been nearly two years since I graduated, a quick sprint up the stairs should have been nothing. I took a moment to catch my breath and regain my composure, and when I looked down, I noticed my arm was clutching my chest, that my bosom ached in a new way, nothing like the growing pains I'd experienced not so long ago. Panic settled in, making it difficult for me to calm. But I had to. I couldn't give myself away to my mother.

A door opened and I steeled myself, a forced grin on my face, to prepare for the family member obviously sent to find me. But no, it was the door across the hallway. "Dottie," a tiny voice called out.

My facade melted, replaced by a genuine smile. "Alice," I said, squatting down to her eye level. "What are you doing roaming when it's about to be *Shabbes*?"

Alice toddled to me, her two-year-old legs roly-polying her along. "Dottie," she repeated, allowing me to sweep her into my arms. I wrapped her in my embrace and picked her up. Her hair was delicate and curly and when my nose brushed against a lock of it, the smell of talcum powder made me wistful for the days when my brothers were this tiny. Zelda often teased me for stealing sniffs of her baby, but that baby scent was heavenly and I couldn't resist. A shiver ran up my spine at the thought of babies.

Stroking Alice's arm, I marveled at the dewy softness of it. "Does your mama know where you are?" I asked.

"Kitty cat," Alice said, and I laughed.

"There are no kitty cats here, you silly goose." I carried her to her door, and pushing it open slightly, I called in, "Mrs. Kaplan? Did you lose something?"

Mrs. Kaplan came out of her kitchen, her hair recently styled for Friday night. "How did you get out?" she exclaimed, taking Alice from my arms. "You naughty little girl."

"Kitty cat!" Alice said again.

Mrs. Kaplan rolled her eyes. "Thank you, Dottie. *Gut Shabbes.*"

"*Gut Shabbes* to you," I said, giving Alice's nose a little tweak before heading back to the hallway, making sure to pull the Kaplans' door tight so Alice couldn't escape again.

The encounter lightened my mood, enabling me to enter the chaos that was my home on a Friday night. The flimsy door slammed against the wall, and I cringed, waiting for the yell I knew was coming: "Don't bang the door," Ma said from the kitchen.

"Sorry," I called as I walked in.

Alfie and Eugene were screaming, running through the house carrying papers folded into airplanes. "Boom boom boom boom boom!" yelled Eugene, dive-bombing his plane into the furniture all around. He ran past me. "Boom boom boom!"

My youngest brother could put a smile on my face even as I suffered the trials of Job. I grabbed him the next time he passed and planted a kiss on the top of his head as I said, "Boom boom boom to you."

"No war on *Shabbes*," Ma said from the kitchen, where she was putting the finishing touches on dinner.

"Boys will be boys," my father called back to Ma from the main room, where he was splayed on the couch, reading *The Nation*, his feet propped on the table. I gave *Tateh* a pointed look—Ma never allowed feet on furniture—but he just put his finger to his lips and gave me a grin.

"Boys can be boys when it's not *Shabbes*. On *Shabbes* they can be a little more God-fearing."

"I'm here," a voice announced loudly from outside the front door. *Bang* went the door as a large man with a jacket that didn't quite reach his wrists entered the apartment. His size dwarfed the room.

"The door," Ma called yet again. "Stamp your feet, Heshie. Don't bring in all the dirt of the city."

"Let your brother be," *Tateh* said. "He just walked in."

That's the way it always went in the apartment. So much noise, so much yelling. Ma and *Tateh* never truly fought, but their voices were loud enough that strangers would think they were constantly bickering. The prying neighbors didn't need cups against the walls to hear every word said.

The smells of home—the ever-present reek of liver, of *schmaltz*, of carp boiling on the stove—caused an uproar in my stomach, immediately deflating my mood, reminding me of my misfortunes. Always the smells permeated, overwhelming even the sweet scent of baking *challah* and roasting *tzimmes*. Ma never escaped them, but I went to great extremes before leaving the apartment to douse myself in the cheap toilet water I bought at Ohrbach's so as not to bring the stink of the East Side into my Midtown office.

I laid my clutch on the table next to the couch, giving my father a peck on the forehead and greeting Uncle Heshie, who plopped down next to him and picked up the *Herald Tribune*. This was the couch I slept on every night, a deep green velvet, fraying at the edges. My lips pursed as I surveyed the scene, like I did every evening, hoping my mother had done something—anything—to improve our home. But no. I used to leave magazines for Ma to look at, to inspire her, but stopped when I saw she had used the pages from the summer issue of *Better Homes and Gardens* to wrap chicken bones. Ma didn't see the wisdom of spending money on "appearances," so we still had the old glass-doored cabinet of books piled every which way, threatening to burst open and rain tomes down on me while I slept. And next to the cabinet was the ancient Victrola on which *Tateh* played the classical records he purchased with money that could have gone for a new couch. The newest object in the apartment was the radio, bought two years ago.

"A good day, Dottala?" *Tateh* asked, barely lowering his magazine.

"Why, yes—," I started, but I was interrupted by Ma walking into the room.

"So, now you're home?" Ma said.

"Good *Shabbes*, Ma." I smoothed out my dress, hoping she didn't notice its snugness.

"Good *Shabbes*, *bubelah*."

Ma bent over to speak quietly to Uncle Heshie. "A letter came from Yussel today."

Uncle Heshie looked up. "And?"

Ma shrugged. "Nothing has changed." From her apron pocket, she pulled a sheet of paper and handed it to her brother, who began to read it right away. "Hesh, don't you know anyone who knows anyone?" she asked while his eyes scanned the page. "Someone at Tammany Hall with the ear of a senator? Someone who could get Yussel a visa?"

Still reading, Uncle Heshie shook his head.

Alfie bounded into the room, screeching, "And the Allies go *boom boom boom*!"

"What did I say about that ruckus on *Shabbes*, Alfie?" Ma said, straightening up, and looking around to see what else needed to be done.

"It's not a ruckus, Ma," Alfie said. "It's the Great War. I'm Frank Luke and I'm shooting down German reconnaissance balloons."

"No war is great," Uncle Heshie said, taking the airplane from Alfie as it flew past, though his eyes never left the letter.

"Aw, Uncle Heshie," Alfie said.

If for nothing more than to stop the squabbling, I asked in Yiddish, "Do you need help, Ma?" Because I was the only girl in the family, it was my responsibility to help with the domestic chores, but it was difficult to keep the reluctance from my tone.

I wished I shared the enthusiasm of my friends. Linda would be marrying Ralph as soon as they could, and she spent every free moment learning how to be a good and dutiful wife. And Zelda, my closest friend, was not only married, but with a baby. While she moaned about her chores—"This life is drudgery," she'd say— she had a grin on her face and a glow in her cheeks. I knew I would have to take on the same tasks when Abe and I married, but I didn't relish the idea. In my dreams, I kept working—either at his store or perhaps, now, at the insurance office—and hired a girl to take care of the house. But those were fantasies.

"Everything is done," Ma said with such firmness that I took it as a reprimand.

My ears reddened as I guiltily remembered how I'd dawdled coming home, and I said, "It's not like I can just leave work whenever I feel like."

"Leave work? Who said anything about leaving work? I just said everything's done. Now shush. We need to light the candles." Ma placed the candlesticks on the thin sideboard crammed between the table and the wall. The room overflowed with furniture: sideboard next to dining table next to couch next to coffee table beside credenza and Victrola. People had to turn sideways to make room for one another, and yet still Eugene and Alfie, with a freshly folded airplane, managed to climb over and under feet as they raced through the small space.

Bustling through the drawers, Ma said, "Where are those matches?"

I shot Alfie a look as he ran past, and he surreptitiously smuggled a box of matches from his pocket into my hand as he continued, "Boom boom boom!" He gave me a mildly worried glance, but I winked at him, willing to keep his secret. If Ma knew about Alfie sneaking cigarettes on the street, she'd hide his backside but good.

"Here they are," I said, handing her the matches. But Ma was no dip and she looked hard at Alfie; he avoided her eye by rushing into the bathroom.

"Go ahead and light the candles," Ma said.

I struck a match on the side of the box. The wisp of smoke and the crackle of the match head brought me a moment's relief as it welcomed in the peace of *Shabbes*. I lit each of the four tall white candles one by one, admiring the silver holders Ma had brought from the Old World, the one treasure her mother had owned, the one thing her mother had sent with her to the New World.

When the flames stood tall, Ma and I both waved our hands over our eyes, and sang the blessing together. *"Baruch atah Adonai, Eloheinu melkch ha-olam, asher kid'shanu b'mitzvotav vitzivanu, l'hadlik ner shel Shabbes."* With my eyes still closed, I took a deep breath. Ma had taught me that right after the blessing was recited, the gates of heaven briefly opened for the prayers of women. A special moment only for us. Silently I sent up my plea. *Please, dear God in heaven. No.*

My solitude was interrupted when I was knocked in the legs by Eugene as he ran past me with his airplane, taking a tumble to the floor. Glancing up, I saw my mother also awakened from reverie. What had she been asking for?

Shaking her head, Ma said, "All of you! Off to your father for your blessings while I get food on the table."

Uncle Heshie rose and scooped up Eugene. "Come on, scamp,"

he said, lifting the boy over the back of the couch and handing him to *Tateh*.

"Isidore," Ma called. "Come out for *Shabbes*."

From the back bedroom the three boys shared, Izzy appeared, tall and thin, on the cusp of manhood but still boylike in his movements.

Ma walked into the kitchen, her limp more pronounced than usual. I followed her in, saying, "I can put things on the table."

"*Shah, shah*. Get your blessing. Then you help."

Blessing. I was nineteen years old and still being blessed as if I were nine. I opened my mouth to complain—again—but my mother cut me off before I could start. "Until you are married, you are a child."

My hand moved to my belly of its own accord. When she found out, would she still think me a child? When she knew the shame of what I had done, would she even consider me a daughter?

Retreating to the main room, I waited for my father to finish blessing the boys. When they were done, I stooped unceremoniously so my father could reach the top of my head from his seated position. I was as tall as he was and the whole process felt humiliating. *Tateh* recited the words in Hebrew. *May God make you like Sarah, Rivka, Rachel, and Leah. May God grant you favor and peace.*

Sarah and Rachel hadn't brought disgrace upon their families. I kissed my *tateh* and, fighting tears, retreated to the kitchen. Ma held a platter of chicken.

"I got it, Ma," I said, and she handed it over. Her steps were uneven. "Is it going to rain tonight?" I asked.

Ma peered out the window. "Do you see clouds?"

"No," I said, walking to the table. "But your leg is bothering you."

Returning to the kitchen for more platters, I saw what I would have sworn was a blush on my mother's cheeks, not that my mother ever blushed.

"My leg has seen worse things than standing all day cooking." She turned away from me quickly.

I stifled a groan. Picking a platter of boiled potatoes with parsley from the counter, I said, "I know, Ma." I had heard the story so many times I could recite it in my sleep. The czar's army. The horse trampling her. Her leg that had never quite healed properly. I snuck a look at Ma from the corner of my eye, trying to picture her as a young woman in the midst of a political protest. But it was too hard to imagine. Ma, with her always-flushed face and her doughy figure, could never have been nineteen.

"Come," Ma said to everyone. "Dinner."

The family gathered. Some *Shabbeses* three or four guests would cram around the table. Tonight only Uncle Heshie joined us. Ma's bachelor brother, who lived all the way up in the Bronx, was a *Shabbes* regular.

I took my seat next to Eugene, where I could easily help him cut his food and keep him away from Alfie. Those two couldn't sit together for more than five minutes without turning into fighter planes or battleships or whatever the game of the day was. Across from me were Alfie and Izzy, and *Tateh* held court at the head of the table. Ma always sat at the foot, ready to dart into the kitchen as needed. She practically ate standing, jumping up and down so often, piling more food on plates, retrieving the forgotten salt, grabbing a rag to clean a spill.

For exactly two minutes and forty-eight seconds—I had often counted it in my head—the table sat quietly while *Tateh* recited the blessings over the wine and the *challah*. And then, the eruption of boys. Hands flew into the platters of food, and—as she did every night—Ma reprimanded. "Boys!" Her tone was stern, but we were all so used to it that we barely paid attention. "Your father and Uncle Heshie first." Her hand reached out and smacked the wrist of the nearest child, who tonight was Alfie.

"Ow!" Alfie said.

"I'll give you something to 'Ow' about," Ma said.

I rolled my eyes. Nothing ever changed. *Tateh* took his time, reaching toward the platters and grabbing one of the chicken legs.

"Aw, I want a *pulke*," Eugene said.

"There are two," Ma said.

"But I want one, too," Alfie said.

"You got it last week." Eugene's little voice rose to match that of his big brother.

While the boys argued, Izzy kept his eye on *Tateh* and as soon as our father's plate was filled and Uncle Heshie had grabbed a breast, Izzy—without a word—grabbed the other leg, brought it to his mouth, and took a big bite.

"Not fair!" said Eugene as Alfie said, "Why, I oughta—"

"Enough!" Ma said. "Stop your bickering. There's plenty more chicken to go around."

Uncle Heshie laughed. "I was hoping for another Braddock-Baer match right at the table."

"I'm Braddock," Eugene said. He sat taller in his seat, puffing his chest.

"Yes, and I'm Franklin Delano Roosevelt," Ma said. "Now eat the chicken you have."

"But I want dark meat," Eugene said.

Ma's temper was nearing a breaking point, so I took a thigh off the platter and served it to Eugene. I leaned close to him and whispered, "This is better than the *pulke*. Bigger chunks of meat for a growing boy like you." So near to Eugene, I breathed in the scent of boy: the salt of his sweat, the faint smell of penny candy lingering on his cheeks, the sweet musk of his skin. For just a moment, the world was right. I kissed him on the temple of his forehead and Eugene looked up and smiled. Sometimes I wished the world could be just me and Eugene. My favorite moments were when he came to me: crawling onto my couch after a bad dream, looking for a bandage when he scraped his knee, telling me what happened in the school yard.

I cut Eugene's chicken into small pieces. To me, the chicken seemed rubbery and sick, which I knew wasn't true; Ma cooked the best chicken. Truthfully, *I* felt rubbery and sick, and I didn't know how I was going to choke down the meat. I took the paltri-est serving I could without attracting Ma's attention, but Ma's eyes were on my plate in a heartbeat.

"You're too good for the chicken? Eat more."

It was easier to place more food on my plate than to argue with Ma. When she wasn't looking, though, I slipped a few pieces off my plate onto Eugene's. Eugene waggled his eyebrows at me, so I stuck out my tongue and tried to touch my nose with it, which made him giggle.

Across the table, Uncle Heshie said to Alfie, "So Baer's hands have been deemed healthy enough to fight Joe Louis."

"Eh, Baer is washed up," Alfie said. "Give me Braddock any day."

"Don't think you can count him out yet," Izzy said, and he and Alfie began to squabble back and forth.

Heshie laughed and winked at me. "Look at these two, fight-ing about fighters."

I smiled, but I couldn't make the edges of my mouth go up quite far enough as I pushed the chicken about my plate. I didn't think there was any way to successfully swallow the food and keep it down, so I just pretended to bring a forkful to my mouth.

At the other end of the table, *Tateh* took a large bite of chicken and said, "Did you read about those crazy British?"

"*Tateh*," I said. "Don't talk with your mouth full." My family ate like we lived in a boardinghouse. I took a chunk of chicken on my fork and cut it delicately into four pieces. My napkin was on my lap and my elbows were off the table.

Ignoring me, *Tateh* went on. "They think Eden puts his foot down and Mussolini abandons the idea of war with Ethiopia? Fools."

Ma snapped irritably, which meant she hadn't had a chance to sit with her *Forverts*. When she did, she enjoyed arguing politics. "I should know what's happening in Ethiopia? As if I have time to sit and read the whole paper? With a bushel of boys and *Shab-bes* to prepare?"

I cut each of the four pieces of chicken into four pieces. Sixteen pieces. Could each one be cut yet four more times? Sixty-four pieces, which I could then make into two hundred and fifty-six shreds. How many times could I divide the chicken into fours?

"Mussolini will not accept economic concessions. He's looking for farmland," *Tateh* said.

"Mussolini and his buddy Hitler are going to drag us into war," Uncle Heshie said.

"Would that be the worst thing?" Ma asked.

"War is a capitalistic tool, Rose." Uncle Heshie waved his fork, as if punctuating the air. "We shouldn't be fighting other nations; we should be banding together to promote the cause of the working class."

"The socialist cause is all well and fine, except that fascism is a greater evil than capitalism. Mussolini supports Hitler. I will stand by the socialists right up to the line where Jewish lives are at stake."

While I often acted as if the political talk held no interest for me, it was hard to stay silent; politics was in the very air in our house. My parents lived their causes, and I could no more remain ignorant than I could not breathe. While lying on my couch at night, I often picked up the *Forverts* from the table next to me, and it was difficult to keep my opinions to myself. "Jewish lives are definitely at stake. Did you read that over a hundred thousand people attended Julius Streicher's anti-Jewish rally in Berlin?" This, however, turned out to be a poor move on my part, as it only drew Ma's attention to my plate.

"Dottala, you think I don't see what you're doing? Stop playing and start eating."

To distract Ma from my food, I set down my fork and knife and announced, "I have news."

"News?" Ma appeared alarmed. "What news? Who's sick?"

Always it was like this. Assuming the worst, assuming something terrible befell family or friends. "No one's sick, Ma." Her pessimism irked me. "Not all news is bad news." Of course, my real news was as bad as it gets, but I was trying not to think of that.

"*Nu?* You have good news? So share already," Ma said.

"I would, Ma, if you'd let me get a word in."

"Now, now," *Tateh* said, ever the calming voice when it came to me and Ma. "What's your news?"

At this point, I didn't even want to tell them, but forced into a corner, I said, "I received a promotion today."

"A promotion!" Ma's face instantly drained of the worry, replaced by a beaming smile. "*Bubelah*. I'm so proud."

The tiniest of smiles crossed my face. "I'm now the head bookkeeper of the office. The girls all report to me."

"A head bookkeeper? My daughter the head bookkeeper." Ma fluttered her hands happily before placing them on her cheeks. She shined with delight. "Wait until Lana hears about this. She was just bragging about her daughter's new sewing job the other day. Not my daughter! No manual labor for her. A head bookkeeper." Ma had spent long hours hunched over pieces of fabric and took pride in the fact that I was not working with my hands. In school, whenever Izzy or I brought home a less than perfect grade, she'd say, "You will work with your mind, not your hands! Do better."

"Didja get a raise?" Alfie asked.

Leave it to Alfie to bring up the money. That boy was a hustler, fast on his way to life as a goon, if he didn't watch himself. He was always scrounging for work, looking to make a dollar. He chopped wood in the street to sell for firewood, which would have been fine if he didn't spend his earnings on cigarettes and crap games. Trying to turn a buck into a five-spot was his only objective.

I arched my eyebrow at Alfie. "It's undignified to discuss finances," I said. *Low-class* was what I was thinking, but I knew that would earn a scolding from Ma.

"Aw, come on," Alfie said.

Izzy looked at me. "Well, didja?"

With a sigh, I said, "I did." For just a moment I hesitated. "A big one."

"How much?" Alfie asked.

I waited for someone to correct him, but not only did no one do so, they were all looking at me for an answer. "I'll be earning"—I paused dramatically, wanting to revel in my new riches—"twenty-three dollars and fifty cents a week." My mind toyed with the numbers. That was $1,222 a year. Every week, I gave my parents $12 of my paycheck. If I now gave them $15 a week, I'd have $442 a year just for me. Enough to have a nice stash of cash for an apartment with Abe.

"Murder!" Alfie said. "That's aces, Dottie."

"Language, Alfie," Ma said.

"Impressive," Uncle Heshie said, and *Tateh* glowed with approval.

A furrow appeared on Ma's forehead. "Maybe now you'll save a little?"

"Ma, I just got the promotion. Let me enjoy it." Ma could sound like a broken record: "Save a little. Save a little. Save a little." Truth be told, I *wanted* to save money, but I couldn't go about dressed in *shmattas*. Especially now. A new dress was called for. After all, the ones I owned didn't seem to fit anymore. I pushed down a rising gag.

"How are you and Abe going to afford an apartment and all the furnishings if you don't start saving a little?" *Tateh* asked.

"Not you, too," I said.

Ma shrugged. "If you don't want to save enough to get married and start your own family, who am I to say anything?"

"And yet that never stops you, does it?" Izzy said. His teasing lightened the mood, and *Tateh* laughed even as Ma sat unsure of whether to reprimand or chuckle. Izzy was filling out; he was taller and less gangly than he had been just a year ago. Though he was seventeen and had graduated high school, in my mind, he was still the little kid in glasses who ran with a bad gang, with Lefty Iskowitz and No Legs Grossman. No Legs had wooden stumps and crutches, but he hadn't let it stop him from being one of the fastest delinquents on the street. But now the gang wasn't so bad and the boys were growing up. Lefty worked as a foreman at the brass and copper company, and No Legs was learning tailoring. Not many jobs for a man with no legs—he'd been crushed by a streetcar as a toddler—but he had good hands and a gentle way with a needle. Izzy, though, was to start night school in September to earn a law degree. Izzy was in-between, not a child, not an adult, and I felt an unease during his moments of maturity, as he turned into a man I didn't recognize as my younger brother.

"Well, this is wonderful. A toast," *Tateh* said, lifting his glass filled with sweet wine. *"L'chaim."*

"L'chaim," we all said, raising our glasses. I tried to hold on to this moment, this joy. Would it be my last? I would have to tell Ma, but not yet. I wanted to clutch this happiness for at least a few days longer. And who knew? Maybe I'd wake the next morning with my courses. Maybe this *was* all a mistake. A miscalculation.

And so we continued our meal as Alfie and Eugene gossiped about Will Rogers and the New York Giants, as *Tateh* discussed union politics with Uncle Heshie, as Ma nervously surveyed the table, making sure everyone had enough. Izzy devoured his third plate of food, while I tried to nibble at the chicken, each swallow accompanied by a hard bone of fear.

Rose

———————— ✧ ————————

AFTER dinner I cleared the table. Dottie jumped up to help, but I knew it was just so she could toss the remains of her chicken in the garbage in hopes I wouldn't see. As soon as the table was empty, she ran off before I could ask her to dry. Did she think I didn't see how she cut her meat into tiny pieces as if that would make it invisible? What waste. That chicken could have made a nice salad. But Dottie was such a jumpy girl these days, and a bit of chicken wasn't worth the fuss.

At the sink, I washed the dishes, carefully dried each one, and put them away in the *fleischig* cabinet. The milk dishes and the meat dishes were from the same set; I needed to be sure to return each to its proper cabinet so as not to mix them. How nice it would be to afford another set of dishes, ones that looked so different, you could tell which was *fleischig* and which was *milchig* with a glance.

But who had that money to spend? Especially when there were bigger worries than mixing the milk and meat plates. All day, every day I worried. I worried about Yussel. How would we get him safely to America? I worried about Ben, going to union meetings. I worried about my boys, running wild in the streets. I worried about Dottie, learning all she needed to be a proper wife. If worrying were a job, I would earn enough to live on Fifth Avenue.

Thinking of money, I decided it was time to fix things for Dottie. Now that my tin held ninety dollars, Dottie would go to school. Her promotion only confirmed what I'd always known—Dottie had an excellent mind—and she should get an education while she was young enough to put it to use at the insurance company, before a family of her own pulled her away from working. In my dreams, Dottala went to a fancy college, a place where she could spend her entire day learning, immersing herself in books. Philosophy, art, literature, plus business classes, of course. But as my mama used to say, "Only in dreams are the carrots as big as bears," and while ninety dollars did not Barnard make, it *could* get her just about two years of night school. The School of Commerce in Washington Square would be an easy commute between home and Dottie's office. True, it wouldn't cover all her books and costs, but with this promotion . . . perhaps Dottie could finally be persuaded to put aside a bit more. That extra could be just enough.

I looked out the tiny window, longing for a star, but all I could see was the tops of the buildings. My leg still ached, and I limped like a horse that had slipped in the snow, but I was pleased: Dottie had great things coming. Head bookkeeper today. Head *accountant* in a few years.

After I put away the last dish, I called to Dottie, who was primping in front of the mirror. "Come sit with me a moment," I said.

"Abe will be here soon." Her voice sounded odd. Squeaky.

"What is wrong?" I asked.

"Why do you assume something's wrong?" she replied. I stood in the door to the bathroom, watching her put on fresh lipstick.

"You sound funny."

"I sound fine," she said, an impatient tone creeping into her voice.

"Sit with me a moment."

"I don't have time." She rubbed her lips together and made a smacking noise. Turning to me, she said, "You should try this color. It would look lovely with your complexion."

"*Psshh,*" I said. "Who has use for lipstick?" Such a waste, covering up a natural beauty.

"You should do yourself up nice, Ma. Make yourself pretty for *Tateh.*"

"I'm not pretty?" I wasn't offended. I knew what I looked like. I knew what Dottie thought of me. She used to leave magazines and books on "improving" around the apartment for me to find. Dottie thought I existed only as I am now, a bit plump around the middle and always flushed from the stove. She didn't understand that my hair didn't frizz in the Russian summers. That I was a handsome woman in my day, attracting the attention of plenty of boys. If Dottie wanted to know the truth, I was prettier than she is now; Dottie inherited just enough of Ben that her eyes were a pinch too close together. But I was pleased to see she was flustered by my question, and she waved her hands uselessly, groping for a response. So I said, "Never mind. Come talk."

She followed me to my bedroom. "Why is your leg bothering you so much?" she asked.

"Old age," I said, though I was having my doubts. "You should never know the problems my leg has had, but here, it is fine."

Dottie groaned behind me. "I know, Ma." Dottie, who knew everything.

"What do you know?" I asked.

"You've told me the story a thousand times."

As if she ever listened to my stories. The impetuousness of the young. She thought she knew my story. But what did Dottie know? Could she have imagined me as I was? So young, so idealistic. I'm sure when Dottie pictured me, it was in a babushka with hunched shoulders, only standing my ground because I was too frightened to move. But truly, I had stood tall and proud, my back straight. I should have been frightened—my father had warned me not to protest, wanted to whip me when he learned how I'd disobeyed him—but I marched into the town square, defiant against the czar's decrees. I had dressed in my finest. My coat, mended by my own hand, appeared seamless. No one would have known how many times it had been ripped, worn nearly to death by my older sisters who'd owned it before me. I was fierce and beautiful as I yelled Menshevik slogans in my near-perfect Russian. I locked eyes with the soldier who sat regally upon a rich chestnut steed. He appraised me as I appraised him, and while his uniform sported many buttons, I saw the cloth was frayed and even bare in spots. His eyes moved from mine and slowly trailed down my body in a way that made me involuntarily pull my coat tighter. His horse whinnied, drawing his attention back to my face. His horse began the march, and as he progressed with a pha-lanx of the czar's army surrounding him, I saw his eyes flicker, but I couldn't read what it meant, whether he felt a burst of anger, of lust, of pity. And as his horse moved forward, I realized that what takes just a moment in time can be stitched into an entire story that lasts a lifetime, can be tattooed and never forgotten. That one moment would stay with me across continents and oceans; through marriage and deaths; against the distance of decades, and that one moment is as real and current as the feel of my sweat on an August day or my son's hand tugging on the bottom of my dress or a kiss from Ben under cover of the dark on a *Shabbes* night.

I didn't feel the horse itself. I wasn't aware of the power of his legs, the heaviness of his load. I didn't hear the whinnies or see the look on the soldier's face at that moment. All I felt was the breath escaping my chest, the feeling of flight as I slipped through the air, the hardness of the packed dirt as my body slammed into it, the thundering of hooves filling my ears.

The next month, my father put me on a ship to America.

What did Dottie know? She knew nothing.

My bedroom was the only place we could speak with a semblance of privacy. I sat on my bed, which felt strange when there was still work to do.

"Shut the door," I said to Dottie. She moved in a step more to close the door. The room barely contained the narrow bed and the dresser. A chair was crammed awkwardly between the wall and the bed. It didn't belong in the room—it was too big for the little space—but when Dottie or Ben suggested removing it, I refused. It was the chair in which I had nursed my babies, and years later nursed Alfie back to health. It was the chair from which I'd tried to save Joey. It was where I'd sat vigil, prayed, and recited blessings for health, applying warm compresses to the twins. To Dottie, it was just a nuisance piece of furniture that was rarely used, but sometimes, still, in weak moments, when no one was home, I sat in the chair and softly sang the *Yiddishe* lullabies I'd once sung to the boys.

Now Dottie plopped herself in the chair.

"Such a lady," I said.

"A lady I have to be, living in this *shtetl*?"

"A *shtetl*? You know of a *shtetl*? This apartment is a palace compared to my home in Russia." That girl with her spoiled American notions. Our neighbors were losing jobs, being evicted from their homes. How many other parents did she know who had their own room and a second bedroom for the boys? Such luxury we lived in.

"You called me in here to scold?" Dottie asked. Her hand went to her stomach and rubbed it, and she toyed with the buttons, trying to adjust her dress. This was a new fidget, and I gave her a sideways glance, trying to suss out if something was going on.

"Things going well with Abe?" I asked.

"Fine, Ma." Her tone was exasperated. "This is what you wanted?"

"So impatient. Show some respect. Honor thy mother, remember?" I leaned closer to Dottie, lowering my voice. Despite the closed door, the walls were paper-thin, and conversations could be carried from room to room without our ever raising a voice. I placed my hand on Dottie's arm, causing her to flinch ever so slightly. "I've been saving some money." I paused. "For you."

Dottie looked both relieved and confused at the same time. Something was up with that girl. I would figure it out soon enough. "For my dowry?" she asked.

"Let your father worry about your dowry."

Now Dottie looked truly befuddled. "Then what else would you save money for?"

I took Dottie's hand in my own. This time, she gave it willingly. "I have been saving since you were born. A woman should always save a little something."

At Dottie's bewildered expression, I smiled and said, "Go to the top drawer of my dresser. Open it."

Dottie did as she was told. The drawer stuck a little when she pulled it, and she jiggled it slightly to make it slide out.

"At the bottom of the drawer, there's a tin. Do you see it?"

"Beneath your underthings?"

"Retrieve it," I said, ignoring the distaste on Dottie's face.

She rifled through the drawer before turning around with an old tea tin in her hand. "This?"

I nodded. "Bring it here."

It jangled as she handed it to me.

"When I had you, my beautiful Dottala, I knew I had to take care of you. A boy? Well, the boys are going to be just fine. They'll get an education—they'll get good jobs. It's easier for boys."

"I don't understand."

I opened the can. Out spilled a pile of change and bills. Dottie gasped. "There must be—" She started poking her finger in the air, counting.

I stopped her before she could get very far. "Ninety dollars and twenty-one cents. I counted it this morning."

She looked at the pile a moment longer before turning her eyes toward me. "But what's it for?"

"For you. For college."

"But, Ma—," she began.

"Hear me out. You will start taking night classes at New York University. The School of Commerce. You will study accounting."

Dottie simply stared at me, dumbfounded. "Accounting?"

"Yes, accounting."

Dottie's hand flew back to her stomach. Her face paled. She sat heavily on the bed beside me.

"What! What?" I asked. Her reaction alarmed me. "You look sick."

"I . . . I don't know what to say," Dottie said. "Oh, Ma." Dottie looked at me with such wide eyes, but her hand was shaky. "This is . . ." She reminded me of herself as a young girl, open, vulnerable, wanting only her mama. "I don't even know what to say. This is . . ." Her voice trailed off.

"This is a way for you to go to college."

She took my hand, but she held it loosely, and for the life of me, I couldn't tell whether she was pleased. A puzzle, that girl was.

"Does *Tateh* know about this?" she asked.

I shook my head. "It's our secret. A woman should always keep a little something from her husband. A 'just in case.'"

Dottie looked downright ill. I placed my hand upon her forehead. "You are sick."

She pushed my hand away. "I'm fine, Ma. College." Her voice sounded wistful. "An accountant." Her eyes returned to the money. It was beckoning her. Beckoning her future. Although Dottie had so little sense, she was probably picturing how many new dresses she could buy with the pile. But no. I was being mean. Dottie was a smart girl, which was why she'd been promoted to head bookkeeper.

Dottie then made me even prouder. She said, "But, Ma, shouldn't we send it to Uncle Yussel? I'm sure he needs it more than I need college."

Shaking my head, I said, "I wish this money could help Yussel. Money, Yussel has. It's the visa he doesn't have."

The money mesmerized Dottie. "I can help you write more letters for visas tomorrow," she said, still not looking up.

"Not on *Shabbes*. We'll do it on Sunday." Dottie was stunned enough that she didn't argue, just nodded her head. "A degree from New York University," I continued, "is nothing to *pish* on. You need to attend now, before you marry Abe, before you spend away your raise. Now is the time."

"I just got my promotion. Maybe I should be head bookkeeper a while before I think of school."

"But schools start in September. You want to wait a whole year? How much more useful you will be at Dover Insurance when you have your degree. You'll need that head bookkeeper raise to help cover the cost of your books."

"Ma," Dottie said. She seemed to be weighing her words carefully. "Yes, I'm not married now, but two years is a long time. What happens when I do get married? How do I have a husband and go to school?"

"Why not? Two years is not so long. And Abe? Abe, he moves like a snail, that man. In two years you will be lucky to be married. And even if—from my lips to God's ears—you do marry sooner, until you have a baby, you can go to school. So you wait a little to have a baby."

Dottie's head shot up. "Wait to have a baby? Isn't that in God's hands?"

I chuckled and leaned in yet closer. "There are things in women's hands, too, my *bubelah*. When you are married, you shall learn." Ruefully, though, I thought, *Have I learned? No, of course I have. I'm too old.*

A voice bellowed in the small apartment. "Hello?"

"Hello, hello," I called back. I took Dottie's hands in my own again. "You will be a brilliant accountant. You will start this fall. Now, go. Your prince awaits. We can talk more about this later."

Giving me a feeble smile, Dottie stood, then leaned down to peck my cheek before going out to greet Abe. But before she opened the bedroom door, she turned back. "Thank you, Ma." I couldn't read her expression. Was it joy? Or sadness? I didn't understand. She surprised me by returning and giving me a hug. "Thank you."

"Shoo, you." I smiled as I released her and she walked out, and I sat on the bed another moment, before putting the money back in the tin. I listened to Ben, Heshie, and Abe chatting in the next room, Alfie and Eugene resuming their airplane battles, Izzy futzing with the radio. Returning the money to the tin, I couldn't help but think, *We've done good. Ben and I, we've done just fine.* I put my hand on my stomach. *Whether this is old age or a new beginning, we'll make it through this as well.*

Dottie

———— ⚱ ————

AS I walked into the next room, my head flooded with confusion. College! And that Ma would do this for me. How she must have scrimped for years to save so much. For me. My heart beat with excitement at the possibility, even as I knew it would never become a reality.

Tateh, Uncle Heshie, and Abe were in a heated discussion, but I couldn't concentrate. Abe stood when I entered.

"I hear congratulations are in order," he said. I could tell he wanted to give me a kiss, but of course he wouldn't dare touch me in front of my parents. He looked around awkwardly, then sat back down in what looked like an uncomfortable perch on the edge of the couch.

I shot *Tateh* an annoyed look. "You gave away my news?"

"News like that I should keep? It's too good not to share."

I could never be truly mad at *Tateh.*

Abe returned to the conversation as if there had been no interruption. "It's nonsense, I tell you. War is an impossibility. That's what we fought for in 'eighteen."

"I wish you were right, Abe," Uncle Heshie said. "Hitler has begun a compulsory draft. Why build an army if you don't plan on using it?"

"Why are we *letting* him build an army?" *Tateh* said.

Abe and *Tateh* were both about the same height, but that was where any resemblance ended. *Tateh* spent his days in the garage, so his skin was pale, his build lean, and his hair a black-streaked gray. Abe, who spent his days unloading crates, stacking goods, carrying groceries for customers at the store, had firm muscles and burnished skin that I loved to run my fingers along. His brown hair flopped ever so slightly into his face, giving me a frequent excuse to brush it to the side. *Tateh* and Abe, side by side, made me feel less unsettled. *Tateh* and Abe would never let anything bad happen to me.

"All this talk of war, and on *Shabbes*. You two are no better than Alfie and Eugene," Ma called from the bedroom, but I knew she didn't mean it. Ma never minded the political talk when she was involved; she just disapproved when she wasn't in the room.

"Dottala, what do you think?" Uncle Heshie asked.

"I think if I start telling you what I think, we'll miss our show." I gave Abe a pointed look, to signal the conversation needed to end so we could be going. The talk of Nazis and Mussolini and war and Jews stuck in Europe was slightly terrifying and definitely depressing, and my mood wasn't the best to begin with. Besides, right then, I had so much else to think about, more important things. College. A promotion. The math that was forcing itself into my head, taunting me with its tallies. May 24. A Friday. Twelve weeks ago. Exactly.

"Our government is letting him build an army because they fear the Communists in Russia," Ma said from the bedroom. Her voice boomed as if she were standing next to us. I could hear her closing her drawer, knowing she was returning the tin. The tin that held my future. Perhaps. Unable to resist the lure of talk, Ma came to the doorway between the rooms. Ma had no compunction about jumping into the fray. Like a freight train coming in from the distance, she would start calmly and quietly, building up steam, until the full roar of her thoughts accelerated, bearing down on you, threatening to run you over with their iron strength and speed.

Calculating forward, I toyed with the numbers again. Nine months. February. The numbers were not reassuring. Sweat pooled at my neck. August in the apartment was oppressive. It felt like the walls were closing in and the droning of everyone's talk was as irritating as the heat. I needed to be outside right away. "We should go, Abe," I said.

But before we could leave, Ma said, "I hear talk that Hitler is going to assume the position of von Schuschnigg. I read—"

I cut Ma short. The political talk would continue all night if I let it. Abe was always more than willing to be drawn into a debate with my parents.

"Ma!" The impatience oozed from me, but I checked myself. An argument would only delay us further. With a saccharine tone, I said to Ma, "We won't make curtain if we don't leave now."

"Of course, of course," Ma said. She made shooing motions with her hands. "Go. See your— What is it you're going to see?"

"The Children's Hour," Abe said.

"Ah, yes. Well, go. Enjoy."

I set my hat on my head and carefully pinned it into place as Abe opened the front door and we headed out.

I hurried down the stairs before anyone else could stop us and Abe rushed to catch up.

"Where's the fire?" he asked as he took my arm.

"Trying to escape the flames of my mother's convictions," I said. I gave him a playful nod with my chin. "Why do you encourage her so?"

"Encourage her? I enjoy the conversation." His smile created tiny wrinkles at the corners of his eyes, a look that made me want to grab him and hold him. But we needed to make our way toward the train.

"Conversation? Is that what you call those battles with my parents?"

Abe chuckled. I pulled his arm closer. I loved when I could make him laugh. The sound was low and rumbling, and it touched me in all the right places. "We'd better hurry. It's at the Maxine Elliott Theatre. If we miss the next train, we'll miss the first act."

Abe and I had known each other since, it seemed, the beginning of time. From grammar school, from the block, from the market. But he hadn't paid attention to me as anything more than a neighborhood fixture in those days. Three years older, Abe had little time for the pip-squeak I was then. While I'd had my eye on him, he had his eye on Sadie Kraus. But just before I turned sixteen, my body began to change, and I found plenty of excuses to stop by Abe's store. A little laugh here, a light touch there, and soon his attentions meandered my way. A few months later, he made his intentions known, and we'd been an item ever since. But Abe was frightfully slow, and after three years, I was becoming impatient. Now I was downright desperate.

As we made our way to the theater, Abe kept me entertained with the gossip from the store. He chatted about who complained the scales were heavy, who tried to pay on credit when credit ran out, what he overheard women telling his ma, and while he spoke, I plotted. Abe was determined we not marry until we could afford our own apartment. Many of our friends moved in with the bride's or groom's parents after the wedding; Abe refused to allow that. He'd saved quite a bit, but it was not yet enough, he insisted.

I pulled him closer, longing to feel his arm around me. When we arrived at the theater, we took our seats just as the curtain rose. But I couldn't follow the story, as preoccupied as I was. My mind tuned in and out like a staticky radio. Yet as words floated past me, a line settled in, nestling into my brain: *Martha and I have been lovers.* They had been lovers. Lovers. Of course.

I didn't need to marry Abe. I just needed to seduce him. How silly of me not to realize that.

But how? It wasn't like I hadn't tried, but before, it had been fun and games. Now it was serious business. Abe was an innocent in so many ways. His parents' store protected him from the harsher aspects of the lower East Side with which Izzy and I were all too well acquainted.

Every day as a child, Abe ran home after *heder* to help his parents. From a young age, he was carting sacks, filling barrels, helping customers, whereas Izzy constantly fell into scrapes with his gang. With *Tateh* at the garage and Ma sewing in the shop down the street, no one kept an eye on us. The neighborhood was territorial, and the street needed to be guarded from gangs from other blocks, and Izzy was into fisticuffs, it seemed, more often than not. Ma did the best she could until Alfie and Joey fell sick; then it was up to me to steer Izzy toward proper behavior, bandaging his wounds, keeping him from the prostitutes who offered their wares on the street corners.

But the truth is, I was not quite immune to the temptations of the street and, out of boredom and curiosity, found myself, once or twice—or a dozen times; who can remember?—in a compromising position with one of the boys in the gang. My virtue remained— more or less—intact, although in empty cellars and on lonely rooftops I certainly pushed the boundaries of decency from time to time. For a while, Lefty Iskowitz and I met in the basement of my building, but it didn't take long for us to tire of each other.

But Abe. Abe was pure and untouched by any hands other than mine. At least that's what he professed. But then again, so did I, so how was I to be sure? Who knows what went on with Sadie Kraus in the back of the store when he was left alone to mind it?

Onstage, the bang of a gun jolted me back to the moment, and I caught the final few minutes. When the lights went on in the theater, I snuggled into Abe's arms and gave him a kiss on the cheek. "That was lovely. Thank you."

"I'm not sure 'lovely' is the right word for a play with such a tragic ending, but the production was wonderful, wasn't it?" Abe said, his eyebrows bopping up and down as they did when he was excited. "Florence McGee was terrific as Mary. Why did we wait so long to see this?"

I took Abe's arm as we stood to walk out of our row. "Because you wanted to catch *La bohème* while it was still playing at the Hippodrome and we *had* to see the Whistler Centenary at the Metropolitan before it closed, and we *couldn't* pass up Leslie Howard in *The Petrified Forest* and . . ." We made our way up the aisle to exit the theater. "Shall I go on?"

With a laugh, Abe said, "Well, I'm glad we finally made it. Such complex characters. I do believe Miss McGee stole the show. Her character was pure deviousness."

As we exited the theater, Abe asked, "Shall we get an ice cream before we head home?"

"Of course," I said, though I worried about my ability to keep it down.

As we walked, Abe returned to the topic of the play. "Isn't it interesting how the story exemplified *lashon hara*?"

"And it always comes back to Torah," I said, trying to keep my tone light.

"The prohibition against gossip is such an important commandment to observe. And it's fascinating to see the relevancy of Torah around us. Even in the *goyishe* world."

Abe still held dear the *mitzvot* of the Torah, spending time studying Talmud even after becoming a bar mitzvah. Unlike other boys who immediately distanced themselves from synagogue— attending only on holidays and the occasional *Shabbes* when their mothers insisted—Abe appreciated the traditions. Even in my own home, the rules were strictly obeyed only because Ma said so. *Tateh* said socialism had no room for religion, but all it took was one fierce glare from Ma, and *Tateh* would be scurrying off to *shul*. "The workers should own the means of production," Ma frequently said, "but there's no reason God can't keep an eye on us while we do it." I once spied *Tateh* eating a sandwich with his pals on Yom Kippur, when they were supposedly praying. That night he came home, and pretending he'd fasted the entire day, he forced himself to eat the lavish spread Ma had prepared for him. How difficult it was to keep from erupting with laughter, as I watched Ma eye *Tateh* with such a suspicious look. "Yom Kippur made you too ill to eat? Here, have some more."

Abe, however, kept the traditions because he found beauty in them. He went to *shul* twice a day to pray. Every morning he placed on his arm and forehead the prayer boxes, the *tefillin*. Yet, he assimilated in many of the same ways as *Tateh*: he kept a clean-shaven face; he no longer observed *Shabbes*; he would sit alone with me.

For the next few blocks, I let Abe pontificate about the play, trying to proffer a tidbit here and there, even though I hadn't paid enough attention to say anything meaningful.

When we reached the ice cream stand, Abe paid for two cones and we found a bench to sit on.

"Oh, I should have bought those with my new raise," I said, scooting close to him.

"It's good you got a raise," he said, "but I will always treat."

Trying to appear coquettish, I licked my ice cream in long, languorous strokes. But apparently it was more comical than provocative, as Abe chuckled.

"With this extra money, we don't have to wait to get married."

Abe nodded. "Yes, it will help. In a year we should have saved enough."

A year. That would never work. But happily, the ice cream agreed with me, and that, coupled with the gorgeous night and the comfort of Abe and my plot to seduce him, made me truly feel like everything was going to turn out fine.

We chitchatted about where we would go on our next date, about our friends, about our families. When the ice cream was down to the cone, I walked over to throw it into the garbage. On returning, I sat on Abe's lap.

"Well, hello," he said.

"Well, hello," I said back.

He popped the rest of his cone in his mouth and snaked his now free arm around my back.

"You have a bit of ice cream on your face," I told him.

"Where?" he asked, drawing his other hand to his cheek.

"Right here," I whispered, and I leaned in, my tongue reaching the corner of his mouth, as I licked the last bits of ice cream. Chocolate mixed with sweat and the deep musky smell of his skin made my body tingle. Abe groaned.

"I think you missed a spot over here," he whispered back, pointing to the other corner of his mouth.

I moved slowly to the other side of his face, and gently brushed his lip with my tongue.

"And you have a bit of ice cream, right here," Abe said as he tilted in to kiss me deeply.

A shock of wantonness spread through me. My body craved his touch. His kisses grew deeper, and his hand slid up the side of my dress, resting just shy of my bosom, delighting me. With a slight twist of my torso, I had Abe's hand cupping my breast in a way that made me gasp in desire. His finger was rough on my silky blouse in a most pleasing manner. I could feel his manliness against my leg.

"Well, I never!" an older woman's voice said.

At that, Abe pulled back, and I shot the couple standing there the evil eye. They were clearly Upper East Side—she in a dress with a fur collar that was ridiculous in this heat—and they looked down their noses at the two of us. In as haughty a voice as I could muster, I said, "Perhaps you should! It's really quite nice."

Abe chuckled as the woman huffed and the two walked off. "Young people today," we could hear the man say. "No morals."

The moment was ruined. Abe and I never had a chance to be alone; the only modicum of privacy we had was benches in the park or dark corners of buildings. Not that Abe would give me much opportunity to be alone with him. He insisted we not proceed too far before our wedding night. The refrain I heard most was *"Es nisht di khale far a-moytse."* Don't eat the *challah* before you've made the blessing.

How would I make this happen? We had only one place where

privacy could be found. Camp Eden, the Jewish getaway up north in Cold Spring, where a couple could be on their own. Camp Eden, where I'd gotten myself into this mess to begin with.

We stood and I smoothed my dress. Abe kept himself turned away, so as not to disturb me with his reaction to our necking. "Walk me home?" I asked.

"Of course," he said. By the end of the block, he was more composed, and he placed his arm around my shoulder and I placed my arm about his waist. We walked in comfortable silence back to the apartment.

When we reached the lower East Side, the very air seemed to change. The fetor of our neighbors' sweat lingered in the air, as the searing temperatures turned the neighborhood into a steamy, seamy pit. When the heat suffocated apartments, the tenants evacuated like ants swarming toward the fruit spilled off a pushcart. Bedding dotted the sidewalks as mothers sat fanning themselves and gossiping on the stoop, while the children slept outside. Others escaped to rooftops, sleeping in the open air, desperate for that rare breeze.

"Do you want to come up? The apartment will be empty. Everyone will be on the roof," I said. My fingers toyed with his shirtsleeve, darting underneath to rub his smooth skin.

Abe shook his head. "I can't, Dottala. You know I can't. It will lead to nowhere good."

I put on my most seductive *Vogue* magazine pose. "How do you know it's nowhere good if you've never been there?"

Abe's wide eyes took me in from head to toe. "Oh, it's clearly somewhere good. This little taste of heaven tells me that. But if it gets too heated, I might not be able to stop."

With an exaggerated sigh, I rolled my eyes. "As you like, my dear." As much as I wanted to press him, I didn't want to scare him away. I needed to get him to Camp Eden. I walked into the front hall of the apartment building, and Abe followed. "You know," I said, trying to sound like I was teasing, "if you just married me already, this could all be yours." I waved my hands down my body.

Abe pulled me close, giving me a long, deep kiss. "I thought this was already all mine."

I whispered in his ear, "But you could have the rest."

He groaned and pulled himself away. "So very tempting, my love."

Trying to keep my tone light, as if the idea just occurred to me, I said, "Say, why don't we go to Camp Eden next weekend? Get away from the heat. Do you think your parents could spare you at the store?" I drew him back in for another sultry kiss, to guarantee the right answer.

"Oh, I think they could," he said, when we took a breath.

"Well, then. Next weekend." And with that, I turned and bounded up the stairs, knowing that Abe was following me with his eyes as far as he could in the darkened hallway.

WITH my family seeking a draft on the roof, I found myself alone in the apartment. All my bravado melted away. My stomach thrashed like a cat at the mercy of a cruel street gang. My worries flooded me, and I agonized about how to make Abe be with me.

Sleep was impossible. The heat. My fears. My stomach. All of them added up to me tossing on the couch, my hand rubbing my belly, as I counted the days yet again. One week. Two weeks. Twelve weeks. Panic swelled in my chest. If this plan didn't work, there was no way out. Soon it would be obvious to the world.

Rose

Saturday, August 17

WITH the breeze on the rooftop and a hint of sun peering over the edges of the buildings, my eyes sprang open that *Shabbes* morning. I guessed it was almost five o'clock. For me, since coming to America, there is awake and there is sleep; nothing between exists. When I was a child, curled next to my older sister Eta in our bed, beneath a full down blanket, those moments between sleep and wakefulness were treasured, that hazy feeling each morning when the angels decided whether to return your soul, the body tugging you back into slumber, the day beckoning you to begin.

But since America, there is no extravagance of angels. On the journey here, my fear on the train that someone would stop me, the roiling of the ship, the terror of what was to come, made sleep a luxury I grabbed in snatches. When I first arrived and lived with my cousins, I was thrust into wakefulness by the worry I would miss a moment of work, of not earning enough to send money to my family back home. And, then, of course, mornings were filled with the sobs of babies, and later, the cries of the sick.

Now that my babes were grown, my family safe, my needs few, lingering sleep would be acceptable. But my cursed body wouldn't allow it. Too unused to it.

Bedding was scattered across the rooftop and I listened to the sounds others made in sleep. Next to me, breathing deeply, was Ben. So soundly he slept, even among the snores and rustles of others. I smiled at the whistle his nose made. Turning on my side, I gently ran my finger down his face, tracing his forehead, his nose, his lips. He didn't awaken, but the corners of his mouth turned up happily in his slumber.

A queasiness in my stomach dismayed me. Inhaling, I tried to settle myself, but the morning air of New York was nothing like the morning air of home, and I breathed in the smell of smoke and dust.

Gathering my sheet and pillow, I rose to head downstairs to begin making breakfast. As I entered the stairwell, I heard a noise behind me, and I turned to see Mrs. Anscher also making her way to her apartment. "Good *Shabbes*, Mrs. Anscher," I said.

"Good *Shabbes*, Mrs. Krasinsky," she replied.

A bubble rose in my belly, and my hand went instinctively to it. It didn't escape Mrs. Anscher's notice. "Try bicarbonate of soda in water," she said. "It settles a stomach."

I resisted rolling my eyes at such obvious advice, but I had another thought. Mrs. Anscher was a good fifteen or twenty years older than me. We walked down the two floors to my apartment, and before she could continue on, I stopped her. "Mrs. Anscher," I blurted.

"Yes?" she said, pausing.

But then I was at a loss. Even I wasn't so bold as to ask such a question. "Never mind," I said.

I must have sounded odd because Mrs. Anscher pressed me. "What is it, dear?" Her Yiddish was the Yiddish of my own region, and I found it comforting to hear her voice.

Shaking my head, I said, "It's not a polite question."

Mrs. Anscher looked at me sympathetically. "Is your mother still with you?"

"My mother never made it to America, and she, of blessed memory, departed this earth long ago."

She placed a hand on my arm. "Go ahead. Ask."

How to phrase it? "I was wondering . . ." I paused. "What I

wanted to know . . ." Mrs. Anscher looked at me patiently. A fierce longing for my mama pierced me. I thought a moment more and finally said, "When a woman . . . changes, is it sudden?" Mrs. Anscher scrunched her nose, confused, so I said, even more boldly, "Do the courses just stop?"

Mrs. Anscher smiled. "No, no. They don't just stop. They come late and early—they come a little more, a little less—but you will know when it happens. It happens slowly." She patted my arm. "How old are you? Forty-three? Forty-four? You're still young."

Indignant, I pulled my shoulders back and stood taller. "Thirty-nine!" It wasn't *such* a lie.

"My apologies. When you're my age, it's so hard to tell. But you have nothing to worry about for another ten years or so."

Forcing a smile, I said, "Thank you, Mrs. Anscher. I appreciate it greatly."

Holding the handrail, Mrs. Anscher resumed her walk to the first floor. "You may come to me anytime, dear."

I stood at our door before entering, letting her comments settle over me. There was no surprise. The suspicion had been growing in me. Apparently, it wasn't the only thing growing in me.

We didn't deserve this.

Friday nights, the start of *Shabbes*, were a special time for a man and his wife. Not a Friday night—except when Jewish law disallowed it—had gone by in all our twenty years of marriage that Ben hadn't fulfilled his duties as a husband. The previous night, before we went to the roof, was no exception. I might be forty-two, but on Friday nights Ben made me giggle like a newlywed.

When I was a young woman, sneaking out into the fields with Shmuel, lovemaking was a loud, boisterous affair. But with Ben . . . That first night of marriage, in his parents' apartment, pretending to be a young virgin, I longed to cry out with desire, but I bit my lip, and admonished Ben to keep his voice down when it rose a touch too high. A parent in the next room, a lodger in the kitchen, a child at the foot of the bed—never have Ben and I truly been able to be free together.

And now we'd wound the clock back to the start.

I needed to prepare breakfast and lunch for Ben and hustle him out the door so he could make the early *Shabbes minyan* before going to the garage.

I opened the door, and quietly passing Dottie asleep on the sofa, I went to dress in the bedroom, fighting back a sob.

What had I done?

Dottie

Saturday, August 17

THAT moment of waking on a Saturday morning was a luxury in which to revel. Not long ago, Ma would wake me early on *Shabbes* to help get *Tateh* out the door for *shul* and to take care of my brothers. But now that I worked in an office, Ma let me sleep in, even though the noise of the apartment made it difficult. I loved, in my sleepy haze, listening to her attempts to quietly shush the boys. "Dottala works hard," she'd say. "Let her rest." Her voice was always louder than the one she was shushing, but she tried. I could hear Ma at the table, not five feet from the sofa on which I slept, serving breakfast to the boys, who had bounded in loudly from the roof about a half hour earlier.

A thin sheet covered me, and I snuggled into it, happy not to be rushing. My Saturdays were always spent with Eugene, taking him to the pictures or the playground at Tompkins Square Park or the library. Saturday evenings I painted my nails. Already I was thinking about what new color I would purchase—coral? Ruby?

And then I remembered. My situation.

The thought came over me like a chill, and I wrapped the sheet tightly around me, as if to hide my dilemma.

And yet? Listening to Ma say the blessings before eating triggered a thought. Maybe, just maybe, this wasn't *my* problem. Maybe I could lay this in the hands of something greater than myself.

I suddenly leaped off the couch, draping the sheet around me. Ma looked up from the table, startled.

"What? A bee stung you?"

"Ma," I said.

"Never have you moved so fast out of bed. Sometimes I can't tell which is sofa and which is you—you stay in so long."

I rolled my eyes and headed to her room.

"What's with the sheet?" Ma asked. "Suddenly you're too modest for us to see you in your nightclothes?"

"I'm a grown woman, Ma. I shouldn't be prancing around in underthings." The truth was I feared her eyeing my bosom, my stomach.

Making my way into her room, where I kept my clothes on a small rack, I surveyed my garments. What to wear for an appointment with *Hashem*? I pulled down my most modest dress, which wasn't saying much—the skirt came to below my knees and the sleeves brushed my wrists, but the scoop neckline wasn't the most decorous. It would have to do. The last time I'd worn this dress was for the Stein funeral.

As I eyed the zipper, I sighed, and I turned to face Ma's dresser. Could I do this? With my eyes half-closed so I wouldn't see her unmentionables, I fished in her top drawer for a girdle. My hands found one, but not before they alighted on the small box. With a quick glance at the door, I pulled out the tin. My future. How wonderful it would be to sit in a classroom, surrounded by numbers. Were there new numbers to learn? New worlds of calculations to discover? I pictured evenings filled with numbers swirling around, multiplying and dividing, leaping along the number line, digits building and snowballing to ever greater sums. I admired the roundness of even numbers in their willingness to halve, the stubbornness of prime numbers in their refusal to divide. I loved the infiniteness of *eight* stretching before me, no end in sight, and the sturdiness of a *five*. Rounded *nine* was maternal, holding within a triplet of threes. But then the thought of maternity brought me crashing back into the moment.

I replaced the tin, shut the drawer, and shimmied into the girdle. Ma was just big enough that the girdle skimmed on easily, which disappointed me; I was hoping it would hide more. But it did enough so the dress slid down my body with barely a struggle.

Before leaving the bedroom, I bolstered myself with a deep breath. There was no way to slip out undetected; I'd just have to deal with Ma head-on.

Ma was cleaning a spill and not looking at me when she said, "Sit and eat." She glanced up and was clearly surprised. "Did someone die?"

"God forbid, Ma."

"Why are you dressed like that?"

Walking to the credenza, I opened the glass doors, hunting for my prayer book. "I thought I'd go to *shul* this morning."

The silence startled me. Ma looked at me openmouthed, and Alfie and Eugene exchanged nervous glances. Finally Alfie said, "Are ya sick or something?"

Ah, there was the *siddur*, behind the photo of Ma's parents. "No, I'm not sick," I said. My tone was taking the singsong quality of an angry child and I checked myself, readjusting my voice by clearing my throat. "No," I repeated, "I'm not sick. It's just been a while since I've been to *shul* on *Shabbes* and I thought I should go."

"What about the movies?" Eugene asked.

"We'll still have plenty of time for the movies when I get back," I said. "Now, if you'll excuse me."

"Wait." Ma's voice was firm. I was sure she was about to insist I eat first.

"Ma—" But she interrupted before I could finish my sentence.

"I will come with you."

"Oh," I said. Now it was my turn to be taken aback. Ma didn't go to *shul*. She sent *Tateh* while she cooked and cleaned. She went for the holidays, but even then she didn't stay long, hurrying home to prepare the house. But here she was looking for her own prayer book and a hat suitable for *Shabbes*.

Alfie shook his head. "Going mad around here."

"Say," Ma said, "why aren't *you* at *shul*? Hooligans! Finish your breakfast and head down. If I don't see you there praying to *Hashem*, I'll give you something to pray about later."

"Look what you did," Alfie said to me.

I shrugged. It took only a few moments for Ma to change her dress and say, "Let's go."

Walking out of our apartment, we made our way down the block. I waited for Ma to cross-examine me, but she looked to be caught up in her own thoughts. Very unlike her. She clutched her prayer book tightly in her hand, and finally, I couldn't stand the quiet.

"So, Ma," I started, but then I halted, unsure of what to say. Was I about to confide in her? No. I felt certain I could pray this away. So what was the point of worrying her?

"Yes?" she said, but her eyes remained forward, focused.

"Um." I scrambled for something innocuous to say. I thought of nothing. "Never mind."

We walked in silence.

Arriving at our *shul*, we went upstairs to the women's section. Down below, we could see a sea of men *davening*, their bodies swaying back and forth as they hunched over their *siddurs*, reading the prayers even though they knew them by heart. There was no point looking for *Tateh* or Abe; they'd been to the early *minyan* before work. The men here were the ones who worked nights or in the afternoon or the pushcart peddlers who made their own schedules, closing on Saturday so they could observe *Shabbes* the way it was meant to be: praying at *shul*, studying Torah, relaxing at home.

The women's area was much less crowded. Most wore large head scarves as they bent over their prayer books, but a few younger and more modern women merely wore hats, and a handful of older women, wigs.

Ma scanned the balcony. Leaning toward me, she whispered, "Do you see Perle?"

Glancing around, I shook my head.

Ma sighed and sat down. "Oh well."

Had she come just to socialize? But then Ma opened her book and began praying with a devotion that felt oddly out of character. She was rapt in her intonations, her eyes closed, her body shaking. Taking her lead, I opened my own *siddur*, and with absolute concentration, I read the prayers softly to myself: *Baruch atah Adonai. Sh'ma Yisroel. Kadosh kadosh kadosh.* And then, when I reached the silent prayers, I put everything I had into it. The Hebrew letters careened and merged within me, and at the end of the prayer, I continued standing, adding in my own private plea. I closed my eyes, and just repeated over and over, my lips moving but no sound emerging, "Please, dear God, let this be a mistake. *Hashem*, make this problem go away. Please, dear God, let this be a mistake."

For two hours Ma and I were lost in our own prayers, and when we were finally done, it was as if we emerged from a deep sleep, refreshed and satisfied.

THAT afternoon, I was so giddy, I let Eugene talk me into a Boris Karloff–Bela Lugosi movie. I allowed myself to be terrified at *The Raven*, confident my problem would be solved. At dinner I laughed, and while eating wasn't easy, the food went down better, which I took as a positive omen. I painted my nails a lovely shade of Sun Rose, before letting Alfie and Eugene coax me into an after-dinner game of pinochle. I fell asleep dreaming of accounting school.

THE next morning I woke excitedly and ran to the bathroom. With a deep breath, I murmured, "Thank you, *Hashem*." I pulled down my underthings and looked.

Clean.

My underwear was completely clean. Not even a spot of blood.

I sat down on the toilet and for the first time—truly, completely, and silently—sobbed.

Rose

✢

Sunday, August 18

NOW that I knew for certain my body had betrayed me, the signs were unmistakable. A sore bosom. An unsettled stomach. My aching leg. My belly protruded, not from too much *kuchen*, but the way that happened when you were with child for the seventh time. The body remembered the curves and bumps and welcomed them back like an old friend.

In the kitchen, always in the kitchen, I prepared the entrails from Friday for our Sunday night stew. I looked impatiently at the clock, willing it to move faster. On Sunday nights Ben and I attended our *kaffeeklatsch*, and I longed for time to confide in Perle. A shred of hope persisted that this child wouldn't take—I had lost babies before—yet if this were truly the third month, then it would appear that this baby would be as stubborn as the others I'd birthed.

Eugene ran into the kitchen, but when he saw me alone at the sink, he suddenly grew shy. "Where's Alfie?" he asked. The child couldn't stand to be separated from his older brother, attached to him like an appendage.

"Where should Alfie be? Reading his Hebrew is where he should be. So on the street causing trouble is where he is."

That Alfie, refusing to study. He would have his hands slapped by the rabbi when he returned to *heder* knowing less than he did the spring before. Alfie hated going, didn't like to be confined, but that boy was going to get an education if it killed him. So many of Izzy's gang had become thugs; *heder* had given Izzy solid footing, teaching him Jewish ethics. Those boys in *heder* with him, No Legs and Lefty, also turned into solid citizens. The boys who didn't go . . . well, they were best avoided. I wanted to keep Alfie away from the gangs. My boys were rough, and the streets of New York were not a safe place for them.

"Thanks, Ma," Eugene said as he ran off, and I called after him, "Don't you dare slam that door," which he was unable to hear for the slamming of the door.

Eugene, what would become of my Eugene? I had so little sense of the boy. Izzy had book smarts. Dottie had math and her Abe. Alfie worried me, but I could see that spark of intelligence in his eyes, the street smarts that made his hands quick and his senses sharp. Alfie was a live wire. He was also my favorite, a fact I tried to hide from the others, but I knew they could feel it, saw the way Eugene watched Alfie and me together. When you come so close to losing someone . . .

But Eugene. Eugene was a stranger. The boy was mature beyond his years, absorbing what went on around him. Yet he was sensitive, aware of every slight, every misfortune. A distance existed between us. I couldn't blame him. It was entirely my doing. When a child is taken from his mother as a babe—and for an entire year at that!— he's bound to distrust. He was just a few months old when Joey and Alfie caught polio, and the doctor insisted Eugene be kept away. I had to choose: send my Joey and Alfie to a hospital, where they'd be alone and terrified and most likely ill-treated, or send Eugene to relatives. It was no choice. Eugene was almost eighteen months by the time he came home to me, a mother he didn't know, a mother who was still mourning the loss of one of her twins.

When he returned, I thought I just needed time. *This too shall pass*, I repeated to myself over and over, the words my mother had whispered to me as a child. I didn't understand that time wouldn't heal this wound, that the mourning would lessen, but the ache would not. After Joey passed, I held on to Alfie with every breath of my body—too tightly, I knew—and he bucked at the reins I placed on him.

The truth is—and this is something I am ashamed to admit even to myself—I considered not calling for Eugene to come home. He had settled in so nicely with Ben's sister. Kate truly cared for Eugene, and to this day, when Kate comes over, he runs to her and curls into her lap for a snuggle, burying his head in her bosom as he sucks his finger with satisfaction. A twinge of jealousy flickers through me when this happens; Eugene never sits on my lap. But I was so exhausted. Nursing the boys, trying to take care of Izzy and Dottie and Ben, making sure the house ran smoothly . . . I could be forgiven—couldn't I?—for thinking life would be so much simpler without my youngest son. Dottie took to mothering Eugene, which gave me a quiet relief.

But still the guilt plagued. Every time I looked at my baby boy, I felt the great weight of my sins. I occasionally spoiled him, letting him get away with things Alfie could never have done—an extra candy before dinner, looking the other way at yet another tear in his trousers—as if the mere act of *doing* could compensate for what I wasn't *feeling*.

Was this new baby supposed to be a chance to redeem myself? Or was it a punishment? Eugene was a longed-for child, and yet, I'd failed him. How could I trust I would do better for a child that I didn't even want?

AT six o'clock, Ben came home from the garage, exhausted as usual, his clothes blackened and torn. I did more darning for that man than for the three boys put together. "Good evening, my *beshert*," he said, giving me a kiss on the cheek.

I playfully slapped him with my dish towel to get him out of my way. "Go. Rest. Dinner will be out soon."

Ben headed to the bathroom to try to scrub the dirt from his hands, a pointless task. As my father would have said, "Like blood-cupping helps a dead person." Once he was as clean as he could get, he plopped himself in his armchair and opened the Jewish newspaper I'd left him on the side table.

Bustling about the kitchen, I ensured everything was ready. Then I went into the living room, to set the table. Since the boys weren't home yet and Dottie was out with her friends, I took the opportunity for a word with my husband.

I swatted at his feet, which were propped on the table. "Feet off," I said.

"I'm tired, Rose," Ben said. "Can't a man rest in his own home?"

"Rest? Yes. But dirty feet all over the furniture? No." I brushed the table with a rag where his boots had been. When I was done, I surveyed the table, satisfied. As I looked around the room, a rush of pride surged through me. Our home was pleasing, with a brand-new radio and a plush green couch. Religious books over-flowed, boasting of the learning of the men in the house. We had the great novels of Aleichem, Mendele, and Peretz, and even some Yiddish translations of Shakespeare and Melville, which I had managed to read over the years. The Victrola played Dvořák's Symphony no. 5, which echoed in the small apartment, making me feel like a fancy uptown lady. But with the pride came a deep fatigue. My entire body felt heavy and my leg ached, so with a sigh, I set myself down on the couch.

As he heard the creak of the sofa spring, Ben looked up from his paper, surprised. But then, looking closer at me, he said, "You're exhausted."

Resting in the middle of the evening was unlike me. A shelf always needed dusting or food needed to be started for the next day's meal or a shirt mended. I closed my eyes a moment before stating the simple truth. "I am." I rubbed the back of my neck to work out a kink. "I'm getting old."

"Old? Or are you . . ."

I raised my eyebrows at him. "Am I what?"

He smiled. I knew exactly what he meant, but I was reluctant to say it out loud, to make it real. Ben took my hand and said, "It's been a few months since you've visited the *mikve*."

I nodded. By Jewish law, a husband is not permitted to be with his wife when she has her courses. When her time is done, she visits the *mikve*, the ritual bath, after which she and her husband may resume relations. So Ben was aware of my time. I'd missed a month or two in the past—I'd never been regular—but this third month meant just one thing.

"Oh, Beryl," I said. I almost always called him by his American name, but at times like these, it didn't feel adequate, and I used his childhood name. "I'm too old for this."

"Clearly you are not," Ben said, with a laugh. "In the Torah, Sarah was in her nineties when she was with child. You think God couldn't do the same for you? You're not even forty yet."

Dear sweet Ben, who thought I was a year younger than him, not two years older. And it made the situation even worse. A child at my age. At forty-two. Enough was enough.

I nodded. "Is it a good thing, Beryl?" My voice caught, and I took a deep breath. "Me, having another child?"

Ben leaned over and placed a gentle kiss on the side of my forehead, lingering for a moment. When the kiss ended, he pulled my hands just a touch closer, squeezing them slightly. Finally he said, "Of course."

"But my work? Esther Friedman is organizing the Women's Conference Against the High Cost of Living. It's this December. I promised I would help on the day of the event, setting up seats, assisting with decorations, organizing the ushers. The Women's Committee of the Socialist Party is counting on me. I've a stack of committee correspondence to which I've promised to respond."

Ben stroked my fingers. "The work will wait, my darling. The world isn't going to be redeemed before this child goes to school. The party can find someone else to assist until then."

"But babies." My voice was close to a whisper. "They are so much trouble. And so much money. Another mouth to feed."

Ben's head bobbed as he thought. "Not so much trouble," he said. "The garage is doing well. The money is fine. Dottie's raise will help. Izzy will finish law school and begin to earn a decent living. And if not, well, we'll make do." He pulled up my chin for me to look into his eyes. "We always make do."

He was right. We always made do. But it felt like such a burden.

"Bringing another Jewish soul into the world is never a bad thing," Ben reminded me.

I nodded.

"Do you need to take it easy?" he asked.

"What do you mean?"

"You may not be as old as Sarah when she birthed Isaac. But you are not as young as when you had Dottie and Izzy. And after Dottie and Izzy . . . well, there were problems."

Thinking back to lost pregnancies, I wrapped my arms around my waist. At the time, that sadness seemed unbearable, back in the days when children were desired, when I was desperate for the soft mewl of a newborn, for the powdery scent of a baby's head. But as overcome as I'd been with despair, I learned later that losing an unborn child was nothing compared with losing one who lived and breathed and played and kissed and laughed and cried. The pure sorrow I felt upon losing Joey was not one I would wish upon the Cossacks. My entire world closed after Joey, and it took years for it to reopen, though it never looked quite the same. Life was slightly grayer, heavier, after the death of my son. I was not the same. How would I be able to let in this new baby? Could I feel for a new child what I felt for Joey? Or would I give birth to another stranger?

Grief must have shown on my face. "I'm sure this baby will be as robust as Dottie and Izzy were," Ben said, and I was sad he couldn't mention Alfie and Joey. And Eugene. Poor, neglected Eugene.

But, pushing that thought aside, I automatically said, *"Puh puh,"* to ward off the Angel of Death.

Ben smiled. "You and your superstitions. You're as bad as my grandmother."

"Your grandmother was a wise woman," I said. Ben chuckled. It was silly of me, I knew, the way I stood at the crossroads of my past and the present, wanting to rid myself of the old customs, but unable, in moments of weakness, to let go of the beliefs that had been fed to me since I was in my mother's womb.

"Yes, yes, she was," Ben said, rubbing my back gently. "Well, at least this time, Dottie will be able to help you."

"No," I said, more sharply than I meant. "Do not tell Dottie."

"Whyever not?"

How could I explain? Dottie must start college. As self-centered as that girl was, I knew she would refuse to go to school if she learned I was expecting. She would insist on helping, would be wary of using the money for anything other than the baby. That girl had such a soft spot for children that she'd probably abandon all to care for it. If I could wait to tell her until after her schooling started, after her tuition was paid, I could guilt her into completing her education. But I couldn't tell Ben this. I still didn't know how I would explain to him from where the college money had come.

"Dottie just received her promotion. I have big plans for that girl. If she knew about this, she'd be more focused on the baby than on her work. She'll figure it out soon enough, but in the meantime, let this be our little secret."

"But you'll need to rest. Dottie will *have* to help out more."

"Nonsense," I said. "No one has ever helped before. No one ever let my mother—may her memory be a blessing—rest. When the time comes, the children will know. Besides"—I paused for a moment, recalling the two lost babes after Izzy—"think of Eugene. The boy has sadness through his soul. I couldn't bear breaking his heart should this not be in God's plan."

"But at least Dottie—"

I interrupted him. "Head bookkeeper will come with its own share of woes. She doesn't need to take on mine now." Forcing a smile, I said, "Besides, Dottie is worthless in the kitchen. It's more work making sure she's doing it right. Let's not worry her now."

Ben placed his hands on either side of my face. I looked at my husband, who at forty already had the countenance of a much older man. The years had treated him well financially, but physically, they'd taken a toll. His hair, which had been a lush brown, was now mostly a wiry gray. Sprouts of hair graced the edges of his ears. His eyebrows were bushy and threatened to take over his entire face. But his eyes were still a mahogany brown and his smile was bright. Every night, Ben brushed his teeth with baking soda, insisting the rest of the family do the same, and unlike many of our friends, he hadn't lost a single tooth.

"A baby," Ben said. His voice was gentle. "A baby is wonderful." He put a finger to my mouth to shush me before I could protest. "I hope it's a girl. A girl just like you."

Ben leaned into me. He smelled of oil and gas from the garage, but it was a clean smell, a manly smell that over the years had come to mean comfort and safety. I had never been in a car myself, but I relished the scent for all it represented. Ben kissed me, intensely, on the lips. The passion between us was unmistakable, and while my heart didn't beat as it once had for Shmuel, my love for Ben was sturdy, durable.

When he pulled away, I glanced at the clock. The smell of the stew wafted from the kitchen. "Where are those boys?" I asked. "Dinner will be ruined." I stood and brushed my dress into place. "I need to get the food on the table."

Ben smiled at me. "I'll go downstairs and call them in."

I returned to the kitchen as he headed out the door. My love for Ben had sustained us through the years. It would sustain me through another child.

Dottie

—⚶—

Sunday, August 18

SUNDAY night, I sat at the café on Second Avenue with my friends, trying to focus on their conversation. It was a struggle. I longed to ditch them so I could confide in Zelda, but there was no point because Zelda's in-laws always came for dinner on Sunday.

When Edith lit a cigarette, I asked for one. I figured if I had something to do with my hands, then perhaps I'd be less fidgety.

"You smoke now?" Linda asked.

"Don't you think I'll look swell with a cigarette in my hand?" Maybe a cigarette would settle a queasy belly. The beer I was sipping didn't.

Linda shrugged.

Edith passed the pack my way. I pulled one out, and Edith flicked her lighter and held it toward me. I lit the cigarette, inhaled, and then gave a good cough. Edith blew out three perfect smoke rings. "Takes a bit of practice, you know."

The entire East Side seemed to be out that night, the evening glowing with the bright faces of girls competing to outshine one another, with hats tilted just so, a dash of powder on their cheeks, and coy smiles tossed to boys, who eagerly caught them. I was not immune. I knew I looked good, as the snugness of my dress, which made my waist so constrained and uncomfortable, also emphasized my blossoming bosom. I sat rather primly at the table in a wood-backed chair, my posture stick straight, my ankles crossed, toes tapping to the song on the jukebox. The café was our go-to place, serving as a dance hall, saloon, and political arena.

Edith and Linda were two of my closest friends. We'd been to the Yiddish theater and seen a series of one-act plays that I'd already forgotten, but Edith and Linda were debating which was their favorite.

I tried again with the cigarette, with a bit of success, covering a gag with a hard swallow. "Not so difficult," I lied. A fan that Edith had wrangled from the corner and aimed at our table blew the smoke back in my face. *Does the cigarette make me look sophisticated?* I wondered. More important, *Does it make me look normal?*

Taking another drag, which went down with less tickle, I glanced around the room and spotted a group of young men at a nearby table. My eyes danced from boy to boy, and I exhaled slowly as the fan's oscillating head turned away. This time the smoke floated sexily above me and I was feeling pleased with myself—until I spotted Willie Klein.

And he was looking right at me.

The aloof demeanor I'd tried so hard to maintain broke completely. I was so upset to see him that I mindlessly crushed the cigarette into the ashtray, crumpling it more forcefully than I meant, tobacco spilling out the sides. I regretted my actions immediately. What was I going to do with my hands?

"That was a waste of a cigarette," Edith said.

"Turns out it's not my thing." I looked back toward the table. Willie winked and tipped his hat at me. I was surprised to see him; Willie hadn't been to the café in months. In fact, I hadn't seen him since . . . My stomach flopped as I recalled the last time I'd seen him back in May. Rumor had it he was working on a story that kept him to the uptown clubs, but here he was now. I could feel my eyebrows begin to furrow, but I couldn't give myself away. Willie smiling at me was nothing more than Willie smiling at me, as far as my friends were concerned. Willie and I always teased each other. At least, we used to.

"You look flushed," Linda said to me. "What are you thinking?"

"Yeah, you're unusually quiet," Edith said.

Placing my hands in my lap so I wouldn't shred the napkin under my beer to bits, I said, "It's hot in here."

"It's hot everywhere," Edith said. "Although it seems to be particularly hot at that table." She nudged her chin toward the boys.

Linda and I both glanced up, only to see Willie staring at us.

"What is that Willie Klein up to now?" Edith asked wearily. She thought Willie was always poking his nose into things for the sake of a good story, and Edith preferred to lead a private life.

Willie Klein was not a topic I cared to discuss. "Who cares what he's up to?" I said. I didn't feel as if I could say his name out loud without quivering. Normally Willie was well worth a conversation; the man was a pip who led the most debonair life, his writing always taking him to the snazziest of places. But not that day. I tried changing the subject. "I saw Zelda the other night. Her ma has a union meeting tomorrow and can't watch the baby, so Zelda won't make it to our gin rummy game."

My friends and I spoke English with one another, even though at home we all spoke Yiddish. We'd worked hard to eradicate the telltale lilt so many of our Jewish peers retained when they spoke English. As children, we'd corrected one another, so we wouldn't be mistaken for immigrants. Even now, though, through a rise in inflection, a slip of a word, our heritage occasionally announced itself loud and clear.

"Zelda never makes it out anymore. That baby of hers is a real pain in the *tuchus*, don'tcha know?" Edith said. She sprawled in her seat, as if dropped in from above, *splat*. Her pantsuit was fashionable, yet daring for this part of town where the greenhorns wore head scarves with their floor-dusting skirts. The way Edith crossed her legs, ankle splayed over thigh, displayed a brazen confidence that I envied.

"Oh, Edith, you're terrible," Linda said. "Little Shirley is adorable and no more of a nuisance than any other baby." The petite

Linda appeared so comically small next to Edith that when the two were alone, they looked like a vaudeville act on the loose. I evened them out, making the three of us look more of a matched set.

"And you've made my point," Edith said.

"Aw, what do you have against babies?" Linda asked. Linda had been with her boyfriend, Ralph, for as long as any of us could remember. She was waiting for him to find a job so they could marry.

"Have a baby and say good-bye to all of this," Edith said, opening her arms wide to indicate the room around us.

This was almost as bad as the Willie Klein conversation. The room pulsated from the heat, from the couples who pushed back tables to dance the Lindy, from the way my head was starting to spin. The air was palpable, suffocating me with its closeness.

The chitchat swam around me, and I became detached, observing, participating without feeling like I belonged. All around us was the patter of conversation as young men and women gossiped and flirted, discussed movies and politics. I was there but not there.

"I would trade this in a heartbeat for a husband and babies," said Linda. She was sweet and simple and being with her was easy. We could talk boyfriends and trousseaux and the latest dreamy movie stars.

"Oy," Edith said. "Babies. Think of all that could be done by the women of this world if they weren't saddled with a clamoring brood." Edith was a more complicated friend, fiercely political but endlessly loyal. She was exceedingly modern about certain things— just look at how she dressed—and her love life was not a topic that was ever broached. Edith, Linda, and I had known one another since toddlerhood, and that bond alone would hold us together through anything. Or so I'd always thought. Had I done the one thing that could tear us apart?

Linda turned to me. "You're oddly quiet on the topic."

My eyes were pulled toward the boys' table, where Willie was now deep in conversation, his hands gesticulating wildly. How I longed to confide in my friends. But as much as I dearly loved them, I couldn't trust them not to be horrified. Even progressive Edith might not think she should associate with, well, with someone like me. I shrugged and said, "I guess I don't feel that strongly either way."

"Liar," Edith said, with a shrieking laugh. "You've been *pining* for Abe to propose. You mollycoddle Zelda's little imp. You moon over your younger brother. Since when don't you feel strongly?"

Since it became a possibility. Since my chest ached and my stomach rebelled and my head felt light and I found myself trapped, trapped, trapped with the upcoming weekend as my only hope. Things with Abe at Camp Eden had to be perfect. Or else . . . What was my *or else?* There was nothing. Me. Alone. With a child.

But of course I said none of that. I merely said, "Why covet something out of reach? I don't see a ring on my finger." My naked finger declared my disgrace. "He says we don't have enough to afford a nice place of our own."

"Don'tcha think you have something to do with that?" Edith said. "Stash some cash, Miss Spendthrift. If you weren't always buying the 'newest,' the 'mostest,' you'd be able to afford a Park Avenue mansion."

I plastered on an insincere grin and raised my voice an octave. "I try, I try! But can a girl help it when a swell new hat calls her name from a department store window? I swear Mr. Gimbel creates those displays to taunt me."

"You and every other girl with a paycheck," Edith said.

"Edith, I think you're jealous," Linda said.

"Of your beaus?" Edith snorted. "I don't think so."

"Oh, come on," Linda said. "Even you will settle down one of these days."

"Who are you, my *bubbe?* I don't intend to marry. It's indentured servitude, is what it is. Marriage. Children. What a passé concept."

"Passé? What? Has *Vogue* decreed marriage gone with the flappers?" Linda asked.

"As if I've ever opened a *Vogue* in my life," Edith said.

"Clearly," I said. I shot an exaggerated, mocking glance from Edith's clunky oxford shoes up to her bare head. Edith laughed her throaty guffaw.

"Arguing about the holy state of matrimony, are we?" a male voice said from above.

A whiff of bay rum drew my eyes up with alarm to find Willie Klein standing by the table. The aroma was dizzying, too feminine for my taste, but the scent brought memories fleetingly to mind, memories I'd worked so hard to force out, memories that brought nothing but shame. I refused to acknowledge the heat the memories also brought. The simmering, brewing fire that infused . . . *No!* I chided myself. *That didn't happen. That never happened.* I stubbornly avoided making eye contact with him and forced my gaze back to my friends.

"And what do you make of it, Mr. Klein?" Edith asked.

"Why, I think it's a respectable institution for respectable people," Willie said.

My hands made their way to the table, where I toyed with my beer glass, twirling it in tiny circles. I wished Willie away. I wished this night over. I would have gotten up and left if I weren't sure he'd follow me—if I weren't worried how that would appear.

"So in other words," Edith said, "it's not for you."

With a laugh, Willie said, "Oh, someday. Mother won't be happy until she has grandchildren to spoil." The lump in my stomach rose to my throat.

"The word on the street says that won't be long," another male voice said from behind. "I've heard rumors about you, my good man."

Don't heave now! I ordered myself. My eyes flitted to Willie's friend, but his glance wasn't at me; it wasn't a jab my way. From my peripheral vision I could see Willie looking at me, but I kept my eyes on the other boys, on my friends, on the fan in the corner, on anything *but* him. I forced myself not to be sick, a disingenuous expression on my face. *Just be pretty and vapid. Not a serious thought in your head*, I told myself. Fresh air. I was desperate for fresh air.

"Lies, I tell you," Willie said. I couldn't help myself; my eyes were drawn back to him. Why did he have to be so handsome?

"Oh, Willie," Edith said. "We've all heard about your pretty little number at that club in Chinatown."

How was it no one noticed how I was suffering? Was I that good of an actress? I must have been, because Edith was smirking at me, enjoying the repartee.

Willie grinned. "She's definitely *one* of my pretty numbers."

"Speaking of lies, Willie," Edith said, "who ghostwrote that *Atlantic* article with your name on it?"

"What?" he asked, tilting his head.

"That piece on the Friends of New Germany? It was well researched and well written, so naturally I assumed someone wrote it for you."

Willie let out a laugh that threatened to swallow me whole. "I hate to disappoint you, Edie, but the words all came from my pen."

"Who knew? There is an intelligent thought or two rattling around in that empty head of yours."

With a side glance to me, Willie said to Edith, "Oh, I've got plenty of thoughts in this head of mine." This time he looked directly at me and added, "If anyone would care to find out."

If I didn't get out fast, I would faint. And wouldn't *that* bring on questions. My friends expected me to flirt back—it was what Willie and I always did—but I didn't trust myself to banter.

Fortunately, the front door of the café opened, bringing a blast of even hotter air. Abe. It was Abe. For a moment, I was able to breathe.

"Sweetie," I said, a touch too loudly. Now it was Willie's turn to be uncomfortable, and he stared at something on the opposite side of the room.

Abe made his way to our table. "A seat for me?" he asked.

I slid over and made room for Abe.

"What are you discussing?" Abe asked.

Was it my imagination or was Willie nervous around Abe? The thought bolstered my confidence.

"Willie wrote an insightful article about the Nazi movement in America," Edith said. When Willie smiled, Edith added, "Well, it wasn't *that* insightful."

I forced a laugh, trying to be my casual self.

Abe shook his head. "The Nazis can't be taken seriously. Hoodlums looking for attention."

"How can you say that?" Willie said. "In Berlin, just this month, two hundred Nazis beat Jews on the street, pulling Jews out of cafés and cars. And that was in the Kurfürstendamm, one of Berlin's most fashionable neighborhoods. Restrictions are being placed on Jewish businesses. Yet Hitler is deporting foreign correspondents, so we don't even know the extent of it!"

"May God strike me down, but I actually agree with Willie Klein," Edith said. "Hitler is eyeing Europe, and the Jews are a minor impediment of which he's looking to dispose."

"Goebbels instigated the riots with his 'If I were God' speech, and—," I said, but I faltered when I saw the withering glare Abe gave me.

"I need a beer," Abe said, looking around. But no waiter came our way, so he said, "I think you're making too much of it. Give it time and the Nazis will prove to be no more than a German fad. They will pass. But what's *not* passing is Torah. If the Jews simply turned to *Hashem*, then—"

The uproar drowned out the rest of his sentence, with Edith, Willie, and Willie's buddies all talking over one another. Linda and I both sat quietly, but for different reasons. Linda hated an argument. I hated an argument where Abe was in the wrong. How could he be so stubborn, so—dare I think it?—idiotic? I longed to dive into the fray, but I didn't want to risk Abe's wrath.

So instead, I stood and put a hand on his shoulder, saying, "Why don't we go for a stroll? Just you and me?"

"I just got here," Abe said. "It was a long day at the store. I'd like to get a beer."

A grin twitched at the corners of Willie's mouth. I swallowed back the taste of panic.

"But some fresh air would be nice," I said, leaning into him. Abe's scent was musky; he wasn't one to disguise his hard work with after-shave. The tart smell of his skin, tinged with the slight pungency of sweat, was more enticing than any manufactured cologne. When I breathed it in, the tension in my belly released ever so slightly.

"One beer and then we can go," Abe said.

Embarrassed, I stood there, unsure of what to do. First, Abe's naive view of the world. Now he'd humiliated me in front of Willie. Of course, Abe had no idea, so could I really blame him? Tears formed in the corners of my eyes. I looked quickly toward the light, trying to discreetly bat them away. I rubbed my eyelash as if a piece of mascara had accidentally gotten into my eye.

With a sly look, Willie said, "Dottie, if you'd like fresh air, I'd be more than happy to escort you on a walk."

I looked at him sharply, eyebrows pinched. But not as quickly as Abe, who seared Willie with his glower. "Excuse me?" Abe said angrily, standing back up. "Are you trying to step in?"

Willie quickly took a step backward and lifted his hands in mock surrender. "Of course not. But if the lady wants fresh air, I'm just trying to accommodate."

The two men stared at each other. Willie was a good five inches taller than Abe, but he lacked Abe's physique. He was a writer with the build of a writer. Not like Abe, who spent his days lifting and hauling bales and crates. Edith and Linda couldn't keep their eyes off the men; Linda was horrified, Edith amused.

Abe turned and took my arm. "Why don't we go for that stroll?"

I realized I was holding my breath. I exhaled. "Thank you," I said quietly.

Abe steered me toward the door as I called out good-byes to my friends.

"We'll see you tomorrow for gin rummy," Edith said.

We walked out the door, Abe pulling me along, slightly roughly.

Out on the street, we walked silently for a block or two, before Abe snapped, "What was that?"

The stores we passed were shuttered for the night, but plenty of people were out; groups of kids, couples, late-night laborers filled the sidewalks.

"What was what?" I said as innocently as I could manage. Now that we were out of the café, my breath returned to normal and I felt the color return to my cheeks.

"Why didn't you back me up? Surely you don't believe that political nonsense Willie spouted."

I couldn't afford a fight, but I didn't know how to let this go. "Abe, my uncle is trapped in Poland. The Jews in Europe are in trouble. The Nazi threat is real."

He threw his hands in the air before stopping and spinning around to face me. "I'm not going to argue politics with you. But was that why you were making eyes at Willie? His great political intellect? Is there something I should know?"

Could he hear my heart beating three times its normal speed? My chin jutted up in feigned indignation. "What are you saying, Abe Rabinowitz? Are you accusing me of something?"

He pierced me with his stare. My stomach reeled, but I couldn't let it show in my face. My best defense was to turn this around on him.

"Why are you so suspicious?" I went on. "Is it because you're feeling guilty? How is Sadie Kraus these days?"

He rolled his eyes, but at least he turned, took my arm, and continued the walk home. "Sadie Kraus has nothing to do with this."

"I'm simply wondering, why these accusations? They often arrive when Sadie is about to come to town."

Abe was silent, and I realized my aimless punch was dead-on. "Sadie *is* coming?"

"The family will be in town next week."

I stopped short. "I knew it!" Sadie Kraus was the only person on this earth whom I truly despised. She was the one who'd started all of my problems. The Kraus family had been friends with Abe's family since their days in the Old Country. Mr. Kraus had made good money in the coat business and moved his family out to Paterson, New Jersey, to be near the textile mills. But they returned to the city frequently, and when they were here, Mrs. Kraus made no secret of the fact that she wanted Abe for Sadie. Even Sadie's brother, Nathan, promoted the match, creating ways for Sadie and Abe to find themselves alone. The Krauses ignored me, treating me as if I were merely a minor hiccup on the way to Abe and Sadie's inevitable future. Mr. Kraus frequently implied that he would set up Abe and Nathan together in business, if Abe were so inclined.

"I have no interest in Sadie Kraus," Abe said. But how could I believe him? No matter how he protested, I was certain he and Sadie had played the same kind of games Lefty and I had played. How could they not? Sadie had luscious curls that needed no perm and her skin was porcelain. Her eyes were such a vivid blue that I wanted to stab them with a fork every time I saw her. I could picture Sadie kissing Abe, seducing him in all the ways he resisted with me. Of course he would give in. He'd be a fool not to, with such a beauty. "But this has nothing to do with the matter at hand. Why did Willie think you might take a walk with him? Were you flirting with him?"

"Of course not," I said. If there was one truth to the entire night, it was that I was most definitely *not* flirting with Willie Klein. Not tonight. And never again.

We were approaching my street, and our argument wasn't abating. It needed to stop. Abe and I *had* to go to Camp Eden this coming weekend. Especially given that Sadie Kraus was coming to town. Swallowing my pride, I pulled Abe closer to me, both my hands clutching his arm, and whispered in his ear, "You are the only one with whom I care to flirt." My right hand slid down his arm, over his belly, gently grazing the top of his thigh.

Abe looked at me, and as I let my fingers stroke him, I could feel his anger melting. Stepping over the children sleeping on the front steps, Abe walked me into the entry of my building, and inside the darkened hallway, he brusquely pulled me in and kissed me with ardor. I could hear Mr. Baum moving about his apartment and I sent up a quick prayer that he didn't emerge.

My fingers combed through Abe's hair as we necked on the stairs. In these hours, I was grateful for the darkness that encompassed the building. His hands roamed my back and sides, never straying too far out of the bounds of propriety. I longed to push Abe a little further, greedy to feel yet more, but after a few minutes I pulled away. No need to rush things. I didn't want to scare him off. The important thing was to get him to Camp Eden next weekend.

"I should go upstairs, check on Eugene. Ma and *Tateh* are out."

"Mmm," Abe murmured, nibbling on my neck.

"We'll have more time next weekend. At Camp Eden. Right?" I said as he moved to my earlobe.

"Absolutely," he said.

I gave him one last kiss and headed upstairs, pleased with myself. This would work. It *had* to work.

Rose

———— ⚜ ————

SUNDAY evening after dinner, I went with Ben to Perle's apartment for the men's card game and the women's social time, carrying a *kichel* I'd made earlier in the day.

"Rose, how is it you walk so fast in your condition?" Ben asked, trying to keep up.

"*Shah!*" I spit on the ground. "You want to tempt the evil eye?"

"Ridiculous superstition," I heard Ben mutter.

"What's that?" I asked, narrowing my eyes at him.

He looked at me and smiled. "Nothing, dear."

"That's what I thought," I said, quickening my pace even more. My leg hurt, but not enough to keep me from hurrying.

"You'd think you hadn't seen Perle in weeks, the way you're moving."

"I want to catch a moment to speak with her privately."

But of course, as luck had it, we were far from the first ones there. The men were already in the living room, playing cards around the table, and the women were gathered in the kitchen. I gave Ben a nod of my head as I left him to his kaluki game.

"Have a cup of coffee," Perle said by way of greeting, pouring me a cup from the percolator.

"Thank you," I said.

Lana and Deborah were both already sitting at the table, and Lana jumped up to offer me her seat. I tried to wave her back down, but she insisted. It embarrassed me when people noticed my lame leg, and now my limp was more pronounced. Yet I took her seat and she pulled a new chair from the other side of the room for herself.

These women were my people, my *landsfroyen*, those of us from the same region of the Old Country. I had known Perle since I was a babe, known Deborah since I could toddle. Lana came from a nearby town, and while I hadn't known her at home, we were related by geography. We all had the same memories: sewing under the watchful eye of a grandmother, secret meetings in the fields with handsome young men, the *rebbe* droning on in the town's only *shul*. For that alone, we would always remain united.

These Sunday evenings we sipped our coffee and gossiped. Gossip important and catty, local and international—everything was covered in these gatherings at one another's homes: tenants' rights, Hitler, Stalin, who was seen out with whom, who didn't have enough for rent, who splurged on a new dining set. So soothing to speak Yiddish in a room full of people who weren't going to reply in English. We all understood Russian, and we were proficient in English, but Yiddish was home.

Taking a sip of coffee, I announced, "So, my little Dottala? A promotion at work." I could feel myself sitting slightly taller with pride. "Head bookkeeper!"

Bayla, who had just walked in, said, *"Mazel tov,"* as she pulled a chair in from the living room and plopped herself down.

"A nice raise, too," I said.

"Now maybe she and Abe can save enough to get married," Perle said.

"From your mouth to God's ears," I said. "Those two, they move like the milk cart in a blizzard."

We chitchatted about our families, slicing slivers of the pastries we'd all brought. Most of the sweets went to the card table in the next room, where we could hear the men's roar of conversation as the smell of their cigars wafted into the kitchen.

As the conversation moved toward politics, I said, "I've received a letter from Yussel. He has given up hope, it seems, of coming here. He is now trying to leave for Cuba. You have all written your letters this week?" That afternoon, Dottie had sat with me for over an hour, making sure my most recent letter to Senator Copeland sounded properly American.

An awkward silence descended upon the room. Blood rushed to my cheeks. "You must write your letters! Those of us who are citizens *must* write our representatives to repeal the Johnson-Reed Act." Passed in 1924, that immigration act had introduced such severe quotas that barely any Jews could now enter the *Goldene Medina*, the golden land.

"We're writing, we're writing," Bayla said. "But surely there are other more pressing things to which we should turn our attention."

"More pressing than our brothers and sisters starving in Europe?" Standing up, I had to fight to control the volume of my voice, which wanted to burst through the ceiling.

"Yussel isn't starving," Perle said.

"No," I said, "but others are. And the Jews are being deprived of rights and stripped of their dignity. And we just sit here and let it happen?"

"We don't just let it happen," Perle said, "but we help those whom we can actually help."

"I'm not helping our comrades here? Who's helping Esther Friedman's women's conference, managing the correspondence and assisting at the event? I agree, it's important. But our people in Europe are being denied jobs. *Killed* in riots. I know most of you have your families here, but some of us are sick with worry about our relatives stuck in the Old Country!" I realized I was yelling when the men from the next room shot worried looks our way. I rolled my eyes at Ben and he shrugged and went back to his cards. This was not a new argument.

Perle walked over and placed a hand on my shoulder, gently guiding me back into my seat. "I write my letters, Rose. And yes, you do much. Yet perhaps you could do more, right here at home.

Conferencing is good. But *doing* is better. So much more needs to be done to feed and clothe and house the families in our own city of New York." She rubbed my arm, as if appeasing an angry child. "I am going to a meeting of the Workers' Alliance tomorrow to formulate our plan for the Workers' Rights Amendment. Come with me."

Waves of exhaustion poured through me, and my whole body sank into the seat. I was fatigued. I was achy. I was pregnant. This was all too much for me. I said much more quietly, "There are lives at stake in Europe."

"There are lives at stake here," Perle said. "People need to earn a living wage to feed and house themselves."

Even if I had the energy to attend a meeting, I knew it was pointless. Why become involved in something new when I'd only have to quit again when the baby came? As it was, I wasn't sure if I could follow through with my commitment to help with the conference. I could already tell: Being pregnant at forty-two was going to be nothing like being pregnant at even thirty-two. But I wasn't going to share that with everyone. Not yet.

Nodding, because it took too much effort to do anything else, I said, "I am sorry, but I am unable to attend the meeting."

Returning to her chair, Perle looked at me quizzically, but I didn't elaborate. "Fight for whatever you feel is important," Perle said. "But actually *fight*. Writing letters and getting coffee for *others* who are speaking is busywork. You need to speak for yourself, Rose."

Embarrassed, I looked away.

Perle and I had practically shared a cradle; our mothers were childhood friends. Perle, my older sister Eta, and I were the only girls who occasionally attended lessons at the tiny school, which bound us even more tightly to one another. Perle's daughter, Zelda, was just months older than Dottie. But where I continued to have children, Perle was unable, so she threw herself into politics. She was the neighborhood's leading member in the Socialist Party, organizing rent strikes and food strikes and sit-ins with the Unem-

ployed Council at the Home Relief Bureaus. With babe in arms, I
tried to follow, all the political fervor I'd possessed in Russia not
just returning but growing. This was America! We could make
changes! My Dottie, Izzy, Alfie, and Joey spent their childhoods
handing out leaflets, parroting slogans, my older two marching
beside me, the toddlers clutching pamphlets in their carriage.
That all stopped when the twins became ill. I left the work behind
as I sat by my boys' sickbed. I knew there was more I should do
now. It was time to throw myself back into the movement. But, as
if to remind me, my leg spasmed, and I remembered, now was *not*
the time. A new burden was arriving.

Oh, if only I could "actually fight." But I couldn't risk it. The
one time since the boys' illness that I'd tried, it had ended badly.

Three and a half years ago, when Eugene was still in short
pants, the *landsmanshaft* learned of a Communist rally in Union
Square. Even though we were firm in our socialist beliefs, we all
agreed to go. Dottie, Izzy, and Alfie were in school, so I had no
choice but to bring Eugene. We walked to Union Square, astonished to find thousands of people crowding in, signs everywhere
reading "Work or Wages" and "Fight—Don't Starve."

At the base of Union Square stood William Foster, the gen-
eral secretary of the Communist Party, who had organized the
steel strikes. I'd read about him in *The Nation*, a magazine Ben
brought home. "Demand food!" Foster was shouting. "Demand
unemployment insurance. Demand wages. We must organize!"

Entranced, I allowed myself and Eugene to be pulled into the
morass. Waves of people swelled, and I looked around, strength-
ened by the faith of those around me. Feelings that had long lain
slumbering rose in me—a heated passion, a longing for revolution
that *I* helped bring on—and I was flooded once again with the
convictions I'd held in my youth, back in the days before the twins
were sick, the confidence that I, myself, could change the world.

Eugene clung to my side, and I felt a rush of tenderness for his
little being, but at the same time, I grasped his shoulder eagerly,

wanting to be in the middle of it all. He held my leg, making it difficult for me to move into the crowd. "No, Mama!" he cried, and glancing down, I saw the fear on his face. I tried to imagine what all these bodies looked like to the tiny boy, and I experienced a pang of sympathy and a slash of impatience at the same time. "Mama, please," he said.

Straining to hear Foster speak, I ignored Eugene at first, but as his pleas became more intense, I yielded. "Come, then," I said, and holding him by the arm, I walked quickly out of the crowd, standing at the back, where I could barely hear what was being said, but where Eugene could stand comfortably. Even in the protests in Russia, I never saw a horde like this. The entire square was filled from avenue to avenue with bodies, some cheering, some shouting, all struggling to hear Foster speak. I tried to follow what he said, but the noise was so loud and the English so quick that I managed to understand only a little.

Out of the corner of my eye, I saw movement on the edge of the crowd, something looming over the throng. In an instant, I realized what was happening; it was the same as that moment in the Old Country. In a split second, I needed to make a decision: to stand my ground with my comrades or to get my son safely away.

At four, Eugene was too old to be carried, and yet I swept him into my arms. The crowd was so vast that even on the edges of Fourteenth Street, it was difficult to pass. I pushed my way through the mob, struggling under the weight of my son. My gimp leg started to throb.

Unused to being coddled by me, Eugene buried his head in my shoulder, and he dug his fingers into my neck.

As I broke free of the crowd, I saw the movement on the edges increase, and mounted policemen rode straight into the protesters in the square. The horses whinnied and for a blink of an eye, I was frozen, back in the town square, the czar's soldiers on their mounts advancing. "Horsies," Eugene called, which was enough to awaken me. I ran, gasping, my leg in terrific pain, and

I squeezed Eugene tightly enough that he cried out. "Hush," I said. "Hush!"

Refusing the temptation of Lot's wife, I ran the four blocks, not once looking back. When finally I arrived at Avenue A, I set Eugene down, and plopped onto a stoop in an effort to regain my breath. Eugene stood silently, curiously. To him, I was inexhaustible. If only he knew.

At the moment, sitting on a stoop like a common housewife, I cursed myself. *What happened to the Rose who had no fear?* Then I looked at my son and knew exactly where that Rose had gone. The hopelessness of my situation, my inability to be both a revolutionary and a mother, filled me with rage. Was this what I was destined to be? Not a fighter, standing up for her beliefs, but a coward running at the first sign of trouble? No, not a coward; a mother. Angrily, I stood, took Eugene by the arm, and walked at a pace that was just this side of too fast, back to our apartment. A mother could bear only so much loss; I couldn't risk another child.

Since that day, my political life hadn't gone further than handing out pamphlets, listening to speakers, writing my letters, and arguing with Ben and whoever came for *Shabbes* dinner. No longer did I march in picket lines. No longer did I stand firm in protest against cops and thugs. No longer did I sneak into factories and sweatshops to leaflet the workers.

And now. Now, just when Eugene would be starting *heder*, his afternoons filled with Torah and Hebrew, now when he no longer needed his mama, now I would be starting all over again. A bitterness filled my heart, a bitterness that caused only guilt, fear, and fury. What kind of a woman felt like this? Was I a monster?

The chatter of the *kaffeeklatsch* continued. Deborah related the neighborhood gossip—Mayer was taking his family to California where a job was waiting; Milton had received a pink slip—and Perle refilled coffee cups. Bayla lounged in her chair, and Lana cross-stitched while interjecting her own tidbits.

I hoped that at the end of the evening, I would be able to steal a few moments alone with Perle, but why should my luck have been any better at the end of the night than at the beginning? It was after midnight when Ben was ready to go, though the game continued and the women went on chatting. The two of us retreated home and I tried to force myself to be grateful for the new chance God was giving me. But in my heart, there was only sorrow.

Dottie

——— ⚭ ———

Monday, August 19

MONDAY after work, I hurried to Zelda's apartment. I prayed she would be home, not that prayer was doing me much good lately. With her ma at a meeting, there was a chance Zelda would go to her in-laws' for dinner. If I could have called ahead to make sure she'd be home, I would have. My parents' refusal to install a phone normally simply frustrated me—"For what do we need that expense?" Ma would say—but given the current situation, it was dire. And the office phone was strictly for work. Not that, realistically, I could speak to anyone from home or the office. But to at least be able to call to see if Zelda was home . . . I sighed. Right then the phone was the least of my worries.

Monday nights were gin rummy at Edith's apartment, but I couldn't face her and Linda. I needed to figure things out before I saw my friends again. What if I broke down sobbing in the middle of a hand? What would I tell them?

As I was walking through Union Square, the display window of Ohrbach's beckoned. Nothing like a peek at the newest styles to cheer a gal. But the stunning outfits wouldn't fit me again for months. Depression cloaked me, and I needed something to perk me up. A hat might do. A hat would fit no matter how large I grew. My sensible side chastened: It was crucial now to save money. But wasn't it just as important to keep up my spirits? Wouldn't feeling blue cause the baby to be born sickly? Besides, with my new raise, what was ninety-nine cents? And there was a darling hat, with a swagger brim and the most intricate lacings down the middle, begging to be bought.

Ten minutes later, new hat in box, I continued on toward Zelda's. Not three blocks down, though, I regretted my purchase. Who cared how fetching I'd look in it? How foolish of me. How would I hide the hat from Ma?

By the time I arrived at Zelda's, I'd worked myself into quite a state. I knocked on the door, relieved when I heard rustling inside. Zelda would know how to take care of my hat.

"Dottie," Zelda said as she opened the door. "I'm so happy to see you. I thought you were that pill from next door coming to borrow another egg." She didn't pause as she walked back in, allowing me to close the door and follow her. "That woman needs to learn to support her own family. Oh, did you hear what's going on with Morris? Seems he got himself a little too close to the strikers in the Workers' Alliance, and Edith—"

At that, I burst into tears. Loud, noisy, unglamorous tears.

"Dear Lord," Zelda said, spinning around to face me. She looked frazzled, but then, she usually did. Her hair escaped the permanent the salon had put in, and streaks of pureed peas ran down the front of her apron. A smudge of flour graced her cheek.

My chest heaved; I was crying so hard.

"Sit, sit, Dottala." Zelda ushered me to the couch, taking a peek at Shirley, who was sitting up in her crib, watching us. I let Zelda guide me to a seated position. "Whatever is wrong?"

I had to take in big gulping breaths before I could speak. "I bought a hat!" I said, giving the box beside me an angry shove.

"A hat?" Zelda said. She shook her head. "I don't understand."

"A hat. A hat. I bought a hat!" I was shrieking now.

"Okay, okay! You bought a hat. How . . ." Zelda was befuddled. "Terrible?"

"It's horrible! It's the worst!" I spoke between gasps. "I can't buy a hat. I have no right buying a hat. What was I thinking, buying a hat like that?" I could feel my nose begin to run.

Confusion was plain on Zelda's face. "Here," she said, taking my purse from my hands. "Let me get your handkerchief." As she opened my clutch to fish it out, her hands stopped on something. Pulling out the two letters—the letters I should have thrown away, the letters that pointed an accusing finger toward me—she raised her eyebrows and asked, "What's this?"

"My hankie, please," I said. A few deep breaths and my tears were beginning to slow.

"Right, right," Zelda said, digging back into my purse and handing me the delicate hankie that Ma had so carefully monogrammed. She returned to the envelopes and looked at the address engraved on the back. "Are these from my aunt Molly? Why is she sending you mail?"

That started me crying anew. This time, my tears set off little Shirley, and Zelda froze for a moment, bewildered about which crying female to comfort first. I waved my hands toward the baby, and Zelda leaped up, took Shirley in her arms, and bounced her up and down until she quieted. Looking back at me, Zelda smiled and said, "If I bounce you, will you quiet as well?"

Blowing my nose loudly, I shook my head. Zelda gave me the room to finish my fit. Zelda, who knew me so well. Our mothers had been together since the beginning of time, so Zelda and I were tethered from birth.

After a few minutes, my wheezing subsided, and I thought I could speak. But an odor in the air gave me pause. "Zelda?" I managed to say.

"Yes?" she asked, eager to hear what was going on.

I sniffed. "Is something burning?"

Zelda jumped up. "*Oy vey, gevalt,*" she said, thrusting Shirley toward me. "My bread!" She ran into the kitchen. Zelda had been married for almost two years, and yet she still fluttered about like a nervous newlywed, unsure of her cooking and mediocre in her housekeeping skills.

I took the opportunity to snuggle Shirley. She had lost some of the new-baby scent, but I still found her smell comforting. Little Shirley was a sweetheart, with the big round eyes and full cheeks of a Kewpie doll, her blond hair beginning to darken and curl. Zelda, an only child, was hopeless at the baby things that came naturally to me, as the older sister to three boys. "Hello, my little Shirley. Hello."

Shirley cooed, triggering a spill of love in my chest. "Oh, my little Shirley, if ever there was an angel, it's you."

"Everything is under control," Zelda called from the kitchen. She came back out, wiping her hands on her apron. "Forgot about the bread in the oven." She sighed. "Guess I'll be headed to the bakery first thing in the morning." She leaned over to take Shirley from my hands, but I refused to let go. Zelda raised her eyebrows at me, so I relented. Zelda placed Shirley in her crib, sat on the couch, and took my hands in hers.

"Dottie, whatever is the matter? And don't give me any nonsense about a hat."

I nodded, but I was having trouble finding the words.

"Does this have to do with the letters?"

I shrugged. Zelda let go of my hands to pick up the envelopes again. Running her finger over the stationery, she experienced the same jealousy I had over the luxuriousness of the paper. She extracted the first letter and read it silently. I had it memorized and let the words roll through my mind: *Will you avoid me forever? Meet me for lunch at the Stork Club this Monday at noon. I promise, Abe will never know. With devoted affection, Willie.* It was dated the beginning of June. Zelda pursed her lips as she folded it carefully back into the envelope. She pulled out the second. The message was nearly identical to the first, but dated July.

"*Nu?* What is going on?"

Her soft green eyes were inviting, comforting. "I'm in a situation," I said softly. Then I lowered my voice even further. "I'm in a family way."

She nodded, pushing a hair away from her face, and I could see she was trying to hide her shock. She didn't do a good job of it. "So you and Abe get married?" Zelda said, more a question than a statement, glancing at the letters. "You won't be the first to have a baby a wee bit early."

I looked down at the ground. Then I looked back at her, fresh tears in my eyes. "It's not Abe's," I whispered, utterly humiliated.

She looked again at the letters before looking back at me. She whistled long and slow before softly repeating, "It's not Abe's?"

I shook my head. I could see her struggling, deciding whether to reprimand or comfort me. I wasn't worried about her pushing me away, though. This was Zelda. My Zelda.

She held up the envelopes with a questioning look. I nodded.

"Willie Klein," she said slowly. "Murder!"

"Murder, indeed," I said, as the drops rolled down my cheeks.

"Dare I ask how this came about?"

I shook my head.

"And there's *no* chance it's Abe's?"

"Not even the remotest of possibilities."

She looked at the ceiling as if gathering her thoughts. "*Oy*, that Abe and his virtue." Glancing back down, she asked, "Okay, what are we going to do about this?"

My love for Zelda grew even more in that moment.

"I don't know."

"Do you want to marry Willie?"

Marry *Willie*? The thought had never even occurred to me, most likely because of the clear answer: no. No, I did not want to marry Willie Klein. I loved arguing politics with Willie, loved teasing Willie, loved hearing about his escapades as he chased stories. But I didn't love *Willie*. I shook my head.

"Are you sure? He's a handsome devil, my cousin. A little

daft, but nothing that should get in the way. Plenty of money. You could be a rich society lady. Oh, that child will be stunning, with your beautiful eyes and his fine cheekbones."

I couldn't help but grin slightly at how Zelda could turn everything into a positive.

She continued. "He has to take responsibility for what he's done. You'll simply have to marry Willie."

"Impossible. Willie Klein is not the kind of man to take responsibility for anything. Besides, I don't *want* to marry him."

Zelda rubbed my hands. "Dottala," she said, "you may not have a choice. And we can make it happen. His family would never stand for this. His behavior is already an embarrassment, being a writer, prancing about town. Aunt Molly has her nose so far up in the air, it's a wonder the birds haven't made off with it yet. She'd be mortified to know Willie knocked up a girl, but at least you're a nice Jewish girl—she'll be flying to the seamstress for a bridal gown. You know Willie's been seen around town with a *shiksa* from that club in Harlem. And Aunt Molly doesn't know the half of it. Last I heard, Willie was cavorting with"—she looked around as if there were someone who would overhear, and she dropped her voice to a low whisper—"*shvartzes!*"

I swallowed down a sob. "If you're trying to make me sweet on him, you're doing a lousy job," I said. "Why would I want to marry a man like that?"

"Do you have a choice?"

I looked at my Sun Rose nails. In the low light of the apartment, they'd lost their luster, looking a sickly brown. "I have a plan."

Zelda's eyebrows shot up. *"Nu?"*

Wiping my nose again, I said, "Abe and I go to Camp Eden this weekend. I seduce him."

Zelda cocked her head. "Oh, sweetie. Do you really think that will work?"

I nodded my head vigorously. "It has to."

"Of course," she said. "Of course it will work." But she seemed doubtful.

"Far a bisel libe, batsolt men miten gantsen leben." For a little love, you pay all your life. "Let me splash some water on my face," I said. "I need to get home to help with dinner." I made my way to the small washroom. The cold-water tap sprayed out quickly, and I patted my face till the swelling of my eyes subsided. If I walked home slowly, I would look presentable. Tired, but presentable.

I came out and Zelda wrapped me in her arms. I let myself sink into her, comforted by the smell of flour and cleaner and baby. It was the smell of home. She hugged me silently. When we broke apart, I looked at the couch and moaned loudly. "The hat. I forgot about that hat!"

"Shhh," Zelda said. "I'll return it to the store for you tomorrow."

Grateful that at least one problem was solved, I said, "Thank you."

Leaving the apartment, I braced myself for another evening at home. I had to hide this from my mother for another week. After the weekend, the problem would disappear. Abe would be the father. And we would finally marry.

Rose

Monday, August 19

DINNER was in the oven, the kitchen floor sparkled, and I sat at the table with my tea and *Forverts*. Which meant, of course, a knock on the door. "*Oy vey iz mir,*" I muttered, heading to the door. "Is it too much to ask, dear Lord, to be left in peace with my paper?"

Opening the door, I looked down to greet my visitor. "Ah, Max," I said, seeing Deborah's young son. "Eugene is out playing. I'm sure you'll find him on the street."

"I alreadys saw Eugene," Max said in the broken English of a child not yet in grammar school. "My ma told me to tell that the Kogens is bein' kicked out today."

With a sigh, I said, "I'll be right there."

Without another word to me, Max ran off.

The evictions had seemed to be decreasing, but the past year was bad, and once again more of the *landsmanshaft* were having difficulty making rent. With the men at work, at least those who had jobs, it fell to us women to keep families in their homes, to stand guard against the marshals tossing furniture and family onto the street. We blocked the doorways, and if the marshals still made it past, then one by one we lugged the pieces of furniture back up again. It was costly for the landlords to hire the marshals over and over, and eventually they would simply give up, and the families could stay in their apartments.

Picking up my hat, I headed down the stairs, the going slow.

Stairs were the hardest for me when my leg acted up, and not for the first time, I cursed that we lived on the fourth floor. I wasn't sure I could manage hauling furniture today, but I needed to speak with Perle. When I'd gone to visit her after breakfast, her neighbor said Perle was at Zelda's, seeing her grandchild.

Grandchild. How unfair that Perle was able to enjoy a grandchild while I was starting all over again.

I was barely out on the stoop when I heard my name. "Roseala!" It was an endearment only Ben would typically use, but Perle and I often slipped into youthful sentiments with each other.

I turned and saw her hurrying toward me, out of breath.

"You heard?" Perle asked.

"You think I'm out here for my health?" I said.

We fell into step easily.

"Toibe told me you were looking for me this morning."

"That woman is such a busybody." Although it was unreasonable, I was annoyed that Perle was so difficult to get alone.

"So *nu*?"

"Oh, Perle."

"What?" she said. The alarm came through clearly. "Is someone—God forbid—is someone sick? Is something wrong at the garage?"

I shook my head and looked up at the sky, trying to gain strength to speak the words aloud. Talking about it with Ben was one thing; he was excited for the new baby. Admitting it to Perle meant admitting how I truly felt. With Perle, there were no secrets.

Our steps were in sync with each other; that's how well we fit. Perle clutched my arm. "Rose, tell me. You're frightening me."

I stopped and turned to face her. All around us was the tumult of every day, women hustling to and fro with marketing baskets, peddlers pushing their carts, children darting every which way. But standing, looking at Perle, I sometimes felt as if we were still young girls back home on the quiet dirt streets of Bratsyana. "Perle," I said. "I'm pregnant."

The widening of Perle's eyes displayed her surprise, even as she tried to keep her voice even. "That's . . . That's . . ." She smiled, but it didn't reach her eyes. *"B'sha'ah tova,"* she finally said, giving me the traditional expression of congratulations on a pregnancy.

I snorted. "That's the best you can do?" I turned and began walking again, and Perle stood for a moment before catching up.

"How can this be?" Perle asked.

"You need a lesson on how babies are made?" I asked.

"Rose Krasinsky, don't you get fresh with me. You forget, I know *exactly* how old you are."

"Apparently, I'm not old enough."

"Forty-two and with child. *Oy vey.*" With Perle I didn't need to explain; she simply understood.

"Tell me about it."

"So, *nu*? What are you going to do?"

I looked at her, surprised. "Do? There's nothing to *do*. I'm going to have a baby."

"But there are . . . ways." Perle's voice dropped, speaking things that should be left unspoken.

"Perle!" I said.

"Look at your walk. Will you even make it to the Kogens'?"

"Of course I'll make it." But the truth was, sweat pooled at the waist of my dress and my leg ached with misery.

"There are ways to not have a baby," Perle said.

I shook my head. "No. Don't be ridiculous. For starters, Ben is pleased. It would devastate him if I lost this baby. Second . . ." I hesitated. "Second, and perhaps most important, I don't have that kind of money."

"So you have considered it."

"No. Why would I consider it? I'm just saying that *if* it had been a thought, it isn't something I can afford."

Perle chuckled. "You make no sense."

"I make perfect sense." I indignantly stood taller and straightened my hat. Perle and I, we were so modern, refusing to cover our hair when we were married as our mothers did. I didn't even know the true shade of my mama's hair, as it was always hidden by a scarf during the week and a wig on *Shabbes*. But was I so modern I could consider what Perle was suggesting—what in truth may have crossed my own mind?

"So you're ready to go through all those years again?"

I shook my head. "I thought I was done with all that."

We walked in silence for a block, each in our own thoughts. "Does this pain you?" I asked. My voice was gentle.

"Not anymore." Perle's strength, I knew, was a front. I was the one who had sat with her, year after year, when her courses never stopped coming, and when they finally did, I was the one to help clean her up after a terrible, late miscarriage. I was the one toting Zelda around with my kids when Perle was too sad to get out of bed. When Perle turned thirty, she declared *enough*, and she threw herself completely into her political work. But I saw the torment in her eyes each time I rounded with child. This time seemed no different.

"I have more important work to do," Perle said. She peered deeply into my eyes. "Don't you?"

Once again I was startled to see an older woman looking at me. When I was with Perle, it was as if we were the same children we'd been back home, and I expected to see a girl in dark braids with smooth skin and twinkling eyes. But Perle's hair was dusted with gray, and lines snaked from her eyes and the corners of her mouth. When had Perle turned into this woman? When had I? "I suppose this part of my life, having babies, isn't meant to be over. It isn't yet my time."

"A woman's duty is to populate the world, bring more Jewish souls into existence," Perle said, a statement that must have been painful for her to utter.

"I have fulfilled the commandment," I said bitterly. "'Be fruitful and multiply.' I produced a son and a daughter long ago." Guilt swept over me as soon as the words were voiced. For Perle, this commandment would forever remain undone.

"Who are we to know God's plan?" she asked. Her voice was quiet, and I knew she spoke for both of us.

"It's not like being a mother is so difficult here in America," I said. "I'll manage. Even at *thirty-nine*."

Perle smiled at my lie. But it was true that life in America was significantly easier. In all the twenty-one years I lived at home, never did I see my mother rest. By the time I woke each morning, Mama was dressed and scurrying, having already milked the cow and stoked the fire. She would hurry me to take the cow to pasture while she baked the day's bread, and when I returned, I'd watch the younger children, who wanted only to be under Mama's feet, while my sister Eta worked at the sewing machine and *Tateh* ate a leisurely breakfast. Even on *Shabbes*, Mama didn't rest, praying as her body swayed to and fro, in her only opportunity to be at *shul*. Never had I witnessed Mama sleeping or even sitting down with her feet up. Yet, here in America, I moan if I miss my tea and paper. Unheard-of luxuries to Mama.

As soon as we could hold a broom, Eta and I were expected to do everything our mother did, cooking, cleaning, milking the cow, and hauling water, but we didn't have her patience. *Tateh* constantly scolded us for not being like Mama and threatened us with the stick when we talked back or bucked against chores. "A woman should be like the moon," *Tateh* would yell in his booming voice. "She should shine at night and disappear during the day." Mama would always calm him with a whispered "*Shah, shah,*" while pushing us out of the house to avoid being beaten. *Tateh* blamed our stubbornness for his inability to find us husbands, when Eta and I knew all along it was a matter of not having the dowry.

When I went to bed, Mama would stay up late, daintily sewing in the corner of the house the dresses she made for women in town, earning money in order for Heshie and the younger boys—and, when she could afford it, me and Eta—to attend school.

Did Mama want all those children? Eleven of us underfoot. And then there were the lost pregnancies. Were those a relief or

a heartache? Did she rejoice or despair as she swelled with each
new child? Did she ever long for a moment to herself, to contem-
plate her world, imagine something more?

"This baby," I said to Perle, "will honor my mother, of blessed
memory."

"So would your work," Perle said, as she came to a stop.

Perle was right. Mama would have taken great pride in knowing I was learned and laboring to help others. All those years ago,
Tateh fumed and threatened to beat me after I went to the dem-
onstration. But Mama coddled me, placing herbs and bandages on
my leg, keeping *Tateh* away from me until it healed. She was the
one who found the money to send me to America. "If the world
will be redeemed, it will be through the merit of children," she
used to say to me. I wanted to be worthy of my mother's dreams.

We were across the street from the Kogens' home. Marshals
were already pulling furniture from the apartment.

Giving me a sad smile, Perle said, "You can't stay here."

"Whyever not?"

"It's not safe for you."

"Shah!" I said. "I'm as fit as a horse."

"No," Perle said firmly. "It is too dangerous if the marshals
become unruly. Besides, you are going to carry furniture up
those stairs? With that leg? And with what you could do to the
child? No, you cannot stay." Perle shook her head again. "I will
come by to report when it's all over."

So I stood on the corner and watched Perle cross the street, to
do things that were surely more significant than bringing yet
another child into this troubled world.

Dottie

———— ✿ ————

Tuesday, August 20

"THERE'S a letter for you," Ma said as I sat at the breakfast table. She tossed me an envelope with a raised eyebrow. "Do you care to tell me why Molly Klein is suddenly corresponding with you? This is the third letter from her this summer."

Avoiding eye contact, I snatched the familiar envelope while making a show of chewing to stall for time. Not that I actually *ate* any egg—though my stomach was feeling better at the moment, I was determined not to put on any extra weight—but I was pretending while moving the food around on my plate. Ma stood with hand on hip, looking down her nose at me. She was already dressed and fed, and had started the baking. The woman never rested. Finally I responded with the first lie I could think of: "Mrs. Klein is looking for young women to join a charitable committee, to bring food to Hooverville."

"She is?" Ma's head tilted to the side. "That woman never had a charitable thought in her life and suddenly she is heading a breadline?"

"Who knows?" I said, with an exaggerated shrug, looking down at my plate.

Ma stared a moment longer, as if trying to suss out my lie. "Wouldn't hurt you to do some relief work," she finally said, returning to the kitchen to pull out food for the boys, who were slowly making their way out of bed.

"Who has time?" I said. "Especially if classes are going to start soon." It was a poor tack to take, reminding Ma of the classes that would be impossible for me to attend, but I needed to dig myself out of that hole.

Luckily, Ma let it go, and shouted into the next room, "Izzy, if you don't get out of bed this instant, you are going to lose that job. Do you know how many people are desperate for work?"

"Coming, Ma!" came a groggy voice from the boys' bedroom.

"Aw, be quiet. Can't the rest of us sleep who don't gotta be at work?" Alfie called.

"Why, you little *pisher*," Ma said, as she headed into their room to drag the three of them from their beds.

Taking advantage of the commotion, I slipped the note into my clutch and headed to work.

NO opportunity presented itself that morning to read the letter. I ran to the streetcar, which was so packed I stood sardined between a man in a crisp suit who reeked of Aqua Velva and another who smelled vaguely of whiskey. The mixture of odors made my head reel. Once in the office, I took my seat at the head of the room, and dove into work. I had to open all the incoming mail, allocate the work each girl would do, then double-check everything they did all while continuing my bookkeeping duties.

The girls filed in and took their seats before the eight a.m. bell. Florence dallied as she set up her desk for the day, and I shot her a menacing glance. I needed to instill in them the same respect for me that they'd shown Mr. Herbert.

When the clock ticked to eight fifteen and Florence still hadn't picked up her pen, I stood. Straightening my dress—Ma's girdle felt a touch more snug today—I walked to stand beside Florence.

"Do you need assistance getting started?" I asked, using the primmest schoolteacher voice I could muster.

"I'm almost ready," Florence said. Her smile could chill the icebox.

"When the bell rings at eight, you should be prepared to begin the workday."

By now all the other girls were looking at us expectantly. Self-consciously, I tugged at the belt of my dress.

"What's the matter, Dottie?" Florence asked. "Your dress a little tight today?"

"My dress is none of your concern," I said.

"I've noticed," Florence continued, ignoring my response, "you're a bit fuller all over. Wouldn't you say, Irene?"

Irene, who had studiously watched us, quickly looked down, picked up a pen, and ran a finger over a column in her ledger. "I noticed nothing," she said, without raising her eye.

"Funny," Florence said. "I have."

"That's enough, Florence."

"Is that what you said to Abe? Or rather, what you didn't say?" She raised an eyebrow at me.

My instinct was to slug her. It wouldn't have been the first time I hauled off and thumped someone—I'd grown up in a house full of brothers, after all. But I was head bookkeeper. A young woman. So instead I balled my fists at my side, took a deep breath, and said, "Florence, you better get to work. There are plenty of women out there who would love your job." I heard Ma's voice coming from my lips, echoing what she'd yelled at Izzy that very morning.

Florence's smile widened. "Whatever you say, Dottie."

I gave her my own wicked grin to hide the lump in my throat. "That's 'Miss Krasinsky' to you, Florence."

As I returned to my desk, I could hear her gasp.

I threw myself into my work as never before, burying myself in numbers. Those beautiful, wonderful, predictable numbers. I swam among the integers, basking in the digits. Like a machine, I made my way through not one but three stacks of invoices. The more I tabulated, the better I felt, until a calmness settled over me.

It wasn't until the lunch bell rang that I allowed myself to replay the conversation with Florence. Did she suspect my secret? Or was she just playing games? I pulled out my lunch and took a small bite of the sandwich, but my stomach grumbled ominously. Of course, Florence was the least of my worries. Let her think what she liked. I was head bookkeeper. I could fire her, if need be. A bubble rose up the back of my throat, so I threw the sandwich in the wastebin, sorry to waste Ma's meal. The thought of meat, though, repulsed me.

Sitting still until I was sure I wouldn't be sick, I took in the silence of the room. I didn't hear any heels on the stairs or chatter in the halls, so I pulled my clutch from the bottom desk drawer. I knew perfectly well that the letter—like the previous ones—was not from Mrs. Klein. Pulling an opener from the pencil holder, I skimmed the long blade in the crease, tearing the paper in one smooth movement.

I hesitated before removing the letter. The first two had served merely to stroke my pride. This one held portentous meaning. I slid it out and unfolded the thick paper. *Dear Dottie*, I read. *I'm sorry if I caused any problems on Sunday. But I would like to see you. Are you going to make me beg? I won't be around for you to neglect much longer. Time is running out. Stork Club, next Monday at noon. Affectionately yours, Willie.*

What did that mean, "Time is running out?" The man knew how to pique my curiosity. Shaking my head, I threw off the thought. He had no business piquing my curiosity.

The letter belonged in the wastebasket. Just as the others did.

I slid it back into my purse, and returned to the pile of papers on my desk.

Rose

Tuesday, August 20

TUESDAYS I did the laundry. I boiled water on the stove and pulled the soap out from beneath the sink. Our apartment didn't have a window facing the rear, so once the clothes were washed, I went to the hall window in the back of the building to hang them on the line strung between our building and the one behind it.

"Alfie," I yelled. "Get the wringer from the basement."

But in response, all I heard was the slamming of our door, followed by the clatter of footsteps down the stairs. A glance out the kitchen window told me that Alfie was not coming back up.

Swearing under my breath, I made my way to the basement. The underground room frightened the children, though they were too proud to admit it. However, the smell of mold and the sounds of mice scurrying reminded me of lazy afternoons hiding in the barn with Perle, plotting the next rendezvous with Shmuel. The smell of the basement brought a smile. Carrying the wringer up the stairs, not so much. The wringer weighed more than two sacks of potatoes, and with my leg pulsating in agony, I cursed Alfie with each step up.

Back in the apartment, I heaved the wringer into the kitchen, using my apron to wipe the sweat from my face. I paused a moment to see if I felt any twitches in my womb. No. This baby was in there for good.

I took the boiled water and poured it into a tub. Just bending like that made my back ache. I piled the soiled clothes on the floor in the corner of the kitchen. The pile was substantial and it was only going to grow. I thought of all the diapers, all the stained clothes. The spit-up. The *kake*. A new baby brought more than its fair share of laundry.

Grabbing a pile of Ben's undershirts and placing them in the metal bucket, I agitated them in soapy water. The hot water combined with the steamy air made me light-headed, my collar damp with sweat. How long had it been since I'd had rags to clean? My courses never were very regular, so the absence of a month or two hadn't brought concern. But this had been three months. I hadn't washed a soiled rag in three months.

Without warning, my hand slipped on a sliver of soap and my arm banged on the bottom of the basin, scalding my forearm, soaking my sleeve. I thought again, *Three months since I've washed a soiled rag.* I pulled out the kitchen chair and sat down, not caring that I was dripping sudsy water onto the floor. Suddenly everything fell into place. Dottie. Her moodiness. Her lack of appetite. The ripeness of her body. *Three months.*

Dottie didn't like the rags that I'd taught her to use when she was younger, so when she began working, she switched to the newfangled Kotex. But every month, there were still soiled under-things to be scrubbed. Except it had been three months. Three months since I'd washed a soiled linen.

"Oh, Dottie," I said to myself. "Oh, Dottala!"

AT nightfall, the house was in shambles, because I'd spent the day not working but plotting. Dottie was so young. True, I hadn't been much older than Dottie when I had her, but this was a different time, a different age. Dottie had so many more choices than those available to me. The more I thought, the angrier I became. Who was Dottie to squander such opportunities? Dottie was supposed to have a better life than mine. As my life was better than Mama's. It was the way it was meant to be. I would be damned if Dottie lost out on accounting school because of a foolish mistake.

The door banged against the back wall, and I yelled by rote, "Don't slam the door," not that it did any good. Why did I even bother?

"I'm tired. I'm going to rest before dinner," Dottie called as she retreated to my bedroom.

Tired, my tuchus, I thought, as I wiped my hands on my apron and followed Dottie into the small room.

"Ma," Dottie said, as she plopped on my bed. I could hear the weariness and for a brief moment, I felt compassion for my foolish daughter. "Can't I have a bit of privacy?"

"Privacy! As if privacy has done you good in the past." *Privacy* was the new fashion. It wasn't a word in my vocabulary, and even if it was, it was a mother's right to go where she was needed.

Dottie rolled her eyes and sighed, turning toward the wall. "Being head bookkeeper is hard. It's a lot more responsibility. I'm tired."

I violently shoved Dottie's legs over and sat on the edge of the bed. "Of course you are tired. Tired comes with your problem. How far along are you, *nu*? Three months, I suppose?"

Dottie flipped back over quickly, panic in her eyes. "What are you talking about?" I could tell she was trying to sound sharp, but instead she sounded shrill.

"I'm talking about you and that baby. What utter irresponsible nonsense, you putting yourself in this position. You are an embarrassment to this family!"

With a gasp, Dottie sat up. "How did—?"

"I am your mother," I said. I looked her deeply in the eyes, trying to impart my fury. "There is nothing I do not know."

Tears filled her eyes. But I put up my hand. "No. You do not get to be upset. You put yourself in this position. You will get out of this situation."

"Ma—," she began, but I cut her off with a *swack* to her leg. "Ow!" she cried.

"You think that hurts?" I said. "That's nothing. Wait till the pain you'll feel when that baby rips you in half. You think you know hurt? Just wait six months and you'll know hurt."

I knew I was scaring her, but I couldn't stop myself. My vision clouded with anger. "You were going to be an accountant. Have an education. And you threw it all away! For what? To slave at home for your children?"

"Ma, the boys will hear." By now she was sobbing, and I knew it was my duty to hold her, to comfort her, but I couldn't, not just yet. The wrath needed to dissipate first.

"The boys are playing outside. And you better get used to 'the boys' hearing. Your life is no longer your own. The baby in your belly is now in charge. Say good-bye to New York University. Say good-bye to your precious numbers. Say good-bye to your evenings out with your friends." I realized suddenly as I raged that I wasn't talking so much about Dottie; I was raging for myself. Abruptly I stopped yelling, which startled Dottie.

"Ma?" Her weeping made her body shake. "Ma?"

I stared at her. Tears rolled down her face, reminding me of when she was a child. She looked now as she had when we lost Joey, and I thought of the way she'd almost disappeared into herself with grief. My anger melted. She was still my baby girl and she was in trouble.

"Oh, Dottala." I opened my arms, and she fell into them. I squeezed tightly, my poor child. For long minutes I embraced my little girl, and felt the weight of her tears on my shoulder.

Finally, I pulled away. "We need to take care of this."

She nodded.

With a sigh, I let my dreams of my daughter as an accountant float away. I brushed her wet cheek with my finger. *Man plans; God laughs.* Time for a new course of action. "You and Abe will need to marry quickly," I said. "Children have been born early;

yours will be no exception. The college money. We'll say someone back home died, sent us the money, allowing you to marry
right away. You'll use the money to rent an apartment, furnish it.
Your impatience, for once, might serve us well. Everyone knows
how you've been suffering to marry that boy."

I could hear Dottie swallow. She looked at me, abject fear in
her gaze. Her mouth moved; she had something to say, but nothing was coming out.

"What? Speak up, girl," I said.

Again, her lips moved, but no sound emerged. Why was this
girl trying me? "Speak!"

Finally I could hear the whisper of her voice. "Abe won't
marry me."

"Of course he'll marry you. Once he learns you are carrying
his child, he'll have no choice. Abe is an honorable man, though
clearly not as honorable as I thought. Putting you into a situation
like this. It's a sin."

Dottie shook her head and the tears sprang anew. Her arms
wrapped around her body, holding it tightly. Her entire body
shook as if taken over by a demon. She said, "No, Ma. No." Over
and over again. I feared she was going mad.

A chill settled on me. "What are you saying?"

"Ma," Dottie said. Her voice was so hushed, I could barely
hear her. "You don't understand, Ma."

"Don't understand?" I shook my head. "Married twenty years,
birthed five children, and *I* don't understand?"

Dottie sobbed silently, which was more alarming than the
noisy weeping. My hands numbed as I tried to imagine what she
had done.

"No," she said again.

"What do you mean, 'No'? Dear God, Dottie, speak plainly."

The words caught in her throat. When she finally uttered them,
I was sure I misheard. What she was saying was simply impossible.

"I can't understand you," I said. I realized my voice was taking on a feverish pitch, but the room was spinning and I set my arm out to balance myself.

"The baby isn't Abe's, Ma." Her voice was quiet, but the words were unmistakable.

"What do you mean?" I asked. Did Dottie notice how the floor was rocking? Or was that merely my stomach lurching?

"The baby isn't Abe's." She could say it as much as she liked, but it simply didn't make sense.

"Of course the baby is Abe's. Did you two have a fight?"

"Ma—"

I desperately tried to block out what she was trying to tell me. My words came fast and frantic. "We can have the wedding next Sunday. Even have a little party at the *shul*. Maybe a *kiddush* after the wedding? You won't have a new dress, but I can fancy up your *Shabbes* dress and—"

"Stop!" Dottie's voice finally found itself. "You have to stop. The baby isn't Abe's." Dottie reached out to grab both my arms, and she gave me a slight shake. "The baby isn't Abe's."

I looked at my daughter with new eyes. Who was this stranger in front of me? A woman so loose? How did I raise such a child? I buried my face in my hands. How? How?

We sat there, each lost in our own grief, until I felt able to speak. Finally, I asked, "Who?"

Dottie couldn't look me in the eye. She stared at her nails—her precious nails she painstakingly painted fresh every Saturday, nails that tickled the backside of whom? Without glancing up, she said, "Willie Klein."

"Willie Klein!"

"Shush!" Dottie said.

I could hear the stirring in the apartment next door, as if someone was scooting to hear us more clearly. I brought my volume down. "Willie Klein."

She nodded.

Willie Klein. That pampered, snooty *putz* of a boy. His mother,

Molly, was too good for her own people. What was Dottie doing getting messed up with a boy like that? "How?"

"In Cold Spring. At Camp Eden," Dottie said.

"At *kamp ganeden*," I said. "Are you sure?"

Dottie nodded.

"Is there even the slightest chance that it could be Abe's?"

Dottie shook her head. Curse that boy. Had to be virtuous with my Dottie. *Schmuck.*

Dottie swallowed hard. "I—" She faltered before trying again. "I have a plan."

I raised an eyebrow.

"This weekend. I'm going to Camp Eden with Abe. I'm going to take care of things. Make sure he thinks the baby is his."

I stared hard at Dottie. Maybe my firstborn wasn't such a numskull after all. I nodded. "Do you think you can?"

Fresh tears formed in her eyes. "I have to, Ma. What other choice do I have?"

What other choice indeed? Briefly, my mind flashed to my talk with Perle, to the idea that there was another choice, but I forced myself back to the conversation with Dottie.

"He's apparently been virtuous so far," I pointed out.

Dottie nodded. "Yes, but I've never put a full effort into it before."

The front door banged. "Don't slam the door," I yelled without even thinking about it.

"When's dinner?" Alfie shouted from the front room.

Dinner. I had nothing for dinner. "You'll get your dinner when I'm good and ready to serve it." It would be a simple meal of herring and bread. The boys would complain. Eh, let them.

I looked at Dottie, her runny nose, her red-rimmed eyes. I took her hands in mine and stared hard at her. "Make this work. You hear me? Make this work."

She nodded.

I stood. I wiped my face with my hands, fighting the sweat, trying to make sure I was presentable. I walked out to the kitchen to begin the dinner preparation. She was going to make Abe think the baby was his? Shaking my head, I knew it was up to me to come up with another plan.

Dottie

———⚲———

LYING in bed, I could hear Ma bustling in the kitchen. I stared at the ceiling, the cracks in the plaster in the shape of a spider-web, weaving its way from wall to wall. Each mark branched into yet more: one line becoming six; twelve lines making seventy-two.

I closed my eyes. Math wasn't going to soothe me now.

My body longed to rest, but my mind wouldn't allow it. I was embarrassed, humiliated, scared. But at the same time, a new sensation took hold: relief. Ma knew. If anyone could fix things, it was Ma. While I knew it was irrational, the fact that Ma knew alleviated much of my fear.

But not my shame.

Last May. How long ago last May seemed now. Last May when I was still young and innocent.

What a fight Abe and I had had. Over those damn Krauses.

I replayed the incident in my mind. We left the theater on a Wednesday night and were wandering the streets, holding hands. Spring gentled its way into New York, and a rain had left large puddles in the road that reflected the streetlamps, giving a holiday twinkle to the cool evening.

I felt light and airy. A night like that was as glamorous as any in the movies. "What do you say?" I asked. "You and I go to Camp Eden this weekend?" I gave him a little squeeze. Just the idea of me and Abe up in Cold Spring was a thrill. In magazines, I read of

folks who escaped the city for an *entire* summer. Even if I could
leave only for a weekend, it made me feel worldly. *I'm going to the
country this weekend,* I'd tell the girls in the office. "It's opening
weekend, and it would be so lovely to go away, you and me."

Every summer all our friends would escape to Camp Eden at
some point. At the small socialist camp, run by the Yiddish Farband,
tents could be rented for a few dollars a night. The chores, in theory,
were equally divvied up—preparing meals, carrying water from the
well, collecting firewood, keeping the grounds clean—but in practice, the roles at camp weren't so different from the ones at home,
with the women doing more of the domestic chores, while the men
built fires and repaired tents. At night, we'd sit around the campfire,
singing the songs of our childhood—the protest songs, the work songs,
the songs we heard our parents sing as we marched in the streets and
cheered at rallies. Talk of politics sprinkled the air. Comedies—
proletarian, of course—were put on, lectures frequently given, baseball games a must. All the socialist talk I could live without. But the
freedom of Camp Eden? I'd take that any day, thank you.

"Cold Spring? This coming weekend?" Abe said. "It'll be
freezing."

"So?" I shrugged. "It'll be cold here, too. But at least there the
spring flowers will be emerging and the nights will be perfect for
strolls in the meadows." I leaned into him, letting go of his hand
to hold him by the crook of his arm.

Abe shook his head.

I changed to a more practical approach. "They need people to
ready the camp for the season." I didn't mind the camp chores.
Anything to be outside, alone with Abe. Camp Eden was the
only place we weren't smothered by people. In Cold Spring, I
was free to slide my hands beneath Abe's shirt, feel the knotty
muscles running along his back, lose myself in his solid arms.
Abe still maintained utter propriety, keeping me at arm's length,
but somehow, his arms never stretched as far in the open-aired
freedom of the country.

"Even if it weren't too cold, I'm afraid I can't. The Krauses are coming to town."

That stopped me short. "The Krauses!" I snorted. "All the more reason to go to Cold Spring."

Abe laughed. "Ah, always charming, my Dottala." He turned and wrapped his arm around me, warming me as the temperature dropped.

"Oh, and Sadie Kraus is so dignified? I've seen the way she looks at the boys when we all go to the café."

Abe stiffened, dropped his arms, and started walking again. "Don't be ungenerous, darling. It doesn't become you."

Not for the first time I wondered about Sadie and Abe. Was Abe jealous of the way Sadie flirted with other boys? Or merely angry that I was insulting an old friend?

"Ungenerous?" I said. "Nathan Kraus has made it perfectly clear he intends you for his sister. He actually said it in so many words." *Don't Abe and Sadie look natural together? If that's not beshert, I don't know what is.*

"Who cares what Nathan Kraus wants? What matters is what *I* want."

"And what *I* want. We'll go to Cold Spring this weekend," I said. "Play some baseball, maybe take a rowboat on the lake, relax by the fire."

"Nonsense," Abe said. "It's too early. And even if it weren't too early, I won't be rude to my friends."

My pace quickened. "Oh, so you're rude to me instead?"

"Dottie." His tone was quickly becoming exasperated. "Don't be like that."

"Fine!" My arms were practically pumping at my side, I was walking so quickly. "I'll go without you."

"That's crazy." Abe's shorter stride kept him a pace behind me. "We'll go in a few weeks, when it's warmer. This weekend, you'll come out with me, Nathan, and Sadie."

Any thoughts of giving in were immediately dashed. "You will not have me and Sadie at the same time."

"Dottie," Abe said, his voice lowering as it did when he was angry. "That is absurd. You are my girl. Nathan and Sadie are old friends. You will come with me when we all go out, and we will have a lovely time."

I stopped suddenly and spun around so quickly that Abe ran into me, practically knocking us both down. "Abe Rabinowitz, you will *not* tell me what to do. You can stay. Sadie can have you, for all I care! *I'm* going to Camp Eden."

"You're being foolish, Dottie."

"Foolish to think I could count on you to stand by my side."

With that, I turned and ran back to my apartment without him, fueled by my anger toward him and my hatred of Sadie.

AND so it was I arrived alone at the Cold Spring train station at 7:33 p.m. on Friday, May 24. At several points over the previous two days I'd thought to cancel my trip—it *was* awfully early in the season; it *would* be cold up there—but I refused to give Abe the satisfaction.

When I got off the train, I looked at the other passengers. No one seemed to be going to Camp Eden. A businessman with a valise appeared to have returned from a sales call in the city. A mother and a babe detrained. But I was the only young person with a suitcase, so with a sigh, I turned to head out to the camp. If Abe were there, he'd talk me into walking the three miles. But he wasn't, was he? So I hailed a cab from the front of the station, where they lined up for the city folk like me who wanted to get away for the weekend. But on that night—so early in the season—there was one lone cab.

Climbing in the back, I hauled my bag in next to me, plopping it on the seat Abe should have been occupying. My bag was small. I didn't need much for the weekend. It was still too cold for swimming, so no towels, no suits. Just shorts for playing sports and a clean pair of slacks for the next day.

The drive was quick, and when we arrived, the driver put out his hand. The meter read ".20." Reluctantly I handed over two dimes and a couple of pennies, sorry I hadn't saved the money by making the hour walk. This only revived my anger toward Abe.

It was late enough that I'd missed dinner, but an old friend from my grammar school days, Beverly, was there, and she scrounged up a snack of black bread and herring for me. After settling my belongings in the tent and eating, I joined the others at the campfire. The turnout was small. Only those especially committed to getting the camp up and running—like Beverly—and those who wanted to escape watchful eyes for a little fun in the country—like me. And Willie Klein.

We all huddled close to the fire, trying to keep warm. The temperatures in the city were starting to rise, but here, under crystal clear skies, the nip was enough to make me shiver if I moved too far from the flames. Damn that Abe. Leaving me cold and alone.

A metal flask made its way around the circle, eventually reaching Beverly on my left. A teetotaler, Beverly simply passed it to me with a "Help yourself."

Even through my thin gloves, I could feel the chill of the metal. The fire did little to warm me. Abe was right in not coming up; it was too early in the year to enjoy a weekend in Cold Spring. My fury grew. What was he doing right then? Had he and Sadie found a quiet corner in a cellar?

Bringing the flask to my mouth, I savored the feel of the liquid sliding down and the burn on the back of my throat. A warm flush rose in my cheeks. I noticed a few of the boys on the other side of the fire eyeing me, waiting to see if I choked on the fiery liquid. But I wasn't as naive as the others thought; I'd drunk before, liked the taste of the amber liquid, the way my insides became toasty.

To my right, Willie raised an eyebrow as I brought the flask to my lips for a second—and a third—swallow before passing it to him.

Willie Klein was as handsome as a movie star, with wavy black hair and high cheekbones. His nose was prominent without being too large, and his eyes were a violent shade of green. His appearance was slightly ambiguous; one could look at him and not know for sure if he was Jewish or Spanish or Italian, a handy trait for a writer in New York. In the city, I didn't see Willie too often. His parents had distanced themselves from the lower East Side, taken to their Park Avenue address with full body and soul. His mother, Molly, was Zelda's aunt, her father's sister, so sometimes Willie visited Zelda. But mostly he stayed in his own world except to partake every now and then in the *Yiddishe* nightlife. His parents thought the cramped and crowded lower East Side—the *shaddachan* making marriages, the peddlers on the street—an embarrassment, a throwback to life in the Old Country, even though neither had experienced it. His mother had been an infant when she came to the States, and his father was American-born. Willie's family was thoroughly modern. No arranged marriages for him.

The thought of arranged marriages made me think of Abe, and what he was doing with Sadie. Was his arm casually thrown about her shoulders? Did her hand rest gently upon his thigh? I thought of the way Lefty's hands, callused and hard, had touched me beneath my clothes all those years ago, how they'd stirred in me feelings of dizziness, but an exhilarating kind, a dizziness that filled me with the sensation of wanting until my body shook with fervor. I knew Abe had no intention of marrying Sadie. Which was exactly why it would be easy for him to act freely with her. No man wants an impure wife; but if she wasn't going to be *his* wife . . . A burst of anger tightened my muscles, made my jaw clench. But when I saw Willie looking at me queerly, I forced a smile. And when the flask came back around to me, my pull was extra long.

One of the girls brought a stack of blankets from a tent and passed them out. They were large scratchy coverings, and I shared one with Beverly and Willie. I tried to relax. The hooting of owls filled the night sky, and stars taunted from behind the clouds, playing peekaboo with the gazers below. Beverly was arguing politics with some of the men, who wanted to express their opinions even more loudly. The voices rose and rose, reaching for the sky. I was desperate for quiet, desperate for peace. No one noticed how silent I was. No one felt my fury. No one noticed the extra pulls I took from the flask, although now I wonder—perhaps I was noticed? Perhaps the man on my right was keeping careful track. But the night was intoxicating. The anger that fueled me, the bourbon on my near empty stomach, the crisp night, the crackle of the fire, the scent of Willie, who somehow seemed a tad closer than he'd been when I sat down. Did he think I didn't notice the way his eyes kept steadfastly returning to my face? A heat infused me, a heat that prickled. I felt beautiful sitting there, light-headed and delightful, admired by a handsome man. I was seductive and sultry. The hell with Abe, I decided. Sadie could have Abe.

No one could see the way Willie inched closer to me beneath the blanket. I observed Beverly from the corner of my eye, but she suddenly stood, moving closer to the boy with whom she was arguing, leaving Willie and me all alone under our cover. I kept my eyes on the fire, pretending I couldn't see him, not until his thigh grazed mine. I was entranced by the flicker of the flame. The fire heated my face to a near burn, but left my backside icy and raw. I settled slightly into Willie, the power overwhelming me. When the flask made its final round, I unabashedly tilted it up, finishing off the contents. Willie slipped his hand around to the small of my back. No one could see, though, when I removed it, enjoying first the consternation on his face, and then the surprised joy when I placed it on my leg.

No one noticed when I stood up. I didn't bother to excuse myself. I didn't glance at Willie, but retreated to my tent, which I didn't have to share, since it was so early in the season. I assumed no one noticed when Willie stood five minutes after.

Later, I lay alone in my tent, listening to the sounds around me, not quite believing what I had done, not quite understanding when it had gotten out of hand. *Were the sleeping bags always so flimsy? Why are the cots so stiff?* I thought, pulling the standard-issue, threadbare cotton sack farther up, trying to bury my chin underneath. May was too early, too early by a long shot. I shifted, rubbing my legs together, trying to ignore the unfamiliar stickiness on my inner thighs. A trip to the outhouse was called for, but it was so cold I didn't want to get up.

I played the night over and over in my mind. Everything had happened so quickly—a simple night of necking had taken a turn I didn't expect. I knew I should feel ashamed. I knew what I'd done was wrong. But as I tried to muster those feelings, I simply couldn't. I was surprised at how *good* it had felt, the way my body cried for his, the way I tingled at his touch. The first moment was one of shock, and when he murmured, "Is this your—" I hushed him with kisses and the shock gave way to heat. My married friends whispered of pain when they gossiped of newlywed life, but I felt none. Only a longing for more. No, it wasn't regret at what I had done. It was regret that it wouldn't—it *couldn't*—happen again. That it had never happened. That I would have to pretend nothing had gone on between me and Willie, that I hadn't felt his smooth hands caress my breasts, that his firmness hadn't slipped inside of me, that I hadn't cried out with such a hunger that I astonished myself.

I simmered in the afterglow of the experience. When Abe crept into my thoughts, I didn't feel worry; I felt only desire. Now that I knew what was coming, I wanted Abe all the more. This would be just a memory. A memory that would fade in time until I wouldn't even be sure whether I had simply dreamed it.

Little did I know. Little did I know that the memory wouldn't stay where it belonged, wouldn't live happily in the past, but would push its way into my present, forcing decisions I didn't want to make.

Rose

———— ✧ ————

Wednesday, August 21

WEDNESDAY morning I forwent my newspaper and tea. Looking into the mirror, I tried to smooth my hair, but it was little use;
gray and brown wisps flew out of my bun. I turned to the side.
Was my bump visible? Since giving birth to Dottie nineteen years
ago, I'd been a bit more round about the waist, so I doubted others
could tell. I rushed through my morning routine, anxious to get to
the *kaffeeklatsch*. All morning my stomach churned with worry.
Dottie thought she could seduce Abe. But that Torah-observant
schmuck was determined to have a pure wife; of that, I was sure.

Rose, I chided myself. How could I be mad at the one person
who held true to his virtue? So his virtue was inconvenient for
me. For that he was a *schmuck*?

Looking at my lined face in the mirror, feeling the exhaustion
that wouldn't diminish, aggravated by the throb in my leg, I
thought, *Yes. For that he's a* schmuck.

Dottie might think she could seduce Abe. And who knew?
Maybe she could. But if she couldn't . . . Well, time was running
out. If there were other possibilities—including the one Perle
had mentioned—they needed to be considered now. Dottie simply couldn't have a baby without being married to Abe. For all
the progressive ideals my friends espoused—my friends, who
had marched as suffragettes, fought against the evictions of their
neighbors, stood in picket lines—they would be appalled at the

idea of Dottie as an unwed mother. A baby who arrived a few months early? Well, they'd raise their eyebrows but then move on. But a baby with no wedding ring? The shame would be too great for Dottie to stay in New York. No man would ever marry her, and then she would have to live with Ben and me the rest of her life. My Dottie deserved a better life than that. The disgrace would touch the rest of us, too: Izzy would have difficulty finding a bride; it could hurt Ben's business.

If Dottie had the baby, she would have to leave New York, move far away where she could claim to be a widow. And where would she go? To Ben's relatives in the South? I could not picture Dottie in Birmingham. How would she support herself? And so far away from me. Who would help her raise her child?

I walked as briskly as my leg would allow to Lana's apartment, where already lounged in the front room were Bayla, Tatyana, Deborah, and Perle. Perle jumped up from the couch as soon as I entered.

"Here, take my seat," she said.

"Oh, is your leg acting up again?" Deborah asked.

"My leg is fine; no need to stand on my account."

Perle pursed her lips at me and I shot her a foreboding glare. She grinned and took back her seat. "Be nice, Rose," Perle said, opening her pocketbook. "Look, I wrote my letters." She pulled out a small stack of envelopes, which she waved at me.

"You want a prize?" I said, as I sat down in a wooden chair, placing my hat on the side table. But I was pleased. I knew that despite Perle's bluster, she worried about Yussel, too.

A plate of *mandelbrodt* was passed around the room, and I took one, along with a delicate linen napkin, which I used as my plate. The talk in the living room was easy. On any given day, the women might change, but never the conversations.

After about a half hour, I worked up my nerve. I swallowed, then swallowed again, willing the words to come. I, who never had a problem speaking my mind, was filled with apprehension.

For whom would they think I was asking? I cleared my throat and jumped in during a break in the conversation. "I have a question. I need . . ." I hesitated, unsure of how to ask.

"Yes?" Tatyana said.

I tried another way. "I have a friend. She has . . . trouble."

Perle looked at me in such an obvious way, a half smile on her face, I was afraid she would give away my situation.

Deborah wasn't too quick. "What kind of trouble? Money?" She took a bite of cookie.

I shook my head. "No. Not money. Trouble. Womanly troubles."

The room went quiet as the kind of *trouble* sank in. For some, it took a moment longer than it had for others. The last to understand, Lana, looked up, slightly shocked. "What does she intend to do?"

Perle chastised her with a look. "What do you think she intends to do? Would Rose have brought it up if this 'friend' were able to have a baby?"

Bayla, turning to me, said, "I may know someone who knows where to go. I can let you know tonight."

Relieved, I said, "Thank you."

WITHIN an hour, the group broke up, all of us returning home to start our dinners. As I was leaving the building, I heard Perle calling behind me. "Rose! Roseala!"

I paused at the bottom of the stairs, allowing her to catch up.

"I'll walk with you," she said.

I nodded.

We walked in silence for a block, before she said, "I know it's not easy. But you will be happy. Not right away, perhaps—"

Shaking my head, I cut her off. "It's not for me."

"What?" Perle's face screwed up in such a comical manner that if I weren't so upset, I would have laughed.

"It's Dottie. She's . . . in a way." Talking about my daughter made it harder to say the words.

"Dottie!" Perle's voice was loud and I shushed her. "But . . ." Perle sputtered slightly, trying to understand. "Why would she need a doctor? Why don't she and Abe simply marry?"

We stepped around a group of boys shooting craps in the street. I eyed them carefully to make sure my Alfie wasn't among them. I glanced up, as if seeking help from above to utter the words I would say next: "It's not Abe's."

"*Oy!*" Perle spoke so quietly and with such vehemence that I was surprised.

"Don't you judge, Perle Gittel Brudner. *Baruch Dayan Ha-Emet.* Only God above can be the judge."

"Who is judging?" Perle said, but her tone betrayed her words. And could I blame her? Wouldn't I hold Zelda in contempt if she did the same? "And the father is?"

Uttering the name of the *shmendrik* was impossible. "It's not important," I said. "Because either Dottie will make Abe think the baby is his or she will get rid of the problem herself."

"Make him think he is the father?" Perle said. Her hand flew to her chest and her eyes opened wide. "But that—how can—"

I let her ramble. Finally she said, "Yes, yes, I see. What else could she do?"

"There is nothing else," I said. "Perle, I failed her."

"Don't be ridiculous," Perle said, but her voice lacked conviction. Back home, protecting a girl's virtue was a mother's most important task. My mama would follow me with a close eye, yet with eleven children, it was impossible for her to be with me at all times. Had I found myself in trouble, Shmuel and I would have married. It would not have been the first time it happened. But Dottie? Was I such a fool for this to happen on my watch? If it was Abe . . . well, that I would have understood, could forgive. But Willie Klein?

"I have to help her now," I said to Perle. "Can you imagine Ben's heartache if he learns of this? If nothing else, I need to do this for him. I need to make the problem go away."

Perle turned and took my hands in her own. "You will. You

will do what needs to be done." She gave a little squeeze before letting go.

Placing my hand on my belly, I said, "May this one be a boy. Girls are too much trouble."

Perle gave me a hollow smile. "From your mouth to God's ears."

THAT night, a knock on the door proved to be Bayla. "I was out for a walk. I thought I would stop by," she said.

Looking in the hallway to make sure no busybodies were about, I said, "I am glad you did."

Ben rose from the couch. "Hello, Bayla. How is Mendel?"

"So-so. He has work, thank God, but his back? Oy, his back. But did I come here to tell you of my troubles? No. Rose, I brought you the name of that new shopkeeper. The one I told you about who needs sewers."

Ben interrupted. "Rose doesn't need to work."

Bayla shrugged. "Just in case. It never hurts to know." She handed me a folded piece of paper. "You should go by, talk to him. Make an appointment to show your work."

I nodded. "Thank you. You never know."

"*I* know," Ben said. "You are not working anymore. Especially not now."

"*Shah*, Ben! Hush your mouth and leave us women be," I said. That man could be frustrating with his determination to spill my secret.

Shaking his head, Ben retreated to the bedroom with a "Stay well" to Bayla.

Bayla whispered, "It's fifty dollars. Have her bring the money with her when she makes the appointment. I wish your friend the best."

"Thank you," I whispered back. "You will never know how grateful she will be."

Bayla smiled sadly, and turned to leave. "Oh, I have some idea."

Dottie

---❖---

Thursday, August 22

ON Thursday, I was ensconced in the numbers at Dover Insurance when the sound of the front door opening registered in the back of my mind. A smattering of giggles tittered throughout the room, but I paid no mind, running my finger down a column of lovely numbers. The bell was about to chime the end of the workday and I was determined to finish the row of tabulations before I left.

"Looking for Dottie, I am," came a familiar voice in broken English. My head shot up at the sound.

"Mother," I said. I'm not sure what was more shocking: my mother's sudden appearance in the office or hearing her speak her stilted English.

Florence laughed. "Of course," she said, not quite under her breath.

"What are you doing here?" I was embarrassed to see Ma in these surroundings. She wore her *Shabbes* dress, but even that was sorely out of fashion. I self-consciously smoothed the front of my frock, as if to flaunt how in vogue I was, while Ma looked more Old Country than lower East Side, never mind Midtown. The girls were enjoying the show, the greenhorn mother out of place in the modern office. My embarrassment was replaced by anger when I realized the others were looking down on me and Ma. It wasn't as if any of their mothers had been born in New York. What my ma was here, their mothers were at home. Worse.

At least Ma could put herself together and get through the city. How many of their mothers ever left their neighborhoods? I threw back my shoulders and gave Ma the slightest of smiles.

Ma said, "I thought we take a walk. An ice cream we'll get. We should go? You are done with work?" I knew how much Ma hated speaking English. Listening to her—the longest stretch of English I'd ever heard from her—I finally understood why. In Yiddish, Ma spoke eloquently, like an educated person. In English, she sounded ignorant.

"Give me a moment, Mother." I spoke firmly, in a tone I never would have used at home, a tone directed more to the room, to remind the others that I was in charge.

By the time I finished my column of numbers, the bell rang and the girls were putting on their hats and gathering their purses. Taking the already neat pile of papers in hand, I tapped them on the desk, lining up the perfectly smooth edges. I wanted to make sure all the girls were gone, so we wouldn't have to walk out together.

As I stacked the ledgers, I snuck a peek at Ma in that *shmatta* she thought of as her finest dress. Looking at her, I couldn't help but think of the poem we'd memorized in grammar school: "Give me your tired, your poor, your huddled masses yearning to breathe free." *Huddled mass* was exactly how I thought of Ma.

Every now and then, I wondered about the journey she'd taken to America. She was brave and strong; I don't know if I could have survived what she'd gone through. From the stories she told me, I pictured her, wrapped in rags and scarves, crowded on the deck of the ship. She gazed at the horizon, willing the shore to appear, each day growing more desperate. Ma told me she would focus on a point in the distance, using every last bit of her strength to keep from getting seasick, because that's how it started; she'd seen it in the other passengers. First they'd empty their stomachs; then, weak and dehydrated, they were laid bare to the thousand diseases crawling on the ship as freely as the mice scurrying on deck. Ma knew even the hint of illness was enough to keep one from passing through the vaunted doors of Ellis Island. She'd heard the tales of those turned away, sent back home, despondent and broken.

Was Ma expecting streets of gold or at the least indoor plumbing and a bathroom of her own? Did she die a little inside when she realized she'd left the life she knew for a cold-water flat up six flights of stairs on the lower East Side, the *shtetl* of New York City?

As mortifying as Ma could be, I also felt a smidgen of pride. *My mother made it.* With a smile, I patted the last papers into place and said, "I'm finished."

"Where do we go for ice cream?" Ma asked, switching back to Yiddish now that the office was empty.

As usual, I responded in English. "There's a place a few blocks away."

We walked out of the office awkwardly. I made way for Ma to exit first, but she stepped aside for me, and we ended up bumping shoulders on our way out the door. How odd to see Ma off the lower East Side. It was as if I were with a stranger. I was doubly proud of her for being able to navigate her way to the office on her own.

As we made our way down the street, Ma glanced around, and if I hadn't known her better, I would have said she looked nervous. But nothing made Ma nervous. Office workers bustled past us, everyone in a rush to get home. Stores were shuttering and the streets smelled of the day's rubbish being put out for morning pickup.

With another skittish look over her shoulder, Ma said, with no preamble, "You'll get rid of the baby."

Her voice was more rumble than words, yet what she said rang clearly in my ears. Her words chilled me, making me shiver on such a warm day, and my hand involuntarily jumped to my belly. Surely she wasn't suggesting what I thought she was. "Ma!"

"It's the only way. You'll get rid of the baby and it will be as if this never happened."

"I told you! Abe and I are going to Camp Eden this weekend. That will make the problem go away."

"Maybe you will, maybe you won't. But if it's 'won't,' then you get rid of the baby."

I couldn't look Ma in the eye. She couldn't mean this. I was upset enough that I replied in Yiddish. "What do you mean, 'get rid of'?" I knew exactly what she meant, but I refused to acknowledge it. All of a sudden, a new thought struck me: "Have someone else take the baby?" I didn't think of this before, but it made perfect sense! *Tante* Kate had watched Eugene when he was a baby. Perhaps she could take this baby? Or . . . it was too much to even think about, but what about Ma? We could go away, me and Ma, and have the baby somewhere else. Pretend the baby was Ma's. Not that I knew if Ma was still young enough to have a baby.

But Ma dashed my hopes before they were even fully formulated. "Get rid of. Don't have. There are ways."

I stopped in my tracks. Ma, oblivious, kept walking. I could hear her voice even as she walked ahead. "I've found the name of a specialist. You'll go." Ma noticed I wasn't with her and turned to face me. She took three steps toward me, maintaining a cool distance between us. "You do it the day before *Shabbes.* Stay in bed the next day and Sunday, too. By Monday you are good. Back to work. Back to Abe."

My body felt like it was collapsing upon itself, my own weight too much to bear. I leaned against the wall. The words swam in my mind, mimicking the turmoil rumbling in my belly. What Ma said made sense—it could make everything right—but my whole body screamed *No!* I looked at Ma and she was blurry.

She closed the distance between us. "Are you all right? Sit, sit." Ma took my arm and drew me toward a bench. She sat me down. "You going to pass out? Put your head down."

I set my head in my hands, which I then rested on my legs. I closed my eyes, trying to calm my body, yet images flew behind my lids, taunting me, images of myself in the office, of me with Abe, of a babe in my arms. Could I not have all of it?

Opening my eyes, I saw Ma, wrenching her hands, unsure whether to touch me. She said, "You can do this."

"It's not so simple," I whispered. Yes, I'd toyed with the idea of throwing myself down the stairs, but I didn't do it. And besides, it might not have done anything; it still would have been in God's hands. If the baby were to disappear naturally, well, there was nothing to be done about it. But to *intentionally* get rid of it?

Ma's hand reached out to my shoulder. "But it can be that simple."

Revulsion shot through me and I shook off Ma's caress. "I can't do that. I can't simply 'get rid' of the baby. It's . . ." It was what? I scrambled to find the adequate word, the word that would encompass every contradictory feeling flowing through me, explaining how as much as I didn't want to be with child, this *was* my child, and I couldn't shed her like last year's lip color. But nothing came, so I alighted on the one word that, while completely inadequate, at least said something concrete. "It's *illegal*."

Legality was the least of my concerns, although the stories I'd heard did warrant a fresh shade of fear, stories of dirty rooms, of crooked men posing as doctors. Stories of women made barren. Or who died. Was this what Ma wanted for me?

"There are ways around 'illegal,'" Ma said.

Get rid of the baby. It hadn't even occurred to me before; that's how foolish this situation was making me. "This is your grandchild!"

"My grandchild?" Ma looked to the sky, shaking her head as if she couldn't believe what I was saying. "Later, when my own children are grown, may God will it, there will be grandchildren. But not now. Now you get rid of it."

The bench felt as if it would swallow me. My limbs were stiff and I needed to move, to escape from these words. I stood and walked. I heard Ma trying to catch up with me.

"You get rid of it," Ma repeated.

"But why kill the baby? It's not the baby's fault." Weren't there other options? And my own ma, who had lost a child . . . How could she even *think* of killing this one?

Ma's voice dropped all notes of sympathy. "A baby? It is not a baby. It is something growing inside of you, but it is no more a baby than we can take an orange seed and call it orange juice. If you keep this baby, your life is done. Will Abe take you after a baby? What respectable man will? You think Willie Klein will marry you? His mother will have you in her fancy-shmancy Park Avenue apartment?"

With envy, I eyed the workers on the street waiting for the streetcar. What's the worst problem they could have? I wished I could be anyone else. I tried to picture myself in Willie's life, but his world was so alien to me, I couldn't even imagine it. "They may not have a choice."

"A choice? Of course they have a choice. *They* have *all* the choices. *You*, though, you have nothing. No money. No husband. No choices. Enough of this nonsense. You go to a specialist. You make the problem go away."

I tried to put this into numerical sense, but nothing added up. One mother minus one baby equaled Abe and college and whatever else I wanted. One mother plus one baby equaled . . . ? That was the question, wasn't it? No easy formula would solve that problem. "How do you even know of such things, Ma?"

Ma shrugged. "You think this problem is new? You think you are the only one with this kind of problem?"

I peered at Ma as we walked another block. Getting rid of the baby. I had to admit, it was the most logical conclusion. But I couldn't erase the vivid pictures in my mind: Eugene's face as he crawled next to me on the sofa in the dead of night, when he was haunted by nightmares and no one else could console him. The torment of losing my brother Joey, the pangs that still struck me in quiet moments when I watched Alfie play, wondering what it was like for him, losing someone with whom he was so intertwined that they breathed the same air, slept the same sleep, practically shared the same thoughts. I remembered Ma, sobbing in her bed, after those times when her belly was full and then, suddenly, it wasn't. Yet, in spite of those memories, I knew getting rid of the baby was the prudent thing to do. Ma made sense. Ma *always* made sense. It made me brim with fury.

"I'm going to succeed this weekend," I said.

"I hope you will," she said. "But even if you do, what about school? What about being an accountant? Maybe you do this even if you do succeed."

"Mother!"

Ma had the decency to look ashamed. "And if you don't succeed?"

"I *will*."

We reached the door of the ice cream parlor. We stared through the picture glass window, looking at cute round tables with curlicued seats for two. The store was made for romance or, at the very least, for young kids who begged their parents for a treat.

Ma turned to me, grabbed my arm desperately in both hands. "If this weekend works, then good. You have the baby. Problem gone. But if this weekend does not work, you will do it. Yes? Promise me. You will do as I say."

"Ma—"

Her voice turned yet more insistent. "You will do as I say, *nu*? You will not throw everything away. If you do not succeed this weekend, you will make it go away. Promise."

I looked in Ma's eyes, seeing the pain there. A twinge of guilt flashed through me, aware that *I* was the one causing that pain. I continued looking, as if searching for some other answer, another solution that might be buried in there. But seeing none, I once again yielded. "Yes, Ma," I said in a near whisper. "I will. I promise."

I looked back into the shop and Ma followed my gaze. We stood staring at the smattering of couples inside. One even had the nerve to share a single-malt glass, sipping from two straws poking out.

After a moment, I said, "Are we going in?"

"Hungry I'm not so much anymore," Ma said.

"Me neither."

And we turned and walked the two miles home in complete silence.

Rose

ON Friday morning I rose two hours before dawn to begin the dough for the *challah*. I pulled out the large tub—the only container big enough to handle the dough—and I placed a cake of yeast in it to proof. I needed to bake ten loaves: two for that night, two for the next day, four for the widower Rogalsky in the next building, and two to send with the committee that brought *Shabbes* foods to the newly landed immigrants in Battery Park. It was a light baking week.

As I waited for the mixture to bubble, I hauled out the flour and pulled the eggs from the icebox. The icebox. Such an unheard-of luxury back home. Keeping foods cold right in the kitchen. What miracles this new country brought. And what heartaches.

My hand went to my back, trying to ease out the soreness. My leg spasmed with each movement, but nothing could be done about that. When I was satisfied the yeast was good, I added the flour, salt, oil, and eggs and, using my arm, stirred it all together. When it held well, I tumbled the entire tub's worth on the kitchen table and kneaded the dough. I pushed and pulled and stretched and punched. The apartment was quiet, but on the streets already I could hear the bustle of those going to work—or coming home— pushcarts being rolled out, the milk wagon making deliveries.

With each twist of the dough, I turned my problems over in my mind. Who was I to judge Dottie? Was I any better? How many times had I snuck into the fields with Shmuel? Even now, twenty-five years later, I could practically feel Shmuel's touch, the gentle caress of his rough hands. His fingers were coarse and callused—he was a leatherworker by trade—but when he stroked my breast, the inside of my thigh, it was as if his fingers were silk. Only luck kept me from the position Dottie was in now. Shmuel and I promised ourselves to each other, even if it meant marrying behind my father's back. My father would never have allowed a love match. If he knew about Shmuel, *Tateh* would have beaten me with such fury, who knows if I would have survived it?

Shmuel's soft blond hair and dark brown eyes filled me with heat, and his physical presence filled a space. But ultimately it didn't matter: Shmuel was conscripted into the Russian army, and he never returned.

Not that I could complain. I had Ben. I loved Ben, intellectually, powerfully, but I loved Shmuel physically, passionately.

Beneath my fingers the dough took on a smooth sheen. I continued to knead, ignoring the way my body groaned. I had come to America to escape trouble. But it found me anyway. A different kind of trouble, perhaps, but trouble nonetheless. For this I made the treacherous journey across the ocean? For this I left my family, my home, and started anew in this strange land?

In Bratsyana, home had been a ramshackle wooden house on a street that was barely more than a muddy strip traversing a village on the outskirts of the outskirts of Odessa.

Tateh was furious that he had to send me to America before my younger brothers. He'd wanted the boys to emigrate, as they would be more useful in the New World, better able to earn money to mail home. But after the incident in the square, he had no choice but to let me go; he didn't think I could be trusted to stay safe, to not bring the czar's police down upon our house. I needed to prove to *Tateh* I could be as good a wage earner as the boys.

Heshie, my oldest brother, was already in America. Christopher Columbus, we called him. But he lived in a house with seven men in two rooms in Brownsville, on a dirt road; it wouldn't have been appropriate—or even possible—for me to stay with him. So instead I went to my cousin's apartment.

Ellis Island was a crush of bodies, a mass of people, and I walked in a daze, my eyes examined, my money checked, and soon I was out on the street, standing alone, unsure of my feet on solid land, my feet, which still carried the memory of the rocking ship. Men accosted me in Yiddish, asking my trade, wanting to know if I had somewhere to go. Other girls, with no one to meet them, let the men lead them to boardinghouses and sweatshops, where I learned later they'd be underpaid until they realized their own worth. But I had somewhere to go. Yet even with that certainty, each step made my knees weak, as the tumult of Manhattan confused me.

"Ver ees Eldridge Street?" I asked passerby after passerby, a phrase I had learned on the ship, until a young woman took pity on me.

"Where are you going?" the young woman asked in Yiddish.

Relieved, I held up the weathered paper with the scrawled address.

The woman nodded. She pointed ahead to a street sign. "Walk up Broadway. At Canal Street, ask for more directions."

"I am so grateful," I said.

"Good luck," the woman said. "You'll need it."

Walking the streets, carrying my carpetbag, which held every possession I owned in the world, I peered at each street sign, not that it mattered; the letters were meaningless. Every few blocks, I stopped someone and said, "Canal Street?" and followed their pointed fingers.

I had never heard such noise. Never seen such a press of people. Boys outside shops trying to lure customers with promises and shouts. Vendors hawking food and clothing from carts on the street. Kids running, darting, throwing balls around. When a rogue ball nearly smacked me, I stood, frozen, as a boy ran past me to get it. He said something in English, but I didn't understand it, could only stare at him. And then he uttered the word that would soon become so familiar to me, that I would hear again and again and again: *greenhorn*.

I was exhausted, but I didn't dare stop, didn't have extra money for the food being hawked, not that I recognized much of what was offered. Here and there, a familiar sound, but mostly alien food, food I couldn't trust to be kosher. My skirts were heavy, the thick cloth made thicker by the coins my mother had sewn into the lining. She had insisted I keep my earnings from my work as a seamstress—had hidden the money from *Tateh*—so I could use it to make a home in America. Little did we understand that this wealth would buy so little in the New World.

The walk was long, but I pieced my way to Eldridge. With the worn scrap in my hand, I searched for the address on the buildings. The paper was a mere formality; I had memorized the address: 27 Eldridge Street.

Finally I found the building. I pushed on the heavy door, and it gave way, leading to a narrow staircase up a dark hallway. With only the light from the small window above the front door, the corridor seemed no better than a black alley. Cautiously I entered, feeling the walls to find my way, climbing to the sixth floor.

A strange hum came from the rooms behind the closed doors, a low buzzing of a sort that I'd never heard before. The sound was constant, a background noise, almost as if a fly caught in my ear were desperately trying to get out.

When I arrived at the doorway, I knocked hesitantly. With my ear pressed against the door, the humming was louder. The sounds were definitely coming from within each apartment. No one answered, so I knocked again, with a bit more force.

A voice hollered inside and the front door was opened by a girl, no more than four years old. She looked up at me with big eyes. "I am cousin Raisa, coming from Russia," I said. When the little girl didn't respond, I wondered if she spoke Yiddish. A voice came from within the room in words I understood. "So? Who is it?"

The little girl turned and yelled in a language I couldn't understand. The only word I could pick out was my own name, although it was said in such a foreign way, with such alien intonations, that I wondered if it really belonged to me. The room was a front room combined with the kitchen, with a large coal-burning stove and three mattresses propped in a corner.

"Let her in already," said the voice, and from behind a machine on the kitchen table, Yetta stood and walked over to me.

Setting my bag on the floor, I embraced my cousin, whom I hadn't seen in almost five years. "Come in, come in," Yetta said, leading me back to where she had been. "Have a seat." She pointed to a chair in the corner. "I need to finish the work. We'll talk while you catch your breath."

I sat on the chair, which at one time must have been plush, but now lumped and sagged in the middle. The chair was the color of the yams we ate back home, and I was struck by a longing for Mama.

Yetta sat back down at the table, on top of which was a graceless metal machine with a large round wheel, a spool of thread atop, and cloth sticking out.

"What is that?" I asked.

Yetta said, "This? A sewing machine. Can you believe it?"

I got up to look at it more closely. The wheel of the black monstrosity was wound with thread, and a giant needle punched up and down as Yetta pumped a pedal with her foot.

"What do you do with it?" I asked.

"I rent it. I do piecework. The store owner sends a runner with the cut cloth—someone else does that part—and I sew it together. I get five cents an item. I'd get more if I could do the hand-sewn finish work, but I'm not so good at it. Your *tateh*, though, wrote me you are excellent at it."

I nodded. At home Mama had taught me to sew, and I became a glove maker, sewing delicate pieces for *Tateh* to take to the market in the next town to sell to the fine women.

"It is good you came. We can make more money."

I sat back down and looked around the room. The sewing machine rested near the only window, which gave barely enough illumination to see the work. I didn't understand at the time what an incredible luxury this window was, how others longed for a sliver of light in their rooms. All I could see was that the glow was dull and the room crowded, with the chair and a settee that someone clearly slept on at night—a blanket and a pillow clustered at one end—and a stack of mattresses. A few photographs, of relatives back home, dotted the meager flat surfaces: the top of the buffet, the side table. An ironing board leaned in a corner. Gaslights remained unlit—gas being too expensive, apparently, to waste during the day, no matter that the apartment didn't seem to allow any light.

"Are you thirsty? Jeanette, get Rose a glass of water."

"Rose?" I asked.

Yetta nodded. "Raisa is Old Country. Rose is American."

"Rose," I repeated.

"Here I am no longer Yetta." Was that pride in her voice? "Here I am Ida."

"Ida." These names twisted on my tongue. So much was changing already; I hadn't expected my name to do so as well.

As I took in the room, Yetta—or should I be calling her Ida?—asked for news of home. Her parents, her siblings, how they were doing.

I told her as much as I knew, searching the crevices of my mind for details I might have forgotten. My head was so full of politics, brimming with excitement at leaving the small town, escaping the village life that seemed so pointless once Shmuel had disappeared, that I hadn't taken notice of much else around me.

After I drank my fill of water and leaned back to relax a moment, Yetta said, "*Nu?* You good? Ready to start work?"

"Work?" I asked. "Already?"

Yetta looked embarrassed, although her tone held no hint of apology. "I know you just got here," she said, "but work needs to be done. This isn't Russia, you understand? This is America. Money is the key to America."

I knew she was right. It was my duty to earn the money to bring over the rest of my family. Plus I needed to earn my keep at Yetta's house.

So I sewed. Every day, twelve hours a day, I sewed. At night, I shared the settee bed with the child, Jeanette, as Yetta and her husband slept on a mattress near the stove, and three boarders, women, slept on the floor—two at our end of the room and one in the kitchen. I knew I was lucky to have a bed to share.

Shabbes as I knew it no longer existed. Yes, on Friday nights we lit the candles, made the blessings, ate the *challah*. But *Shabbes* was no longer a day of rest. Work must be done. Seven days a week.

I spent most of my days in that cramped apartment, doing the fine finishing details. My work was beautiful enough to garner the attention of the shop owner who commissioned my work. He gave me more intricate pieces, lace work to do. My rates rose, until I was doing elaborate pieces that would be sold at Macy's, earning me ten cents an outfit.

At night, as tired as I was and as cramped as my back felt from hunching over the delicate pieces of fabric, I made sure to go out. I left partly to escape the bickering of Yetta and her husband—I quickly learned that time alone for a man and a woman was a luxury of the rich in America—as well as to see this new country. Two nights a week, I went to the Educational Alliance, where I learned English. Many nights, I attended free lectures and discussions— Dr. Magnes discussing his trip to Palestine; Morris Hillquit and Samuel Untermyer debating "Should the government own and operate all the trust?"; Congressmen Sulzer and Goldfogle protesting the Dillingham Bill. When I could splurge on a cup of tea and a pastry, I would visit Café Royal, where young people gathered every evening to reminisce about home, to play chess, and to discuss politics.

It was over tea that I met Ben, a young labor organizer, a

union man. After giving a rousing impromptu speech, mixing both English and Yiddish, about the benefits of workers banding together, he sidled up to me.

"What do you do?" he asked me in English.

The words were basic enough that I could understand them, but I replied in Yiddish, "I don't respond to men who don't speak to me in the *mame-loshen*." I tried to appear coquettish as I said this, when in reality, English made me feel stupid.

Ben grinned and repeated the question in Yiddish. As a union man, Ben made himself useful with his fluency in English, Yiddish, and Russian. He, and often he alone, could communicate with the various groups.

"I do piecework," I told him.

"And do you belong to the International Garment Association?"

"I belong to no one," I said coyly.

With that, Ben gave me a broad smile. He was a short man, perhaps even an inch shorter than me, but he had deep brown eyes and a furrowed brow that gave him an air of intelligence. I took an instant liking to him.

"In that case," Ben said, "would you care to accompany me to the theater?"

I raised an eyebrow at him. I had never attended the theater before. I had never gone out in public alone with a man. I thought back to Shmuel. He was gone and yet I felt as if I were betraying him.

"The Yiddish theater," Ben added, with the grin that would become so familiar to me. "That is, if your parents will allow it."

"I am a woman of"—I hesitated for the barest of seconds, seconds in which I chose to leave Shmuel behind in the Old Country, to reinvent myself as an American—"eighteen. I require no one's permission." A small lie. Three years shaved from my age. I didn't want Ben to think I was a spinster. This was a fresh start in a fresh country, and I wanted to start it as a young woman, not an old maid.

Ben and I knew each other four weeks before we announced

our intention to marry. And two weeks after that, with a quick visit to the *rebbe*, with only the newly arrived Perle and my cousin Yetta as witnesses, as my brother couldn't miss a day of work, we were married. Just like that, I no longer lived on the settee with Jeanette.

Ben and I lived with his parents in a one-bedroom apartment where the walls were so thin that I reddened when I saw his mother in the mornings. But Mama Krasinsky always smiled at me, saying little. She was a caring woman, but she wasn't my mama. I dreamed of bringing Mama to America, of giving her this life where girls were expected to learn their letters and marry for love and join in the political conversation without fear. When news arrived of Mama's death, I cried for six days. I named my firstborn, Dorothea, for my ma, Deenah.

Until Dottie was born, my primary concern was earning enough money for my family back home, and Ben's was saving enough for our own apartment. In the summer, the work wasn't so bad. I was extremely mindful not to let a drop of my sweat taint the fabric; I was expert enough to keep my cloth pristine. In the winter, though, the work was miserable. The sewing was too intricate for me to wear gloves—I couldn't make fine stitches if I didn't have complete movement of my fingers—so while the rest of me sat bundled in coats, my fingers were bare. Fingers that were icy hurt that much more when accidentally pricked with a needle. And my fingers were constantly raw from the chill, so I had to take great care not to snag the wispy fabric. Heat was nonexistent. A tiny flicker of warmth seeped out of the stove, but it didn't make much difference. Visiting the toilet meant a trip down a dark, dank hall to the unheated room that was shared with the other three apartments on the floor. It was almost as bad as the outhouse back home, even if I didn't have to go out in the rain or snow.

My fingers never recovered from the work, and I was still a youngish woman in my twenties when they first felt the pain of arthritis. *Never*, I promised myself, *never will my own children work with a needle and thread.* My children would use their wits to make their way in the world. And true to my word, I made sure I never taught my children—especially Dottie—more than the basics, kept from them the skills that helped me to survive in this strange New World.

While our days were backbreaking, we enjoyed all the East Side had to offer at night. We continued going to speeches and cafés, and on a few occasions, Ben was the lecturer. How proud I was to sit in the audience and listen to his inspiring talks on the labor class and the capitalist machine. A Jewish man speaking politics in the open with nothing to fear! It amazed me. I strutted like a peacock on those evenings. Yet as much as I believed in the theories he espoused, I worried about Ben's day-to-day involvement with the union—people were known to get hurt doing what he did. But Ben brushed off my concern, and went out from early morning often until late at night, canvassing workers, imploring them to unite, joining picket lines, occasionally coming home with a bruised eye or a sore rib, which he would dismiss with a wave of his hand. But I was not a woman to be easily dissuaded, and after few years of marriage, I convinced Ben he must think of our future, of the second child we were expecting. Ben needed a job that paid better. So Ben borrowed money and purchased a garage with his cousin, who had recently returned from Detroit, where he'd worked at an auto factory. They made good money housing and fixing the cars that were rapidly taking over the streets—enough to repay his debts and for us to move into the apartment we live in today—and although they often stayed late washing and servicing the cars, I stopped fearing for his safety. By the end of many years, Ben and I had saved up a nice bundle of money, and we sent over enough for various members of both our families to make the journey to America. My *tateh*, though, refused to come, as his own mother was too ill to travel. Besides, he didn't want to leave Yussel alone—Yussel, who would be denied an international passport until he passed the age of the draft.

I continued to do garment work during the day, but Perle and I—with children in tow—always found a few hours every week to visit the cafés to discuss the garment union with new immigrant women or to distribute flyers outside the sweatshops. We spent many hours marching for suffrage and were disappointed we couldn't attempt to vote, as we were not yet citizens. We were prepared to be arrested with the other women. Ben's garage was successful enough that I was poised to leave the needle trade behind and take a lower-paying position in the union. "In the office, where it's safe," I'd say testily to Ben, when he teased me about entering the world that I had made him leave.

And then the twins became sick. Nothing else mattered. Alfie, thank God, recovered quickly, and even the telltale polio limp disappeared in a year or so. But Joey. I spent every day with Joey even when, toward the end, he was taken to the hospital, which had the new machine, the iron lung. But for Joey, it was too late. And by the time he passed, I felt it was too late for me. A spark had been extinguished. I buried myself in the children, focused my efforts on procuring a visa for Yussel, tried to do good works in the neighborhood. My life was filled, too much for me to reflect upon my place in the world. But every now and then—when the children were sleeping, with Ben at the garage and the bread baking in the oven—I thought of Russia; of *Tateh*, toiling to care for my grandparents; of my mama, who died without me by her side. I longed for my older sister Eta, who had left Bratsyana shortly after I, headed for Palestine. "I'm a *halutz*," she wrote when she arrived, a pioneer. Her big ideas and sturdy frame were exactly what the country needed, but selfishly, I wished Eta had chosen America.

I continued sending money back home every month, money I hoped would pay for firewood, for food for the harsh winters, until *Tateh* wrote that my envelopes were arriving opened, the money gone. At that point, I put aside every extra cent in the name of my daughter. For my daughter to make something of her life. To go to school. To become an American.

Was this what an American was? Unmarried with child?

Now *Tateh* had returned to Mama, Yussel was trapped with his family in Warsaw, and I, with child yet again, felt infinitely alone.

Just when I thought my arms couldn't take any more, the dough became pliable, soft. Using both arms, I scooped it back into the tub and, covering it with three dish towels, left it to rise.

Looking out the window, I could almost see a few stars. Closing my eyes, I prayed to the heavens that Dottie would get this right, that she would make the right choice. *Be smart, Dottie*, I implored. *Please*, Hashem, *guide her.*

Dottie

I couldn't shake the bad feeling from my talk with Ma on Thursday night, and it put a pall on my eagerness for the weekend. I packed listlessly, the trip taking on funereal tones. If I didn't succeed, it was the end of my baby.

Abe received a shipment to unload at the store late Friday afternoon, so we decided to leave Saturday morning. The knock on the apartment door came soon after *Shabbes* early *minyan* would have ended. Ma jumped at the sound. I shot her a look. Nothing could be amiss. This was a normal weekend away.

"*Gut Shabbes*," Abe said as he entered. His smile was broad and he gave a slight bow as he said, "Is Mademoiselle ready to go?"

My laugh felt forced, and Ma stood at the kitchen door, wringing a cloth in her hands. I willed her to bring up Europe or rent strikes or FDR or any of her other topics that drove me crazy, but she stood mute. I needed to get Abe out before he realized something was off.

"We should hurry along. Don't want to miss the train."

"Yes, yes," Ma said. "Off you go." She retreated quickly to the kitchen. Abe gave me a questioning look and I shrugged. Why did Ma abandon her tirades now?

"Let me get your bag," Abe said, reaching for my small suitcase. Lifting it, he said, "Yikes, what's in here?"

With a light smile, I said, "Oh, the usual. My iron. Alfie's baseballs. A roasting pan."

Abe's laugh calmed my nerves and we headed out.

On the way to Grand Central Station, I tried to pretend nothing was awry. Just me and Abe off for a ruckus on a summer weekend. We bantered, but I felt more like an observer than a participant.

Stepping up to board the train, I thought again of tripping, of falling. If I dove from the train, would I die instantly or would I be racked with pain? What would the baby feel? What would she say when she greeted me in the world to come?

No! I chided myself as I followed Abe to empty seats. He lifted my bag and placed it upon the mesh shelf above us. We sat next to each other and I curled my body into Abe's as the train pulled out of the station. He was warm and soft and comfortable. Sweet Abe, who was as familiar to me as the couch in my living room. He molded to me, fit me in all the right places. I watched the scenery pass, trying to forget the importance of this weekend. But it occurred to me, if my plan worked, this would be my last trip to Camp Eden. Forever. I couldn't go if I was expecting and once I had a child . . . well, everything would be different then, wouldn't it?

My life was about to take a sharp turn, and I'd never come down this path again. Whether I married Abe or did as Ma said, the break was final. Before and after. I'd either be a wife with a home and a child or be a career gal with the ghost of what could have been. No longer innocent and carefree, I'd cross a line, become an adult. All I wanted to do was mourn for the life that was spent.

The trees whisked by the window, blurring into a mass of green. I said to Abe, "How many trees do you think we pass on our way to Cold Spring?"

Abe laughed, as he paged through last week's *New Yorker*. "I don't know, but I have a feeling you're about to tell me."

My finger idly traced on the window, outlining the trees as they whizzed by. "Well, if there is a tree every four feet, then there would be one thousand three hundred and twenty trees in a straight mile. How many miles do you think it is from Grand Central to Camp Eden?"

Abe shrugged. "Fifty? Sixty?"

"If it's fifty miles, then it would be sixty-six thousand trees. If it's sixty, then seventy-nine thousand two hundred trees." I tilted my head back against Abe and considered. "Although they wouldn't be evenly dispersed. Fewer trees in Manhattan, more in the Hudson Highlands."

Abe kissed the top of my head. "My brilliant mathematician." Closing the cover of the magazine, he held it out to me. "Would you like to read this? There's a piece on Paris fashion." I went to take it, but he playfully pulled it out of reach. "But don't go getting any ideas. Your raise won't cover—whatshername? Vanilla Chanel?"

"It's Coco Chanel," I said, but looking up, I realized he was teasing me. I laughed, but to my ears, it sounded off.

"Coco Chanel, then," he said, picking up *The Nation* magazine.

I scanned the article, but frankly, it held little interest, given the state I was in. Concentrating was nearly impossible. I flipped through the pages and noted the articles, all light and fluffy: a letter from Paris by Genêt about nothing more controversial than the Tour de France, a favorable review of Mrs. Lindbergh's book *North to the Orient*, short stories, an article called "The Advance of Honorifics," whatever that was, and a report on the races at Saratoga. Thinking of Yussel and the argument between Abe and Willie, I looked for something—anything—about what was happening in Europe. In all its sixty pages, the only hint that trouble stirred abroad was two sentences hidden in "Of All Things": "As we understand it, Goering and Goebbels are Hitler's G-Men. Their job is to stamp out the pernicious churchgoing element." That was it. Our world was falling apart overseas and it was comedy for *The New Yorker*.

Abe must have seen something in my face, because he asked, "Are you okay?"

Banishing my thoughts, I smiled broadly, saying, "I can't wait to arrive."

I tossed the magazine aside and curled into Abe. This weekend would be a success.

A baseball game was ending as we arrived. "Shall we hurry and
join them?" I asked. I needed to please, to make Abe happy.

"Nah," he said. "There's always tomorrow. I want to relax."

We separated into our own tents. Abe's was shared—it was
cheaper that way—but I'd splurged on a tent of my own, the better to make good on my plans.

Before dinner, I took extra care. Normally I cultivated a casual
look at Camp Eden, making myself look pretty without appearing
to have tried. But tonight I took more time, with a less outdoorsy
look than usual, applying a little lipstick, trying to look refined,
my hair flawless. Instead of the slacks I usually wore at dinner and
around the campfire, I put on a new skirt. I struggled to button it
and finally gave up, leaving the top button undone. How could my
stomach have blossomed so? With my blouse untucked, no one
would notice and the skirt showed off my legs to my advantage.
When I peeked down at my bosom, my first instinct was to hide
how it had begun to swell of late. But then I chastised myself for
such a priggish notion, and instead undid one clasp on my top, just
enough to emphasize my roundness. I surveyed myself as best as I
could without a mirror. Lovely and ripe, I thought. Abe might not
notice the difference, but he would sure notice me.

Camp Eden was a haven, a place to simply be. The first time
I'd ever come was with an older cousin, who was now married
and no longer escaping to the country. I was fourteen and I'd
never spent the night away from my parents, never slept without
the sounds of the streets in my ears, away from the noise of the
neighbors through thin walls. Even the train was an adventure,
its Pullman cars with sleepers and luggage racks above the seats
to stow my small suitcase. I dreamed of a time that I'd travel far
enough to lounge in a Pullman.

When the cityscape gave way to open rural space, I could only stare in awe. Land. With no one on it. My entire life subsisted between the monoliths of New York City, where people lived on top of people, in apartments piled high on crowded streets. I had never seen a place where space existed without people. When I described the scenery to Ma, a faraway look entered her eyes, and I knew she was thinking of her home.

Once we arrived at Camp Eden, my cousin led me to the tents, and I was amazed at the idea of sleeping outside where there was no smog, no smelly bodies pressed against my own, no street noise below. Sleeping in the woods—with only a thin layer of canvas between me and the heavens—was as far removed from sleeping on my roof at home as Schiaparelli gowns were from the *shmattas* the women of the neighborhood wore. I didn't sleep a wink that first weekend, mesmerized by the sounds of nature. Who knew such a different noise belonged in the world?

Ah, such a time of innocence. No more. Tonight Camp Eden was not to be a haven. It was a duty. I had one job: make Abe think this baby was his.

Yet, as much as I dreaded what I needed to do, a part of me thrilled at the idea. In all this misery about the baby, I hadn't allowed myself to think about what had put me in this position. That night. With Willie. I knew I should feel ashamed thinking about it, but I didn't. I felt, well, lustful. And I longed to share that with the man I truly loved. To feel Abe's hands caress me, to feel his kisses deepening. I craved the touch of his hand, sliding up my side, stroking my breast. The mere thought of his body pressed against mine gave me a warm determination.

At dinner I laughed at his every joke. I held his gaze for moments too long. I needed to be in control of the night. When he put a distance between us, I flirted with the boy next to me. Nothing made a woman more desirable than being wanted by someone else. And it worked.

Sitting around the campfire, when the flask passed my way, I

took a long swig before handing it to Abe. Though I tried to coquett-
ishly ignore him, I couldn't help but notice Abe's hearty gulps of the
amber liquid. A young man played his guitar, and the boy with
whom I'd flirted at dinner asked me to dance. I stood but had barely
entered his embrace when, as expected, Abe was soon at my side.

"May I cut in?" Abe asked.

"Ah, cork it," said the boy, and I laughed a little drunkenly.

"I'm sorry," I said to the boy, "but I'm all his."

I turned to Abe and rested one hand on his shoulder, and he
took hold of my other hand. The guitarist played "Don't Fence Me
In," and one of the girls sang as more dancers dotted the grass.

The music was seductive, enhanced by the bourbon, and I pulled
nearer to Abe, allowing him to lean in and kiss me. As we glided, we
sidled into the shadows of the trees, which cast long, lean markings
on the ground in the moonlight. We danced and kissed, oblivious to
those around us. As the kisses deepened, I carefully brought myself
close enough to Abe that I could clearly feel how much he wanted
me. My hand tightened on his neck, and I pressed my breasts against
his body, grateful for the way they spilled out of my blouse.

The magic of the night was taking over. I was lost in the moment,
happier than ever before, my body humming in such an intoxicating way that I couldn't wait for what was next. I was drunk on the
music, the stars, the alcohol, and Abe. Together we moved even farther from the others, till we were hidden by the woods and he
leaned me against a tree. The bark dug into my back, but I ignored
the discomfort as his body moved rhythmically against mine. I
pulled up my skirt so I could feel him, through his pants, on the
skin of my thigh. My hands teased the top of his pants, working the
buttons, and I slipped my hand, tentatively, slowly, between his
pants and his waist.

My body was alight, my head spinning with arousal, and I needed
to feel him inside me. In that moment, that singular moment, I knew
perfection. Me, Abe, the moonlight, the only sounds the ones of our
lust. This was the moment I would hold with me the rest of my life,

the moment I would retreat to whenever there was trouble, disappointment. This exquisiteness made me delirious with happiness. This was the moment that would sustain me, the moment when the world was just right, and I knew in my heart I was about to get my happily ever after.

And I clung to that thought. I clung to it like a drowning woman to a life preserver; I clung to it with every hope and every breath even after he began to gyrate at a quicker pace, even after he gave a violent thrust against me, even after he groaned loudly, calling out my name in a deep rumble. I held on to the thought even as I realized it was too late, that my thigh was damp from him, that my plan had failed utterly. For once it was me who had been too slow.

My body still needed to be touched, still needed him. I hoped to recapture the moment, to arouse him again, so, fighting the desperation in my voice, I whispered, "Abe," as I nibbled on his neck. I needed his hands upon my chest, between my legs. I needed. But he pushed himself away, disgusted. "Oh, Dottie," he said, refusing to look me in the eye. "I am sorry."

"Don't be sorry," I said, my voice still raspy with desire. I pulled him back, drawing his hands toward me. "Just don't stop."

"Dottie," he said. "I've sinned enough for one night." I could hear the embarrassment in his voice. "*We've* sinned enough."

"How can it be a sin when it feels so right?" I attempted to kiss him on his earlobe, but he shook his head and took a step away from me and the tree.

"Dottie, we can't," he said. "This was wrong. I can't be trusted around you."

"But why?" I asked. I tried to keep the pleading notes from my voice, but I feared I was failing. "We are in love. We will be married. And it feels so . . . nice." I took a step toward him and stroked his face, but he pushed away my hands.

"Dottie," he said more gently, hiding his body in the shadows so I couldn't see his humiliation. "We've been through this before. You know why it is not right."

My body screamed for him, begged for him. "I don't understand."

"Of course you understand," Abe said. "You simply choose not to." His voice lost its distress and took on a more patronizing tone. "What we've done tonight is a sin. An act against God."

Looking around, I spotted other couples, far off, in various stages of necking and petting. Nothing was truly visible in the night but the movement of bodies, and the low murmur of sweet nothings carried on the evening winds. "Abe. This is 1935. New York. It's not 1880 in the Old Country."

Abe took another step back and looked at me condescendingly. "Virtue is not dictated by time and place. Dottie, I do not wish to be with the woman I am going to marry before our wedding night."

That stopped me cold. "What does that mean?"

"What does what mean?" Abe asked. His confusion sounded genuine.

"Does that mean you've been with a woman you *don't* intend to marry?" I asked.

"Of course not," Abe said.

Was I reading too much into his words? But how else could he stay so pure? He *had* to be *shtuping* someone. "Have you been with Sadie?"

"I am horrified that you would even accuse me of that," Abe said.

His tone told me I was pushing things too far, but now that I had started, I couldn't stop. "That wasn't a no," I said.

"Dottie, I won't entertain such a disrespectful accusation."

"Is this why you won't be with me? Won't marry me? Because you'd have to give up Sadie?"

Abe's voice was strained with fury. "We will marry when I have the money for us to have our own apartment. I don't want to be one of those couples who move in with their parents. We need to stand on our own two feet." He looked upward and took a deep breath. Clearly he no longer wished to argue. "Or rather four feet," he said, trying to lighten the mood.

Or six feet, I thought.

"I suppose I should be flattered by your jealousy," he said, rubbing my arm gently, but keeping his body away. "Dottala, I promise, there is no one but you, and there has *never* been anyone but you. Our wedding night will be so very special." He placed his hands on my arms, turning me so I was looking him in the eye. "For both of us."

I stood there, too confused to cry. I had completely misread the situation. Sadie meant nothing to him. Which made my tryst all the more of a betrayal. My entire body was hot and angry, but I was as angry with myself as I was with him. I desperately wondered what Ma would do in this situation. Ma, who always managed to bend *Tateh* to her will, without him even being aware of it.

I batted my eyes, as if pushing away tears, when really I was trying to dispel my anger. "I'm sorry, Abe. I want so much to be married." A thought occurred to me that had flitted through my mind before: "You work for your parents. Why can't they give you a raise?"

He pulled his hands down and smiled at me. "My parents are generous with my wages. By spring," Abe said. "By spring I'll have enough money."

"I have money saved," I said.

"But not enough."

"But I do! My mother has saved ninety dollars that's just for me. We will use that. That's four months' rent."

Shaking his head, Abe said, "We can't take handouts from your mother. Not when spring isn't so far away."

I placed a hand on his chest. "Abe, I don't want to wait until spring. I want this." I stroked him and crept closer. "Now." I leaned in to kiss him.

"Dottie. No," he said, moving definitively away. "You'll feel better about this in the morning. When the bourbon has worn off," he teased.

"Abe—," I tried again, but Abe merely leaned in and gave me a chaste kiss on the cheek.

"Good night, Dottie. I'll see you in the morning."

He left me standing there; I watched him walk off to his tent. For a desperate moment, I forgot about the baby and thought only of my own desire, my own longing, my own fury, my own desperation. I hungered for the feel of his body and wanted to scream at him for his refusal to take me. I knew I was attractive; I knew I was desirable. Willie made that abundantly clear.

The thought of Willie instantly sobered me. Willie. My condition. No solution. It was all over.

The next day, Abe kept a distance, emotionally, physically, as if afraid of repeating the night before. Clearly he'd meant what he said.

I tried to get close, but he kept his smile frozen and our normally easy way was stiff and formal. When everyone went swimming, I pretended I'd simply forgotten to pack my swimsuit. My body was too round at this point to put on such a display.

On the train home, Abe thawed, knowing he was safe from my advances. He tried to cuddle, but what was the point? No future existed for me and Abe. Not unless . . . Ma's logic was inviolable as always.

Looking out the window at the scenery that at one time had so enthralled me, I saw only emptiness, nothingness. Maybe the country didn't hold the answers. Maybe getting lost in the city was the only way to truly survive, to disappear among the masses.

Only one answer remained. I wondered if the blackness settling over me would be with me for good.

WHEN I walked into the apartment, Ma looked at me expectantly. I pushed past her, suitcase in hand.

"Make the appointment," I said as I stepped into Ma's bedroom and shut the door behind me, falling into sobs upon the bed.

Rose

⚡

Monday, August 26

MONDAY morning, Dottie left early for work. She spent extra time making herself look pretty, I imagine to distract herself from what was coming. I knew my pitying looks were only pushing her away, but I couldn't stop myself. My poor baby.

Izzy and Ben left for work and I shooed Eugene and Alfie out the door. I put on my *Shabbes* dress. Seemed I was wearing that thing daily, and I was starting to see Dottie's point that a new dress wouldn't hurt, not that I could buy any clothing when I was about to blossom. Even now the buttons strained and I had only a couple more weeks I'd be able to put it on.

From my bosom, I fished out the piece of paper with the address Bayla had given me. I'd kept the scrap on me—God forbid I lost it or that Eugene made a paper airplane out of it. From my top drawer, I removed the tin can. Opening the lid, I looked at the money it had taken me nineteen years to save. Nineteen years. And what was I buying with it? I choked back a sob as I fished out a wad of bills. Slowly I counted out fifty dollars. Such a price! Of all the things I'd dreamed about for this money, this was not one of them. Never. Couldn't have even imagined it. Ah, but such thoughts would get me nowhere. I tucked the money into my purse and steeled myself for the day ahead.

The walk was a long one, farther down on the lower East Side than I usually went. Would I ever be allowed to return to my morning paper?

The heat was sweltering, and sweat streamed down my back in rivulets; my limp made the going slow. Heading south, I was greeted by street peddlers and hawkers. The aroma of baked goods mingled with the stink of the fishmongers' wares, the stench of the rubbish in the streets, the gassy exhaust of the automobiles.

"*Knishes!* Bagels!" called the food men. Other carts held kitchenwares and trinkets. Good thing I had already eaten. The smells of the freshly baked items were tempting, but I didn't trust the food in this unfamiliar neighborhood.

Crossing Delancey, I looked at the strangers around me and held my purse tightly against my chest. Carrying so much money made me eye everyone with wariness. In my neighborhood were the Jews from Russia, the ones who spoke Yiddish with the same accent as mine. Here the Jews were from other lands: Germany, Romania, Poland. Spotting the greenhorns was easy; they still dressed as if they were in the Old World. They weren't acclimated as I was, with my modern style, wearing dresses that stopped at the knees, shirts that didn't reach much past my elbows. My head was topped by a hat and not one of those ragged scarves worn back home. I stood a smidgen taller knowing I was a real American.

The streets were crowded with people. When a car came through, the horn would sound continuously, but the masses rarely moved out of the way, slowing the car's progress, eliciting ugly oaths from the driver.

Eventually, I reached my destination. I compared the address on the paper to that on the stoop. No name on the door. The building looked like any other. The number matched the one on the basement apartment, so I went down the side stairs, where I knocked loudly on the plain wooden door. No answer.

I peered through the window, but if anyone was there, it was too dark to tell. Returning to the door, I knocked more. Louder. Harder. If this address was wrong, if there was no doctor . . .

Soon it would be too late for Dottie. Panic rose in my chest until I was pounding on the door.

Finally it swung open. "What are you trying to do, bring the whole neighborhood in here?" a young woman asked, her tone menacing.

Using English, I said, "Sorry, I am. I didn't know if you were here."

Blocking the entrance, the girl looked from my feet, up my body, all the way to my eyes. Her own narrowed. "What do you want?"

"I—I—" How to explain what I needed? "I need to make an appointment."

The young woman grabbed me by the wrist and pulled me inside, shutting the door behind me. I nearly lost my footing and stumbled. Such cheek. And yet, it appeared I was beholden to her.

A small front room, with a couch and a desk, greeted me. The young woman went to the desk and opened a bound book. "How far along are you?" she asked without looking up.

"Far along? What does that mean?"

"How pregnant are you? When are you due?"

"It's not—" I tripped on my words. The girl looked at me without moving a muscle on her face. "It's not for me."

She nodded. "Of course not," she said. "How far along is she?"

"I am not sure. It is important?"

"If she's more than three months, it costs more. Sixty bucks if it's early. Seventy if more than three months."

"Sixty dollars!" My hand involuntarily went to my throat. "I thought it was fifty. I only have fifty."

She sighed and rolled her eyes. "You were misinformed."

Was I misinformed or was she skimming money off the top for herself? I was in no position to negotiate. The woman rapped her nails on the book, brightly polished crimson nails that *tap tap tapped* in an irritating way. The girl, probably the same age as Dottie, was the kind of girl Dottie would have befriended if they worked in the same office. *What did her life give her that this is the work she does?* I shuddered, all the more convinced we were doing the right thing for Dottala.

"So," she asked again, "is it less than three months?"

"Yes, yes, less than three months," although I suspected it was longer.

The young woman eyed me carefully, trying to detect the truth. I stood straight and looked her in the eye. Finally she peered at the book. "Thursday. Be here at one."

I shook my head. "Friday. It must be a Friday evening."

"No," she said. "Thursday at one."

How could Dottie miss so much work? A Friday night, she could recuperate on the weekend and be back in the office on Monday. A Thursday at one meant a day and a half's loss of work.

The young woman grew impatient. "Listen, do you want it or not?"

"Yes, I want it." We would create a story for her boss.

"Don't eat before. We don't want you—I mean your friend—vomiting on us. Bring extra rags. You'll need to help her get home. You should meet her on the street four hours after the appointment. Make sure you don't come to *this* street, though. Meet her a few blocks away. She'll be sore and cramped."

I nodded.

"I need the money up front."

I hesitated before saying, "I thought it was only fifty."

"It's sixty."

"But I only brought fifty."

She slammed the book shut. "Then come back when you have sixty."

"No! Please. We can't wait."

She looked at me expectantly.

"Please. I give you fifty now. Bring ten more on Thursday."

My desperation must have been clear—although who came here who wasn't desperate?—because she said, "I'm not supposed to do that. But okay. Make sure you bring the extra ten."

That I was grateful to her showed how low I'd sunk. I reached into my purse and pulled out all those bills. The woman grabbed them.

"Do I get a receipt?" I asked.

"A receipt? Of course not!"

"But how will you know I paid?"

"Because everyone pays first. And I've marked it in the book."

It was a lot of money to be handing over without a record, but I didn't have a choice. The woman counted the bills.

A thought occurred to me. "It is a doctor, no? A doctor who does the procedure."

She looked up suspiciously. Her eyes were a shade of green that would have been lovely in any other setting. "You from the health department?"

"No, no. Make sure, I want, that it is safe."

She went back to the money, starting to count again. "It's safe. Don't worry."

But how could I not? The girl didn't glance up again, so I showed myself out.

Dottie

———— ✿ ————

Monday, August 26

ALL Sunday night, I worried the problem in my head, not getting an ounce of sleep. I tossed on the couch, unable to find a comfortable position, constantly jabbed by the reality of what I would have to do. But would I? There was one other option, wasn't there? Zelda's question echoed in my mind: "Do you want to marry Willie?" That was the only choice other than Ma's drastic measures. I couldn't think about Abe. Abe was no longer an option unless I went through with Ma's plan.

Could I marry a man I didn't love if it meant keeping my baby? The thought required a complete shift in my perspective, a total upturning of all I had envisioned for myself. No, I didn't love Willie. But I admired him. He spoke so passionately of politics in a way that made me feel like I was at home; he had the same fiery mind as Ma and *Tateh*, and while I professed that their debates were tedious, I was usually drawn in. Willie's writing was thought-provoking and the life he led was exciting. Willie was intriguing, to say the least. Abe made me *feel*. But Willie made me *think*.

I loved Abe. Of that, there was no doubt. But my maternal instincts were kicking in. And I suspected that as much as I loved Abe, I loved this baby more.

* * *

THAT Monday I took special care getting ready for the day. I dabbed on a bit of extra toilet water, pinched my cheeks to bring my color forward. A new lipstick graced my lips, and as I surveyed myself in the mirror, I thought I looked quite fetching. If only it were for Abe.

I left early for work, as much to avoid Ma's looks as to get enough work done that I could take a longer midday break. I didn't have an exact plan, but I knew I must do something. And that meant going to lunch.

At my desk, I snuck the card from my clutch for what seemed like the hundredth time. Looking around to make sure no one saw, I opened the card.

> *Time is running out.*
> *Stork Club, next Monday at noon.*

About twenty minutes before the bell chimed for lunch, I made a beeline for the door, taking the other girls by surprise. It was the first time I'd left for lunch, never mind that I was going early. But Willie had written *noon*. We were supposed to take only a half hour, but I mumbled something about delivering papers for Mr. Dover. I don't know if anyone believed me.

Though I hated the crowd and the smell, I took the subway to Fifty-first Street, as it was faster than a streetcar, and then walked as quickly as I could in my heels to the restaurant.

Arriving at the formidable entrance to the Stork Club, I hesitated as doubt crept through me. I took a few deep breaths, trying to calm myself, patting my hair, hoping it was still in place. I'd been so concerned about making it here quickly that I hadn't thought about the actual meeting. What exactly did I expect to say?

In his crisply ironed suit with the gleaming buttons, the

doorman opened the door. I had never been out for a meal that involved a doorman.

Feigning indifference was an utter failure, and I couldn't hide my awe when I entered the room. Men and women dappled the tables, wearing the finest fashions straight out of the windows of Gimbels and Macy's. Everyone was eating and smoking and drinking and laughing, and I was reminded there existed an entirely different New York from the one I inhabited, one from which I was excluded. A pang of bitterness tainted my admiration.

"Good afternoon, miss. May I help you?" asked a tuxedoed gentleman at a front dais.

Swallowing my fear, I said, "Mr. Willie Klein is expecting me."

"Follow me," the gentleman said.

He wound his way through the throng of tables to a small two-top in a corner. "Mr. Klein," he said, "your party has arrived."

Willie was reading the *Times*. He looked so dashing, so . . . like he belonged. Why did he have to be so handsome in his crisp suit and blue silk tie? Was it from Brooks Brothers? It certainly wasn't from my neighborhood.

Putting down his newspaper, Willie looked up, surprised. "Dottie! You came." His eyes grazed my body and I tried to suck in my stomach. Belatedly I realized that only emphasized my bosom, which was not what I intended.

I attempted to look nonchalant. "Only because you made it sound so dire. 'I won't be around for much longer.'"

With a genuine chuckle, Willie said, "Well, it worked."

"Miss," the gentleman said, pulling out a chair.

"Thank you," I said, hoping I sounded demure. It would take a few tries to land on the correct persona for the Stork Club.

"Mr. Klein, your drink will be here momentarily."

"Of course, James."

"And what can I get you, miss?"

Wishing I knew what Willie had ordered, I hesitated a moment. If I ordered poorly, I would stand out like the greenhorn I probably resembled. Thinking back to a recent article in *McCall's*, I said, "A whiskey sour, please."

"Excellent." With a slight bow, the gentleman left.

"Whiskey sour?" Willie had an amused smile on his face. "You know, that's Dorothy Parker's drink."

I did know that, from the article, which was why I'd ordered the drink in the first place. But it was with a skewer of jealousy that I asked, "And how do you know Dorothy Parker's drink?" I was positive he wasn't reading *McCall's*.

"That's my news."

"Dorothy Parker is your news?"

He laughed a deep laugh, a laugh that shimmered with class and money. The sound filled me with a strange heat. "My news is I've taken a position. As a writer. For *The New Yorker.*"

"No!" I said, my hand flying to my chest in a well-practiced maneuver. "How marvelous. And you've already met Dorothy Parker?"

Leaning back in his seat, he said, "No, not actually. But the practices of the Old Guard are well-known, including their drinks."

"Well, this is wonderful news." Better than wonderful news. Willie was no longer cobbling together different assignments, unsure from where the next paycheck would come. He was an employed writer. With the means to support a family.

"It is. Doesn't pay much, I'm afraid, but it'll keep me." Willie's eyes crinkled in the corners like the folds of a fan. Magnetizing, his eyes were. "Mother, of course, isn't happy; this ends her dream of my following in Father's footsteps. Can you picture it? Me, day in and day out at the bank? Home every night by five fifteen."

Actually, I *could* picture it. Willie coming home after a day at the office, sitting in his chair with a drink in his hand, while I laid out dinner with the recipes I found in the magazines, the baby cooing gently from the next room. Yet, in my mind, the picture wasn't Willie; it was Abe—*Stop it!* I chided myself. I couldn't let Abe interfere. Abe was done. It was now or never.

Taking a deep breath, I was ready to tell all. "Willie—," I started, but he cut me off, still on his own train of thought.

"The hell with Mother!"

I laughed even though I was completely taken aback at his disrespect. Startling me, a hand reached in front of me and placed a glass on the table, and every ounce of my courage fled.

I nodded and looked at the short glass with the yellow liquid. I hadn't known what to expect.

"And your martini, Mr. Klein," said the waiter. "Have you decided what you'd like for lunch?"

"Oh," I said. "I haven't even looked at the menu."

I glanced down, unsure of what half the items even were. *Oeufs? Nicoise? Chiffonade?*

As if sensing my distress, the waiter said, "Might I suggest the sole?"

"That sounds lovely," I said, handing back the menu, when in truth, I had no idea what sole was. I only hoped it would be palatable.

"I'll have my usual, Sam," Willie said.

"Of course, Mr. Klein."

As the waiter departed, I said, "Your 'usual'? Do you come here often?"

"Father started bringing me to the Stork Club when it was in its previous location on Fifty-eighth Street. At the time, it was the only place he could have his martini. It was our Monday lunch ritual. 'Recovering from the weekend with your mother,' Father used to say. 'Fortifying myself for the week ahead.' I still come every Monday even though Father, once Prohibition ended, found places closer to his office to drink."

Looking around again at the fancy hats and lacquered nails, breathing in the heady scent of Chanel mixed with the earthy smell of steak, hearing the tinkling of glasses and silverware that sounded more like a party than a lunch out, I wondered, could I become accustomed to a place like this? Or would I always feel like a visitor?

When I looked back at Willie, he was smiling with amusement. Hurriedly, I reached for my drink, raising it. "A toast. To your new job."

"A toast," he said, "to the lovely lady who finally agreed to lunch with me."

Blushing, I clinked my glass to his and took a sip. The drink was surprisingly strong but quite delicious, with sweet undertones. Much better than the hooch I was used to drinking. "Mmmm," I said. "Like Dorothy Parker." Trying to appear cosmopolitan, I asked, "So, what is the *New Yorker* office like?"

Willie launched into a monologue about the bedraggled crew who came in and out; how an article he wrote for *The Atlantic* had gotten him noticed; how the boss, Harold Ross, was buffoonish, but had an excellent eye for prose; how the magazine was surviving the Depression. I tried to follow along, but I kept sipping my drink, which really was quite delightful, and taking in Willie's handsomeness and the hubbub of the room, and I felt light-headed and lovely, as if I were in the middle of a Cole Porter song. *I could be very happy here,* I thought. I knew I must tell him, but this was all so heavenly, this little oasis from the problems of my world, that I didn't want to spoil the ethereal mood with the gross realities of my life.

By the time the waiter returned with our meals, my drink was nearly empty, and before I could stop him—I needed to return to the office, after all—Willie ordered me a second. With my plate in front of me, I was relieved to learn *sole* was simply fish, albeit fish swimming in butter, but quite tasty, I discovered.

"How is your meal?" Willie asked.

"Delectable," I said.

"You must try mine," Willie said. "They make the most superb crab salad."

I looked up with a start and saw that Willie's hand was outstretched. Surely Willie knew me better than that. But of course he did. This was a test.

"I shouldn't," I said, trying to smile demurely. "A girl must watch what she eats."

"Truly, Dottie," Willie said, "it is simply wonderful." Seeing the distaste in my face, he narrowed his eyes slightly. "You don't keep kosher. Do you?" His voice took on the vague tones of censure. If he were Abe, I would have slapped him. Of course I kept kosher. Of course he knew I kept kosher. But I needed Willie, so I tamped down the rush of fury. I gave a smile, hoping that would be response enough. It was not.

For all my talk of *modern* and *progressive*, I had not yet tasted *treif*, unkosher food. This was not so much a conscious decision as a way of life. Ma bought from the kosher butcher, never served milk with meat. I didn't eat with *goyim*, brought all those lunches from home. So no one had ever offered me *treif*. And I never *wanted* anyone to. Just as I would never walk out of the house in only my undergarments, I would never think of eating a pushcart sausage. And yet here was Willie, seeing how inflexible I would be. Ma would be mortified if she saw me sitting here with Willie, a pile of shellfish waving beneath my nose. My situation, the *treif*—I suspected the sins were equal in Ma's mind.

"Try it. It's wonderful."

Willie and his family belonged to the big *shul* uptown, the German one. The Reform one. Their rules were flexible, and *treif* didn't exist for them.

It wasn't right. But right was not important here. What was important was making myself attractive to Willie. What was important was making myself marriage-worthy. So I offered him a wan smile and said, "Why not? Life is about new experiences, *nu*?"

Oy! I thought, mortified by the *nu* that had snuck out. I covered it by trying to delicately open my mouth, allowing Willie to feed me. The act was intimate, one lover feeding another, and

Willie lingered as my lips closed around the fork. He stared at me with such intensity that I was embarrassed to chew, but I forced myself to make tiny nibbles. A nausea rose, which I tried to gain control of; I liked Willie's gaze, didn't want to put him off by becoming sick. The crab was rubbery and rather bland, coated as it was with mayonnaise, which I didn't like even on the best of days. Placing my napkin over my mouth, I forced myself to chew and swallow. Lightning did not strike me.

"Well?" Willie asked.

"Delicious," I said, extracting a smile from somewhere deep within.

Willie placed another large helping on his fork before shoveling it into his mouth. "Would you like some more?" I'd apparently sailed through the exam.

"Thank you, but my sole is excellent as well. Would you care to try some?"

He shook his head, and rested his chin on his hand as he gazed at me. "You know, Dottie," he said, "you are really something else."

With a blush, I said, "Thank you." Hiding my nervousness, I took another sip of my drink. Maybe this was the moment to bring up the subject. But how?

With an overly deep sigh, Willie lifted his head and returned to his meal. "I'm going to miss you like crazy. Not that I ever had a chance with you. I know," he said, raising his fork, with a sardonic chuckle. "You and Abe, *besherts*."

The crabmeat careened in my stomach. Why had he brought up Abe? My mouth was suddenly Sinai dry, and I reached for my drink.

"Abe and I, well . . ." I let the thought dangle, hoping to imply that Abe and I weren't exactly a done deal.

Willie looked at me more closely, rubbing his chin between his fingers, as if trying to evaluate me.

"And what do you mean," I asked between bites of fish, trying to erase the lingering taste of crab, "that you'll miss me? Are you going somewhere?"

He teased me. "I told you I wouldn't be around to bother you for long."

A fever passed through me, reaching my head, where the weight of the drink took hold, leaving the beginning of a headache in its wake. "Oh?"

"It's the *New Yorker* job." He sat straight in his chair, the picture of nonchalance, as he spooned a large helping of crab salad into his mouth.

Fingers of pain scratched at the corners of my eyes. "Yes?" The scent of perfumes mingling in the air, which only moments before had smelled so lovely, now cloyed, suffocating me.

He put down his fork. "The job is in Paris." He watched my face closely, trying to assess the impact of his news.

"Paris?" I didn't know what to do with my hands. I picked up another piece of fish, although my appetite had departed completely. "That's—Paris." I hoped to be giving off an air of detachment, as if this didn't destroy my last shred of hope.

"Well, it starts in Paris. I'll be all over the Continent. I leave on September twelfth, just over two weeks." Waggling his eyebrows, he said, "You shouldn't have waited so long to join me for lunch."

"How fascinating." I chewed my fish, no longer tasting it. Confusion overwhelmed me, a daze, as if I were just waking up, knowing I'd had a good dream, but unable to grasp it before it slipped away, replaced by the cold reality of morning. I knew there was music, laughter, drinks, and food, but I couldn't piece it together, couldn't see the picture anymore. I hadn't known what to expect from the lunch, but this certainly wasn't it.

"The opportunity is phenomenal. Ross thinks I'm going to cover the cultural scene, but this is my opportunity to expose the Nazi Party for the threat it is. Oh, I'll do one or two fluff pieces for Ross to keep him happy, but my real work will be investigative. The American press has been an embarrassment in its coverage of what is happening in Europe." He leaned toward me, and tickled the tops of my fingers with his own. "I'll write exposés that will have *New Yorker* readers demanding American intervention."

If I hadn't been so shaken, I would have been impressed. "It sounds admirable. But . . ." I struggled to find the words amid the flotsam clogging my mind. ". . . aren't you concerned? This is a dangerous time to be a Jew in Europe."

He chuckled. "I'm barely a Jew! Besides, I'm an American. I can take care of myself."

I simply nodded.

Lowering his voice, his fingers sliding more deliberately across my hand, Willie asked, "May I see you before I leave? More . . . privately?"

Startled, I looked up at him. Willie's gaze was matter-of-fact, as if he'd simply proposed a cup of coffee at the deli.

My eyes weren't focusing properly. The million lights were blurring into a blinding headache. I feared passing out or retching or humiliating myself in some other fashion. My hand fluttered to my face. "Oh my. It's getting so late. I must powder my nose and head back to the office."

Before he could even stand up, I pushed back my chair, and made a beeline for the back of the dining room, where I hoped I would find the ladies' lounge, which, to my relief, was clearly marked.

In the bathroom, I hurried to a stall, and realized I *was* sick. Wafts of perfume floated in the air and my stomach turned in somersaults. In a most undignified manner, I crouched on the floor and emptied my stomach into the toilet. Thank goodness no one was in the room to hear, other than the attendant, who sat on a seat between the sinks. With one hand on the wall, I made certain every last bit of *treif* exited my body.

When I'd regained a shred of decorum, I stood up and used toilet paper to wipe my mouth. I exited the stall, and the attendant handed me a paper towel, which I gratefully took to clean myself further while inspecting myself in the mirror.

The attendant gave me a motherly smile. "How far along?" she asked.

My eyes quickly moved from my own reflection to the colored woman in the white apron. My first instinct was to deny it, to pretend I had no idea what she was talking about, but what was the point? Soon everyone would know. My shame would be worn like a scarlet letter upon my belly. How was it so clear to this stranger when it wasn't obvious to the one who needed to know? "Three months, I think."

The woman nodded, but her smile faltered when she noticed my hands. She was too polite to say anything, but I saw the change in her mien and knew what she was thinking.

All those months listening to Zelda moan gave me a quick response. With a false smile plastered on my face, I blatantly waved my left hand and said, "Wouldn't you know? I've swelled up like a balloon in the Macy's Thanksgiving Parade. My rings already don't fit!"

I must have said the correct thing, as with a knowing nod the woman offered me a mint. I accepted it, left a nickel on the silver platter, and returned to the table.

Willie sat, looking morose. He stood as I approached the table.

"Listen—," he started, but I wasn't about to let him finish.

"I had no idea how long I'd been sitting here. I must get back to the office."

"My driver—"

"Thank you so much for lunch."

Turning and hurrying out, I pretended not to hear him calling, "But, Dottie, wait!"

MORE than twice the half hour designated for lunch had passed by the time I returned, but I refused to give Florence the satisfaction of pretending to care. I had more important worries at the moment. I slowed down before entering the room, taking a breath, pinching my cheeks, and calmly opened the door and sauntered in as if I hadn't bolted down the street like Gallant Fox. I walked toward my desk, past the girls, who stared at me, surprised to have seen me leave the office. All lingering traces of light-headedness dissipated along with the hopes I'd nurtured.

At my desk, I tried to immerse myself in the numbers, my safe haven with their black-and-white answers to every problem. I let the click-clack of the tabulating machines wash over me.

But they did nothing.

The numbers didn't quell the nausea. They didn't erase my worries. They didn't lure me into an analytical trance. All I could think was that Ma was right. I had no other choice. No option.

The girls eyed me suspiciously, sensing something. I tried to ignore them, but felt overwhelmed with the urge to snap at them and their sniveling ways. How was it that out of all the girls in the office, *I* was the one to find myself in a situation like this? This didn't happen to nice Jewish girls.

For the first time, I found the work painful. I double-checked the numbers on a long sheet of tabulations, and frustrated to no end, I barked, "Florence!" My tone was harsher than it should have been. "You missed an entire column of numbers here. You'll need to do it again."

Florence walked to the front of the room with an exaggerated swivel to her waist. "Yes, boss," she said, in a mock-obedient tone.

The rest of the room giggled and I glared at them. "Behave!"

"What's the matter?" Florence asked. "Got your monthly?" Her eyes twinkled in a wicked way, and my hands twitched at my sides, clenching and unclenching.

"That is an improper way to speak to me. I am your supervisor."

"It's just you've been so moody lately. You must have your monthly. Although it's odd." She paused and dramatically brought her hand to her chin as if she were in deep thought. "For someone who is so careful about what she eats, you're a little soft around the belly."

Tittering spread throughout the room. My control rapidly slipped away. "That's enough, Florence."

"Is it? Is it enough?" Her taunting cut me deeply. Her voice dropped to a near whisper. "Why, Miss Krasinsky, it looks to me like *you've* had enough."

My hand shot out faster than Florence could have expected, and it made a cracking sound as it sliced across her face. Gasps came from around the room.

"Ow!" Florence said, genuine tears springing to her eyes.

And wasn't it my luck that at that moment Mr. Dover chose to return to the office?

"Good grief," the deep voice said from the door. "What on earth is going on?"

The flush consumed my body, but I stood firm. "Florence has been impertinent, disrespectful, and sloppy in her work. She should be fired."

"Fired!" Florence was ruffled. "You can't do that." With more uncertainty, she turned to Mr. Dover. "Can she?"

He looked back and forth between the two of us. Silence stretched and I stood terrified. Finally he said, "Both of you. In my office."

Meekly, we trailed behind him.

"Shut the door," he said, and I obeyed.

He sat behind his desk, a large mahogany affair with leather accessories. He intertwined his fingers. He did not invite either of us to sit. "Dorothea, tell me why you think Florence should be fired."

"Mr. Dov—"

"Silence." He held up his hand. "I want to hear from Dorothea."

"Florence's tabulations are inaccurate almost more often than they are accurate. She is frequently late for work. She wastes an inordinate amount of time gossiping. And a few moments ago, I asked her to correct one of her mistakes and she became insubordinate. Plenty of qualified girls are hungry for work and willing to do the job properly." I held my breath, waiting to see if Florence would bring up my long lunch. Luckily for me, she decided upon a different tactic.

"But, Mr. Dover," Florence said as she pouted her lips and leaned toward our boss. My eyes widened when I realized that—somehow—the top two buttons on Florence's blouse were undone. It was clear Mr. Dover noticed as well. "I try sooooo hard." She was trying to sound seductive, but to my ears, it came out as a whine. Mr. Dover, though, apparently heard something else, as he templed his fingers, touching them to the tip of his nose. He nodded his head.

"Dorothea, let me have a word with Florence, please."

Florence gave the slightest hint of a puckish grin as I looked from her to Mr. Dover. Straightening my back, I said, "Of course, Mr. Dover."

I turned to leave when his voice came again. "Please close the door, Dorothea."

I returned to my desk, humiliated. Florence was the one behaving shamelessly. Yet I was the one who felt hollow.

I went back to the numbers, but it was no use. I'd be getting nothing else done. All the girls in the office had their eyes on Mr. Dover's door, and they glanced nervously at one another.

After twenty minutes, Florence emerged with a big grin on her face. Mr. Dover trailed behind her, his tie slightly askew.

"Dorothea, Florence and I have chatted. Florence, you have something to say to Miss Krasinsky?"

With her eyes cast toward the floor, Florence said, "I apologize for my insolence. It shan't happen again." Without lifting her head, she looked up at me, raised her eyebrows, and gave a catty smile.

"Dorothea, Florence will remain at Dover Insurance conditionally. Her work must be perfect." Mr. Dover glanced at the clock. "It's already four fifteen. Why don't you girls go home? I told Florence I would personally go over the procedures again to make sure she understands exactly what needs to be done."

"Leave? Now?" I asked uncertainly, as the other girls gathered their belongings. "But I can help Florence."

Mr. Dover shifted uncomfortably. "I want to make sure she learns properly, so I'll teach her myself."

Looking around, I realized I was the last to comprehend. "Of course, Mr. Dover." Taking my purse, I left my work where it was. How was it these double standards worked for other folks, but not for me?

As I walked out of the office, I heard Florence calling after me, her voice dripping with syrup. "Have a lovely evening, Miss Krasinsky."

The door slammed loudly behind me. *Damn her*, I thought. *Damn her. Damn Mr. Dover. Damn Willie and Abe, too.*

I began the long walk home.

Rose

⚓

SHELLING beans at the sink, I was overcome with melancholy. I yearned for my mama to wrap me in her arms, her hair smelling comfortingly of yeast and cooking smoke. I wanted to sit with Eta in the barn and hold hands while we plotted our grand futures. I pined for a simpler time. This pregnancy wasn't sitting well with me—the aches and the fatigue—and even worse was Dottie's. How did I end up here?

When the door banged open, I yelled, "Alfie, wipe your feet."

"It's not Alfie, Ma. It's me," Dottie called.

Oy vey, what was the matter now? I threw down my beans, wiped my hands on my apron, and was about to walk into the front room when Dottie entered the kitchen.

"What happened? Why are you home? Did you get fired?"

"Ma." Dottie rolled her eyes at me. But then she peered at me. "Are you all right? You look flushed."

"Why are you home?"

"Mr. Dover let us go early."

I stood at an awkward angle, favoring my good side.

"Your leg is even worse," she said, placing a gentle arm around my back. It was such a tender gesture that for a moment I thought I might fall upon her in my grief.

"You will be paid for the full day?"

"I get paid weekly, Ma. Not by the hour. Now, what's wrong?"

Dottie led me to the front room, seating me on the sofa. It was so maternal that my eyes teared. When had my baby girl turned into this woman? Where was the toddler who got into my threads, grabbed at my needles, and begged for one more poppy seed cookie?

"Ma," Dottie said again, "what's wrong?"

Bringing the hem of my apron up to my eyes, I blotted the tears I imagined were there, the ones that hadn't actually fallen. Perhaps Ben was right. Perhaps now was the time to confide in Dottie. If anyone could understand the unwelcome situation, it would be my own daughter in a similar place. "A child," I said. "A child is such work."

I heard a loud sigh and looked up to see the exasperation on Dottie's face. "I know, Ma." Her voice was laced with whininess. "Don't you think I've given thought to every possibility?"

Of course Dottie thought I was speaking about her. Why wouldn't she? She had no idea.

"Actually, Dottala—," I started, taking her hands in mine, but Dottie continued as if she didn't hear me.

"I saw Willie, Ma. Saw him at lunch today."

I pulled back my hands. All thoughts of confession fled. Did I raise such a fool? "Willie? What does he have to do with this?" Dottie was not a friend in whom to confide; she was my daughter, who still, apparently, needed the firm hand and level head of her mother.

"What do you mean, 'What does he have to do with this'? You know perfectly well what he has to do with this."

"Oh, Dottala. This is not *his* problem. Did you tell him? Oh, God above, please tell me you didn't say anything to him."

Dottie shook her head. "I didn't get a chance. Before I could say anything, he told me he's leaving. Moving to Europe to work as a writer."

"Europe!" I threw up my hands. "Does he not know there's going to be a war there? Is he a complete idiot?"

"He's not an idiot, Ma. That's why he's going, to prove that there's a real danger. It's a great opportunity, to be a writer for *The New Yorker*."

"To be a writer for *The New Yorker* he has to kill himself? A man like that you need? Thank God you didn't tell him." I dotted the sweat on my forehead with my apron. "Now everything is clear, *nu*? You know what you have to do."

Dottie looked more closely at me. "You are definitely ill. You look peaked."

I waved my hands in the air to brush away such notions. "It's August. How should I look?" I pushed back my hair and repeated my question. "Everything is clear? You understand what you need to do?"

Dottie looked down and twisted the hem of her dress in her hands. I wanted to bat her fingers away, tell her not to ruin a good dress, but I bit my lip. We had enough problems without quarreling over her fidgeting.

"I can't get rid of this baby."

The heat was making me woozy. "Of course you can."

"No, Ma. I can't. I *won't*."

What she said made no sense. She was with child. The child was not Abe's. The child must go away. How much plainer could it be? "You *can't*? You *won't*? This I do not understand."

"What if," Dottie said, "you took it? What if you pretended the baby was yours?"

"What?" She couldn't have shocked me more if she said she was traveling to the moon. Me take her baby?

"You can take it. You're still young enough to have a child of your own, aren't you?"

If only she knew. "A child of my own?" I said.

"We'll go away. The two of us. Spend a few months somewhere else. Your cousin Freyde in Baltimore. We tell people she's sick, that she needs your help. Then we use the money you saved for my schooling to pay for a place for us, maybe in the Catskills. When we return with the baby, we'll tell everyone it's yours. No one will be the wiser. You can raise the baby. I'll pretend to be its sister."

My body twitched as if I were a caged animal. "That's . . . that's . . ." My mind reeled at the thought. It was impossible. Simply impossible. What, I would leave and we would have twins? But even if I weren't with child, to take on the burden of someone *else's* child? "That's ridiculous."

"Why?" Dottie's eyes were wide and innocent. How ludicrous. No one would believe us *both* leaving the family. The household needed a woman to run it. Absurd. "Why won't it work? It solves all our problems."

"First of all, we don't have the savings anymore. Fifty dollars I spent on the appointment and I still owe another ten dollars. And more importantly, it doesn't solve all our problems because I don't want to raise another child." The guilt those words caused made me apologize in my heart to *Hashem*. *I'm sorry I don't wish another child. Not even the one in my own womb. Forgive me,* Hashem.

"But I'll help. I can do most of the work. We'll pretend the baby is yours."

"And what happens when you and Abe marry? When you move out? I'll be stuck at home with the baby."

"'Stuck with the baby'? That's how you feel?"

"I have raised my children. And if *Hashem* intends it, I will raise more of my own. But I do not intend to raise anyone else's children."

Dottie stood, and paced the room. "Ma, this isn't anyone else's child. This is *my* child."

My eyes were completely dry now. "That, my daughter, is exactly my point." I got to my feet. Turning to face her, I said, "You have an appointment. Thursday at one. It's already been paid for. I expect you to be there." And I exited to prepare dinner and brood about my own problems.

Her sobs sounded throughout the apartment. As I returned to the bowl of beans, I heard fast footsteps and then the slamming of the door. *Fine*, I thought. *Let her go. Let her mull on her mistakes.* The rhythmic task of snapping the ends of the beans with a paring knife and pulling down the stringy stems was calming. How could Dottie ask such a thing of me? To care for yet another child? I should have simply told Dottie about my own child, explained to her the impossibility of the situation. But Dottie proved herself, once again, to be a mere girl, unable to handle such problems.

Dottie was so delicate. Would she be able to handle the procedure? Would she recover? And what would happen when she learned of my baby? I feared she would be furious that I had kept a child when she had to give hers up. Every time she looked at this new baby, it would be a reminder of what she didn't have. She would resent me, resent the child. I could only pray her anger didn't consume her, didn't drive a wedge between us. She had to understand. There was no choice: If she had the baby, she would have nothing.

The green beans were trimmed. Wiping my hands on my apron, I stood and walked over to the sink. I had to hope Dottie would forgive me. But first, I had to boil the beans.

Dottie

---✦---

AFTER I stormed out of the apartment, my head was swimming. My physical symptoms might have abated, but my head was a flurry. How could Ma say no? How could she want to see this life ended?

For an hour, I walked the streets, trying to make order in my mind. Playing gin rummy at Edith's sounded like an atrocious idea, but given I had nowhere else to go, it's what I ended up doing. I bought a *knish* at Yonah Schimmel's for my dinner and walked till it was time to meet my friends, my mind reeling at what I was going to have to do. How had it come to this?

Before entering Edith's building, I tried to pull myself together. I needed to give the appearance of a carefree girl, even though I would never be one again.

Edith was the youngest of three, her older brothers both married. One of them lived with his wife's family; the other was fortunate enough to have his own place. On Monday nights Edith's parents went to the *Arbeter Ring*, working up their socialist fervor, so we had the apartment to ourselves.

At the top of the stairs I gave my hair a final pat and let myself into the apartment. "Hello, hello," I called. "I'm ready to play." My voice sounded tinny to my ears.

In the old days, the cardplayers gathered and broke off into games of two, but of course with Zelda busy with the baby, we were now a threesome, so we ended up playing the more awkward three-person round-robin version.

"Now you join us? After standing us up last week? Where have you been?" Edith said from the kitchen.

"Sorry, sorry," I said. "Ma and *Tateh* went to a lecture and Eugene didn't want to be home alone." It was a lie made easy by the fact we didn't have a phone; I had no way to get in touch if I wasn't going to make it.

"Well, you're here now. Sit," Edith said. "I'm getting the refreshments." The coffee Edith inevitably burned was the last thing my stomach needed, but I poured myself a cup from the percolator on the table anyway. I sat in one of the dining chairs as the front door opened again.

"I'm here," Linda said.

I gestured to the center of the table. "I'll pour you coffee."

Linda hesitated before whispering, "Did Edith make it or her ma?"

I took a sip. Wrinkling my nose, I said, "Edith."

"None for me, thanks," Linda said, as she sat next to me.

Edith came out smiling, holding a platter. "Sweets." On the platter were the most misshapen, lumpy cookies I ever saw, not to mention blackened at the edges.

"They look . . ." Darling Linda, searching for something kind to say. "Homemade?"

"Damn right they're homemade," Edith said. "Ma said if I didn't learn how to do something domestic, she was going to send me to the Educational Alliance to learn to cook."

"Don't swear, Edith," Linda said, her voice soft. "It's not becoming."

"Since when is Edith 'becoming'?" I picked up a cookie and banged it against the table. It didn't crumble a smidgen. "So light and delicate," I said. "Forgive me if I pass. I'd like to keep my teeth."

"What about you, Linda?"

"They do look so lovely, but I . . . um," Linda said.

"Aw, hell." Edith fingered a cookie. "I'll save these for *Tateh*. He'll eat 'em."

I doubted that.

"I think Ma has a package of Lorna Doones around here somewhere." She popped back into the kitchen, where we heard lots of rattling of cupboard doors.

"God help the man who marries her," Linda said. Her tone was mournful, which was out of character for our Pollyanna. I looked closely at her, trying to read her, but she looked away.

"Okay, *store-bought* cookies. Are your teeth happy?" Edith plopped the cookies on the table.

"Delighted." Since Edith wasn't going to do it, I removed the Lorna Doones from the package and spread them nicely on the plate.

"Who's dealing?" Linda asked.

Edith shuffled, offered the cards to Linda to cut, then dealt.

"What's with your mother's sudden interest in you learning to cook?" I asked.

Edith shrugged as we all gathered our cards in our hands. "She wants me to learn the domestic arts. Thinks it will help me when I move out."

I snorted. "You move out? How on earth would you pay the rent?"

Edith worked at the International Ladies' Garment Workers' Union, although I wasn't sure it counted as work when Edith was paid less than the women for whom she advocated. After high school, she'd started a liberal arts course at Hunter, but dropped out because she thought the classes too bourgeois and began working for the union, thus guaranteeing she would live with her parents indefinitely.

"Exactly! And Ma is an excellent cook. Who would do the laundry if I moved out?"

Linda said, "Someday you'll need to cook and clean and do the laundry for your family."

To my ear, Linda sounded bitter, but perhaps it was my own feelings coloring what I heard. I nibbled on the plain buttery cookie without too much difficulty. I should have been famished after the episode at the Stork Club—a *knish* and a cookie did not a meal make—but my appetite had diminished. *Is that good or bad?* I wondered.

Edith said, "Linda, how many times do I need to tell you, I don't ever intend to have a family?"

The cookie crumbs were dry in my throat, and as disgusting as it was, I took a swallow of the coffee to wash them down. How I longed to discuss my predicament with my friends, but I didn't dare. Edith might be sympathetic on a political level, but she'd be disdainful on a personal one. Linda would be horrified.

"It's unnatural not to marry," Linda said. Her voice broke, and I looked up, startled.

Edith placed her hand on Linda's. "It's going to be okay, sweetie."

"Uh," I said, "did I miss something?"

Edith glowered at me. "Don't miss a gin rummy night and expect—," but Linda cut her off.

"It's okay." Looking at me, her eyes brimming, she said, "Ralph received a job offer last week." She batted her eyelids quickly to keep the tears at bay. "In Baltimore."

"Oh," I said, my surprise clear. Ralph had been trying to find work for months. A bright man, he'd struggled financially to earn an engineering degree at MIT, one of the few Jewish men to make the yearly quota. Jobs for a Jewish engineer, though, were few and far between.

Linda looked at her cards and discarded a four of hearts. Without looking up, she said, "He needs to leave in a week. He wants us to marry so I can go with him, but I can't abandon *Tateh*." Mr. Tewel had been ill for ages, infected with painters' sickness, but a year ago June, he became bed-bound. All year he seemed to be near death, but he never gave his family the relief of actually passing away. The family relied on Linda's typing wages and on the small amount her ma made cleaning at night. "I marry and desert my family. Or I never marry. It's as simple as that."

"Well, what if—"

"There is no 'what if'!" she said. "I've thought of every possibility and in none of them does it work out." She tossed down her next card almost violently. "Can we talk about something else? I'd prefer not to think about it for an evening."

We completed another round of choosing and discarding cards in silence, searching for a safe topic.

Finally, Edith spoke. "Actually, I have news to share." She cast off an ace of clubs, which helped me not at all.

"Do tell." I nibbled at another cookie.

"Word on the street is Willie Klein is headed off on assignment in Europe."

I gagged.

"You okay?" Edith pounded my back. I took another sip of the god-awful coffee, trying not to cough.

"Fine, fine," I managed to say. "Went down the wrong way." I swallowed more coffee.

"Europe?" Linda said, gathering the cards in her hand. "How terrible." Her voice was back to neutral. "What did he do wrong that he's being sent there?"

"Wrong?" Edith said. "This is a plum job! Don't anyone repeat this, but I applaud the man for it."

"You do?" I asked.

"Sure," Edith said. "I plead with workers all day long to stand strong, join the union, but they don't seem to want to improve their lives. Willie is actually *doing* something that could make a difference. And that leads to my news: I was so inspired that I inquired today about a job at the Joint Distribution Committee. I start next Monday."

"The what?" Linda asked.

"The JDC. It's a relief organization that helps Jews around the world. After the war, they provided loans to Jews in Eastern Europe to stimulate the growth of the Jewish communities. Now they—or rather *we*—are raising funds to help German Jews emigrate."

I perked up a moment. "The JDC? Will you have connections? Will you be able to help Uncle Yussel get a visa?"

Edith pursed her lips and placed her hand on mine. "I'm sorry, sweetie. The priority right now is Germany. If things get worse . . ." She trailed off and gave my hand a halfhearted pat, before going back to her cards. "Well, let's hope it won't get any worse."

"Sounds very noble," I said, trying not to appear as deflated as I felt. "Will you earn more money than you did at the union?"

Edith looked abashed. "Well, less, actually."

"Less?" I chuckled. "Is that possible? How will you survive?"

Edith grinned. "Didn't you hear me? Ma is an excellent cook."

"Don't you think Willie's putting his life in jeopardy?" I worked hard to keep my voice even, as if my concern were no different from nor any greater than theirs.

"Probably," Edith said. "But that's a risk he has to take if he's going to do great things."

The numbers on my cards danced before me. I had three *threes*. Three plus three plus three equaled nine. Three squared? Nine. That stupid number, nine. Why should I care if Willie was risking his life? I was going to take care of my situation, and Willie would be of no concern to me. Yet, something in me ached with worry, and I was pretty sure it had nothing to do with the baby.

I picked up a card. Another *three*, which completed the set. I put down the match and drew a queen.

"Isn't anyone going to congratulate me on my new job?" Edith said.

"Congrats," I said. "At the rate you're going, you'll be paying your employers soon."

Edith laughed good-naturedly. "Well, while I still have a few pennies left, why don't we go to the pictures this Sunday? There's a new Jean Harlow that *The New Yorker* liked."

"I suppose," Linda said, before announcing, "Gin."

"Aw, I was so close," said Edith. "Your deal, Dottie."

I grabbed the cards and shuffled. So much to think about: Linda losing Ralph; Willie putting himself directly in harm's way; little hope for Yussel. Little hope for *me*. As I passed out the cards, one by one, I wondered when we'd stop being dealt losing hands.

Rose

Tuesday, August 27

DOTTIE spoke no more than two words at a time to me: "Yes, Mother." "No, Mother." The *Mother* was new. Apparently I'd lost the right to be called *Ma*.

I served the boys' breakfast, keeping an eye on her. She bypassed my food and simply lopped off a hunk of bread, at which she barely picked.

All three boys were at the table, which was unusual. Izzy normally left early for his work as a clothes presser. "Why are you still here?" I asked him.

Dottie rolled her eyes.

"Hirsh Weinstein got his hand caught in the mangle yesterday. Since we're short a man, Mr. Silberberg told me to work a double today: afternoon and night."

"Dear God! Mr. Weinstein, he is all right?" I asked, my hand flying to my mouth.

Dottie shot me a scornful look. "*Him* you worry about?"

"Oh, Dottala," I said. "The man may have lost his livelihood."

She threw down her napkin. "But he has his life."

With that, she grabbed her clutch and hat and, without even putting the hat on her head, stormed out of the apartment.

I looked to the heavens. *Oh,* Hashem, *guide me.*

Walking back into the kitchen, I heard footsteps behind me. Izzy.

"Here, dry," I said, handing him a wet dish. He took a cloth and wiped the plate. Izzy was so meticulous. Dottie was careless, leaving streaks of water behind, but Izzy was thorough.

"Ma," he said, but then stopped.

"*Nu?*" I scraped the pieces of shell from Ben's egg cup into the garbage pail.

He placed the dish in the cabinet and waited for the next. He wanted to say something. I wouldn't rush him. Izzy came to his thoughts in his own time.

"Ma," he said again. With the yolk finally scrubbed off, I ran a soapy dish towel around the cup. Another rinse, and it went to Izzy.

Finally he spoke again. "I've . . . I've heard things."

I froze, the cold water running from the tap, the bucket of hot water cooling next to me. "What things?" I asked without looking at him. My eyes were trained on the sliver of sunlight coming in the small window.

"About Dottie," he said quietly.

I nodded. Odd how I could sweat so and still be chilled. "About Dottie," I repeated stupidly. "Who says things?"

From the corner of my eye, I could see him shrug. "Just on the street. No one important. One kid said something." Izzy appeared bashful.

"What did you do?"

He shrugged again. "I slugged him."

Smiling was too painful, but the image of my little Izzy—well, not so little, I suppose—punching someone for his sister's honor pleased me. "What exactly are they saying?"

"Ma, the dishes," Izzy said.

Willing my body to move, I picked up the next plate soaking in the warm tub. "What are they saying?"

Izzy shifted from foot to foot. "Nothing real specific."

I turned to look at him dead-on. "What are they saying?"

He stared at his feet, reminding me so much of the little boy he once was, caught skipping *heder* or sneaking a piece of *kuchen* before dinner. I reminded myself that he was a grown man of seventeen. The mere thought took my breath away.

"They say she's a bit of a piece."

"A bit of what? Look at me when you're speaking." I put my hand under his chin, surprised at the stubble, and lifted his face so I could peer into his eyes.

"Dottie has been having some fun lately. That's what they're saying."

"Fun with who?"

"No one specific," he said, but I was pretty sure he was trying to protect me.

Rather than push it, I let go of his chin. "You hit a guy for that?"

He nodded silently, waiting to be scolded.

"Next time you hear something like that"—Izzy looked chagrined—"make sure to punch him even harder."

Izzy grinned, relieved.

"Now go. Make sure your brothers aren't causing any more trouble than usual this morning." I gave him a peck on his head and he ran out. I finished cleaning up as I turned his words over in my mind. Did people know things for sure? Or was this simply the talk that happened, the bored meddling that exaggerated and created stories for entertainment? Either way, it would have to stop. Either Dottie would get rid of the baby and live such a pure life that no one could doubt her moral nature, or she would marry Abe and the talk would die off of its own accord.

After everyone left, I sat with my tea and newspaper out of habit, but I had no interest in the *Forverts* that day. My mind couldn't focus on the world at large, not when my world within was falling apart so rapidly. The frustration I felt. I should have been worrying about what might happen to Yussel with Hitler's influence spreading east in that backward Old World, not what might befall my daughter in the modern age of the *Goldene Medina*. It was time to take matters into my own hands.

I headed down the stairs at a slow pace. My dress that morning was snug. Luckily it was belted and I was able to loosen it two notches. But soon I would need the larger sizes that still lay in the back of my bottom drawer, those dresses I'd worn countless times during my pregnancies. Even without my saying a word, just putting on those old dresses would announce my current state to all my friends.

With my cloth bag in hand, I turned toward the Rabinowitz market. I didn't shop there often; they charged thirty cents for a five-pound bag of flour, when if I walked two blocks more, I could buy the same flour for a quarter.

The door was open to allow for a little breeze. The space inside was tight, with cans and boxes piled everywhere. Mrs. Rabinowitz sat behind the counter, chatting with a woman I recognized from the street. They made small talk while I waited patiently. Mrs. Rabinowitz was small, but squat, as if her body had melted into itself, all those hours she spent on that stool behind the counter. If you asked me, the woman was lazy. Abe did all the heavy lifting, and Mr. Rabinowitz either worked on the books or studied Torah. Mrs. Rabinowitz took great pride in reminding folks that her husband was a learned man.

The woman finally left, and I approached the counter.

"Ah, Mrs. Krasinsky," Mrs. Rabinowitz said. "We haven't seen you in a long while."

I nodded. "I usually send the boys to do the errands." This was a lie, but I hoped it might ease the awkwardness of my not shopping there regularly.

But of course, Mrs. Rabinowitz was not one to allow the easy way out. "Hmm, I don't recall seeing them."

Changing the subject, I asked, "Where is Abe?"

"Off at the piers, retrieving a shipment of goods."

I had hoped to speak to Abe directly, to learn of his intentions, but time was of the essence, so Mrs. Rabinowitz would have to do.

"With what may I help you?" she asked.

I didn't want to buy much, given the inflated prices. But I needed to purchase something. "I'd like a dozen eggs, please."

She turned to a box behind her and pulled them out. "Is that all?"

My smile was forced. "Yes. My last two were bad and I was in the middle of a recipe."

Mrs. Rabinowitz's body stiffened. "Well, I'm sure you didn't buy them here. All our eggs are good."

"Of course, Mrs. Rabinowitz," I said. "I came now because I know how fresh your eggs are."

Appeased, Mrs. Rabinowitz placed the eggs in my bag. "That will be thirty-five cents."

I dug the coins out of my purse. Thirty-five cents. Ridiculous. But I smiled as I handed over the change.

"So, Mrs. Rabinowitz," I said, as if making random small talk, as if a thought just popped into my mind. "Abe and Dottie have been sweet on each other for a long time now."

"Yes." Mrs. Rabinowitz gave a sigh that I couldn't decipher. Was it frustration? And if so, with what? With Abe's slowness? Or that he was with Dottie?

I couldn't allow myself to become ruffled, so I continued. "Don't you think it's time the two married?"

Mrs. Rabinowitz stared at me with shrewd eyes. "What's the rush?"

"Rush?" My shoulders squared themselves of their own accord. "It's been three years and Dottie is now nineteen. She will be an old maid soon. I would hardly call that a rush."

Fingering the papers on the counter, Mrs. Rabinowitz spoke, seeming to choose her words carefully. "I am sure when the time is right, Abe will decide on marriage. But he has many things to consider first."

Consider first? What was there to consider? "I know money is a concern," I said. "If it's simply a matter of financing a home, I'm sure Mr. Krasinsky and I could help with an apartment. And perhaps you and Mr. Rabinowitz could assist as well."

Mrs. Rabinowitz nodded, idly playing with the receipt pad. "Well, yes, finances are always a concern. But there are others."

The confusion must have been plain on my face, so she continued. "You are aware our family has been quite close to the Kraus family for many, many years. And Mr. Kraus is very successful in his garment business."

The Krauses! "But . . ." I was speechless. Was this Mrs. Rabinowitz speaking? Or Abe?

"Mr. Kraus and Mr. Rabinowitz have been discussing an expansion of the store. Perhaps we will begin to sell clothing."

Words were difficult, so offended was I for my poor Dottala. "Thank goodness we no longer live in the Old Country, where children were married off like chattel for family betterment."

Mrs. Rabinowitz's eyes narrowed to slits. "When Abe is ready to marry, I am sure he will take many things into consideration. Including the opinion of his parents. He is a good boy, that Abe."

My Dottie. How much insult could one child take? This was ridiculous. "My Dottie is a wonderful girl," I said, more defensively than I would have cared.

"Of course she is," Mrs. Rabinowitz said. "Good day."

That was it? I was being dismissed? I forced a nod at Mrs. Rabinowitz and bid her a "good day" as I marched out of the store.

My poor Dottala. Her choices had run out. It was the appointment on Thursday or a lifetime of shame. I wondered, though, if she could survive either one.

Dottie

※

Wednesday, August 28

ALL week I'd been snapping at my brothers, short with *Tateh*. And I was concerned about Abe. I hadn't seen Abe since Sunday, and while that wasn't unusual if things were hectic at the store, it was worrisome after Camp Eden. Was he avoiding me? Or was it as simple as a busy week? Not knowing ate at me.

Wednesday, as I did my morning toilet, Eugene shot into the tiny bathroom, nearly knocking me over.

"Alfie has more planes than me. Help me make more," he said, flashing me those big eyes that always got him what he wanted.

But that morning even Eugene couldn't alleviate my suffering. "Can't I get a minute's peace, even in here?" I said. My tone was sharper than I intended, and when Eugene slunk out, I saw the hurt streaked across his cheeks. Still in my slip, I took my dress, a smart navy blue from Ohrbach's, from the back of the door and slid it over my head. I needed my mother to do the buttons up the back.

Emerging from the bathroom, I saw Eugene at the table with a stack of old *Forverts*, neatly tearing squares to be folded into the flying toys.

Glancing at the clock, I knew I didn't have much time, but Eugene was so earnest in his work that I couldn't help myself. I sat next to him and took a square. "I suppose there's always time for an airplane or two."

Eugene didn't look up, but a smile tickled the corners of his mouth.

He was getting so big. How did it happen so quickly? When he was a babe, stashed away at *Tante* Kate's home, I used to sneak off to visit him. I was forbidden to travel so far from the apartment by myself—*Tante* Kate's home was over a mile away, down on Essex Street—but I hated coming home after school, hated having to prepare dinner, clean the house, and, worst of all, see my brothers Alfie and Joey lying there, sick, in Ma and *Tateh*'s bed. Izzy and I shared the second bedroom and *Tateh* slept on the couch. Ma would fall asleep sitting in the chair next to the boys' bed. And then the worst: Joey was sent to the hospital. The emptiness of the apartment chilled me, and I wanted to be anywhere but there. The only way to escape first the stench of illness and then the loneliness was to leave the apartment.

In those days I was fast on my feet, and I could quickly cover the distance to *Tante* Kate's, giving me time to spend with Eugene but still get back before Ma noticed I was gone. Not that Ma noticed much in those days, certainly not the dust gathering in the living room nor the burnt bread I produced.

Tante Kate was always happy to welcome me, eager to run errands or socialize with friends without Eugene underfoot. I would sit with him in her apartment and play patty-cake, teach him nursery rhymes, feed him treats I'd pinched off the food carts. I made sure to speak only English to him. Eugene wasn't going to be subjected to the humiliation I'd suffered in grammar school, when in kindergarten I couldn't keep up because I didn't speak English. No one believed I was American born, as all I could speak was Yiddish. I worked extra hard to catch up, determined to be not merely an equal to my classmates but their superior. And in math, at least, I succeeded, excelling, winning awards for arithmetic every year, even beating out the boys.

No, I made sure Eugene started school as an English speaker, a point in which I took great pride. Every day I spoke to Eugene in English, sang to Eugene in English, read to Eugene in English. His accomplishments would be as much my own as his. The rush of love I held for Eugene was unlike anything I'd ever felt for anyone else. Until now. Until this feeling that was stirring for a creature inside of me that didn't even yet exist.

Looking at Eugene, old enough this year to start *heder* after Rosh Hashanah, to begin learning Torah. I couldn't imagine how empty my life would have been without him. His face had lost its roundness and he had a sureness in his ways he'd lacked mere months ago. His hands were steady as he ripped the paper, then folded each sheet with precision. Eugene had kept me levelheaded when the house had fallen apart.

What if the baby was the same? How could I look at Eugene and even consider not having this baby?

I'd folded two airplanes to Eugene's five when we were interrupted by Ma coming out of the kitchen.

"*Ach*, look at the time. What is this nonsense you are doing?" Ma asked.

Looking at Ma, with the halo of hair floating about her head and her midlife belly starting to protrude, I thought to myself, once again, how attractive Ma would be if she watched what she ate and took some care with her clothing and hair. Maybe a dash of lipstick?

With an arched-eyebrow glance to Eugene, who gave a not-so-quiet snicker, I said, "I need you to button me up, Ma, and then I'm ready to go."

"No breakfast? You must eat."

"I'm not hungry," I said. I took a hard look at Ma, to see what I was to become. Feeling cruel toward her, I said, "Perhaps you should skip a meal or two. Pass on the *kugel*, maybe? You're starting to grow a belly." Would my body, like Ma's, curve permanently once it began carrying babies?

My eyes were quickly drawn up by Ma's sharp intake of breath. "Never you mind my plumpness. If a woman my age can't allow herself to become a little fuller, then what is the point of it all? Now spin around."

Would I ever again not be angry with Ma? I turned my back so she could do up the dress. The buttons did not give way easily, and Ma struggled to match the two sides. The dress squeezed about me.

Finally Ma said, "You need to find another dress. This one doesn't fit."

"But it fit last week." I turned to scowl at her.

She shrugged. "And next week, it will fit again. But for now, you must find another dress."

"Too much *kugel* for you, too," Eugene said, with a laugh.

"Shush yourself," Ma said, a touch too harshly. She turned to me. "Go. The green dress should fit. Change quickly and get to work. Head bookkeeper cannot be late. Especially as tomorrow—"

"Hush, Ma!" Tossing my head in the direction of Eugene, I said, "Little pitchers have big ears."

"Aw, I always miss the good stuff," Eugene said.

Without another word, I retrieved the green dress from Ma's room and slipped into the bathroom to change. I left the navy dress in a heap on the floor, certain it would never fit again.

THE morning passed in a flurry of numbers, and at lunch, as always, I was alone. As the girls gathered to go out, a stab of loneliness gutted me. I longed to be included, to be frivolous and carefree, even as much as I despised Florence.

Florence. Florence, who paraded her new status, knowing her job was safe. Florence, who, I was sure, would wait patiently for Mr. Dover to propose, who clearly didn't read the *Times*, which last weekend had announced his engagement, a spring wedding in Connecticut. A few weeks ago, I would have flaunted the paper, shown up Florence as just another girl who got herself into a bad place. But now, oddly, I was sympathetic, even a little sad for her. Although as bad as Florence had it, it wasn't nearly as low as where I was.

I needed to make one more try. One last-ditch effort. When the office cleared out for lunch, I picked up the phone. "Operator, please get me the offices of *The New Yorker*."

The phone rang long enough that I feared no one would answer, but finally a woman picked up. "*The New Yorker*. Finest magazine that apparently cannot afford a receptionist. How may I direct your call?"

Momentarily confused, I said nothing.

"Hello. I haven't got all day. Is someone on the line?"

"Yes, I'm sorry," I said. "Is Willie Klein available?"

"May I tell him who is calling?"

"Dottie Krasinsky."

I heard a muffle on the other end and then the woman's voice calling out, "Klein! There's a dame on the phone for you."

After a moment, a rustle and then a masculine voice. "William Klein here."

"Hello, Willie. It's Dottie."

Another rustle and voices in the background. "Dottie!" Willie was clearly startled. "What a surprise. I thought— Well, I'm enchanted to hear from you."

"I'd like to meet up. We need to talk."

Willie hesitated, and finally said, "I would love to see you. Did you mean—"

"I need to *talk* to you," I said.

"Talk." Was that disappointment in his voice?

Panicked he would refuse, I added, "I hurried out hastily on Monday, and I feel we left things . . . unsaid."

He chuckled. "I would be delighted to talk, but I don't have an abundance of time. I need to prepare for my trip. Do you want to meet after work on Friday?"

Another one of his silly tests. He knew I would be rushing home for *Shabbes* on Friday night. Besides, Friday night was too late. Trying to put a purr in my voice, I said, "What about this evening?"

Silence on his end. Clearly he was wondering what I was up to.

"Hmm," he said, and I could hear tapping, as if he was rapping a pencil against the receiver. "Sure, I could see you tonight." I could hear people chatting in the background. "I'm putting together a piece on the Fernand Léger exhibit at the Museum of Modern Art. Meet me there and we'll see where the night takes us."

Sickened by his assumptions, I merely played along. "That's perfect. What time?"

"Five fifteen."

"Till then," I said, trying to force a seductive lilt to my voice.

AT exactly five fifteen, I waited nervously in front of the Museum of Modern Art. I wasn't acquainted with this museum, which was only about five years old. When I was a child, *Tateh* had often brought me to the Metropolitan Museum, and I loved losing myself in the sumptuous building and the stories in the paintings.

But the town house that contained the Museum of Modern Art didn't have the gravity that an institute of art should maintain. Instead of a grand staircase, four simple steps led to a regular door. As a museum, it was as out of place as I.

Midtown bustled as well-dressed folk streamed past, men hurrying home, women with a *click-clack* of heels dancing past me on their way to meet friends or beaus. These were the people for whom Ma made clothing when I was younger. I could still picture Ma hunched over the garments, the needle flying rhythmically. In those days, I longed to help, begged Ma to teach me. But Ma refused. "You are too good for this," Ma told me, many times over. "You will do great things. You will never need to sew for other people."

Glancing at my watch, I saw Willie was ten minutes late. It took every ounce of willpower to keep from pacing the sidewalk;

it wouldn't do to look anxious when he arrived. I tried for nonchalant, although my body longed to give in to fatigue, to plop indecorously on the front stoop like a rag doll tossed aside, tired and worn and discarded by all who used her. Where was Willie? "Fashionably late" was all the rage with the swell set, but I fretted that he'd changed his mind.

At half past five, Willie casually strolled up the sidewalk. "There you are," he said, as if I were the one behind schedule. If he'd been Abe, I would have given him a piece of my mind. But of course, he was not Abe. Willie kissed me on the cheek. "Shall we go in?"

I nodded, not trusting my voice to hide my irritation, and I let Willie take me by the arm. As we walked in, he said, "I think you'll be impressed by the exhibit. Are you familiar with Léger's work?"

The lack of grandeur in the front hall disappointed me, and I debated momentarily if I should fake knowledge before admitting, "No. He's new to me." Willie led me up the stairs to the second floor.

"His work is probably unlike any you've seen before. His aim is to create 'democratic art' for and about the working class, with bold color and, as he calls it, 'mechanical' form."

We reached a closed door at the top of the stairs. As Willie went to open it, a guard spotted us and said, "I'm sorry, sir. That exhibition isn't open to the public yet."

Willie tipped his hat and said with a tone that was both authoritative and colluding, "My dear friend Mrs. Crane would have called ahead granting me permission for a preview."

The guard stood a little straighter. "Mr. Klein, I presume? Of course." He walked over with a set of keys and unlocked the door, holding it open for us. "The museum closes in twenty minutes."

"Thank you, my good man," Willie said, turning back to the door.

"Who is Mrs. Crane?" I whispered to him.

"Mrs. Crane of the paper company? Her husband was a business associate of Father. She's a member of the museum's board of trustees. Come, let's go in."

As we walked into the room, I gasped. Willie was right. This art was like nothing I had seen before.

Willie watched me carefully as I meandered from painting to painting. The colors were muted—gray and yellow and black—yet dynamic. I was drawn first to a painting of three women lounging in a living room. They were nude, but not like the nudes I had seen at the Metropolitan. Their bodies were plush and rounded yet strangely disjointed. From behind me, Willie spoke softly, intimately, in my ear. "What do you think?"

His voice made me shiver in a delicious way and for a moment, I was simply a girl out with an incredibly handsome boy at an exclusive exhibition, and I was in heaven. His hand slipped onto my waist, and I panicked he would note the extra flesh, but it also felt good, so I let it sit. We were alone, so it felt safe. "It's remarkable," I said, "how they are so feminine and oddly beautiful, yet completely masculine."

When Willie was silent, I turned to look at him and saw him appraising me. "Yes," he said, and I was pretty sure I had passed another test.

The closeness suddenly made me uncomfortable, reminding me of how I'd gotten into this situation in the first place. Where Abe was warm and sturdy, Willie reminded me of my times in the back alleys with Lefty—all sizzle.

To gain a little space, I walked to the next painting, forcing his hand to drop, and asked, "So what is your story about?"

Willie straightened, adjusting his hat. Was it possible I flustered him as much as he flustered me? "Are you aware that Hitler has denounced Expressionist art? And that he's decreed there's no room for modernist experimentation in the Third Reich?"

I shook my head, spellbound by a painting that completely dominated one wall. The signs for many of the paintings weren't up yet, but this one had a tiny plaque identifying it as *La ville*. A city gone mad, it was even denser than the lower East Side. Lines overlaid lines; billboards were sliced in half; scaffolding angled in the distance.

"Art must be 'pure,' according to Hitler," Willie continued. "His artistic tastes are insensate. My piece explores what is so 'ignominious' in these paintings."

I looked up, surprised. "But *you* don't find them ignominious, do you? I mean, look at this one! Both claustrophobic *and* expansive. So contradictory. Yet mesmerizing."

"Yes, exactly," he said, moving behind me and dropping his hand onto my shoulder. "I like the way you put that. I might borrow your words."

The physicality of his body pressing against mine sent shocks of electricity through me—and reminded me why I was there. I had forgotten my nerves in the pleasure of the art and his company. I wondered if Abe could ever be enticed into coming to the Museum of Modern Art. In my heart, I knew he would find the work too shocking.

Abe. Willie. These paintings, which suddenly made me feel confined in the lines and the colors. I became warm, breathless. I trembled. Willie could feel it.

"Are you all right, Dottie?" he asked. His voice held genuine concern.

Barely nodding, I asked, "Tell me again. When do you leave?" My voice quivered, and I cursed myself for my fragility.

"Two weeks from tomorrow."

"Aren't you worried about heading into Europe?" I kept my eyes on *La ville*, though I could feel his gaze boring into me.

"Worried?" Willie chuckled. "Worry is for mothers and weaklings."

"I would think your family would worry sick about you," I said.

"My mother frets about hangnails." Willie took me by the waist and drew me to a bench at the side of the room. "Of course she's worried. But my father understands—or at least pretends to, which is good enough. At some point my parents will expect me to settle down, start a family, but this is my time. And it's not so easy for a parent to meddle when you're thousands of miles away."

He sat me down and really looked at me. My smile was frozen, but tears taunted the corners of my eyes. I blinked rapidly, willing my expression to change.

Willie's eyes narrowed a touch as he tilted his head. "Dottie?" His gaze was fierce, and all I wanted to do was cower in the corner. "Why did you want to see me?"

My mien didn't change. I stared at him, blinking, blinking, blinking. I forbade the tears to fall, but like with everything else, I was powerless, and they dripped inelegantly. Dismayed at my lack of grace, I pulled my hand from his and tried to cover my face. This was not how I'd planned to present myself.

"Dottie, what's wrong?" His voice held both pity and disgust. I could imagine what he was thinking: He was looking for a carefree romp, and instead I was crying on his doorstep.

I couldn't look at Willie, instead staring at the walls.

For a while I didn't speak, trying to keep my terror under control.

After what seemed an infinitely long time, Willie spoke again. "Dottie, why did you want to see me?" But his tone was resigned, as if he knew exactly why I was sitting there, with him, in the Museum of Modern Art, trying not to sob like a schoolgirl.

"That night. At Camp Eden."

Willie tensed. "It was lovely."

With an uneven breath, I steeled my nerves so as to look Willie in the eyes. "It's still with us."

"Still with . . . ah," Willie said. "You are sure?"

I nodded.

He paused, trying to formulate the words. "But you have a boyfriend. . . ."

I shook my head. "It's not his." My voice was ragged around the edges. "I even tried . . . I wanted Abe to think it was . . . but . . ."

With raised eyebrows, Willie said, "You mean you two have never?"

"Never." My voice was barely more than a whisper.

"Damn puritan."

I longed to defend Abe, to protest this slur, but unfortunately, Willie was right. *Damn puritan.* Ruining my life.

Gently, Willie took my hand back in his. Speaking in an untroubled voice, he said, "I'm leaving for Europe."

I nodded.

"I—" He hesitated. "I know people."

Jerking my head up, I stared at him, dumbfounded. Not him, too!

Gently stroking the back of my hand with his fingers, he spoke soothingly, as if appeasing a small child. "It's not pleasant, I know. But there is a way to take care of this. I know a doctor. I can pay for it. The recovery isn't too bad; you should be able to return to work in a day or so. Or if you need to take extra time off, I can help with your wages for that week."

Willie's words settled over me. Dear God. "You've done this before, haven't you? Taken women to doctors."

His silence was all the answer I needed. He continued to stroke my hand. What kind of man was he?

"I—no," I said, trying to be firm, trying to muster a shred of dignity.

Willie took my chin in his hand and gently turned my face so I was looking directly at him. "I know this is difficult. But I *am* leaving for Europe on the twelfth. You need to take control of this situation. You need to fix it."

Letting go of my face, he opened the left side of his jacket, reached into his pocket, and retrieved a gold monogrammed money clip that held a wad of bills. He counted out all that was there. "This is forty-five dollars. It won't be enough, but I can get you more. I can arrange things for you, if you'd like."

I stared at the money in revulsion. "I am not a working girl."

"Of course you aren't. You're a good girl in a bad situation, and I want to help you out of it."

"A bad situation that *you* put me in."

"Now, now," he said, a chill entering his voice, "I don't remember you discouraging me."

Mortified, I turned away.

The door opened, and the guard poked his head through. "Mr. Klein, you have five more minutes until the museum closes."

"Thank you, sir," Willie said. Turning back to me, he said, "You need to take care of this. I don't see a choice." From under my arm, he removed my clutch and snapped it open. It looked so delicate in his hands. He took the money and slid it inside, as if he were a husband giving his wife her weekly allowance.

I wanted to take the money and throw it at him. I wanted to yell at him to take responsibility. I wanted to lunge into his arms and have him hold me tight and say everything would be all right.

"I can make the arrangements," he said again.

Words wouldn't come, so instead, I took the coward's way out, grabbing my purse, running through the room, pushing open the door, and scurrying down the stairs out onto the street. *Come after me*, I prayed. *Come find me. Do the right thing, Willie.*

But as I stood on the sidewalk, tear-streaked and out of breath, I was alone. Completely alone.

Rose

✧

Wednesday, August 28

DOTTIE'S seat at the dinner table was empty.

"I have a meeting tonight," Ben said, shoveling calves' liver into his mouth. "Mechanics' union."

Ben was as bad as the boys, all of them racing to eat, as if there wouldn't be enough. There was always enough. "Slow down. All of you. That food took me hours to prepare and it disappears in seconds."

With a full mouth, Alfie said, "But it's so good."

I removed the serving plate from the table before Alfie could grab more. "Save some for your brother."

"Where is Izzy?" Ben asked, spearing another bite with his fork. "And Dottie has been out quite a bit."

"Izzy is working double shifts," I said. "And Dottie? Who knows where that girl goes?"

"Probably with Abe," Ben said. He grabbed a hunk of bread to mop up the mushroom sauce on his plate.

Probably not, I thought. But I was concerned she wasn't home yet. Tomorrow was her appointment. I wanted her to get a good night's sleep.

At close to eight, as I was finishing the washing up, the front door banged open.

"Don't slam the door," I said. I assumed it was the boys, returning for more pillows to make a cozy nest to sleep on the roof. In these brutal days, the roof was the only relief from the torrid heat, though little good it did. "You need what?" I called out.

When I didn't get a response, I wiped my hands on my apron, and walked out to see Dottie sitting on the couch, hat still on, purse in hand, looking straight ahead but not seeing anything at all.

I sat next to her, taking her hand in mine. For moments we sat in silence. Finally, I said, "You are frightened."

Dottie didn't respond. She sat rigidly, staring forward. I knew she feared that if she spoke, the tears would start and never stop. I knew this because *I* felt it. That if I didn't remain strong, I would shatter into a million pieces.

I wrapped my arm around her shoulder and pulled her close. "You will survive, my *bubelah*. You will go on to be an accountant, get married—" Although to whom? I couldn't tell her about my conversation with Mrs. Rabinowitz, couldn't bear to break her heart any more than it was already broken. "—have many, many children, if you so desire."

She swallowed loudly. In a whisper of a voice, she said, "I do. I do desire."

I nodded. "You will have them."

She turned her face to me and I saw big wet drops brimming in her eyes. "What if I can't?" she said. "What if they mess up? I've heard stories. I've heard of women . . ." And with that, she buried her head in my shoulder and sobbed.

"Hush, my *bubelah*, hush. God will guide you. He won't abandon you. You will have children. You will be up to your ears in diapers and feedings. When the time is right."

A rap came on the front door. "Everything all right in there?" Mrs. Kaplan called from outside the front door. "I thought I heard crying."

I rolled my eyes at Dottie, but she didn't even glance at me to notice. "We're fine, Mrs. Kaplan. Thank you for checking."

"Oh," she said, disappointment ringing in her voice.

I pulled Dottie closer. Her tears warmed my neck, slid down

my shoulders. Her body shook. I held her, my baby girl; I held her as I hadn't in many, many years, rocking her back and forth and back and forth as she gripped me with the desperation of a little girl who wants her *mamelah*. That moment held a lifetime, yet lasted mere moments, before the boys came bounding in, oblivious to the grief of women.

Dottie

———————— ⚜ ————————

AFTER everyone retreated to the roof, I remained sitting on the couch, unable to move. Ma hadn't wanted to leave me alone, but I promised I would get ready for bed and join the others soon. And I would, as soon as I could lift my heavy limbs. Usually I craved solitude, but that night, the night on the precipice of my life before and my life after, I knew I would evaporate on my own.

Finally I slid on my nightgown and climbed slowly to the roof. Looking out at the sea of sleeping bodies, I sought my family. Finally I recognized the mounds on mattresses. Carefully stepping around the others, I crouched next to Eugene.

"Shove over," I whispered into his ear, and in his sleep he smiled and rolled over. I stretched out next to him, staring at the stars that dangled overhead. I listened to the sounds of the roof—the snores, the sighs, the simpering, and the staccato breathing—and the sounds of the street—the rumble of cars, the shouts of boys out too late, the cries of a baby in another building.

Eugene turned toward me, his arm snaking over my body. His breath was warm on my face, and when I nuzzled closer to him, I smelled its sweetness. I leaned into him and gave him a peck on the cheek.

Eugene stirred momentarily, mumbling, "Sweet dreams, Dottala," before rolling back on his other side. I turned onto my back and stared at the stars, which the lights of the street made dim.

I knew sleep would help, that I needed my strength for the next day, but every time I closed my eyes, the image of my baby formed beneath my lids. How clearly I could envision her, the way her entire newborn face would pucker, seeking me, her mother. Her wisp of a hand. The downy hair. The softness of her belly. A tightness in my throat made me gulp for air. I let myself cry silently, the tears leaking down the sides of my face, wetting the mattress. Ma said this wasn't my baby, that my babies were yet to be. Why couldn't I accept that?

When my tears were spent, I pulled Eugene close to me. I lay there, looking upward, unaware of when the stars receded and sleep overtook me.

Rose

———— ⚘ ————

Thursday, August 29

I was a bundle of nerves.

Dottie arose an hour earlier than usual. She came down from the roof and changed into her work clothes even before Ben awoke.

Sitting at the breakfast table, alone, she moved as if in a fog. "It's a beautiful day," she said, and the sorrow in her voice made me want to pull her into my arms, want to run away with her, protect her, my sweet, darling Dottala. But of course, that wasn't possible. "I thought it might rain, but the skies are crystal clear."

I nodded. "Do you want some toast?"

She looked at me with the glassy stare of a Flossie Flirt doll. "I thought I wasn't to eat. Is toast permitted?"

"I'm sure a piece of toast and some tea won't hurt," I said, but what did I know?

I put a plate in front of her as well as a glass of tea. I brought out a bowl of sugar cubes. "Help yourself. I won't look," I said, trying to cheer her. Normally I doled out the sugar, watching how much she took, but I'd do anything to see her smile.

"One o'clock?" she said.

Swallowing hard, I nodded. "One o'clock, it starts. You must be there at twelve thirty. You have the address?"

"Do I need to bring money?" Her voice was monotone. "You said we need to pay more?"

I shook my head. "Don't worry about it, my Dottala. I have the ten dollars. You save your money. Spend it on something pretty."

She nodded, but I wasn't sure she heard me.

Not knowing what else to say to her, I retreated to the kitchen. But there was nothing for me to do there, so I leaned on the sink and stared at the sky.

A few moments later, the door closed, in a quiet, gentle way. Going back to the dining table, I saw Dottie's food, completely untouched, the sugar still stacked in the bowl.

I cleared the table and began to fix breakfast for the boys.

Dottie

Thursday, August 29

MY plan was to go to work early. I would get through a few stacks of papers in the morning, and then tell Mr. Dover that my ma was ill, that I was taking her to a doctor's appointment and would need to leave work at the lunch hour. On Friday I'd send Alfie to Dover Insurance to let Mr. Dover know I needed to take care of Ma for the day, but I'd be back at work bright and early on Monday morning.

That was my plan.

ON my way to the streetcar, I detoured south a block to pass by Abe's store. Mrs. Rabinowitz was cranking open the awning, and I stopped to greet her. "Good morning, Mrs. Rabinowitz."

She looked up, startled. "Morning," she replied. She didn't invite me in to see Abe or encourage any conversation, so I stood outside, staring at the lettering on the window, debating what to do. RABINOWITZ MARKET, it read first in English and then again in Yiddish beneath it. *Kosher*, read the sign below it, this word only in Yiddish.

My eyes focused on the letters, so I didn't notice for a few moments that Abe had spotted me and was making faces in the window. Relief washed over me. He wasn't still angry about our Camp Eden "sin." I laughed at his goofiness. He popped outside.

"Dottala." His warm voice filled me with hope. It was a voice I could sink into, lose myself in. "What brings you out so early?"

"Going to work. Trying to catch up on the stacks of numbers that need inputting," I said.

"So diligent." He smiled at me, and it made my stomach drop. I wanted to let him comfort me and take care of me and make the world right again. My face must have betrayed my emotions, because Abe came out of the doorway and put a hand on my arm. "Dottie? Are you okay?"

I shook my head. Mrs. Rabinowitz said, "Do you need to sit down, dear? Is the heat too much for you?" Her words were caring, but her voice lacked even a smidgen of sympathy.

Ignoring her, I said to Abe, "Perhaps we could sit somewhere alone? Have a little chat?"

"Alone?" Abe said, glancing at his mother. I was sure he was thinking of last weekend at Camp Eden, but it was not even seven in the morning on a Thursday. What kind of beast did he think I was?

I chewed my bottom lip, not sure how to respond. But I think he realized the foolishness of whatever he was thinking, so he said, "Of course. Let's have a cup of coffee upstairs." Abe's family lived above the store, and as we walked up, Abe said, "*Tateh* is at *shul*. I'll put on the coffee."

"I don't want any coffee," I said as we entered the front room.

"Well, I'd like a cup." Abe was a focused man, always finishing what he started. It was a trait I both admired and found to be exasperating.

When the percolator was finally set on the stove top, he sat down at the kitchen table. I hesitated before taking a seat across from him. I didn't know how I was going to begin.

"Abe," I said.

"Yes?"

What exactly was I trying to say? "I hate my job." The words surprised me. They were the furthest thing from the truth, and yet here they were flowing from me.

"What?" Abe laughed. "You love your job."

I shook my head. "I love the numbers. But trudging uptown. Dealing with those girls. My demanding boss."

"But your promotion," Abe said.

I nodded. "So much pressure. I didn't realize how much more work would be involved." I took Abe's hands in mine. I glanced around the room, as if looking for answers in his kitchen. "I want to be working in a smaller business. A family business." I looked into his eyes, which stared at me quizzically. "*Our* family business. Abe, it's been three years. It's time we married."

The coffee percolated, and Abe stood slowly, deliberately. "Are you sure you don't want a cup?" he asked, as he poured the steaming liquid. I shook my head.

"Abe, are we going to be married or not?" I put all my cards on the table. What was it going to be?

"Of course we are," he said. "In the spring, perhaps."

My voice caught in the back of my throat and a burning sensation began in my chest. "Not *perhaps*. Now. I am ready now. I want to marry you. I want to run your business. I want to start a family." At that, I choked on the words. "I need to be married now." I closed my eyes briefly. *Why did I say* need?

Abe looked at me curiously. "Why now?"

"Because I'm nineteen and it's time for me to be married."

"But why not when you were eighteen? Why not when you're twenty? You know your ma was here making the same suggestion to my ma."

My cheeks warmed. Ma was here? Should I be angry at her for meddling? Grateful she had tried to help me avoid . . . unpleasantries? "I didn't know."

Putting his cup on the table, he sat down across from me. "Why the push now for marriage?" His voice took on a discouraging tone. "Does this have to do with what happened last weekend at Camp Eden? You were quite determined."

I reached for his hands, but he pulled his away, so my hands were left open in the middle of the table, untouched. "I don't understand," I said.

His voice was now harsh. "*I* don't understand. Why do you want to marry now?"

"Last weekend at Camp Eden made me realize how much I want to be with you. Be *married* to you. I've been wanting to be married for years. It's no secret. Everyone knows," I said, unsure of what I was defending.

Abe pushed away from the table and paced the small space in the kitchen. "You know I don't listen to *lashon hara*. I don't believe in gossip."

Gossip? I placed my hands in my lap and fidgeted with the buttons on my dress.

"But perhaps there's something to it? I've heard the things Willie Klein has been saying."

I didn't mean to. I don't know how it slipped out. But I gasped. And that gasp gave away everything I was trying so hard to keep secret.

Abe stared at me. The seconds lengthened into a lifetime, but flashed so quickly. "Get out," he said.

"Abe, let me—"

"Get out!" He yelled his words, and the sound was terrifying from a man who never so much as raised his voice even to cheer at a baseball game. I was looking down, so when I heard the smash, I jumped, banging my leg on the table. When I looked up, I saw a streak of coffee across the tablecloth, and the remains of Abe's cup splintered on the floor. Abe looked venomous, and for the first time, I was frightened of him.

"Abe, no!" The tears let loose, and I sat frozen until Abe came over and grabbed my arm, lifting me from the chair, shoving me to the door.

"Get out. Now!"

Rapid footfalls sounded on the stairs. The door opened, and Mrs. Rabinowitz yelled in, "What is going on?"

Abe pushed me toward the door and said, "Dottie was just leaving."

Anger contorted his face into an ugly scowl, and I couldn't help but notice the pleased look on Mrs. Rabinowitz's face.

Without another word, I ran out the door, down the stairs, and out of the store. I sprinted to the streetcar. *Maybe I'll trip*, I thought. *Maybe I'll fall and lose the baby, and then everything will go away and it will all be out of my hands.* But of course, it was too late for that. Even if the baby were gone, I'd still be lost. Abe was gone. Forever.

Rose

HOW does one dress to take her daughter to rid herself of a baby? Clothing was not something I cared about, but I needed to be strong. Dottie told me many times that clothing could change the way you feel. But I had no choice. I put on my *Shabbes* dress, leaving the buttons at my waist undone because they wouldn't squeeze closed.

So much had to be done. Dinner needed to be started. The floors were filthy and should be washed before *Shabbes*. The *kaffeeklatsch* was meeting at Perle's. I needed to write letters for Mrs. Friedman for the Women's Socialist Conference. I'd promised to make a meal to deliver to the immigrant society. Alfie's pants needed altering so they could be passed down to Eugene. And the entire day's worth of work needed to be squeezed into the hours before noon, when I would leave to meet Dottie.

Placing my hat on my head, I took my clutch in hand and sat on the couch. All that work to do. And for the next four hours, I could only stare at the clock and wait.

Dottie

———— ✛ ————

BY the time I reached the Third Avenue streetcar, I was out of breath and my feet hurt. My ankles were swollen, and I longed to slip off my shoes.

When the trolley pulled up, I swung aboard. The car was crowded, so I stood, even though the fatigue was almost unbearable. A young man caught my eye and, with a smile and a wink, stood to give me his seat. Gratefully, I slunk into it, and it took a moment for me to realize that the young man continued to stare at me, his eyes roving up my legs. Shame swept through me, and I tugged at my dress, crossing my ankles.

My future was written. I would have nothing. Not Abe. Not my baby. Nothing.

At Twenty-third Street, a young woman came aboard with two small children. She held a shopping bag and the kids pulled at her dress. "Not now," she snapped at the two, and I wondered if I should be relieved this would not be my fate.

Despite my tiredness, I stood up, gesturing for the mother to sit. She did, without a thank-you, as if it were her right to a seat on the car. The two children leaned on their mother's knees. I couldn't help but observe them, and I was taken aback when the mother turned a tender look to her *kinder*. "I'm sorry I yelled, my little angels," she said.

"That's all right," said the older of the two, a boy no more than five.

"That's all wite," mimicked the younger, a girl probably three.

The mother laughed and the girl leaned over and gave her mother a kiss.

It was as if a dagger assaulted my stomach. My hand went of its own accord to rest on my belly.

When the streetcar pulled up to Thirty-fourth Street, I had every intention of getting out. I was going to get off, walk up the street to Thirty-fifth and Lexington, and open the door to the office building. I would press the button for the elevator and stand in the lobby staring at the oil painting of a Cape Cod seascape, waiting for the doors to open. Others would gather beside me, all staring ahead, all waiting for the little box to arrive. When it did, one of the gentlemen, also waiting, would hold open the doors as I stepped in. As the elevator was a new, automatic one, he would ask me what floor, and when I said, "Three," he would push the button for me. We would stand, close, but not touching, each looking forward, pretending the others weren't there, at least until the elevator stopped, at which time the gentleman would hold open the door for me and wish me a pleasant day.

I would step out of the elevator, and approach the frosted-glass door stenciled with DOVER INSURANCE COMPANY. I'd open the door, walk through the room, which would surely be empty, and arrive at my desk. I'd remove the pin holding my hat in place, and set my hat and clutch upon the desk before situating myself in my seat, and letting myself disappear into the numbers.

That was what I intended to do.

MY feet were still firmly planted on the floor when the streetcar reached Sixty-fifth Street, and I had to shake them loose. I pushed my way through the crowd and stepped off. Up here the roads looked different. Wider. More trees.

As I walked westward, I considered what I was doing. This could end badly. But with each footstep, I grew more determined.

What was it Willie had said to me? "You need to take control of this situation. You need to fix it."

Abe was lost. Whether or not I had the procedure, Abe was gone. The procedure was meant to guarantee my future with Abe. But he was no longer my future. Abe was my past. I thought of the doctor, of what he would do. Would he use knives? Needles? Would he cut or scrape? Would I be numb or would I feel every movement? Would the baby? A shiver of horror broke through my anesthetized feeling.

With each footstep, the words played in my mind like a Victrola stuck in a groove: "You need to take control of this situation." Well, that's what I was going to do. Take control. Fix it. Ma always told me where to go, whom to see, what kind of work to do. Ma was the voice of the family. I'd never needed mine before. It was time for me to find my own voice.

I had stared at those letters from Willie often enough to memorize the return address. Of their own volition, my legs walked toward Park Avenue. The apartments here were larger—I could tell by the size of the windows—but there were fewer people on the street.

Upon arriving at 654 Park Avenue, I hesitated for the first time. The building was grand, with ornate flowers carved around the entrance, and an expansive awning jutting out. The street was broad and lush, like something in a movie, not existing in real life in New York City. At least not in *my* New York City. *This isn't right*, I thought. *I should turn around now.* But then the doorman smiled at me. "May I help you, miss?"

Too frightened of what lay ahead of me if I walked away, too terrified of what I would face if I went upstairs, too mortified by the morning's encounter with Abe, I did the only thing I could: I dropped into a faint.

When I came to, I was on the bench in the lobby. "Now, now, miss," the doorman said. "You gave me quite a fright there." The doorman's accent was rich and Irish, and I wished I could listen to it all day and make the rest of the world go away.

"I'm—I'm sorry," I said, beginning to rise, but the doorman grasped me.

"Now, you sure you are okay to stand up, miss?"

"I'm fine, I'm fine," I said, although I wasn't. My legs were shaky and I blinked to make things appear in focus.

"Is there something I can help you with, miss?"

Before I could allow the fear to overwhelm me again, before I could allow myself to change my mind, I said, "I'm here to see Mrs. Klein."

With a raised eyebrow, the doorman asked, "Whom shall I say is calling?"

"Kindly tell her Dorothea Krasinsky is here to see her about a very important matter."

The doorman gave me a little nod and walked to the telephone. My light-headed feeling gave everything a strange glow, amplifying colors. I noticed the way the doorman's red uniform contrasted with the pale marble lobby, the way the buttons on his golden epaulets reflected the light.

I could hear him saying my name. "Dorothea Krasinsky. One moment, while I check."

The doorman appeared disconcerted as he turned to me. "I'm sorry—could you tell me to what this is in reference?"

"Please tell her I'm Dottie. Rose and Ben Krasinsky's daughter," I said. "Zelda's friend. I have an urgent matter to discuss."

The doorman repeated my words into the phone, then nodded and hung up the receiver. "Mrs. Klein would be happy to see you. This way."

He rang for the elevator, which soon arrived at the lobby. The door opened and a colored man sat inside, wearing a similar, but less fancy, version of the doorman's outfit.

"Please take Miss Krasinsky to Mrs. Klein's apartment."

"Yes, sir," said the man perched on a squat wooden stool. I stepped in and the man closed the door and pulled a lever. With a jolt, the elevator rose. As it ascended, I thought about what I would say to Mrs. Klein.

I didn't have long before we bounced to a stop. "Watch your step, miss," the elevator man said, as he opened the door. The elevator was an inch or two shy of the floor. Only a mild step up and yet I still stumbled, catching myself before tumbling to the ground. "Careful, miss. Apartment 6A, miss," the man said.

The hallway was broad, with a pair of doors at the end of the floor, one marked 6A and the other 6B. The walls leading to the Kleins' apartment held giant mirrors on both sides, so I saw myself reflected infinitely: a scared young woman slouching beneath the weight of her fear. I forced my shoulders straight. A lush carpet lay on the floor beneath me. *And this is just the hall!* I thought. I knew Willie's father was successful, but I'd had no idea the family was *so* well-to-do. I should turn around right now, I once again decided. I would leave and never come back.

I was halfway to the elevator, when the door to 6A opened, and a voice called out, "Miss Krasinsky? Mrs. Klein will see you in the parlor."

With a deep breath, I turned back. The servant was a young girl, also with an Irish accent. She wore a crisp uniform of black and white, her hair tucked in a bun. She held open the door, and with an inelegant gulp, I entered.

The apartment was even more magnificent than I'd imagined. A large oil painting graced the wall opposite the front door, an almost life-sized portrait of Mr. and Mrs. Klein, with Willie as a young boy.

"This way, miss," the housemaid said, and she sashayed to the next room.

As I followed her into the parlor, I took in shelves filled with elegant pieces of porcelain. A table with a lovely vase, white with a blue floral design. An overstuffed couch. Mrs. Klein sat in a chair by the window with a small piece of cloth in her hand and an embroidery needle. It had been a few years since I'd last seen her, but her hair was still an unnatural light brown, without a hint of gray, and it was perfectly coiffed, not a stray hair flying out, unlike Ma's hair with its frizzy halo around her bun. Mrs. Klein's face was lightly made up, with a faint sheen of powder dusting her nose in an elegant, *Vogue*-like way. The room seemed mammoth, with high ceilings and broad windows that overlooked Park Avenue. The apartment even smelled different. It took me a moment to place it; there were no odors of liver frying or chicken roasting or fish stewing. The only scent was the vague fragrance of lilies.

"Dottie," Mrs. Klein said, not bothering to stand, forced cheer on her face. "What a surprise to see you. Or do you go by Dorothea now?"

"Dottie is fine."

"Please," Mrs. Klein said, stretching her arm toward the sofa. "Have a seat." Her voice was thin, unwelcoming beneath the pleasantries. Mrs. Klein nodded toward her maid, who left the room.

"Thank you, ma'am," I said, as I sank into the plump cushion covered in a lavender toile.

"Were you looking for William? He's already left for work." She shook her head. "You've heard of his cockamamy plan? Going to Europe to be a writer? His father and I are appalled."

"Willie mentioned it to me." I could hear the catch in my voice and I tried to hide it. "It sounds like quite the adventure."

Looking into Mrs. Klein's face, I realized she heard the same catch, and the older woman's eyes narrowed. With a slight scowl on her face, her resemblance to her son was unmistakable.

"To what do I owe this pleasure?"

"Mrs. Klein . . ." I fumbled for the right words.

Her face was now plastered in suspicion. "Yes?"

With a deep breath, I fixed my eyes on the country landscape hung over the fireplace. The Impressionist painting looked familiar. Could it be an actual Monet? Pretending to be lost in the fields, I closed my eyes, and said, "Mrs. Klein, I am in a situation." At the lack of response, I plowed on. "I am with child."

I heard a sharp intake of breath, then, "And what does this have to do with me?"

Opening my eyes, I forced myself to look directly at Mrs. Klein and hold her gaze. Now was not the time for weakness. I was not going to cower. I needed to prove myself Mrs. Klein's equal. I asked, "Do you truly need me to explain myself?"

Mrs. Klein broke eye contact first, and I silently heaved relief.

"No," she said, returning to her embroidery, "I'm afraid you don't. You are not the first girl to appear on my doorstep."

Horror must have been reflected in my face.

With a sardonic chuckle, Mrs. Klein said, "I am sorry to disillusion you, my dear. Did you think you were the only one?"

I thought of Willie and his knowledge of doctors. I shook my head.

"Did he not offer to take care of it? I am well aware my son has his . . . connections."

I nodded. No tears threatened this time. Perhaps I was cried out. I was grateful for small mercies. The hitch in my chest, though, threatened to engulf me, to swallow me whole. I peeked up slightly and noticed Mrs. Klein evaluating me.

"I take it that you do not wish to have the situation taken care of?" she said briskly.

Not trusting my voice, I shook my head.

"I'm curious, dear. You are not typical of the . . . of the girls with whom William has had difficulty. I thought you were such a good girl, Dottie. How did this occur?"

Toying with the belt on my dress, I said quietly, "At Camp Eden. Last May."

"At Camp Eden!" Mrs. Klein said. "At Camp Eden," she repeated, shaking her head. "I always said sending him there was utter nonsense, but my father-in-law insisted, said William needed a connection to Judaism, to Zionism. Now look at what it's done. Given him this ridiculous idea that he needs to 'save the Jews' and . . . this."

Daring to glance up, I saw Mrs. Klein gnawing on her lower lip, her lipstick chipping off and lodging on her front tooth. She stared out the window. Her eyes held a faraway gaze that was unreadable. "That greenhorn mentality. Camp Eden was supposed to instill strong values in William. And look what he does."

The minutes of silence stretched until finally she said, "Well, I can't say I'm surprised by William, but I will say I'm surprised at *you*. I would have thought you came from better stock."

I straightened my spine. With the lipstick on her tooth, Mrs. Klein seemed less formidable. "I come from excellent 'stock,' I'll thank you," I said. "I didn't intend for this to happen. It was a onetime occurrence, an evening that clearly got out of hand. Despite what you may think, this is not what I would have chosen for myself. I was planning to marry another and have a family with him, but alas, that is not to be anymore. My intended will not have me in this condition. Willie has a responsibility."

With a raised eyebrow, Mrs. Klein gave the tiniest hint of a smile. "Have a streak of spunk, do you?"

Staring Mrs. Klein dead in the eye, I said, "Willie told me I need to take control of the situation. Which is precisely what I am doing."

Mrs. Klein looked out the window. She thought for a few moments before asking, "What does your mother say?"

When I didn't respond, Mrs. Klein glanced back. "I presume your mother is aware of the situation?"

I nodded.

"And?"

I tried to keep the firmness in my voice. "She thinks I should make the problem go away."

Mrs. Klein nodded. "Your mother has always been a sage woman." She finally set her embroidery down on the carved and polished table next to her. I could see the beginnings of cross-stitched birds. "I take it from your appearance today that you have chosen not to take your mother's advice."

I nodded even though I was still unsure. If this went poorly, I'd hop a subway downtown and meet Ma as planned. But Mrs. Klein didn't need to know that.

"If you did as your mother wished, it would be as if this problem had never happened. No one need ever know."

"*I* would know."

Once again, Mrs. Klein surveyed me. Her eyes first took in my shoes, a new fashion with a strappy front piece that revealed slices of my foot. They'd seemed so stylish when I bought them at Mays in the beginning of the summer, but now they felt clunky and cheap. I watched as her eyes moved to my legs, covered in the stockings that seemed to rip at the mere thought of a snag, then to my dress. At least that was smart and stylish, thanks to Ma's handiwork. I was never more grateful for how she could make a store-bought dress look like the ones in the magazines.

I willed my hands to be still in my lap. "I'll be frank," Mrs. Klein said. "You are not who I intended for my son. But . . ." She pursed her lips in thought and I sat in silence, fearful of saying something foolish.

"Perhaps," she said at last, "we can be of assistance to each other. Ah, but where are my manners?" She rang a bell and in a moment the parlor door opened and the maid entered.

"Yes, ma'am?" she asked, eyeing me with open curiosity.

"Please bring in some tea. And cake."

"Right away, ma'am," the girl said, closing the door behind her.

"You must keep up your strength, mustn't you?" Mrs. Klein said, her eyes twinkling maliciously. "So, we seem to have a bit of trouble here."

"I do not mean to cause trouble."

"You may not mean to, but it most certainly appears to have followed you here." Her smile gave me a chill.

The maid returned with a tray holding a tea service and a cake, which she set on the table before the sofa. The water must be kept to boil in the kitchen at all times for it to have come out so quickly.

"You can leave those, Fiona. I'll pour."

"Yes, ma'am," Fiona said, clearly preferring to eavesdrop.

Mrs. Klein noticed. "Be sure to clean the upstairs well, Fiona," she said. "I noticed dust gathering beneath the beds."

"Yes, ma'am." I was a little surprised she didn't curtsy before leaving the room. But then I thought about Mrs. Klein's words: *upstairs.* Imagine an entire second floor for one family. It was hard to fathom.

My reverie was interrupted when Mrs. Klein placed a slice of coffee cake on an elegantly flowered plate and handed it to me with a slim silver fork before pouring the tea into matching cups. They were dainty china teacups, not the plain glasses we drank from at home. "Eat, eat," she said, gesturing toward the plate in my hand. The words relaxed me ever so slightly. Mrs. Klein may have been an uptown woman, but she was still a Jewish mother at heart, and I knew she'd want what was best for her son.

I realized I was ravenous, having skipped dinner last night and breakfast that morning. I took a bite of the cake. It was soft and airy, not like the dense loaves Ma baked. I felt guilty, as if I were betraying Ma, but as lovely as her cakes were, they suddenly seemed old-fashioned and Old World, with a heaviness this American cake didn't hold. I longed to devour the slice but compelled myself to take slow, small bites.

Mrs. Klein watched me and shook her head slightly, a hint of a smile forming. Leaning over, she cut a second, larger slice, which she placed on my plate. "I remember. I was always starving. Eat more."

Not wanting to appear greedy, I continued to cut delicate pieces, but I was thankful for the small kindness.

With a cup of tea held gracefully, Mrs. Klein took a sip. "As unlikely as it may seem, perhaps we could make this work to both our advantages. It's safe to say, I believe, that you do not wish a *mamzer.*" I flinched at the Yiddish word for *bastard*, but nodded. "And I"—Mrs. Klein placed her cup upon the table and leaned forward, as if to take me into her confidence—"do not want my foolish son returning to the land we fought so hard to leave."

For the first time, I looked hopefully at Mrs. Klein. I forced myself to put down my plate, the cake unfinished, although I longed to lick up every crumb.

"Let me be clear," Mrs. Klein said. "You are not my choice. But you are sturdy and Jewish and come from a decent family, and, to call it as it is, you are white."

I gasped. I thought the rumors about Willie were merely idle chatter. But if even Mrs. Klein heard them . . .

Mrs. Klein shook her head. "Let's not be naive, dear. In the lot of them, you are certainly the best who has come along. You shall do." With growing determination, Mrs. Klein repeated, "Yes, indeed. You shall do just fine. And William, for once and for all, will have learned his lesson."

"I am to be his lesson?"

"There are worse things you could be." Mrs. Klein stood and paced as she gnawed on her lip again. "He plans on leaving soon for Europe, so there is not a moment to lose. You will return tonight. Five p.m. sharp."

"Tonight?" I repeated in confusion.

Mrs. Klein smiled broadly at me, but it held no warmth. "We must solve this little problem of yours quickly, of course. Now, run along. I've a lot to do."

"Shouldn't Willie be consulted? This is his situation as well."

"William was consulted last May at Camp Eden. You may show yourself out." And with that, Mrs. Klein left the room, bellowing to her maid, "Fiona! We have our hands full."

As I let myself out the front door, Mrs. Klein called back to me, "Five o'clock. Don't be late."

Rose

—⚓—

AT twelve thirty exactly, I arrived at the address. Had I really just been here on Monday? Years had passed in this one week.

The avenue was busy, with hawkers and carts and children playing in the streets and women bustling about, doing their shopping, pausing to gossip with friends. On one stoop, boys were shooting craps, yelling loudly as they rolled the dice, arguing over who owed what to whom. The scene was exactly like the one on my street, but here it had an ominous overtone, as I knew what else lived on this street. In my own neighborhood, Alfie often played craps, betting the pennies he earned selling firewood. What a ridiculous waste of time and money, but no use telling Alfie that. Izzy was the same. I used to forbid Izzy from gambling, imploring him to study, but he only found new ways to evade me. Yet he still kept up with his schooling, so who was I to complain? If only Alfie had half the brains of his older brother, I wouldn't have to worry so much about him. Strange how my *kinder* were so utterly my *kinder*, yet also these foreign creatures. My children were . . . What was the word I was looking for? It struck me. Americans. My children were Americans.

How Yussel would have loved these stoop games and stickball. I couldn't shake my image of Yussel as the twelve-year-old I left behind, the boy who woke early for *shul*, spent his mornings learning, and then his afternoons apprenticed to the bridle maker.

When Yussel had sent me a picture of his family, I could barely see the boy beneath the man. I tried to swallow the knot forming in my throat. It would do no good to think of Yussel now. I had more immediate concerns. My hand instinctively went to my belly.

My head was beginning to throb like my leg, so even though I would never do something so undignified on my own street, slowly I lowered myself to sit on the front stoop of the building next door to . . . the place. My eye took in the street, the rows of tenement buildings so different from my home. Back in Russia, our little house was cramped, and even though it was tidy, dirt from the floor covered every surface, no matter how my mama tried to chase it out. Mama and *Tateh* slept in one room, all us girls in another, and the boys in the main room. But it was all ours, with windows on every wall. And when you stepped outside, there was sunlight. I had a hard time getting used to the darkness of America, the apartments so small and suffocating, with hardly a place to take a breath. Even in the streets, the buildings fenced you in, closed you off, kept themselves between you and the sky.

Mama was sweet and mild, not like the loud, outspoken girls to whom she gave birth, girls who were forever getting themselves in trouble with their mouths. Eta and I were mischiefmakers, not so different from Alfie. I remember when the teacher would smack Yussel's hand with a stick when he read too slowly. How it infuriated us. One afternoon, Eta and I made a pretense of visiting the teacher's house to inquire of his wife, who was cooking *Shabbes* dinner, if she needed anything sewn. Eta distracted her while I slipped a small field mouse into the closed soup tureen. As we snuck away, we could hear her shrieks.

I blessed Mama's memory for making sure we received an education, such as it was in that little room with so few desks I had to sit in the corner on the floor, not that I minded. When the money was short and there wasn't enough for me to take a lesson, she made me practice my letters anyway, tracing them over and over in the dirt. I was so proud of those letters, and I wanted Mama to learn them, too, to show her how they went together to make magic. "It's too late for me," she used to say, "but you have all the time in the world." Even as *Tateh* grumbled that it was a waste of time to educate girls, that the money could be better spent, Mama always did whatever she could to save a few kopecks to pay the teacher.

I blessed her memory again for stopping *Tateh* before he beat me to death after I attended that rally. "Do you want her to end up in Siberia?" she asked, as loudly as I'd ever heard her speak.

Before I left, I was a confusion of emotions. I was like the whip *Tateh* used on the horse, flying free in the air one moment, coming down hard on the hide the next. At night, I clung to Eta, as if trying to fix in my mind the curves of her body, the feel of her hair, the scent of her skin. As much as I wanted to go, I wondered if I should stay with my family. Wait for Shmuel. I feared desperately I wouldn't see my family again.

The day before I left, I was watching Mama sew for me, hiding things in my skirts, ensuring my clothes would last, and my dread washed through me. "Mama, how can I leave you?" My voice cracked.

Mama put down the cloth and needle and opened her arms to me. "What is there for you here? You want to live the same life I live?"

"What's wrong with your life?" I asked, even though I knew my answer to her question was *no*.

"You are destined for greater things than what Bratsyana can give you. Go to America."

Choking back sobs, I said, "I don't see how I can leave you."

With a sly smile, Mama said, "Leave me? Or leave the hope that Shmuel will return?"

I was shocked. "What do you mean?"

She laughed. "I saw how you used to sneak looks at him in the market and at *shul*."

I exhaled, relieved she didn't know the extent of the sins Shmuel and I had committed.

"Shmuel is gone. He may never come back. You need to forget him. In America, you will be someone new. Here, your father would never have permitted a love match." With a gentle squeeze of my hand, she said quietly, "But your father will never know what you do in America. It's a fresh start. In America, you can have your politics *and* find yourself a good man. You will raise a family. Start anew." With Mama's words in my head, I pushed Shmuel from my mind, and allowed myself to fall in love with Ben.

Where was Dottie? I looked at my wristwatch. The minutes dragged on, and I held the timepiece up to my ears every few moments to make sure it was ticking.

I'd told her twelve thirty; I was sure of that. I didn't want to be late, didn't want to miss the appointment. And I longed to speak to her, to make her realize I understood. I wanted to assure her that one brokenhearted moment wasn't going to ruin her future. And what a future Dottie had. She'd become educated, be an accountant. She would marry. Have a houseful of children when the time came and plenty of money with which to take care of them. Maybe they'd even move out of the neighborhood, to Washington Heights, or a nice apartment building in the Bronx.

On the street, a young woman trotted down the sidewalk, one hand holding her clutch in front of her, the other keeping her hat from flying off her head. Finally! I stood to greet her. But as the woman came closer, I realized it wasn't her. This woman was squatter, with lighter hair, and I couldn't imagine how I'd mistaken her for Dottie. Impatiently, I willed Dottie to come along faster. What on earth was taking her so long? Sometimes the elevated would stop for no apparent reason; today, of course, that would happen, the day it was so important for the elevated to *not* stop for no apparent reason. Dottie must be stuck, panicking, waiting for the train to begin moving again.

I sat back on the stoop and continued my wait, yet in my heart I was coming to believe it was futile.

I looked around at the stores, the fashions, the children playing: After all these years in the *Goldene Medina*, I still marveled at what went on around me. For so long, I'd had nothing and it felt like enough; poor Dottie had everything, but it was never adequate.

My children roll their eyes at my stories of the Old World, of how we had a wood fireplace for cooking and oil lamps for the evenings. They see nothing miraculous about electric lights.

I had never seen a city until I got to Hamburg, where I would sail to America. I thought it was so busy, so big. But that was before I saw New York. Closing my eyes, I could still picture Hamburg, that huge ship with the roaring smokestack, the tiny windows, and the masses of people. A ship that was bigger than my entire village.

While waiting to board, I saw the most curious thing—a young boy had a long yellow object. He broke open the top, and pulled down the sides, revealing a white-fleshed fruit, which he ate in large bites. When he was done, he threw the yellow part on the ground, and moved with the crowd toward the ship. Looking around to make sure no one saw me, I bent over and picked it up. It felt strange: On one side it was thick and smooth, almost like the leather strap on *Tateh*'s horse, and on the other it was mushy and stringy. I held it to my nose, but all I sniffed was a bitter scent. Tentatively, I bit into it, but the taste was sour. My face puckered as I looked up, only to be embarrassed at the amusement of a nearby man. "There is a reason he threw that part away," the man said. His Yiddish was tinged with the accent of a country that wasn't Russia, and I couldn't place it. The mere fact someone spoke my language but in such a different way startled me. "The inside is the good part. It's like an orange. You eat the inside and toss the peel." My face must have looked blank, because he laughed and said, "You've had an orange, haven't you?"

"It's a color, no?" I asked.

The man chuckled. "It's a color, yes. *And* a fruit."

Back in the present, a church bell rang one o'clock and startled me out of my memories. No Dottie.

The thought that Dottie wasn't coming took firmer root in my mind. Yet it didn't elicit the anger I would have expected. Dottie wasn't coming. I craned my neck to look both ways down the street, and with certainty, I understood. Dottie wasn't coming. I said it aloud. "Dottie isn't coming."

The idea settled on me in a comfortable way. I had known, hadn't I, that Dottie wouldn't be coming? Dottie wasn't meant to give up her baby; I was. Dottie wanted her baby; I didn't want mine. That's what my mama would have done: sacrificed herself for her child. Mama would understand that I needed to give up a potential child to save my existing one.

If I were to have the procedure, then, yes, we would go away, have Dottie's baby in secret, and I would still be saddled with her child, but it would be only temporary, wouldn't it? We would settle this ridiculous Kraus nonsense once and for all, and Dottie and Abe would marry—in their own sweet time, when they had enough money. A pretense could be given—my leg worsening; an illness could be fabricated. The baby could be given to Dottie for care. I would only need to sacrifice, what? A year? Maybe two? I could have my freedom. But more important, I could take care of *my* baby, my Dottala. That was what my mama would have done. It was what I would do.

I heaved myself to a standing position, and made my way down the stairs to the basement apartment. It was one o'clock. It was time.

Dottie

FROM the Kleins', I rushed back downtown, heading straight for Zelda's.

When I arrived at her house, I was breathless, but full of hope. The baby. I was going to keep my baby. Nothing else mattered, because my baby would be mine. I wanted to jump and sing and dance and scream my joy out to the world.

"What do you think Mrs. Klein is planning?" I asked Zelda in a rush.

"Why, your wedding, of course," Zelda said, and she laughed happily.

I didn't relish forcing Willie into marriage, but it wasn't the worst thing. Hopefully he'd see that, too. True, I wasn't the best cook, but I'd learn. And who knew? Perhaps, with the kind of money Willie's family had, I'd be able to hire a nanny. And then with the free time, maybe accounting school wasn't a fantasy.

I was getting ahead of myself. But could I be blamed? In one morning, my life had turned completely around.

"Oh, Dottie," Zelda said. She was kneading bread dough on the counter and flour flew everywhere. Zelda might not have been a great cook, but she was certainly enthusiastic. "We'll be related. Cousins!"

I picked up Shirley with a grin. "You're going to have a playmate."

Bringing the baby close to me, I inhaled deeply. "Zelda, we'll shop together and the kids will play together and we'll—"

Zelda interrupted with a laugh. "Hardly. You'll be living the swell life uptown, while I swelter away in this pit." She opened her arms broadly, indicating the cramped space and the foul smells, raising a cloud of flour as she did so.

"Don't be ridiculous." But I wondered if there was a shred of truth in what she said. When one of our neighbors did make it out—by marriage, because someone's father made good—she rarely came back. The one left behind felt out of place uptown and the one who made it out, well, she generally didn't want reminders of where she'd come from. But I'd be different. I'd never leave my loved ones behind.

"Do you think we'll have an actual wedding?" I asked. "With bridesmaids and all?"

"Maybe," Zelda said, folding the dough over itself and pushing down.

"You'll be my bridesmaid."

Wiping her sweaty forehead with her arm, Zelda left a streak of white powder across her forehead. "I'm no maid."

"Okay, my bride's matron. I don't care. You and Edith and Linda. Although—I don't know. Think it will be a sore point with Linda?"

"You like to dream big, don't you? You'll never get Edith in a dress." Zelda punched the yeasty mess in front of her. "Say, what will you wear? I suppose white is out of the question."

I grimaced. "I'm sure Mrs. Klein will have some ideas."

"That woman is going to run you ragged," Zelda said. "Aunt Molly is a forceful woman." She looked at me as Shirley's hands squeezed my nose. "You want me to come with you tonight? Stand up for you a bit?"

Never had I loved Zelda as much as I did in that moment. "Would you?"

"Let me first get the bread made. Stanley won't be home till after nine anyway. I'll leave Shirley with Ma."

Ma. That was the one thought that sent my stomach into loop-de-loops. I pictured Ma, waiting at the abortionist, furious I didn't show up.

"Not your ma," I said.

Zelda looked at me quizzically before she realized what I was thinking. Perle could keep nothing from Ma, especially concerning me. Her ma would go running immediately to mine. I wasn't ready for that. "Of course," she said. "I'll leave her with my mother-in-law. Will you let your mother know where you're going?"

With a glance at my watch, I realized that at that very moment she'd be waiting for me. I shook my head. "She's not home right now. I'll tell her after Mrs. Klein has made our plans. No need to worry her needlessly now." This plan would not be to her liking. Giving up college, marrying a man of whom she thought little. The money wasted on the unused procedure. So many things she wouldn't like. I didn't want to face her anger, her disappointment. I would make everything work out, and then present it to her with pride. I was a grown woman. I was taking care of things.

Rose

———— ✿ ————

I made my way down the steps, back to the basement door, and rapped, tentatively. The door swung open and I stepped inside.

"You're late," the girl said.

"Just a few minutes," I said. "Did . . . did anyone else come?"

Her eyes narrowed at me. "Who are you expecting?"

Clearly she didn't remember I had made the appointment for someone else. "No one," I said.

Standing there in that little room, I felt strong and confident for the first time in weeks. I was always the one meant to be here, not Dottie. Images danced in my head: Mama, illiterate and alone, for all the good *Tateh* was, practically a slave in her own house, caring for a thoughtless husband and chained to the children who kept arriving year after year; Dottie and the life she was meant to lead, which was now a different life, but a good one yet; Joey, whom I longed for every day, his sweet smile, his soft breath; Eugene, who deserved so much more in a mother than the tired, unhappy woman I was becoming. I thought of Ben, and how hard he worked at the garage, such long hours to give us all such a good life. I thought of the stench of the boat ride from the Old Country and all the sweet bananas I'd eaten since then, and how now I knew an orange was not just a color but the perfect way to brighten a dull gray day, with the delicious tang on the tip of the tongue as the juice slid down my throat. I thought of my glass of tea and the *Daily Forverts*. I thought of Perle and the work we had yet to do.

"Ready, I am," I said in English.

"Do you have the rest of the money?"

I opened my clutch and pulled out ten dollars. I handed it to her, and when I looked down to shut my purse, I was startled by the girl's attempt to pull a cloth across my face.

Jumping away, I said, "What are you doing?"

"Blindfolding you. That way you can't tell where you went."

Dread swept through me. "It is not done here?"

"Course not. We'd have the cops breathin' down our necks. I put this on you—then I take you out the back door. A car is waiting to take you to where you need to go."

"A car!" In all my years in America, I had yet to ride in a car. A streetcar, yes, but not an honest-to-goodness car. Ben drove cars at the garage, fetching them for customers, moving them around so he could work. He'd taken all the kids for rides in them at various points, but I always refused. Such silliness. Now I was ashamed to admit the idea of riding in a car terrified me as much as what I faced at the end of the ride.

The girl moved again to place the cloth around my head and I submitted. It was made of rough cotton, and it itched my nose. But when I went to scratch, the girl snapped, "Don't take it off," so I pulled my hand down, lest she get the wrong idea.

The girl took me by the elbow and walked me to what had to be the back of the office. She smelled of jasmine, and it saddened me when I recognized it as the same scent Dottie wore.

As I lost my footing on a step, the girl said, "Watch where you walk. More stairs ahead." Her tone hinted she enjoyed watching me stumble.

The sounds in the alley were muted. I could still hear noises from the street, but they seemed to come from a distance farther than the other side of the building.

I heard the creak of a door opening, and the girl, none too

gently, pushed me into the backseat of the car. I bumped my head on the doorjamb and cried, "Ow."

"Shhh!"

I slid onto the seat.

"Lie down," the girl said. "We don't want you seen back there." The door slammed shut.

As best I could, I leaned over into a horizontal position, my feet awkwardly draped to the floor while my head bumped against the other door. The fabric was pitted and smelled of cigarettes. Reflexively, I put my hand out as the car jolted forward, and I met the back of the front seat, which I leaned against to steady myself. The windows of the car were closed and smoke wafted from the front seat.

Forcing myself not to cough, I tried not to slip into hysteria. What in the name of *Hashem* had I gotten myself into? The car bounced up and down, jouncing me in the seat, and I thought I would roll onto the floor. My legs cramped from being bent and the roar of the car was frightening.

For this I came to America? I thought, overwhelmed with doubts about what I was doing. For this my family suffered so I could live the dream? Was this the dream? Back in Russia, I knew of women who brought their courses on, either on their own or with the help of a midwife. It was nothing like this. What if I didn't survive? Who would make sure Ben had his livers on Sunday or that Alfie and Eugene made it to *heder*? Who would make Izzy continue his studies, get his law degree? And, most important, who would guide Dottie through this mess she was clearly making of her life?

But then I had a second thought: Better I suffer this than Dottie. I clutched the seat tighter.

After five minutes or thirty—I had no way of telling—the car stopped. I heard the door open, and I gratefully breathed in the flood of fresh air. A female voice, different from the young girl's, said, "C'mon out now." This woman took me by the arm and helped me into the building. She was kinder, and told me about

the steps before I reached them. Her voice was gravelly and comforting, her scent a more familiar one, like that of baking bread.

Once we entered the building, the woman tugged at the back
of my head and pulled off the blindfold. I was shocked to see she
was brown, brown as the milkman's mare. I had seen colored
people, of course; they lived in nearby neighborhoods, walked the
same streets I walked. But folks tended to keep to themselves,
Jewish, Irish, Italian, Negro. Everyone had his own problems.

"Follow me," the woman said. "I'm your nurse today."

"A nurse, you are?" I regretted the disbelief my voice held.

"You have a problem with that?" she asked. She didn't sound
mean or even angry; it was a sincere question.

I shook my head.

"Good," the nurse said. "Let's get you ready."

She led me upstairs, to a small room with a long table. "You can
take off your skirt and underthings—leave your blouse on—and
put this on," she said, laying a white apron on the foot of the bed.

"But a dress. A dress I have on," I said, dismay rising in the
back of my throat.

She shook her head with what seemed like sorrow. "Then
take off your dress. I'll return in a moment." She left the room,
leaving me to do her bidding.

I did as instructed, undoing the buttons, folding my dress
carefully, and laying it on the chair in the corner. I unclipped my
stockings and rolled them down, followed by the girdle. I draped
the apron about my middle and lay on the table, feeling more
exposed than ever before in my life, half-naked, alone in a strange
room.

I lay there praying to *Hashem* over and over to see me through.
Finally the door opened, and the nurse approached the bed.
Without a word, she strapped down my arms.

Alarmed, I half sat up, but she gently pushed me back. "Is it
necessary?" I asked.

She nodded and went on with her work, like it was a perfectly normal job. She picked up a razor and said, "Bend your legs, and put your feet on the table."

I realized I was to be shaved between my legs. The last time I'd been shaved there was when I gave birth to Eugene. I ought to be embarrassed, but I wasn't; I felt only relief that it was finally beginning.

When the shaving was done, the nurse returned to my side.

She draped a towel over my eyes, then went to open the door. I heard footsteps returning; then something covered my mouth and a deep voice said, "You'll go to sleep now," and I inhaled something sweet and, within a few minutes, fell into a dreamless slumber.

"WAKE up. Time to wake up."

I groaned and went to rub my face, but my arms held fast at my sides, and immediately I struggled, not sure where I was or what was happening.

"It's okay, it's okay," came a soothing voice. "We don't need these anymore."

Opening my eyes, I saw the nurse, and everything came flooding back to me. As soon as my arms were free, my hands went right to my stomach. What had I done? Was it all gone? My mind was hazy, and everything seemed slightly out of focus.

"What's wrong with me?" I asked.

"That's the ether. It'll wear off before you know it. Here, sit up."

I gingerly sat up, only to be hit with an excruciating pain across my midsection. I bent over, my head almost in my lap.

"That'll pass," the nurse said. "I need you to get dressed. You brought rags?"

I nodded, not trusting my voice.

"Fine. I'll help you."

It was mortifying, but I had no choice. I could barely stand on my own. "Did it—did the doctor—is it . . . ?" I couldn't seem to form the question I longed to ask.

"It's all taken care of," the nurse said. "You'll be in some pain for the next few days, but really it's no worse than losing a baby before its time, if that's ever happened to you."

I nodded. But of course, this was much worse. Losing a baby was an act of God. This was the work of man.

The nurse took me by the arm and helped me off the table. I saw my legs were covered in blood and looked at the nurse, feeling helpless.

"Here's a towel for you," she said, handing me a dingy white cloth. I shuddered to imagine who else had used it, but I cleaned my legs anyway. Carefully, she helped me make my way into my clothing, but I shoved the girdle into my purse—it would hurt too much to put on.

My fingers fumbled at my buttons as I realized the enormity of what I had done. I thought I might fall, so I threw my hands out to steady myself, grabbing hold of the table, lowering my head. Hashem, *forgive me.*

"Still feeling dizzy?" the nurse asked.

I didn't respond. I tried the buttons again, then smoothed my hands along my dress. Without the girdle, it bulged at the waist. I was no thinner. Not yet.

With a deep breath, I worked up the nerve to ask what was roiling in the back of my mind, though my tongue was thick and the words came out muddled. "Was it . . . Did I . . . ?"

"Excuse me?" the nurse asked.

Clearing my throat, I tried again. "Was it a girl?" I had a hunch it was a girl, and now it seemed imperative to know.

"Oh, honey." She laid a hand on my arm gently. "It wasn't anything."

Nodding, I bit my lip. Of course it was something. My child. Or it had been. Now it was simply gone.

"You'll be fine," she said. "Are you ready to go?"

"Go? Don't I get to rest?" My leg ached, my belly throbbed, my entire body longed to lie down, and my eyes hungered to close. I wasn't in any shape to move.

But the nurse shook her head. "We need the room again. And it's not a good idea to have women lingering."

"Oh." I was at a loss for words.

The nurse led me from the room and walked me down the stairs. Before we left the building, she picked up the strip of cloth again. "I'm sorry, but I've got to cover your eyes."

I allowed her to tie it around my head, after which she carefully led me to the car. She was tender, and she told me about every step, every crack, every bump that could get in my way. She was so kind that I imagined she herself must once have been in the same situation.

Placing her hand on my head so I wouldn't bump it on the car doorframe, she helped me bend down and lean in. "Try to rest in the car," she said. "Lie down and relax."

I curled into a fetal position on the seat, which helped ease the cramps. But the rough car ride was torturous. Each jolt was a knife to the womb, and made the bile rise in my throat.

When we arrived, the girl was waiting; she opened the door and led me back into the office, where she removed the blindfold.

"Okay," she said, "you're done. You have someone waiting on the next block to help you home?"

Looking down, I shook my head.

"No," she said. "No one ever does."

Dottie

AT exactly five p.m. Zelda and I arrived at the Kleins' building. This time, the doorman knew who I was.

"You can go right on up, miss," he said. "Mrs. Klein is expecting you."

On the brief elevator ride, all the optimism and courage I had felt at Zelda's slowly drained from me, replaced by fear of what lay ahead. Zelda, sensing my emotions, held tightly to my arm.

When the elevator stopped, I experienced déjà vu. The uncertainty, the upset stomach, the panic. My stomach bubbled like fizzy soda, which made me think of dates with Abe. Abe. A flush crept up my neck, settling in my cheeks. I burned with the humiliation of my last conversation with him, of how utterly he had rejected me. As I stood in the hallway, time stretched with elasticity, and in that moment, I saw everything: Abe was gone; I was too late for the appointment; my mother would be furious over the lost money and, more important, the lost prospects. I saw my future child; a life with Willie; cooking, cleaning, and caring for a baby and a husband while trying to study accounting at night; being tethered to a man with a roaming eye and no interest in being a husband or a father. In that moment, the hallway elongated, narrowing at the Kleins' door, showing me the singular path my life would now take. I had no other choice. Even if I ran away, how does a single woman feed, shelter, and clothe herself and a babe? Ma hadn't come to America for this. For all the misery I caused that woman, I had to admit she was strong. Ma would never have been in a situation like this. For all her Old Country ways, Ma knew how to handle things. Some modern girl I turned out to be, doing things the most old-fashioned way.

Zelda pulled on my arm, nudging me toward their front door. "Come on, love," she said. "It will all turn out fine."

I walked as though my feet were moving through molasses. I knew what waited at the end of the hallway. Mrs. Klein would force Willie to marry me. If Ma knew, she would tell me it wasn't so bad. Plenty of women had arranged marriages, and they all worked out one way or another. I would grow to love Willie. And if not? Well, it wasn't the end of the world, was it? I already loved this child. That would be enough.

I tried to imagine the wedding Mrs. Klein would plan for us. It would have to be soon, but I was sure she would arrange something lovely. I'd get a new dress. Maybe not white—Zelda was right; that would be inappropriate, and it would fool no one about the reason for our sudden marriage. Yellow might be pretty. Or pale pink would suit me nicely.

My arms froze at my sides, so Zelda knocked firmly on the door. It swung open quickly, revealing the maid from that morning—Fiona, I thought—but this time she appraised me, running her eyes up and down my body, lingering at my stomach. Even the help knew about my situation.

Zelda stepped in, looked around the place, and whistled. "My, my. Every time I come here, it gets even fancier."

"Mr. and Mrs. Klein are waiting for you in the parlor," the maid said, ignoring Zelda as she shut the door.

I tried to imagine what it would be like to visit this apartment on a regular basis. To come here with my child—someday, perhaps, *children*—for holidays, for meals, to spend time with their *bubbe* and *zayde*. What would the children think of then going to see *my* parents in their meager little apartment? In my mind, I was already defending *Tateh* and Ma.

When we walked into the parlor, Mr. and Mrs. Klein looked up from the sofa. Mr. Klein lowered the newspaper he was reading, but neither rose to greet us.

"Zelda, darling. What a nice surprise," Mrs. Klein said, her voice conveying her insincerity.

"Aunt Molly, the pleasure is mine," Zelda said in her schmaltziest tone. She walked over and leaned down to buss her aunt on the cheek. Zelda moved to her uncle, who at least gave her a little peck back, the newspaper crinkling between them.

"Always nice to see you," Mr. Klein said to Zelda, without putting down his paper.

"Where are your parents, Dottie?" Mrs. Klein asked.

My flush deepened as I said, "I didn't know they were supposed to accompany me."

Mr. Klein bobbed his head in an annoyed sort of way and his wife said, "Don't you think they should be here for this?"

"For what exactly?" I said.

"Your wedding."

The whole room turned topsy-turvy on me, and I thought my legs might give way. "Tonight?"

Mrs. Klein looked at me oddly. "Well, what did you think was going to happen tonight? You are in trouble, aren't you?"

"Oh, for gosh sake," Zelda said. "That is ridiculous. Who would have thought it would happen tonight? Let's plan a little to-do. Make a nice little wedding."

"Of course it has to happen tonight. Do you think William will simply wait around while we plan a 'little to-do'? If he heard a whisper of marriage, he'd be on a boat first thing tomorrow."

My shame knew no bounds. I was something to escape, to avoid. Shaking my head, I looked down at my feet.

"No, the wedding will take place tonight, as soon as Willie

gets home for dinner. Don't you think your parents should be here?"

"I didn't—I hadn't—" I wrung my hands.

"Well, let's give them a call. What's the number, dear?"

"My parents don't have a phone." My voice cracked. "And if you call a neighbor, all of New York will know."

"They don't have a phone?" Mr. Klein said to Mrs. Klein, as if I weren't standing there. "What kind of people don't have a phone?"

"Lots of people don't have phones. Have you heard of this thing called the Depression? My parents only installed a phone last May and you know it," Zelda said.

Looking from Zelda to Mrs. Klein, I could scarcely believe they were related, that Zelda's *tateh* and Mrs. Klein were brother and sister. Mrs. Klein was so American, you would never know she was born in the Old Country. But of course, she came over as a babe, whereas Zelda's *tateh* was almost a teenager when he immigrated, too late for American schooling, too late to lose the accent.

"Are you sure about this, Molly?" Mr. Klein asked Mrs. Klein.

"No, of course I'm not sure."

"Aunt Molly!"

I gave a silent thanks to *Hashem* for Zelda's presence.

"Pish, pish, it'll all be fine," Mrs. Klein said, sounding as much as if she was convincing herself as she was Mr. Klein. "Dottie's family are good people. This is the right thing to do. It will keep William out of trouble and in New York. Put an end to those rumors."

The doorbell rang, and a moment later, the parlor door opened. "Rabbi Shulman here to see you," Fiona said.

"*Rebbe* Shulman?" Zelda said. Her face twisted into a moue of disgust. "Couldn't you find a real *rebbe*?"

"Enough," Mr. Klein said, forcing even Zelda to cower. Silenced, she took a seat on the couch.

"Now, Ira," Mrs. Klein said, "let's not air our dirty laundry in front of the rabbi."

Right then, in walked a man with a close-cropped beard and a *yarmulke* on his head. He wasn't wearing the hat or the long coat of the *rebbes* in my neighborhood. I peered at his waist and saw no sign of a *tallis*. What kind of *rebbe* didn't wear a prayer shawl? He must be the *rebbe* of the big Reform synagogue on the Upper East Side. Was a marriage performed by a Reform *rebbe* even legal? I suddenly flashed to the crab salad Willie had eaten at lunch. What would Willie say when he learned I would keep kosher? With two sets of dishes plus an extra set for Passover?

So many things I'd never considered.

"Good evening, *Rebbe*," Mr. Klein said. "This is . . ." He seemed to be searching for my name. "This is Dottie."

The *rebbe* said, "How do you do?" and he reached out to shake my hand. Startled, I accepted his hand. A rabbi touching a woman to whom he was not related? I'd never heard of such a thing.

"Do you have witnesses?" the *rebbe* asked.

Mrs. Klein nodded. "Matthew and Colin will be our witnesses."

"Matthew and Colin?" I asked.

"Our house servants."

"But they're not Jewish," I said. "It won't be legal if we don't have Jewish names on the *ketubah*." The wedding contract was a vital part of a Jewish marriage ceremony.

"Isn't it a little late to be worried about Jewish names on the *ketubah*?" Mr. Klein asked.

"Zelda will be our witness," I said, determined to exert some control over my own wedding.

"Sure, I can do that," Zelda said from the couch.

I realized no one was going to invite me to sit, so I took a seat next to Zelda. She scooted over a pinch to give me a little space. Until she did that, I hadn't realized how closed in I'd been feeling.

"If you're going to have a woman, you might as well have a non-Jew," Mr. Klein said.

"It's as kosher as we're going to get," Zelda said.

Mr. Klein scowled at the word *kosher*. "Fine. Zelda can witness. What do I care?"

I knew I couldn't allow myself to cry, but this was mortifying. This was not how I ever saw myself getting married, wearing a navy blue suit, with no parents to give me away, no canopy to stand beneath. Would this *goyishe rebbe* even recite the seven blessings? Tears filled my eyes, and my face went hot. Zelda quickly dove into her purse and retrieved a handkerchief for me. I blotted my eyes, but felt my nose begin to run.

"Say," Zelda said, "don't you need a marriage license? We had to apply for ours a month in advance."

My eyes widened. Forget kosher; would this marriage even be legal in the City of New York?

Mr. Klein laughed, and I was startled to hear it was Willie's laugh. "In New York, anything can be had for a price. Including marriage licenses."

Relieved, I let myself sink slightly into the sofa.

"What do we do now?" Zelda asked.

"We wait for William," Mrs. Klein said.

The *rebbe* must have known a scene would erupt when Willie appeared. "I'll look over the *ketubah*," he said—clearly an excuse—and retired to the parlor. A silence fell over the room as the minutes passed. Zelda held my hand, rubbing it gently. The gesture was soothing, but it didn't erase the insanity of the situation. What was I doing here? This apartment was like a palace. It was everything I'd ever admired in the pages of my *House & Garden* magazines, with the rich, full curtains, the fireplace, the library with books lining every conceivable wall, the tables made of brass and glass. But never once had I thought to live so royally in real life. Not as Abe's wife. I didn't want the fanciness; I wanted Abe.

With deep breaths, I calmed myself and reminded myself of why I was there. It wasn't for me; it was for this baby. Ma had traveled across the ocean and worked her hands into an arthritic mess so I might have a better life than she, a life where I could go to school and earn a diploma, a life where I could get a job in a Midtown office, a life where I was never in want of food or clothing. How different my childhood was from hers. And now it was my turn. As much as I'd had growing up, I would do what it took for my child to have even more. *My daughter won't sleep on a couch; she'll have a bed in a bedroom, with a door she can close. I'll scrimp and save so we can go away to the country on weekends, as a family. My daughter won't just finish high school; she'll go to a college and earn a degree.*

I have no idea how long we sat there before the door slammed. "Hello, hello," called Willie's voice, and I could hear the rustle of a hat being placed on a side table, the handing off of a briefcase to the maid. "Mother, is dinner about—" As he walked into the parlor and saw us sitting there, his eyes jumped from his mother to Zelda to me. At me they lingered, and as our eyes made contact, his expression flinched, his surprise reshaping itself, taking the form of a slow, simmering anger. "What is this about?" he asked.

"No need to be coy now," Mr. Klein said.

"My dear," Mrs. Klein said, "I think you know exactly what this is about. You seem to have gotten yourself into quite an unfortunate position."

Willie walked to the bar cart and unplugged a crystal decanter. Without meeting anyone's eyes, he said, "You can't even be sure it's mine. She's been seeing Abe Rabinowitz forever."

I couldn't speak. I'd already told him! Did he really believe . . . ? What was he saying about me?

Using tongs, he plunked two ice cubes into a glass, the sound of which echoed loudly in the silence, before pouring in more than the proper amount of amber liquid.

Helplessly, I looked at Zelda. Her eyes were brimming with fury on my behalf. "Willie Klein, you know full well this child is yours. Abe Rabinowitz is as pure as the snow on Saint Patrick's, and I know Dottie as well as I know my own mother. Dottie never lies. This is your problem as clear as clear can be."

It took every ounce of willpower to not bury my face on Zelda's shoulder and sob.

Willie, still facing the cart, took a deep swallow of his drink. He shrugged. "You never know." He topped off his not-empty glass before turning and facing the room.

"Indeed. I made my own inquiries, and it would appear you are undoubtedly the father, William."

With a sharp inhalation, I looked at Mrs. Klein.

"What, my dear?" Her voice held a touch of ridicule. "Did you think I would simply trust you? It's not like you'd be the first poor girl who tried to better her situation." Seeing my alarm, Mrs. Klein tried to tone down her derision. "Don't worry. I promise I was extremely discreet. Which, I might add, is more than I can say about you two. Your little friend Beverly was able to confirm the night at Camp Eden. And I hear that both you and your mother have been in a hurry to arrange a marriage to Abe." When Willie rolled his eyes, his mother turned on him. "And you, young man. Must you have bragged to your friends? Word spreads quickly, you know."

"Mother," Willie said, "you seem to have mistaken me for a greenhorn." He took another gulp of his drink, and his voice became calmer. "You cannot force me into marriage."

"I am well aware I cannot *force* you to marry," she replied, "but I can cut off your monthly allowance."

Willie froze, his glass halfway to his mouth. His eyes focused on his mother as his eyebrows knotted on his forehead, revealing a web of wrinkles. He tossed back the rest of his drink.

"What is your new salary?" Mrs. Klein said. "Twenty-seven dollars a week? Or is it twenty-eight? Whatever it is, I'm sure it will keep you in the luxury to which you are accustomed. You don't need that meager allowance anymore, do you?"

"Why, Mother," Willie said, "I do believe that's blackmail."

I was surprised that he no longer sounded angry. In fact, he seemed almost . . . amused. He walked back to the bar cart.

"Don't you think you've had enough?" his mother asked.

"Oh, I don't think I've even begun." He poured yet another glassful. "Father, are you really going to allow this charade?"

Willie wouldn't even look at me. And why should he? I was merely a bargaining chip.

"Pour me one of those, would you, Will?" Mr. Klein said. "You know full well I may bring home the money, but I don't control the purse strings. Besides, your mother has a solid point." Willie handed his father a glass. "It doesn't seem so bad to me. I think Dottie will make a fine wife and mother."

I was being discussed as if I were chattel.

In the doorway, a throat cleared. "Are we ready?" asked the *rebbe*.

"Are we?" Mrs. Klein asked Willie.

"This is ludicrous," Willie said, but his protests were hollow. "A farce." He finished off his third drink while he considered. "I marry her," he said, "and you will continue my allowance?"

"Absolutely," Mrs. Klein said.

"And there will be no other restrictions placed on me?" he asked.

"No other restrictions."

The *rebbe* gave an awkward cough, to remind us he was standing there.

"Well?" Mr. Klein said.

Willie swirled the empty glass in his hand before sighing and placing it back on the cart. "Let's get this over with, shall we?"

For the first time he turned to really look at me. Something in my swollen crimson face must have softened him, because he gave me a gentle smile and held out his hand.

Zelda placed her hand on my lower back and helped me to a standing position. I dabbed my eyes one last time and tried to discreetly wipe my nose as I took Willie's hand in mine.

Before we could follow his mother and the *rebbe* into the formal living room, he held me back for a moment and leaned toward me. "Don't worry," he whispered into my ear. "It won't be so bad."

For the first time in days, a small pang of relief in the fog of pain enveloped me. It would be okay. It wouldn't be the marriage I'd dreamed of, but it would be marriage. Solid and sound and I would have my family and I would make it work. I flashed a relieved smile at Willie. A smile that dissolved instantly at his next words.

"We only have to stay married until the baby comes. Then we get divorced. I'll even present you with—what's that thing called? the Jewish divorce?—a *get*? Nice and kosher, I promise. And I give you my word, I will always provide for the child."

I stumbled, and he caught my arm, a smile on his face. *A divorce?* A disgrace that had never happened in my family before. Divorce! That was for Hollywood actors, not for real people. Divorce had never crossed my mind. How was it the possibilities to shame my family seemed endless? With panicked desperation I thought, *I have a year! One year to change his mind.*

Marriage was not going to be the answer I'd hoped.

In the formal living room, I discovered, were two white couches. Such elegance I would never dream of sitting on, like something from George V's palace. In the corner, silently watching, was one of the Kleins' servants. The non-Jewish witness, I supposed.

"Come here," the *rebbe* said, beckoning us to a desk on the far side of the room. "This is your *ketubah*." A paper lay on the desk, the sacred wedding contract; it seemed like a mockery to sign it, but I did as I was bid. I wrote my name as I'd learned it at home, in Yiddish letters. Willie leaned over the paper, looked at my signature, and glanced back up at me. With a smirk, he signed his own name in English. *So that's how it will be*, I thought. *I am Old Country. He is America.* I wanted to protest, *I was born here, too.* But I knew he was right. For all my pretenses, I fit into his world as well as Ma fit in at my office.

"Shall we begin?" Mrs. Klein asked.

Mr. Klein and Zelda held a tablecloth over our heads, a

makeshift *chuppah* for our makeshift wedding. The *rebbe* murmured prayers, leading us in what to say and what to do.

My eyes darted to the door leading out to the foyer, drawn by an invisible pull, a magnetic force, waiting, waiting, waiting for Abe to break down the door, to rescue me at the last second like the hero releasing the heroine from the tracks just moments before she is run over by the freight train. I couldn't look at Willie; so sure was I that at any moment my *beshert*, my true soul mate, would burst in. I could hear the train rumbling in the distance, and my heart beat fast, as I hoped, prayed that I would be freed, that my protector would carry me off in his arms. So distracted was I that it wasn't until I felt the cold chill of the band sliding onto my index finger that I realized the train had run right over me, eviscerating my very being.

It was too late.

I was Mrs. William Klein.

"You may now kiss your bride," the *rebbe* said in the most American of ways.

Willie turned to me and to my utter shock gave me a passionate kiss. As I heard Mrs. Klein cough with embarrassment, I realized the kiss was for show, designed to needle his mother. I tried my best to remember I was kissing my husband, but all I could think of was Abe. I pulled away.

As Willie released me, he murmured, "At least there's one thing marriage is good for, no?" I blushed. The pleasure I had taken in our night at Camp Eden was now something that could be freely repeated. I tried to take comfort in that, to look forward to the pleasure he'd brought me that night in Cold Spring. But all I felt was empty.

"Isn't he going to break a glass?" Zelda asked.

"Not my Waterford crystal, thank you very much," Mrs. Klein said.

With a sigh, Zelda said, "Well, at the very least, let's put something in that Waterford crystal. How about a toast?" When she saw that neither Mr. nor Mrs. Klein had any intention of responding, she said, "Aw, I know you have a bottle of bubbly somewhere around here. Your only child got married. If that's not reason to celebrate, then what is?"

Mrs. Klein's face held a tight smile. "Yes, of course. Fiona," she called out, and Fiona popped in so quickly that I realized she'd been standing on the other side of the door the entire time. "Please bring out champagne."

"None for me," the *rebbe* said. "I'm needed at the synagogue. I ran out on a board meeting."

"And we appreciate that," Mrs. Klein said. I wondered how much the Kleins donated to their synagogue that they had the *rebbe* at their beck and call. "Five glasses of champagne, Fiona."

"Yes, ma'am," she said before running off to the kitchen. Duty as a witness done, the houseman followed her.

"Well," Mrs. Klein said. "Well."

"Yes, indeed," said Mr. Klein.

Zelda came up and whispered in my ear, "Your wedding band. Switch it to your ring finger."

I looked at my hand, the plain gold ring around my index finger as required by Jewish law. But I couldn't move. Zelda gently took my hand, slid the band off, and placed it on the proper finger. There it was. My manacle.

"*Rebbe*, are you sure we can't entice you to stay for one drink?" Mrs. Klein said. "It's real French champagne. None of that American copycat nonsense."

"Thank you for the offer, but no, I must go." He turned to Willie. "Congratulations. May you have a fruitful marriage."

"Seems like that's already been taken care of," Mr. Klein half mumbled under his breath.

"Please," Mrs. Klein said.

The *rebbe* exited as Fiona returned with a silver platter bearing five glasses and a champagne bottle. The elegant crystal flutes fizzled with golden bubbles. A chill of realization dawned on me: This was now my family. A family that served champagne at home. This would be my life. I'd have a fine apartment and my children would dress in clothes from Bergdorf Goodman. Would I have a maid?

Fiona walked around with the tray, serving Mr. and Mrs. Klein first. I looked at Willie and tried to comprehend that we were married. I needed to make this work. To make him forget all about a divorce.

I reached for a glass of champagne, attempting to feel elegant and modern, but failing miserably.

"A toast," Zelda said. "To the happy couple."

"To a more stable life," Mrs. Klein said, looking directly at Willie.

Willie grinned and looked at me. "To my beautiful wife."

The heat in my cheeks felt like a blush instead of sadness. For a moment, I allowed myself satisfaction. He was incredibly interesting, cultivated, passionate about his writing. And I couldn't ignore the fact he was a terribly handsome man. He wasn't my *beshert*, but he would be a good provider. I was a young bride. My future awaited. I wasn't happy. Not yet. But perhaps I would be.

Everyone drank, so I brought the glass to my mouth and took a small sip. The bubbles tickled my tongue in a pleasant way, but the champagne was tart, and though I smiled, I didn't like the taste. But the others greedily drank theirs and Willie even reached for the bottle to pour himself more.

"I've taken the liberty of arranging a room for you at the Pierre Hotel tonight. It wouldn't do to have your wedding night in your parents' home. You can begin looking for an apartment tomorrow," Mrs. Klein said.

I hadn't thought about where we'd go that night. In my neighborhood, the parents' apartment was exactly where newlyweds went, with little money for anything else. The Kleins' apartment was so large, I'd assumed we'd stay there. A hotel was an undreamed-of luxury! I had only ever slept on my own couch or in a tent at Camp Eden.

"Thank you, Mother. We'll enjoy the hotel tonight," Willie said, winking at me to my chagrin and to Mrs. Klein's disapproval. "But there's no need to go apartment hunting."

"Nonsense," Mrs. Klein said. "I can't believe you would want to live here and not in your own place."

I sat, once again a bystander to the decisions being made about my life.

"Listen, Mother, this marriage doesn't change the fact that I leave for Paris in two weeks."

With a sharp inhalation, I reminded everyone of my presence. "Paris!"

"No!" Mrs. Klein said.

"Now, my boy," Mr. Klein began.

"Paris! Murder!" Zelda said.

"Paris," Willie reiterated. "Why is this such a surprise? Every single one of you knows I am going to Paris for *The New Yorker*. I'll be traveling all about the Continent."

"But, but . . . ," I sputtered, knowing how foolish I looked.

"What did you think? Now that we are married and having a child, that I'd throw away my writing? That I'd settle down and take a job in my father's office, becoming the kind of drudge who works eight to five and then takes in a show?"

"That's exactly what I thought," Mrs. Klein said, and if I was being honest, I'd thought the same thing. "You have responsibilities now. A family to care for. You can't go gallivanting to the Continent now."

"Especially now," Mr. Klein said. "There's a war brewing over there, you know."

"Which is exactly why I need to be there," Willie said. "Can't you get that in your thick skulls? To write, I need to be where there is something to write *about*. I need to show the world what is happening."

"What about me? And the . . ." I couldn't bring myself to say *baby* out loud.

"The choice is yours. You can stay behind or you can come with me to Paris."

My heart pounded. What would my parents say? How could I go so far from home when I needed Ma the most? She had left her family to start a new life in a new country, but I wasn't as brave and strong as she was. I was terrified.

"Just think: Paris!" Zelda said, with a dreamy smile. "You'll have first dibs on those Parisian styles."

"On his income?" Mr. Klein said.

Willie raised an eyebrow at his father. "Mother promised you would continue my allowance. No restrictions."

"Mother promised we would continue your allowance. And we shall. But if you go to Paris, there will be no increase to support your growing family. If you stay, we will make it possible for you to live in the manner to which you are accustomed. Otherwise, you will have to live as three on the income of one."

With a grimace, Willie realized he'd been bested. "Very clever, Father. I suppose I should have expected nothing less. But it doesn't change anything." He turned to me. "So? Paris with me? Or New York by yourself?"

I looked from Mr. Klein to Mrs. Klein to Zelda. Each face seemed to be sending me a different message. Mr. Klein showed indifference. Clearly he wasn't concerned with Willie's fate; he merely wanted to keep his wife's fury in check. Mrs. Klein was hoping I would stay, that I could yet force Willie to remain for the child's sake. Zelda's face reflected longing, the dream of a life of adventure, far away from drudgery. But once I was a mother, it would be the same drudgery in Paris. I loved this baby, but could I manage being a mother in a country where I didn't speak the language, didn't know the customs? Yet, was I going to stay here alone, everyone knowing my husband had left without me? I would be humiliated. And it would give Willie an excuse to divorce me the moment the baby was born.

Then there was Mrs. Klein, who surely wouldn't allow her

grandchild to be born on the lower East Side. I would be under the thumb of this shrew if I stayed. And if I left, I could return with the child and no one would need know how early it had come. Everyone would think I was simply foolish Dottie: angry at Abe, so I rushed into marriage with another. No one would know the truth.

I looked into Willie's eyes. Did he want me there? Or was I merely a burden? Well, it didn't really matter. Willie had played an equal part in the mess I was in. At last here was something *I* could decide. I could choose.

"Yes," I said. "I will go with you to Paris."

Mrs. Klein threw up her hands. "This is madness! You'll be completely on your own," she shouted at me.

With steel in my voice, I said, "No, I won't." I threw back my shoulders and stood tall. "I'll have my husband."

Willie rewarded me with a genuine smile and held out his arm. "We have a wedding to celebrate. Let us go, Mrs. Klein."

That was me.

I took his proffered arm and walked side by side with him out of the apartment, ready to try on the life of a married woman.

Rose

❧

THE journey home was twice as long as the one that had taken me there. Briefly I considered taking a streetcar—my belly throbbed and my leg ached—but my wooziness overruled my pain. I feared the jostling would make me ill. Slowly I walked, the cries of the neighborhood children piercing my ears. What had I done? Who had I become? Thinking of the daughter I wouldn't hold, the sweet scent of a baby's head, her skin as soft and delicate as *challah* dough, I cried. I cried for the baby who wouldn't suckle at my breast, who wouldn't greet me with coos and sighs. I cried for the child who wouldn't trail behind me, pulling at my skirt, begging for sweets. I cried for the young woman who wouldn't love and despair and have babies of her own. The depth of my sadness took me unaware. I thought of all my babies, the ones still on earth and those already departed to the heavens. *Forgive me, daughter,* I thought.

Yet, amid the sorrow, another feeling grew. I couldn't identify it at first. As it slipped through my body, a sense of calmness bathed me, and soon I recognized the feeling for what it was: relief. Pure and total relief. With my hand on my belly, I felt sadness but not regret. It was possible, I found, to both mourn a loss and yet be grateful it had happened. All around me, children shouted, fought, sang, and cried while they played stickball, shot marbles, and swarmed the stoops, and my convictions were confirmed; my days for bearing children were over.

Dottie, though, was just at the beginning. Decisions had to be made. Abe, it seemed, was a lost cause, but her idea of going out of town could work. A place in the Catskills was impossible, of course. How would we pay for it? This was not a vacation. But cousin Freyde could be trusted and we could stay with her in Baltimore. When we returned, I could claim the baby as my own, as long as she was willing to care for it. Or would a few weeks with a child show Dottie how difficult motherhood could be? Would she consider a foundling hospital? No, probably not. And what would we tell Ben? I wished my mind weren't hazy from the ether.

As I walked, I thought again of Mama. How she did nothing for herself but sacrificed everything for her children, toiling until exhaustion for eleven hungry mouths, eleven dirty faces. For eighteen years her belly rounded, with children born and children lost. For eighteen years, she fed babies from her breast, day and night without ceasing. I wasn't that kind of mother. I loved my children and gave that love generously, but wasn't I important, too? Standing up for what was right, being able to fight for the jobless, the homeless, the Jews under threat in Europe—this was important. Time for me and Ben to be alone was important. My children were important, yes, but they were not the only ones. Why did I see this when so many women didn't? Wasn't the work that Perle was doing as important to mankind as bearing children? I'd need to wait a few more years, but my time to return to that work would come soon enough.

A sharp pain in my abdomen made me stop and buckle over. Was this a sign, a reminder from *Hashem* that I was still Dottie's mother, and my thoughts should be with her? Yes, I would claim Dottie's child as my own, but she would have to compromise, do much of the tending. I could save her reputation and still fight for the lifting of immigration quotas, save my brother, and even attend Workers' Alliance meetings with Perle.

With each step, blood oozed down my legs. The rags weren't enough. Despite the pain, I tried to hurry home. I needed to find Dottie. She must know it wasn't too late. I would take her baby. We would figure this out.

BY the time I got home, the sky had darkened and I knew my family would be worried. The stairs were pure agony, and I leaned heavily on the rail as I climbed the three flights to the apartment.

As I opened the door, the last of my strength gave out. "Beryl," I called, but my voice was barely more than a whisper.

He must have heard the front door open. Ben came in from the other room. "Rose, where have you been? There's no supper and—" He stopped suddenly when he saw me. "Good God, Rose! What's wrong?"

The pain overwhelmed me, and crying, I said, "The baby. I'm bleeding."

Ben sprang at me, put his shoulder under my arm, and helped me to the bed. Ben was half a head shorter than I and about thirty pounds lighter, but he hoisted me as if I were no heavier than a sack of potatoes.

"Izzy!" he called out. "Go to Mr. Baum's apartment and ask to use the phone. Call the doctor. Tell him to hurry. Go!"

The doctor! "No!" I said. "We don't need a doctor's bills." As soon as he saw that I had been shaved, the doctor would know exactly what I had done. "I've gone through this before," I said. "I know what to expect. Just have Perle come over."

"Nonsense," Ben said, wiping sweat from my forehead. "You have a fever. We can afford a doctor. This is not the time to be worrying about bills." He rubbed my brow gently. "I should have listened to Dottie and installed a phone. Next week, I tell you. Next week we get our own phone."

"Get Perle. Please." I was sweating profusely, the heat engulfing my body.

"Fine, fine. Perle. *And* the doctor." Shouting again into the next room, Ben said, "Alfie! Alfie, stop that racket and listen. Your ma needs you. Go, run get Perle. Tell her your mother needs her urgently."

A knock on the door, and I heard Mrs. Kaplan's voice. "Everything all right in there?" The busybody, looking for gossip.

"Yes, yes, fine," Ben shouted. I could tell, though, she didn't budge, perching in the hall to listen to every word we said. The whole street would know of my loss within the hour.

Turning back to me, he said, "Oh, Rose. I am so sorry. So very sorry."

How should I act? Should I pretend to be sad? Admit what happened? No, of course not. I kept plenty of secrets in my life. One more was a mere grain of wheat added to the mill; it would mean nothing.

I slipped in and out of sleep as Ben fussed over me, bringing water, dabbing my forehead with a cool cloth. I had no sense of time passing before I heard the door open and close and voices murmuring in the front room.

Dr. Auerbach came into the bedroom. "Mrs. Krasinsky. I'm so sorry." I was in such a haze, I didn't have the energy to protest his presence. And this time, I admit, was nothing like when I'd lost babies before. This pain was much more intense, the bleeding much worse. "Mr. Krasinsky said to let you know he's taken the boys to his sister's," the doctor said. "Now, let me examine you." His Yiddish was accented, the Yiddish of an American-born boy. Dr. Auerbach was probably a few years younger than me, with deep blue eyes and hair already graying. His long face lent him gravity even when he was attempting a joke—something he didn't do very often. Perhaps it was the job, but he had a seriousness about him that belied his years. He had grown up in the neighborhood, and had practiced with his father, now old and ailing. It was his father who'd saved Alfie. It was his father who'd lost Joey.

A moment later the front door slammed open again. In my heart, I wanted to call out, "Don't slam the door," but I had not an ounce of energy.

"I'm here," Perle's voice called from the front room.

"Perle," I said, but my fever muted my voice, and the doctor didn't hear me. I repeated, a little stronger, "Perle. I want Perle in here." That slight exertion took all my stamina.

"But I need to examine you."

"I want her here."

He hesitated, clearly reluctant, but finally he nodded and called for Perle.

When Perle walked in, she was startled to see me lying on the bed. "You!" she said. "I was expecting—" With a glance at the doctor she stopped abruptly. The doctor looked from one of us to the other, trying to glean her meaning.

Coming to sit in the chair by the bed, the chair that had been my perch for those long months nursing the twins, Perle said, "My poor *bubelah*." She sat, held my hand and comforted me.

The doctor knelt at the foot of the bed. "Let's take a look," he said. "Slide down and bend your knees."

My bad leg resisted and it took a moment to arrange myself. Perle took my hand in both of hers. Her skin was rough and dry from hours handling the pamphlets for leafleting. When she was younger, we'd experimented with balms to soften them, but eventually Perle gave up. Hands were important for what they could do, not for how soft they might be.

The doctor squeezed into the small space between the dresser and the mattress. He began his examination by pressing on my belly, which drew a moan from my throat. So tender. Then he cleaned the blood between my legs so he could get a better look, and I heard his cluck of disapproval when he saw the bareness of my skin. I closed my eyes and tried to imagine I was somewhere else. Preferably in the future, where this could all seem like a bad dream. This too would pass. Dr. Auerbach continued his ministrations, but his sighs of censure were as clear as the *hazzan* on the Day of Atonement.

"Oh, stop your huffing," Perle said.

I opened my eyes in time to see the doctor glare at Perle before returning to his task. I gave Perle's hand a weak squeeze.

The minutes stretched in silence while I waited for Dr. Auerbach to speak. But I couldn't stand the tension, the quiet. "I told Ben we didn't need to call you. We've all miscarried before. We know how to manage."

The doctor continued his silence. After finishing the examination, he said, "Clean rags?"

Perle jumped up and rummaged through my drawer till she found some. Without a word, she handed them to Dr. Auerbach and returned to my side.

He replaced my rags and then said, "I'm going to wash my hands. I'll be back in a moment to talk."

The minute he left the room, Perle leaned close and whispered in my ear. "Rose, I thought this wasn't for you. Why didn't you tell me? I would have—"

"Shhh." I nodded toward the door. I didn't want the doctor to hear.

Perle gripped my hand more tightly as the doctor reentered the room.

He looked fiercely at us. "I have to say I've never seen a miscarriage quite like that."

Perle returned his sternness. "Oh, I don't believe that for a second."

"Don't antagonize him, Perle." I didn't fear the doctor would turn me in to the police, but he might gossip, and I couldn't bear the idea of the truth getting back to Ben. He couldn't find out. Not ever.

"You've lost a tremendous amount of blood," he said. "I've tried to stanch the bleeding, but if you continue to soak through your rags in the morning, you'll need to enter the hospital."

My eyes widened with fear.

He looked down his nose at me. "There are reasons that woman shouldn't interfere in the work of the Lord."

Trying to look contrite, I nodded.

"Why would you do this?" he asked.

Light-headed, I closed my eyes. *Why had I done this?* There wasn't a single answer I could give that he would understand. Luckily, Perle spoke up for me. "Men cannot be expected to understand the trials of women."

He shook his head as Perle continued: "Now, I trust you won't go telling that wife of yours. You might not approve, but no need to harm Rose further by spurring malicious gossip. And it would cause Ben great pain if he knew."

The doctor's eyes sank into the hollows of his face as he turned to glower at Perle. "I would never repeat the misfortunes of others."

Perle harrumphed. "Yes, sure. That's why we all knew when Mr. Lebowitz caught—"

"Enough! The good doctor understands your point." I looked at him, trying to work my face into a solemn expression. My voice was barely a whisper, but in the small room, it came through clearly. "I'm sure the doctor understands and will do what's best for everyone."

After a moment of scowling, Dr. Auerbach reached into his bag and pulled out a small bottle. "You may take this for your discomfort." He handed me the bottle. "I will tell Mr. Krasinsky to keep the boys at his sister's. You will need peace to recover."

With that, he donned his hat and left the apartment without so much as a good-bye.

"Well, that's a fine how-do-you-do," Perle said. "As if he's so high and mighty. Why, I bet he's just upset that he didn't make any money performing the procedure himself."

I managed a small laugh.

Perle stroked my hair and looked at me with a kindness that

reminded me of my mama. Being taken care of by Perle made me feel protected, like nothing truly bad could happen.

"Do you want some of the medicine?"

I nodded. Perle retrieved a spoon from the kitchen and returned. She poured some of the syrupy brown liquid from the bottle and fed it to me. I drank it greedily.

A thickness fell over me, as I hovered between wakefulness and sleep. As the medicine took hold, all those emotions the pain had tamped down rushed to the surface. I was flooded with relief and anger and heartache and confusion and optimism and despair, but my mind was so hazy it was impossible to settle on any one. My eyes fell closed, as if my lids were weighted, and in the darkness of my mind, I was greeted with a vision of the child that was not to be: a lovely towheaded baby resting happily and cozily in the arms of Mama, with Joey and the other lost babies by her side. I knew she would be protected, loved, and cared for in the world to come, and a sense of peace washed over me.

I fell into a deep, sound sleep, comforted by my certainty that I had done what was right for Dottie. I had done what was right for her baby. And, perhaps most important, I had done what was right for me.

Dottie

⚓

Friday, August 30

THE sun tickled my eyelids as it rose the morning after my wedding night. I woke in confusion to the plush pillows and the downy comforter that enveloped me. Remembering where I was only made my unease grow. My husband was asleep next to me, his mouth slightly agape, breathing heavily in a deep slumber. *My husband,* I thought, looking at my ring finger to confirm it was true. I twisted the plain gold band, and it spun easily, too large for my small hand. Mrs. Klein had picked it up, of course. I'd have to have it fitted.

I sat up in the bed, pulling at the sheets to cover my bosom, self-conscious about my nakedness. As if to emphasize my feeling of exposure, Willie rolled onto his side, pulling most of the sheet with him. I thought about last night when we'd arrived at our hotel room and the bellboy eyed our lack of luggage suspiciously. All we had was a bottle Willie had pilfered from his father's liquor cart.

When the bellboy unlocked the door, Willie plowed in, setting his hat on the bureau as I waited behind.

"Ahem," I said. "Aren't you going to carry your bride across the threshold?"

With a laugh, Willie played along. "Oh, I plan on doing more to her than that." The bellboy scurried off, and I was embarrassed by Willie's crassness. But he picked me up and carried me to the bed, where he set me down with more of a plop than I thought was needed. He grabbed two glasses from the side table and poured us large servings of bourbon.

"*L'chaim,*" he said, and I repeated, "*L'chaim,*" clinking my glass to his. Needing the courage, I downed the entire glass in one swallow.

"Whoa," he said.

"Another," I said, with a smile. I figured a good-time girl— like the girls Izzy ogled, the ones who liked strong drink, spent late nights out at the clubs, and were easy on the eyes—would be most appealing to Willie, and for the next year, my only job was to be appealing to Willie.

After a few more glasses, our hands explored each other's bodies. My memories of Camp Eden were mild compared with what happened on our wedding night. Willie seemed both surprised and pleased by my enthusiasm. When I faltered, unsure of what to do, Willie guided me.

"Am I doing this right?" I asked once or twice, and he would moan with pleasure.

When Willie touched me in my most private of places, I startled at first and then relaxed with a purr. He laughed gently. "Tell me everything you like," he whispered.

"I don't know yet," I said, "but this is definitely nice."

He nibbled my ear and said, "I really was your first, wasn't I?"

As I sighed with lust, I said, "First and only."

Willie pulled back and looked me in the eye, evidently pleased with this idea. "All mine," he murmured.

"All yours," I said. I moved his hand back to where it had felt so nice, which excited him even more, and we became truly husband and wife. I took comfort that even if we had our differences, physically we were as compatible as could be. It wasn't much to start a marriage on, but it was something.

Just thinking about the previous night made my body tingle, and I ran a finger lightly down Willie's spine, hoping to arouse him again. I stroked the back of his neck, but he merely groaned and rolled over. Willie appeared to have no qualms about sleeping the day away.

With a sigh, I stood and walked to the window. Never in my life had I paraded about fully unclothed. Dressing at home was a quick affair, as someone always needed the bathroom or the bedroom. Even bathing, I removed my clothes furtively as I slipped into the tub. Standing in the hotel room completely naked felt both terrifying and delicious as I savored the warmth on my skin. It was a gorgeous late summer morning, rays of sunshine so determined that they forced their presence through the diaphanous curtains. I pulled aside the silky drapes and gazed out at the most beautiful view of the city I had ever seen. I was just miles from home, but I was worlds away.

Glancing back at my sleeping husband, I wondered how long he would stay in bed. According to the clock, it was already six thirty a.m. I rarely slept past six. With Ma bustling in the kitchen and *Tateh* hustling off to the garage, sleeping in was a luxury unimagined.

It looked like I'd have to wake Willie. We needed to tell my parents what we had done. They would be worried. Zelda had promised to let them know I wasn't coming home last night, but Ma would know something was amiss. Unless I was at Camp Eden, I never spent the night out. Between the missed appointment and my disappearance last night, Ma would be both worried sick and beside herself with anger.

I went back to the bed and slipped beneath the covers. "Willie," I whispered. He didn't move. "Willie," I said louder, shaking him gently.

He gripped my side and pulled me toward him, still half-asleep.

"Willie, we need to go tell my parents we're married."

His grip loosened.

"We need to go before they worry."

Cracking open an eye, Willie looked at the clock. He groaned and closed his eyes again. "It's still the middle of the night. We'll go later."

"*Tateh* will leave for work soon. We need to go now." A little frantic, I gave him another small shake.

"You go," he said. His speech was thick with sleep and barely more than a mumble. "I'll go another day." And he rolled back onto his side, away from me.

I'd have to go to my parents alone. Sitting up again, I looked for my clothes, which in our passion Willie had flung across the room. I tried to make do in the bathroom with a washcloth and a bar of soap, but I had nothing fresh to wear, so I put on yesterday's clothes. I was sorry I didn't have a hairbrush or a toothbrush to make myself feel more presentable. I scrubbed my teeth with my finger, swishing water around my mouth. From my purse, I fetched lipstick and face powder. It would have to do. Glancing in the mirror, I saw I looked passable. Not my best day, but certainly no one would guess what I had gotten up to last night.

When I was set for the day, I leaned over my sleeping husband, hesitating only momentarily before giving him a kiss on the cheek. "I'll be back later," I whispered. We'd agreed last night we would stay in the hotel until it was time to leave for Europe. Just the thought of Europe made me catch my breath.

Before leaving, I scrutinized the near stranger with whom I was now locked in matrimony. His hair was disheveled and one slender arm lay atop the covers. His chest was pale and smooth, with barely a hair upon it. He looked innocent. Vulnerable.

He looked like a boy compared with Abe.

A sharp sense of regret mixed with last night's bourbon made my stomach lurch. No point dwelling on what was lost forever. But still . . .

What was I doing here? Here in this opulent hotel room, with an Asian-style ceramic vase filled with fresh flowers, a pale green chaise longue tucked in the corner, the double bed piled high with sumptuous pillows. This was the room I wanted Ma to make. This was the life the magazines promised. Well, I would embrace it. I was going to do everything it took to guard that it didn't slip away. To make sure this was the life to which my child would become accustomed. Even if it was no longer the life I wanted, my child deserved every bit of it.

Rose

———— ⚘ ————

Friday, August 30

MY body still felt feverish when I awoke Friday morning, but it was no longer boiling. My abdomen burned, but my energy was returning. Peeking beneath my clothes, I saw that the bleeding was slower, and a tremendous relief washed over me: I wouldn't have to go to the hospital.

Outside the bedroom door, I heard movement. "Ben," I called, but my voice was hoarse. Clearing my throat, I tried again. "Ben."

The door opened, and Ben peered inside. Seeing me alert, he smiled. "You're awake. How are you feeling, my *beshert?*"

The warmth in his voice soothed me like nothing else. When the world was falling apart around me, Ben could always hold me up. "Better," I said. "Much better."

He came in and kissed my brow. "I'm so relieved. Perle will be back later this morning. I had a heck of a time getting rid of her last night. I thought she was going to sleep right there on the floor by the bed."

Though it sounded weak to my ears, I laughed. "Where's Dottie?"

"Zelda came by last night. Said Dottie would be staying with her to help with Shirley."

Help with Shirley? That was odd. What kind of help would Zelda need? "Why didn't Dottie come herself? And why—" I was interrupted by the sound of the front door opening and Dot-tie's voice calling, "Ma? *Tateh?* Are you still here?"

Ben kissed me again and said, "Ah, speak of the devil. I'll go talk with her."

From the bedroom, I could hear their muted voices, Dottie's ris-ing in exclamation, Ben hushing it down. I was confused: Why would Dottie have spent the night at Zelda's? Her apartment wasn't big enough for Zelda, her husband, Shirley, and a guest. Why on God's earth would Zelda need any help from Dottie? She had Perle for that. Although I supposed since Perle was with me . . . But no. Zelda's mother-in-law was also available. And wouldn't Dottie come to tell us herself if she was going to spend the night out?

Slowly a delightful notion rose like bubbles in my mind, bub-bles delicately floating heavenward, light and beautiful. Of course Dottie hadn't been with Zelda. Dottie had succeeded! Dottie had spent the night with Abe.

In the midst of my pain, hope surged. That *must* be what Dottie had done. I would plan a wedding. The hell with Mrs. Rabinowitz. I'd have to work quickly, as the baby would appear to be quite early, but this wouldn't be the first time it happened. The engulfing relief worked its magic in reducing the pain. I needed fabric. I would sew Dottie a lovely dress. Finally my skills as a seamstress would be put to use on a labor of love.

As Dottie dashed into the room, I couldn't suppress a smile.

"Ma," Dottie said, rushing to the chair by my bed. I could hear Ben in the kitchen, making coffee. "What have you done?"

"What have *you* done?" I asked, my voice singsonging with joy. "And who were *you* with last night?"

Dottie shook her head. "Ma, tell me what you did."

"I did nothing," I said.

"Of course you did something. Why are you here in bed, sick, if you did nothing?"

"Oh, my Dottala! Don't worry about me. Tell me what you did!"

"Ma!" Dottie's voice held the same threatening tone mine did when I was speaking to the boys. "*What* did you do?"

"I did nothing," I said. "But I did lose a baby. I was with child. I miscarried. I didn't want you to worry."

"*Lost* a baby? Is that what you call it?"

"Dottala, I am sick," I said. "Don't make me strain myself."

She stared at me. "*Lost* a baby. How convenient that you *lost* a baby, the very same day I had . . ." Her voice faltered. She threw her shoulders back and took a deep breath. "The same day I had an appointment." She looked at me hard. "You can say what you will of me, Ma, but you didn't raise a fool."

"Coincidences happen," I said. "Now don't torture your old ma." My voice teased her. "Were you with Abe last night?"

Dottie was clearly reluctant to change the subject, but finally she took a long deep breath and shook her head. "No," she said. "I wasn't."

The bubbles started to pop.

"You weren't with Abe?" The ether should have worn off. But I was confused.

"No, Ma," Dottie said. "I was not with Abe."

And with that, the bubbles went flat, like seltzer left out overnight. Reality returned and the pain in my midsection cried for attention. Well, it wasn't as good as it could have been if Dottie had seduced Abe. But we were no worse off than we were ten minutes ago, and it would all work out.

"Ma," Dottie said, "why didn't you tell me you were with child? Why did you do this?"

"You had your own problems! Why should I trouble you with mine? Besides, I did nothing, my *bubelah*!"

Dottie looked at me hard, as if trying to see through me. But I, who had kept so many secrets, could keep one more. Swiftly she stood. She marched to my dresser and opened the drawer.

"Dottala . . . ," I warned, but my voice was weak, and I was so very tired.

Pulling out the tin, she opened the top and dumped the contents into her hand. Barely glancing at the stack, she said, "If you did nothing, you should have forty dollars left. You paid fifty. You owed ten more. So if you did nothing, why are there only thirty dollars here?"

"Oh, Dottala." I reached my hand out toward Dottie, beckoning her, hoping that would be answer enough.

She put the money and the tin back and returned to the chair by my side. "Don't lie to me after all this. Don't you think it's time for you and me to stop keeping secrets from each other?"

I stared at my little girl, so grown-up, and gave her only the barest of nods. "It was my problem, not yours. And now it's gone."

The tears came on suddenly, her body shuddering with her sobs.

"Don't you understand, *bubelah*? Everything is again possible. We will be able to take care of your situation. Now we can raise your child. We will figure out a way to make this work. You will have to quit your job anyway, so now you go to school full-time when we return. We don't have the money anymore for Washington Square, but you'll go to City College."

The conversation exhausted me. She reached for a handkerchief from the side table to dab her eyes. Wasn't this just like her? I was the one sick in bed and she was the one carrying on. "Stop your tears. There is no more crying. We will go away; you will have the baby. We return and tell everyone the child is mine. *Tante* Kate can keep an eye on Alfie and Eugene while we're gone. When we return, you will have all the time in the world. Your education. Marrying Abe. There will be no rush."

Shaking her head, Dottie said, "It's too late, Ma."

Despite the fever, a shiver ran through me, a premonition of what was to come. I tried to sit up, but failed. It was like speaking with a toddler. "What do you mean, Dottala?" When Dottie continued to sob, I put my hands on her arms and raised my voice. "What do you mean?"

"Everything okay in there?" Ben called from the kitchen, before moving to the bedroom doorway. "I hear crying."

"Yes, yes," I said. "Dottie's upset about my loss. You should be going to the garage."

"The garage can wait. Dottie, you shouldn't be distressing your mother like this."

"*Shah*," I said. "Leave it to a man to not understand the grief of a woman. Go. Let us be."

Ben eyed us for a moment, before giving a curt nod and retreating to the next room.

I turned back to Dottie and spoke in a loud whisper. "Tell me now. What did you do?"

Dottie tried to calm herself, so I gave her a moment, stroking her hair and brushing it from her face. "Tell me, *bubelah*," I said, "It's all right. We can fix most anything." I picked up Dottie's hand and right away I felt something hard and smooth. I looked down. At the sight of the plain gold band, I dropped her hand in shock and stared at her finger as if it were a pork sausage in my kitchen. Dottie made no move to hide her hand. In fact, she began to twist the band around her finger.

I looked into Dottie's face. "You married Abe?" I asked, but even as the words left my mouth, I knew this wasn't the case. But the only other possibility was too horrifying to even consider.

Dottie's voice was hardly more than a murmur. "I married Willie."

A gasp flew out of me.

"Last night. We married at his house." She wouldn't make eye contact with me. "It wasn't supposed to work out like this."

"I—I don't—" I was speechless. I looked helplessly at Dottie, waiting for her explanation.

"I told Mrs. Klein about the baby. She sprang the wedding on me. I had no way to let you know."

"You married Willie?" My stomach hurt in a new way.

She nodded. "Yes."

So many thoughts fought for space in my mind, I didn't know where to turn first: Dottie didn't marry Abe. Dottie married

Willie. What was Willie? A spoiled layabout. A seducer. Willie Klein was going to take care of *my* Dottie? The Kleins were now my *machatunim*? My daughter married and I wasn't there to see it? "You didn't want to try again with Abe?"

"Abe is done. He guessed my secret."

I nodded. I wasn't surprised.

"Do you—" I wasn't sure what I was supposed to ask. "Do you love Willie?"

Dottie sat taller. "I'll grow to love him. That's what you said about *Tateh*. That you barely knew him. That first you married. Then your love grew."

"But it was a different time." My voice softened. "Nowadays, people marry for love."

Dottie stiffened. "Well, I loved Abe. And he didn't want me."

"But does Willie?" The idea of my baby hobbled to a man who didn't want her crushed my heart.

"He didn't have a choice," Dottie said, her voice catching. "And neither did I."

"But—" So many questions. Where to begin? I picked the most obvious. "Will you live with his parents?"

Dottie trained her eyes on the ceiling, a trick of hers when she was trying not to cry. "No."

"But then where? Can he afford his own home?"

Dottie brushed a stray hair behind her ear, the same way she'd done since she was a child, getting her hair out of the way to brace herself to be tough. "Willie is not giving up his job."

"His job? Speak plainly. You are going around in circles. What does an apartment have to do with his job?"

She gave her eyes a last swipe with the handkerchief and then spoke in a tone that would brook no doubt. "Willie is a writer. *The New Yorker* is sending him to the Continent."

New Yorker? Continent? What continent? Our conversation from earlier in the week came rushing back to me. What was it she'd told me after she'd lunched with Willie? He was going to be a writer in Europe. *He's one kind of* dummkopf *if he thinks he's going to Europe. He's another kind of idiot if he thinks I'm going to allow Dottie to go with him.* "Absolutely not. I forbid it."

"We leave for Paris on the twelfth."

"Paris! There's a war brewing on the other side of the ocean. I'm struggling to bring my brother out of that treacherous place, and you are *going* there? What kind of fool is this Willie that he thinks it's right to head into trouble with a wife and child?"

"He's the kind of fool to whom I'm married. Willie is going to Paris. I am going with him."

Who was this stranger sitting across from me? Such determination I'd never seen.

"You cannot go. Who will help you with the baby in Paris?"

"I'll have to manage on my own."

"But how?"

"Ma, you managed on your own when you came here. You traveled all the way from Russia by yourself. Found work. Found *Tateh*. When you had me, you didn't have your parents here to help."

"But I had my brother, my cousin Ida. I had the *landsmanshaft*. I had Perle. And I didn't have a choice. There was nothing for me in the Old Country. I had nothing to lose."

"There is nothing for me here." Dottie's voice remained firm and calm, but I slipped into desperation.

I wanted to scream, to let myself wail, but I needed to keep myself quiet so Ben didn't hear. "Nonsense. You have your parents. Your friends. Your future as an accountant."

"I have a child on the way. My future as an accountant is gone with this child. If I stay here, I stay in shame. Everyone will know I betrayed Abe, and then they'll say there must be something wrong with me when my new husband deserts me. And when the baby comes in six months . . . No, Ma. There is nothing here for me."

I leaned back in the bed. Dottie was right. I knew that. But I couldn't accept it. "No, my child. This cannot be."

"Don't worry, Ma," she said. "I'll have Willie. I'll find my way."

I closed my eyes. A heaviness settled over me and I longed to drift back to sleep, to wake up later and not remember this terrible dream. "No," I said again. "I forbid it."

When I opened my eyes, I saw Dottie looking down at her hand, not to avoid me but to gaze at her ring as if it were giving her courage. "I'm a married woman. I am expecting. You cannot forbid me."

I studied her face. She was no longer my red-cheeked toddler who ran wild in the streets, barefoot till the first snow, and even sometimes after. She was no longer the girl who longed to sew like her ma, who managed to always be underfoot. She was no longer the little mama who cared for her younger brothers. No, she would *be* a mother. My melancholy deepened. "What will Eugene do without you?"

Dottie startled. I'd found the chink in her armor. Eugene.

But she refused to be rattled for longer than a moment. "I can't think of Eugene," she said. "Eugene is *your* baby. I have my own baby to consider."

Nodding, I said, "Yes, he is my baby." The time had come, it appeared, for me to take care of the children I had left. "So? Where is this husband of yours?"

"He's . . ." Dottie hesitated in such a way as to make me wonder if I was about to hear a lie. "He had to be at work early. I came home to tell you and to pick up some of my belongings."

"What kind of a man is that, not accompanying you to greet his in-laws?"

"Ma, it's not like it was. These are modern times." But a flicker in her eye belied her tone, and I could tell she was hurt.

"My little Dottala. All grown-up and married."

She gave a half smile, but I could see the tears gathering once more.

"Come here, my *bubelah*." She leaned in and I wrapped my arms around her, pretending one final time that she was my little girl and that I could make everything better with a kiss and a cookie.

Dottie

SEEING Ma weak was almost as shocking to me as knowing what she'd done. Why hadn't she confided in me? But then again, if I were her, would I have confided in me? I was a mess. I didn't know where to begin, what to feel. Heartache. Guilt. Fear.

In the kitchen, *Tateh* was bustling about trying to start the soup, which needed to simmer all day to be ready for the *Shabbes* dinner. He wore one of Ma's aprons, and as silly as he looked in that floral print, I could see the despair in his movements, the heaviness of his body as he shuffled about, his sorrow filling the room. The last time I'd seen him like this was after Joey died. How much worse would it be if he knew the truth about Ma's loss? I would make sure he never found out. As it was, I knew my news was going to devastate him.

"Come, *Tateh*. Give me the apron." I held out one hand, the other balled on my hip.

For a second it looked like *Tateh* was going to protest. He shook his head. "You look so much like your mother, standing there."

Glancing down at my body, I realized I'd mimicked Ma's stance when she was waiting to retrieve something—a bottle of milk, the morning paper—from one of us children. With my curving belly, I looked all the more like her.

Tateh untied the apron and handed it to me. I took it and tied it around my waist, as if I had done it my whole life, which was not the case. The motion was familiar—how many times had I seen Ma do it?—and it was one to which I must become accustomed. This was my life now. Wearing an apron. Cooking. Retrieving things for and from children.

"Sit," I ordered *Tateh*.

Without a word, he sank into the chair by the small kitchen table.

I surveyed the counter. "Look," I said. "You forgot to put in the chicken bones. The bones need to be boiled first. Otherwise the vegetables will become soggy." Ever since grammar school, when *Tateh* and I spoke without Ma in the room, we used English. His English was as good as his Yiddish.

I reached for the carcass and broke it down into smaller pieces. It's astounding how much I knew simply from observing Ma all those years.

"I told her not to work so hard," he said. "I told her to let you take some of the burden. Look at how well you do. She shouldn't have worked so hard." His eyes were blank, and my chest ached at what I had done. He clearly blamed himself for what had happened, and yet it was my fault.

With a *chop chop chop*, not daring to look up, I said, "I'm sorry I haven't been more help."

"Look at you in the kitchen. A *balabusta* in the making."

I sliced through the thick tendons, separating the bones, dropping them in the pot of boiling water as I pulled each one free. "*Tateh*, I have to tell you something." I put down the knife and rested my hands on the counter. I could feel myself hyperventilating, the breath coming hot and fast. I needed to spit this out quickly, yank off the bandage.

"*Tateh*, last night, Willie Klein and I were married." I wanted to turn to face him, but my body was leaden, my head bent, the weight of it too much for me to hold up. I stared at the wooden counter, grooved and nicked. The linoleum floor needed a mopping; dirt was beginning to show in the crevices.

"You were what?" His voice sounded confused, sounded old.

"We were married."

"Married?"

I nodded without turning. I couldn't look at him, knowing how much disappointment I was about to cause him.

"What do you mean, 'married'?"

I was being a coward. I turned around. "Last night, Willie Klein and I were married." I held up my hand with the band. "*Khasene,*" I repeated in Yiddish, so there'd be no misunderstanding. "Willie Klein and I were married."

Tateh looked wild, like one of those men from Hooverville. "I understand the word," he said in English, fury in his tone. The shock of Ma, the shock of this. I dreaded telling him my next piece of news. "Married to Willie *Klein?* Married to that . . . that *schmuck?*"

My skin chilled. While Ma occasionally let her language become coarse, *Tateh* never used vulgarity. I wanted to defend Willie, defend myself. Giving in to my misery would have been the easiest thing to do, but I reeled in my emotions. Falling into a hysterical mess would do neither of us any good. As I turned back to the counter to continue breaking down the bones, I said coolly, "Willie Klein is my husband."

"But what about Abe?"

"Abe has nothing to do with this." Tossing the last bones in the pot, I began with the vegetables, which *Tateh* had already started. I counted the pieces as I cut them. The carrot, sliced in half, made two pieces. Slice the halves again, and there were four.

Tateh leaned heavily on the back of the chair. "Willie Klein."

I continued dicing. Eight pieces. Sixteen.

"You have been seeing Willie Klein?"

Thirty-two pieces of carrots. Using the knife, I slid the orange slivers into a bowl to await the soup pot. Two carrots would give me sixty-four pieces. If I had five carrots, I'd have one hundred sixty. The numbers weren't working. I could feel the blood rushing to my head, my breath unsteady. "I am married to Willie Klein."

"You love him?"

Looking around the counters, I located the onions behind the salt dish. "I will grow to love him." I removed the thin layers of peel and put them in the waste bucket on the counter.

"I don't understand."

When I sliced the first onion in half, the fumes immediately rose, burning my eyes. But I refused to let even onions make me cry. I was done crying. There was no escaping what I had to say. Putting aside the half-chopped onions, I forced myself to look straight at *Tateh*, to stare him in the eyes, to speak boldly. "I am with child."

His eyes were fixed on me, but I could tell they weren't focused. His mouth was agape. For a moment I was afraid he was having a seizure.

I knelt in front of him and took his hands. "Did you hear me, *Tateh*?"

The silence frightened me. His gaze never left my face.

"*Tateh*?" I swallowed a sob. No more tears. "*Tateh*, please say something."

Finally his voice was whisper soft, but ice-cold. "You are *what*?"

I looked down at his hands. The moons of his nails were permanently blackened, dark hairs gracing his knuckles. Hands that had comforted me so many times over the years. Those hands had kept me safe. But they couldn't keep me safe any longer. "I am expecting a baby."

He shook his hands free from mine and stood up—to do what? To get away from me? To hug me? To slap me? He paced the small room, his hands at the side of his head, gripping himself as if he was afraid he would burst apart. His eyes darted about the room, refusing to land upon me. "With child?" He paced like a caged animal in that small space. "You are with child?" Finally he gazed right into my face and spit out the words, "You are *pregnant?*" The word sounded profane coming from his mouth.

"*Tateh,*" I said, panic rising. "It's not so bad." My voice sounded pleading.

"Not so bad?" he repeated, shaking his head. "You are head bookkeeper. You had a big raise. You and *Abe* had a future. Not that *shmendrik* Klein."

I sent up a quick prayer of thanks that he didn't know about Ma's plans for me to go to college. That I forfeited an education would have devastated him.

"You, with your fancy clothes and your uptown accent? You go to the theater—you have a high school diploma, an office job! You were going to do so many things." He put both his hands on the back of the chair and for a moment, I feared he would pick it up and throw it across the room. But instead he loosened his grip, one hand covering his face, and I realized he was crying. "Pregnant before husband? You were too good for that."

"*Tateh,*" I said, going over to put my hand on his shoulder, but he pushed it off.

"You are my little girl," he said, tears flowing down his face, and it terrified me. The only other time I had seen him cry was at Joey's death. "You *were* my little girl." Would he sit *shiva* for me? Was I going to be dead to *Tateh?*

He sank back into the chair and put his head in both his hands on the table.

"*Tateh,* I'm still your little girl." I could hear the despondency in my voice.

He shook his head. "What have you done?" He lifted his head so I could see his reddened eyes. "What have you done?"

I put my hands on his back, and this time he let them rest there. Emboldened, I reached around, hugging him from behind. "It's okay, *Tateh.* Willie is a good man. A smart man. He will take care of me. He will take care of the baby. This baby will want for nothing. *I* will want for nothing."

"Did you really want for so much? We gave you all we had." His tears slowed, but his voice was full of sorrow.

My chest shattered into a thousand shards at his words. "Of course not, *Tateh*. You gave me everything. I was never grateful enough. You gave me everything, and I was happy, *Tateh*." I squeezed him tighter and he put his arms around mine. Despite all my efforts, the tears were flowing from me. "I love you, *Tateh*. I'm sorry. I'm so sorry. But it's going to be okay. I promise." I buried my head in his shoulder, squeezing him as tightly as I could. He clutched my arms as if to a life preserver, and quietly we stayed like that.

After a good while, with a deep breath, *Tateh* regained his composure. He let go of my hug and stood, saying, "We better get this food made. The soup won't cook itself."

I nodded. With a deep breath, I moved back to the onions while *Tateh* sliced celery. We worked in silence, moving about the kitchen, preparing the beginnings of the evening meal.

As the soup was set to simmer, the front door banged open. *Tateh* and I exchanged glances; I'd have to tell the boys.

Wiping my hands on the apron, I called out, "Don't slam the door. Ma is resting."

Tateh nodded toward the living room while he cleaned up our mess in the kitchen. I knew what I had to do. Walking out to the front room, I passed Izzy as he went in the bedroom to check on Ma.

Alfie was splayed on the couch like a bum, but I could tell by the way he kept looking sideways from the corner of his eye toward the bedroom that he was worried. "How is Ma?"

"She will be fine," I said, sitting down. "I need to talk to you."

Eugene looked up, as if expecting more bad news. The boy had had so much grief in his short life. And here I was about to deliver more. I despised myself for what I was doing to my family.

Izzy came back out. "Ma's feeling better, though we should probably stay at *Tante* Kate's a little longer."

"No," I said. "She needs her family here."

Izzy said, "But the noise—"

"The noise will be fine," I said. "She needs her boys around her." I knew the silence of the apartment would make her crazy, make her think too hard about all that was done, about all that was missing. "Sit, Izzy. I have something to say."

With a quizzical look, Izzy squeezed onto the couch between Alfie and Eugene.

"I know this will come as a shock, and things certainly didn't turn out the way I expected, but last night, Willie Klein and I were married."

Izzy's eyes locked on mine, and with sadness I realized he wasn't surprised, that he'd heard the same rumors that Mrs. Klein had.

"Willie?" Alfie said. "But what about Abe?"

"Abe and I split up. I married Willie."

"Congrats, I guess," Izzy said.

I nodded crisply. "I need to finish getting the *Shabbes* dinner ready. If you'll excuse—"

"Will Willie move in here with us?" Eugene asked.

I didn't want to look at Eugene. I knew he had the power to make me fall apart. But how could I not look at my sweet baby boy? I regretted it the moment I did. His eyes were so trusting, I could barely get out my next words. "No, Willie will not be living here." I toyed with the gold band, which still felt alien on my finger, as if trying to make it fit better. "Willie has a job writing. In Europe."

I heard a knife clatter in the kitchen. Looking up, I saw *Tateh* standing in the kitchen doorway. "What did you say?" he asked.

Closing my eyes for strength, I said, "Willie has a job with *The New Yorker*. It's in Europe. He will be a foreign correspondent."

"Does he not understand what is happening in Europe?"

"He understands, *Tateh*. That's why he's going. To write about it. To make sure Americans know about it."

"So when he goes to Europe, you'll still live with us?" Eugene asked.

Tateh's hands balled into fists at his sides. Speaking slowly, as if daring me to disagree, he said, "What kind of a *mamzer* leaves his pregnant wife and travels to Europe?"

"Pregnant?" Alfie said, eyes wide.

"This is ridiculous," Izzy said.

Willing myself not to collapse, I enunciated carefully, trying to sound resolute. "I am going with him." Somehow I managed to keep my voice steady.

"What?" *Tateh*'s voice was thunderous. I could hear movement in the hallway and I knew Mrs. Kaplan was listening to our every word. "Absolutely not!"

"I am leaving for Paris two weeks from yesterday. My *husband* and I are moving to Europe."

"But what about me?" Eugene asked, on the edge between fury and sadness.

"Oh, Eugenie," I said, bending down to take his hands. "I need to be with my husband."

"But it's far, isn't it?"

"On the other side of the world," Alfie said, and I realized even my middle brother would miss me, and that I would grieve for him.

"No," *Tateh* said. "I will *not* allow it." His hands shook, and while I knew he would never strike me, I feared he would hurt himself.

A soft voice floated from the bedroom. "Beryl."

"Rose," *Tateh* hollered, "stay in bed."

"Beryl," Ma said again, as she appeared in the doorway, leaning on the frame, her face pale. "She must go. She must be with her husband."

"Rose Krasinsky, under no circumstances am I—"

"You are going to argue with me now?" She waved her hand weakly. Her housecoat was wrapped loosely around her, showing her long nightgown. I had never seen her in nightclothes during the day. Guilt flooded me anew. "Dottala has to leave."

"But—"

"Keep your voice down," Ma said, heading back to bed. "I need my rest."

"Can I c-come with you?" Eugene asked, his voice breaking midsentence.

I bent over to hug him. "Oh, sweetie," I said, but as I reached my arms out, he pulled away. He looked like he was going to say something, as if he was about to cry, but instead his face twisted into a fist of anger, and he stormed away, slamming open the door and running from the apartment down the stairs.

Rushing behind him, I yelled, "Eugene!" but an arm pulled me back into the apartment.

"I'll get him," said Alfie, running after his brother.

"What are you thinking?" *Tateh* asked. "Europe? Now?" His words had lost their anger and were tinged instead with despair. His hands lay flat against his sides, as if the emotion had simply drained from him.

"I don't have a choice."

"Of course you have a choice."

Embracing my stomach with both arms, I shook my head. "No. There is no choice."

Izzy came up behind me, placing a hand on my shoulder. It had been a long time since Izzy and I had touched, and it felt nice.

"You'll be okay," Izzy said. "I know it. You *have* to be okay."

I nodded and felt an emptiness when Izzy pulled away his hand.

"How in *Hashem's* name did this hap—," *Tateh* began, but I couldn't let him finish, couldn't answer the questions he wanted to ask.

"Let me finish cleaning. Then I need to pack. I have to get back to Willie."

Tateh looked at me, as if trying to comprehend a foreign language I was speaking. "Help me understand," he said.

How gray *Tateh* had become over the years, from the struggles and the heartaches. And now here I was, causing yet more sadness. I wanted to explain to him I hadn't meant to make this mess, but now I was taking responsibility for what I'd done. I wanted to promise him I would be an excellent mother and give him a houseful of grandchildren. I wanted him to know I would make this marriage work. The passion Willie had exhibited last night must mean *something*. He had to care about me at least a little. I wanted to tell *Tateh* that Europe wasn't all bad—I would see new places and not live in a crowded tenement anymore. That Willie was smart and he could be decent and he was doing the right thing by me. That I was exploding with joy at the thought of becoming a mother. That having a baby was one of the things I'd always wanted. That it was going to make me happy.

But I couldn't get out any of those words. So all I said was, "I'm not sure *I* understand," and I returned to mop the kitchen floor.

A couple of hours later, dinner was on the stove, and I packed my meager belongings in my old Camp Eden suitcase to return to the hotel. Would Willie still be there? He'd said he was going to his office—it was a workday—but I had no idea how Willie spent his time; a writer could theoretically be anywhere, with anyone. We hadn't made any plans and part of me feared he would disappear.

A knock sounded at the door. I assumed it was Perle, who had come over earlier to check on Ma and make the *challah* dough. She'd run home to prepare for *Shabbes*, but I knew she'd be back.

Opening the door distractedly, I was surprised to see Irene from the office. She stood uncomfortably in the dark hallway, grasping her pocketbook with two hands, as if afraid someone was going to run off with it.

"Oh, Irene," I said. "I meant to send a note." Of course, in all the madness, I had forgotten. My chest felt hollow when I realized I'd skipped out without a word.

"Mr. Dover sent me over. Said you didn't have a phone. Wanted to make sure you were all right." Shifting from foot to foot, Irene seemed ready to fend off attackers. The lower East Side was foreign territory.

"I'm all right," I said. With a meek smile that I hoped belied my misery, I held up my left hand. "I got married."

Irene nodded. "So you won't be coming back?"

"No," I said. "I won't be coming back." This didn't feel right, announcing my departure to Irene. "Wait. Let me get my hat. I'll go tell Mr. Dover myself."

"Don't bother. Florence told him you probably wouldn't be back." Irene reached into her purse and pulled out an envelope. "So he sent me with your pay for the half week, in case that was true."

I could feel the flush rising in my cheeks. I'd just confirmed all of Florence's suspicions.

"Thank you. Tell Mr. Dover—" *Tell him what?* I thought. *That this was the best job in the world? That I was so grateful he gave me the opportunity? That I am a terrible person for not living up to his expectations?* "Tell Mr. Dover I am sorry."

"Will do," Irene said, and, clearly relieved her dangerous mission was now at an end, she turned and bounded down the stairs.

Rose

———— ☥ ————

LAST week had been our final *Shabbes* together and I hadn't known it. I tried to recall it, but all I could remember was the bickering. If only we'd talked more, laughed more . . .

Now a pall set over the table, even with Heshie there. Dottie's absence filled the room in a way her presence never had. It felt like a house of mourners.

It was hard to sit up, but I came to the table to sample the meal Dottie had prepared. The soup was salty, the chicken dry, and the *kreplach* chewy. But it was passable. At least Dottie and Willie wouldn't starve.

No one was talking, until Heshie tried to lighten the mood. "Did you see that the Brown Bomber arrived in New York?" he asked Alfie. "Seems to be in good shape to fight Max Baer."

"Yeah," Alfie said, his eyes on his soup.

Eugene slouched next to him, using his spoon to play with his *kreplach*, bouncing them up and down in the broth.

"Get your elbows off the table," I said to him.

Instead of arguing, he simply slid them off.

"Eat," I said.

After twirling the spoon a few more times, Eugene brought it to his mouth and slurped the soup.

"Don't—," I started, but I halted myself. All eyes looked at me expectantly. Eugene's eyes didn't look as fearful as they did tired, as if all the family's worries made him weary. It was not a look a seven-year-old should have.

"Never mind," I said. My despair was worse than my pain. I couldn't help Yussel. I couldn't help Dottie. And now I was failing Eugene. Was I a failure as a woman?

Silence draped us. We all picked at the food, even Alfie, who usually couldn't shovel it in fast enough. Looking at Eugene, I worried what would become of the boy. His life was too full of gloom for someone so small.

"I think there is cake for dessert. Perle brought over one of her special *babkas,*" I said, hoping to bring a smile to someone's—anyone's—face. But no one budged.

"Not really that hungry tonight," Izzy said.

Eugene glanced up from his plate, and he looked around the table, staring each of us in our eyes, one after another. "Is that it?" he said. "Is that all? Isn't anyone going to *do* something?"

Heshie, closest to Eugene, patted him on the back. "There's nothing we can do."

"But Dottie is going to leave if we don't *do* something!" His voice tottered between baby and boy.

"Oh, *bubelah,*" I said. "Dottie is a wife now. She's going to be a mother. Her place is no longer with us."

Eugene threw his spoon across the table and shrieked, "Her place is with *me!*"

"Eugene!" Ben said sternly, but I shushed him.

"It's okay. Eugene is angry. We are all angry."

"Why did she do it?"

"She didn't mean to," I said. "Mistakes are sometimes made." I thought of my own youthful escapades, of Shmuel, and I realized, if I could go back in time, I wouldn't have done anything differently. Shmuel was my mistake. *This* was my family. My love for them was infinite. And Dottie would feel that way for her own child, her own family. "But sometimes mistakes can end happily. Eugene, you will be an uncle."

"I don't want to be an uncle! I want to be a brother." He jumped up from the table so fast his chair knocked over backward, and he ran to his room.

Dottie's words echoed in my mind: Eugene was my baby; it was time for me to care for him. I needed to go after him. I needed to cuddle him and hold him tight and make him know he was still a brother and, more important, he was still my son.

As I stood, my abdomen shot with pain. I leaned on the table to hold myself upright.

Ben leaped up to help me. Placing my arm around his shoulder, he helped me toward our bedroom.

"Eugene," I said.

"You need to lie down."

I nodded. "I will lie down. Eugene."

Ben shook his head, but he led me to the boys' room. Eugene lay on the bed sobbing.

Carefully, Ben helped me down. He stood there, until I shooed him out.

Lying on top of the bedding, I stroked Eugene's back. I wanted to pull him to me, but the pain was too great.

Eugene rolled toward me, but when he jostled the bed, I involuntarily moaned and he kept his distance. So instead of hugging him, I wrapped my arm around his neck, and he wrapped his about mine. We lay there, head touching head, just being. I stayed there until I heard his breathing steady and I knew he had fallen asleep. And then I stayed an hour more, stroking the head of my baby boy, before I allowed Ben to help me up and back into my own room.

Dottie

—⚜—

Saturday, August 31

ON my second morning as a married woman, I again woke well before Willie. The sun streaming in gave me a contented feeling, but when I glanced at my husband, my mood soured. *Where did he go last night?* I wondered. After a torturous dinner with his parents—a *Shabbes* with no blessings, no *challah*, no candles—I was left alone in our grand room at the Hotel Pierre, where I put on my silkiest nightie, and tried to lie seductively on the bed as I flipped through magazines and listened to *Hollywood Hotel* on the radio. I don't know when I fell asleep, and I don't know what time Willie woke me with his hands sliding up my gown, but his rough passion was enough to temporarily quell my doubts.

At dinner, Willie's manner had been polite, solicitous. His arm lay casually about my shoulders. He signaled for Fiona to offer me the serving plate first. When Mrs. Klein looked away, he rolled his eyes conspiratorially at me. A tiny thrill coursed through me when Willie spoke of "we." "I am sorry you disapprove, Mother," he said at one point, "but *we* have made our decision and that is final." I smiled and nodded agreement at everything Willie said to rebut his mother's endless complaints. The biggest benefit of leaving the country would be avoiding these horrific dinners with the Kleins, dinners we were apparently still expected to attend while in New York.

Yet, as dreadful as the evening was, Mrs. Klein did seem to be warming up to me ever so slightly. Before the dinner, Mrs. Klein pulled me aside. "You'll need a great deal to set up a house," she said. She peeked into the hall to make sure no one was listening. "I've left word at my stores—Bonwit Teller, Lord and Taylor, Macy's—that you may put things on my account." She gave me a crafty look. "But don't tell William or Mr. Klein. The accounts are sent straight to Mr. Klein's moneyman. Mr. Klein has no idea how much I spend." As chummy as we had been, though, it didn't stop her at the meal from voicing her displeasure—again—about our traveling abroad.

Despite our pretense of wedded bliss, the moment we walked out of his parents' apartment, he gave me a peck on the cheek, helped me into a cab, and was gone before I could even think to ask, "May I join you?"

The memory of our late-night passion, though, made his whereabouts less important. *He came home to me. That's a start. I just need to keep him coming home to me.*

Well, I couldn't stay in bed. I had *shpilkes*, ants in the pants. What was the point of lying in bed when all of New York was waiting for me? It would be one thing to laze about if Willie were awake to join me, to suggest ordering up room service and snuggling in bed, but given how late he'd come in, he would be asleep for a good many more hours.

Once more I found myself dressing alone. A day earlier Ma had reminded me of all the things I needed to do before my departure. Clothing purchased and altered. Basic kitchen supplies found. Towels, napkins, and other household linens. And with Ma still not feeling well, I needed to help with the boys. Not to mention that I still hadn't told Linda and Edith what I had done. Best that I headed down to my parents' apartment to begin the work at hand.

After making sure my hat was just so and my lipstick smoothly applied, I walked to the door. Something on the dresser, though, made me pause. Lying beside Willie's money clip and handkerchief was a blue-and-white zebra-striped matchbook. I'd recognize those stripes anywhere. I picked up the matches and turned it over in my fingers. The El Morocco. One of the swankiest clubs in town, where the rich and famous gathered. I'd always wanted to go there. Holding up the matchbook, I thought I smelled the faintest wisp of perfume. No, I told myself. Just the pregnancy playing tricks on my nose.

I set down the matchbook, glanced back at my husband, and left for what still felt like home.

CLIMBING down from the elevated, I surveyed the neighborhood I'd never thought I would miss. But seeing the families hastening to *shul*, the kids playing, the *goyishe* vendors hawking their wares, I was struck with nostalgia for a life I'd never thought I desired. Had I married Abe, this would have been my forever, and that had seemed just fine. Now, from my view as an outsider, it seemed even better. Compared with the cold formality of the Kleins' dining room, the scene in front of me exuded life and warmth. My reverie was broken when a ball rolled into my foot, and a ragamuffin, no more than seven, came running up to grab it, with a mumbled, *"Zay moykul."*

This was what was going to set me off? I batted away the unwelcome tears, suddenly struck with an urge to find my brothers. A peek at my wristwatch reminded me that they should be at *shul* for the late *minyan*. I turned south, hurrying the few blocks down to our large synagogue, which dominated the block.

Inside it was bright, with a large, ornamental chandelier in the center of the sanctuary and stained-glass windows allowing in the summer light. The wood pews gave the room a pleasantly musky scent, and I was sorry I hadn't come more often in recent years.

Climbing to the women's balcony, I was so busy looking down at the men's gallery to see if I could spy my brothers that at first I didn't notice the women sliding away from me and covering their gossiping mouths with their prayer books. It was only when I caught my name that I looked up. Disapproving stares followed my every move, and the women not-so-subtly skimmed their eyes down my body to peer at my belly. Several clicked their tongues.

I froze, unsure whether to give in to my humiliation and run from *shul* or stand my ground.

Before I could make a decision, I was saved by a firm hand on my elbow. "Dottala," the voice said in a loud whisper. "Your mother sent you to get me? Thank you for coming." And with that, Perle led me from *shul* as she shot a ferocious glance at the women who were still blathering.

On the street, I turned to Perle and asked, "How do they all know?"

Leading me back toward my parents' home, Perle said, "How could they not know? That Molly Klein called around to check up on you. Mrs. Kaplan heard quite a bit through the apartment walls. Abe's mother talks."

How could I have been so naive as to think I'd escape undetected? Of course people knew.

As Perle led me home, every eye seemed to stare at me; every whisper sounded like tale-telling. The neighborhood, which a half hour before had felt like home, was now enemy territory.

Without thinking, I began to walk up the avenue toward Tenth Street, but Perle turned me onto Seventh so we would have to walk up First Avenue.

"This is the long way," I said.

"Best we not go up Avenue A." Perle's voice was gentle.

Only for a moment was I befuddled. On Avenue A, close to Tenth Street, was the Rabinowitzes' home and market, where Mrs. Rabinowitz often sat outside on a *Shabbes*, gossiping with passing neighbors.

Swallowing hard, I said, "Of course."

With a knowing smile, Perle patted my arm. "This too shall pass."

The tightness of my waistband and the heaviness of my bosom, though, belied the sentiment. Some things, I realized, never passed.

Rose

⚓

Saturday, August 31

EARLY that morning, I remembered twelve more things that needed to be done. From my bed, I called out, "Bring me my list and a pen. Dottie left them in the front room."

For once, Alfie jumped. "I got it, Ma!" I cringed hearing him stomp around the front room, looking for them.

"Look on the credenza," I said.

Last night I had tackled the chore that rankled me the most: I wrote to Molly Klein. As much as it churned my stomach, she was now my daughter's mother-in-law, and basic courtesy required we invite her family for *Shabbes*. This marriage might not have been made under ideal circumstances, but manners were manners, and I would do what was right. Certainly that Molly Klein would never think of it herself.

"Got it!" Alfie burst like a firecracker into my room.

"Thank you," I said, reaching for the pad and pencil, but when I went to pull them toward me, he held fast.

"I can write down what you need. I can help you, Ma." His eyes were wild, and I realized for the first time how terrified he was seeing me as an invalid. And why wouldn't he be? He was young when he lost his brother, but a memory like that can't be erased by time.

Taking Alfie by the wrist, I stared steadily into his eyes. "I am going to be fine, *bubelah*."

"But how can you be sure?" The sadness in his voice cracked open my own heartache.

With every ounce of energy I had, I brought the strength back to my voice as I said, "Because I have to prepare your sister's trousseau. Because I have to make sure you and Eugene have clothes for school next month. Because your father needs someone to cook and clean for him. I'm needed too much to go anywhere." I granted the boy a rare smile. "Now give me the paper. I have lists to make."

Reluctantly he handed over the paper. But before he could leave, he threw his arms around my neck and planted a kiss on my shoulder, something he hadn't done since he was still in short pants. "Swear to me, Ma. Swear you'll be okay."

My children wouldn't stop breaking my heart. Trying to sound firm and healthy and like my normal self, I said, "No swearing. It's *goyishe*."

He pulled back and looked at me, his eyebrows creased over his nose in concern. "Please, Ma." His nose was running.

Swallowing the lump in my throat, I nodded. "I swear." He leaned back in to give me another kiss, and I whispered again in his ear, "I swear."

Dottie

Sunday, September 1

SUNDAY morning I woke with a mission: to make up with Eugene and Alfie. Saturday they'd left before I arrived, and didn't come home till after I'd gone, even though I dawdled at the apartment until the last possible second, hoping to catch them. The whole day was spent tending to Ma and running errands. But now, I needed my boys. I couldn't bear my brothers' anger.

Down on the lower East Side, I searched the stoops and lots till I found them in a stickball game in an alley. Eugene was coming up to bat. He swung at the first ball, cleanly missing it, to the jeers of his friends.

"You're holding the stick too high up," I called to him.

He looked over at me with a glare.

"Hold on," I said, coming to stand next to him. "Here, you hold it like this."

"I got it," he said, twisting away from me.

"Don't be dippy," I said, getting behind him. I placed my hands over his and slid them farther down. "Go ahead," I yelled to the pitcher.

"You can't have two players," the pitcher yelled. "And what kind of baby needs his sister to play for him?"

I squinted into the sun. "Saul, is that you? Aw, you've gotten so big since I was changing your diapers." I grinned maliciously and Eugene giggled.

"Aw, jeez," Saul said, and he tossed the ball. I swung with Eugene. The ball went sailing.

"How did you do that?" Eugene asked.

"Go on, silly. Run. I can't do it for you." He dropped the stick and ran.

I stood to the side and watched the rest of the game. Alfie's movements on the asphalt field, his leaps and turns, were almost balletic. Eugene still played awkwardly, but his throwing skills were improving. Someday he would own that game and it made me tear up, knowing I wouldn't be there to see it. I dabbed my eyes discreetly. I didn't want anyone to see me cry.

When the game ended, the boys dragged their feet coming out of the alley. My brothers were torn—wanting to see me, yet still upset with me.

"C'mon," I said. "I'm buying you ice cream."

"Ice cream?" Eugene said. "It's only ten thirty in the morning."

"So don't tell Ma, you dope," Alfie said, running ahead to the parlor. Eugene didn't need to be told again, and he took off in a sprint.

By the time I caught up to them at the store, they had already chosen their flavors. I bought them each a scoop and followed them to a table.

Alfie shoveled his ice cream into his mouth, taking huge spoonfuls. Eugene was more meticulous, taking small, careful bites to make it last.

I brushed a hair from Alfie's face, and he moved to object, then changed his mind. It must have taken all his courage to ask, "Why are you going, Dottie?"

I shrugged at him. "I don't have a choice."

"Why don't you have a choice?" Eugene asked.

"Because I'm married. Where my husband goes, I need to go. And he's going to Europe."

"And there's a baby? Inside you now?" Eugene asked.

I wished he didn't know that. I nodded.

"How did it get there?"

Alfie and I exchanged looks. "Uh . . . ," I began.

"I'll tell ya later," Alfie said.

I raised my eyebrows at him. "You know?"

His turn to shrug. "I've heard."

Not trusting whatever Alfie had heard on the street, I said, "Maybe you should both ask Izzy."

"I'm still angry at you," Alfie said.

"I'm still angry at me," I said.

He nodded. The two finished their ice cream quietly. They were clearly still angry with me. But they were speaking to me. And I'd take that as a start.

THE rest of the day I listened to Ma's instructions about where to shop and what to buy. She wanted to come with me, insisting she was feeling well enough to be up and about, but I kept pushing her down and telling her to rest more. In the evening there was another torturous dinner at the Kleins'. Willie and I couldn't make our exit fast enough.

When we left his parents' apartment, the air held the slight coolness that hinted at autumn. I always looked forward to it—the changing colors, the promise of Rosh Hashanah, the excitement of a new season of clothes. What would fall be like in Paris?

"I still haven't told Linda and Edith about our marriage," I said. "I should have stopped by yesterday, but there's so much to be done." It was an excuse. I was terrified at what they'd think.

"So do it tonight. What do you say we make our grand appearance?" Willie asked, taking me by the arm.

"What do you mean?" I asked.

"Let's hit the café on Second Avenue."

I leveled my gaze at him. What was he up to? "Do you think it's the best idea?"

"Why not?" He grinned, and I realized I was his prize to flaunt.

He had his girls. He had me. Willie Klein was having his cake and eating it, too, and he wanted the whole world to know it.

The idea chilled me. I wasn't ready to face Edith and Linda, and on a Sunday night they would surely be there. Wasn't tonight the night they were going to the Jean Harlow pic? It was a year ago that Edith had suggested going to the pictures, but really, it had been only last week. We always went to the café after a movie. And what about Abe? Would Abe be at the café?

But Willie whisked me off in a cab, deaf to my protests, and we barreled down to the lower East Side. This was crazy. Downright insane.

A half hour later, we stood at the entrance. Inside was the normal busyness of a Sunday evening. Outside, the temperature seemed to have dropped by twenty degrees. I shivered.

"You'll be fine," Willie said, and I wondered when he'd stop testing me.

We opened the door and stepped in. As eyes darted to see who'd entered, a silence enveloped the room. Clearly our news had preceded us.

Willie seemed a little nervous as he looked around the room, perhaps wondering if he'd grossly miscalculated.

I caught Edith's wide eyes; then she deliberately looked across the room. I followed her gaze.

Abe. And next to him: Sadie Kraus.

My breath caught in my throat. Willie saw me staring and looked in the same direction. When he saw Abe, a malicious smile stretched across his face. He threw his arm around my shoulder and led me in another step. Addressing the room, he said, "Isn't anyone going to offer the newlywed couple a beer?"

Abe stood abruptly, the table tottering as his friends grabbed hold of it. Raising his arm, he smashed his beer glass to the ground.

"Let's go, Sadie," he said, grabbing her arm roughly. He stormed toward us—or, rather, toward the door. Sadie looked at me from beneath her eyelashes, a look of victory, and she gave me a half

grin as she tried to keep up with Abe, stumbling in her fancy
heeled shoes. Willie and I were blocking the way, and as I scrambled to move, Abe and I locked eyes, and I knew his expression
would haunt me for decades to come. I wanted to reach out to
him, to stroke his cheek, to ease his heart. My hand stretched out
of its own accord, but I pulled it back. There was no point. Abe
pushed between us. My last view of him was his hunched, angry
shoulders. Sadie turned around for one last look, eyebrows raised
triumphantly as the door closed behind them. Abe was gone.

Willie pulled me from the doorway into the room.

"Well, Will," one of his friends called from across the room,
"you always did know how to make an entrance."

With that, the spell was broken and the room buzzed. A count-
erman cleaned Abe's mess. Willie laughed and headed over to his
friends. I was shattered, despondent. *Abe.* I wanted to run after
him, to hold him, to comfort him. But I was Mrs. William Klein,
so I swallowed my misery and made my way to Linda and Edith.

The two girls stared at me as I sat down.

"What in good God's name have you done?" Edith said, a hiss
to her voice.

"Now, now," Linda said, always the peacemaker.

"No, I'm not going to *now, now.* Is it true? You're married?
And"—Edith spit out the word—*"pregnant?"*

The tears came unbidden. I didn't even care who saw them,
not that anyone was paying attention to me; Willie commanded
the room.

Edith's voice rose dangerously. "How could you do that to
Abe?" Linda put a hand on Edith's to signal her to quiet.

I took slow, deep breaths to avoid heaving sobs. Linda pulled
a handkerchief from her purse and handed it to me.

Edith said, "How could you do that to *us?"*

For a minute, I gave in to the tears, Linda rubbing my arm,
Edith wild-eyed and angry. But they waited for me to cry it out.

Finally, when I was composed enough to speak, I said, "It was an accident. I didn't mean to do it to Abe. I didn't mean to do it to myself." I dabbed my eyes, afraid they'd start welling again. "Look at me. Look at the mess I've made of my life. Saddled with that . . . that . . ." I looked across the room at Willie drinking a beer, the life of the party. I dropped my voice to a whisper. "That buffoon."

With a snort, Edith said, "You made your bed. And clearly you've already lain in it."

"Edie," Linda said. Anger tinged her voice. "Dottie is our friend. Show her sympathy."

"Sympathy?" Edith wiped the corner of her eye, and I realized she was close to crying. Edith crying? What had I done? "What about sympathy for us? Why didn't you tell us? We could have helped you. We *would* have helped you."

"How?" I asked. "You would have taken me in with the baby? Helped me diaper it and walk it in the carriage?" I shook my head. "This was the only way it could have happened. You know that. If I had a baby on my own, I would be shunned for the rest of my life. Now at least I'm an honest woman."

Linda took my hand in her own. I looked gratefully at her. "I'm so sorry, Dottie," she said. "I understand. You did what you had to do." With a glare at Edith, she said, "Happy endings are only in fairy tales."

Around us, the room roared along as usual, with squealing and chitchat and flirting. But Linda and I were two unhappy women, lost in our thoughts of Abe and of Ralph. Of happiness and of necessity.

Finally, Edith said, "Are you really going with him? Are you really leaving us for Europe?" Her voice was quiet now, but full of anguish.

"I am," I said.

We sat another minute.

"Well," Edith said, "let me at least buy you a beer."

Rose

⚥

Monday, September 2

THE invitation arrived in the afternoon mail, the same heavy cream card stock and the same engraved return address on the back flap. But instead of being addressed to Dottie, this card came to me.

I gently opened the flap and ran my finger over the lining. Never had I touched such rich paper. Such luxury put one in more pleasant spirits.

Pulling out the note, however, erased my good cheer. "The nerve of that woman," I said.

Hovering anxiously at my shoulder was Dottie. She was making me a little crazy the way she didn't want me to do anything. But I was fine. A couple days of rest and now it was back to work. And so much work there was, preparing for Dottie's departure. But this, I knew, wasn't about my overdoing it; she recognized the envelope.

"What? What did she say?" Dottie asked.

Disgusted, I tossed down the note. "She invited us to dinner. Tomorrow. Not even for *Shabbes.*"

Dottie fell with a *plop* on the couch, and for a moment I thought she fainted, but quickly realized she was only being melodramatic.

"She wants . . . us? All of us? To dinner?"

"Isn't that what I said?"

"Do you think . . ." Dottie paused, carefully weighing her words.

"Do you think you should be going all the way uptown? You're not yet fully recovered."

So worried about her mama. *Feh.* That girl was worried about how we would look, how we would act in Molly Klein's fancy-shmancy uptown apartment.

"I can't sit on a streetcar? Lift a fork to my mouth? I'm recovered enough for a dinner uptown."

I continued my stitching. I had much to do if Dottie was going to have a proper trousseau to take with her to the Continent.

Dottie picked up the letter and scanned it for herself. "Why did you accuse her of *chutzpah?*"

My fingers ached slightly, but my stitches were as delicate as ever. Something in which I could still take pride. "I invited the Kleins here."

"You did *what?*" Dottie leaped up and paced the small room.

"She's too good to come to us?" I finished the corner of the linen I was working on, tore the thread off with my teeth, and then switched to the next side. "Remember, Molly is Perle's sister-in-law. I knew that family well. Too good for our home? *Chutzpah.*"

"I still don't see why you had to invite her here!"

Dottie glanced around, and I knew she was trying to picture the Kleins here. That Dottie, she could be a prideful one. Our home was lovely; she didn't appreciate it.

"You're making me dizzy with this back-and-forth. Sit."

Dottie sat in the chair next to mine. "Why did you invite her?"

I set my sewing in my lap and cupped her chin in my hand, forcing Dottie's gaze to my own. "Because meeting with your daughter's in-laws is the proper thing to do. That Molly Klein would never have done the right thing on her own, and while I don't relish an evening with her, it's what's required. They are our *machatunim* now, and we need to have them over." As I released Dottie, my eyes grazed the note that was still in her hand. "Ridiculous!"

"Of course," Dottie agreed. "It's insulting! We should not go. That will teach them."

I arched an eyebrow. "What, I was born yesterday?"

She had the common decency to appear chagrined.

"We will go," I said. "Of that you can be sure."

THE next afternoon, while Dottie awkwardly sewed linens, I dispatched Alfie to the garage to remind Ben to come home early to clean up.

"I need to run an errand," I said, putting my work aside and standing. My body felt stiff and my abdomen ached, but it was nothing I couldn't handle.

"Absolutely not," Dottie said. "I'll do whatever you need me to do. Don't go rushing off."

"Who's rushing?" I said.

"I'll go," she said, getting up.

"No. I'm just going to Perle's. I'll be fine."

"If you need Perle, I'll get her and bring her back here." Dottie's eyes scanned my body as if she was waiting for it to fall apart. Her concern was sweet. And annoying.

"I am going to Perle's." Looking at the cloth in her hand, I sighed. "Rip out those stitches. They are too wide. They'll never last."

Despite her protests, I made it out of the apartment and over to Perle's. Not that I would ever admit it to Dottie, but I was nervous about dinner at the Kleins'. What would I wear? What would we talk about?

"Don't you worry about that old biddy," Perle said to me when I arrived and after she admonished me about making the journey. But sitting in my apartment made me cranky, and the fresh air did more for me than all that bed rest. "My sister-in-law has a fear of her Old World roots being exposed. Remember her father was a horse trader back home. The lowest of the low." Perle laughed maliciously. "If it weren't for Ira, Molly would still be living in the mud. Now, let's see to your outfit."

Perle went through her closet, looking for something elegant.

As a representative for the Workers' Alliance, she sometimes had occasion to dress well. She found a deep green suit that, while a smidgen short and a tad snug in the bosom, did the job nicely.

"You look high society," Perle said.

"What happens when I open my mouth? What if I embarrass us?"

"That woman should be trying to impress *you*. Don't you worry about what she thinks. She needs to show you that she's worthy of the Krasinsky family."

I nodded and studied myself again in the mirror, bending this way and that to try to see myself in my entirety. I looked good. Uptown. For the first time, I could *almost* understand Dottie's concern with clothes. There was something nice about feeling so elegant. Perhaps I should sew myself some new clothes. Through my sadness for Dottie and the baby, one thought had been furtively lurking: I was free to resume my work. As soon as Dottie's trousseau was prepared, I would purchase some cloth for myself. I'd have new things to wear when I met with officials for the Women's Conference. To wear when I worked for the union again. Because I had decided. It was time. I would return to the union. It needed me.

"You look nice." Perle put her hands on my shoulders. "You will do fine at the Kleins'. The only thing you need to remember is to use the silverware from the outside in."

"What on earth are you talking about?" I asked.

Perle laughed. "You'll see. She'll have enough silverware for four meals at that one dinner. From the outside, in."

I glanced again at myself, pleased. "From the outside in."

Dottie

AS we entered the building, I kept a sharp eye on Ma, trying to gauge her reaction. But she showed no emotion as I gave our names to the doorman, entered the elevator, and walked down the endless hallway to the apartment. Ma looked sharp in a green suit I'd never seen before. When I asked where it came from, she just gave me a sly smile. But I was pleased she was trying. I was also relieved that Ma had suggested the boys stay at home—the *boom boom boom* of the Allied planes would not go over well at the Kleins'—but as much as I tried to suppress it, I was self-conscious about the smell of oil and gas that hovered about *Tateh*. He had scrubbed himself in the tub—an unheard-of luxury for a Tuesday evening—but the smell would never completely disappear, and his hands advertised the inky black of his profession.

When the maid opened the door, Ma nodded at her, as if she were accustomed to servants, and held her head haughtily as she walked in. If I hadn't known better, I would never have guessed that four days ago she was bedridden. *Tateh* handed his hat to the maid, who disappeared with it into another room.

"Ah, Rose, Ben. So good of you to join us," Mrs. Klein said in English as she walked into the foyer to greet us in a beautiful dress of pale peach chiffon. Her words were welcoming, but her bearing was stiff. She shook Ma's hand and then barely grasped

Tateh's, no doubt concerned the dirt of the garage would soil her. At that moment, I despised her. But I willed myself to smile.

"Dottie," Mrs. Klein said, leaning in to kiss my cheek. The gesture was almost warm, almost convincing.

"Mrs. Klein," I said.

"Ours is the pleasure, Molly," Ma said awkwardly in English. "Where is Ira?"

"He'll be joining us shortly," Mrs. Klein said. "Delayed by business."

Under his breath, *Tateh* muttered in Yiddish, "But *I* had to leave the garage early?"

"*Shah,*" Ma whispered back.

"Why don't we step into the parlor? Willie will fix us cocktails."

Mrs. Klein led the way as *Tateh* barely contained his laughter. "'Cocktails,'" he whispered. "La-di-da."

Ma was trying not to giggle. "Behave yourself, Ben."

"Of course, my dear," *Tateh* said, placing his arm about Ma's waist.

"Ma! *Tateh!*" I said. "Please."

Ma gave me a wink as we followed Mrs. Klein. I was alarmed that Ma was not taking the evening seriously.

The parlor was every bit as intimidating as I remembered, but this time, I noticed the flaws: the crack in the wood by the fireplace, the way the fabric on the backs of the chairs didn't match the fabric on the fronts, the uncracked spines of books that were clearly meant only for show. Was it possible that imperfections made it even more perfect? It was so . . . high society.

"How do you do, Mr. and Mrs. Krasinsky?" Willie said, standing to greet us. He came over to shake *Tateh*'s hand. I noticed Willie wince as *Tateh* grasped a touch too firmly. I longed to scold *Tateh*, but didn't dare.

"We are family now," Ma said to Willie. "We are Rose and Ben."

"Rose, then," Willie said, kissing his new mother-in-law's hand.

"Darling," Willie said to me, kissing me gently on the cheek. Then he whispered into my ear, "If I keep the cocktails extra strong, we should be able to get through this."

I forced a giggle that I hoped sounded conspiratorial. I looked toward Mrs. Klein, waiting for her to ask me to call her Molly. Nothing. To nudge her, I asked, "Mrs. Klein, shall Willie make you one of his famous drinks?" but Mrs. Klein merely replied, "That would be fine, dear."

"What can I make you, Rose? Ben? A Ward Eight? A champagne cocktail?"

"A Manhattan is nice." Ma's accent was thick but understandable. Where did Ma learn about Manhattans?

Willie splashed liquids from various bottles into a glass and, using a long silver spoon, stirred, making the ice clink. As he poured a second for *Tateh*, Mr. Klein came into the room.

"Good to see you," he said, shaking hands with my parents.

Willie handed out drinks, and *Tateh* took a hearty gulp of his. I tried to mentally convey to him to drink more slowly.

"Please, have a seat," Mrs. Klein invited, gesturing around the room.

Ma and *Tateh* sat on the couch. As *Tateh* leaned back, he sank into the plush cushions, tipping his drink. My eyes widened, but Ma saw, too, and she shifted her body so as to cover the damp spot. *Tateh* inched his way to a more dignified position.

The six of us remained in uncomfortable silence, and I frantically tried to think of a safe topic of conversation. Mr. Klein jumped in first, though. "So, Ben, what do you think of this cockamamy idea of moving to Europe?"

This was *not* a safe topic. Luckily, *Tateh* said, "I confess it distresses me greatly, but I'm sure they will manage just fine." Bless *Tateh*. If I could have given him a big kiss on the spot, I would have.

"Manage? Our grandchild is going to be born in a *shtetl*!" Mr. Klein said.

"Don't be ridiculous, Father," Willie said. "We will be in real cities. Paris. Rome."

"It will be a grand adventure," I said.

"Of course it will," *Tateh* said. "As long as you're sensible. Things aren't looking good in Europe. Promise to get out before things escalate."

"But that's when it's going to get interesting," Willie said, causing a knot to form in my stomach. There was going to be no talking Willie out of this ridiculous idea.

"Returning to Europe is a step backward," Mrs. Klein said. "Next thing you know, you'll be working as a storekeeper, as my father did in the Old Country."

Ma registered surprise. "A horse dealer, your father was."

Mrs. Klein's entire face flushed a blood red. "Nonsense. He was a storekeeper." Mrs. Klein's hands tapped the base of her glass in irritation.

I caught Ma's eye and saw she was biting back laughter. I confess I was rather pleased to see Mrs. Klein brought down a peg. Park Avenue's Mrs. Klein the daughter of a horse dealer? Now who was too big for her britches?

The maid entered the room. In her Irish brogue, she announced, "Dinner is ready, ma'am." I leaped to my feet, relieved to move the evening along.

As Mrs. Klein guided us into the dining room, I sent up a silent prayer that nothing *treif* would be served. Ma was doing well, but fireworks would erupt if crab salad emerged from the kitchen.

The grandeur of the setting—of the large mahogany table, the high-backed chairs, the silver gracing the center of the lace tablecloth—gave me a shot of pleasure. As fancy as our previous dinners had been, Mrs. Klein had pulled out all the stops tonight. The dining table was set for royalty. If I was going to be forced to live this life, I might as well revel in the beauty of it. I fought an urge to pick up a plate and check the underside to see if it was Wedgwood.

When the maid served us each salad, Ma reached for the fork to the far left. Both *Tateh* and I watched and mimicked her movements. In all situations Ma moved with an assurance I envied. Yet Ma's fork hovered over the plate. I looked down. The leaves of lettuce were drenched in a creamy sauce, not much different from mayonnaise. Dreadful.

Speaking in Yiddish, Ma said, "When you return from the Continent, we shall have to throw a proper party to introduce you as a couple."

Silence washed across the table. The Kleins looked as put out as if someone had passed gas. Was Yiddish such a crime?

"I apologize, Rose," Willie said. His stiff bearing showed his distaste for the Old World language. "I never learned to speak Jewish."

"No," *Tateh* said. "How can that be?"

Mrs. Klein's smile stopped short of her cheeks. "We speak English in this house. Always."

I hadn't noticed before how tight Mrs. Klein's skin was, like a canvas stretched across a frame. I wondered what creams she used.

"But your grandparents?" *Tateh* said to Willie. I knew *Tateh* would be doing most of the speaking that evening, with his perfect English. "How do you converse with them?"

"You know my parents passed years ago," Mrs. Klein said.

"But Ira's parents?"

"Oh, we don't see much of them." Mrs. Klein spoke breezily. "They live in Brooklyn. A nuisance to get out there."

"And they don't relish the journey to civilization," Mr. Klein said. He cleaned his salad plate, leaving a *schmear* of dressing on his mouth.

My shock was as great as Ma and *Tateh*'s, but to my relief, they didn't say anything. But it did make me wonder: Did Mr. and Mrs. Klein expect me to leave my own parents behind? To live a life like theirs and toss my parents aside like a bundle of rags?

Ma repeated, in English, her offer of a party, as the maid came to clear away the salad plates.

"I'm not sure how practical that will be," Mrs. Klein said. "After all, Dottie will be far along by the time they return."

"Far along?" Willie said. "Don't be ridiculous. By the time we return, we will have our son."

"Or daughter," I said, my stomach rolling at the thought of being away from my family for so long.

Willie gave me a humoring grin. "Of course. But it will be a son."

"For how long do you intend to be on the Continent?" Mr. Klein asked.

"For as long as it takes to expose the Nazi threat and to make my name as a writer."

"Say your good-byes now, dear," Mr. Klein said to his wife. "It seems our son will never return."

A wave of embarrassment for my husband washed over me, and I rose to his defense. "Willie is an excellent writer. Have you not read his work? I wager he'll succeed in time for us to be home before the baby's *bris*."

For the first time since the wedding, Willie gave me a truly appreciative look, a look that bespoke a kindness—or was it thankfulness?—that I hadn't seen from him before. For a moment, I was grateful for this dinner, which had given us an opportunity to be something new: allies.

"Who has time to read?" Mr. Klein said.

"Well, you should," *Tateh* said. "That book review Willie wrote in last week's *New Yorker* was impressive."

"You read it?" Willie asked, sounding pleased.

The maid returned carrying plates filled with something that resembled chicken.

"I'm curious," *Tateh* said to the table at large. "If Willie is going to 'expose the Nazi threat,' how will he do so without speaking Yiddish?"

"Willie speaks perfect French and Spanish and highly passable

Italian. Why on earth does he need to know Yiddish?" Mrs. Klein said, delicately cutting her chicken into tiny nibbles.

Willie shoveled large bites into his mouth and spoke without swallowing. "We're starting in Paris. The relief organizations there operate in French and English. If we move to Spain, my Spanish is excellent and I can even make out Portuguese."

"But the French and Spanish Jews aren't the refugees."

"Diplomats speak French. And Spanish. And English."

"But won't you gain more from speaking to the refugees escaping the German Reich? Those refugees are coming out of Eastern Europe and Germany. I can't imagine they'll be speaking even imperfect French, Italian, or Spanish," *Tateh* said.

Willie paused midbite, considering. Self-consciously, he chewed and swallowed what was in his mouth, preparing to speak, but I smiled broadly for the room and placed my hand on Willie's forearm. "Willie's thought of that, of course. One of the reasons he asked me to join him in Europe is because I'll be able to assist him. He will speak to politicians and dignitaries in the Western languages. I will speak to the refugees from Eastern Europe in Yiddish. I will translate for him."

Ma shot me a look and raised an eyebrow.

Willie turned to me and gave me a thoughtful appraisal. "Yes," he said. "That's exactly what I had thought." I could feel his eyes lingering on me, and it was pleasant.

Changing the subject, Mrs. Klein said, "Dottie, remind me before you leave tonight, I picked up some darling baby clothes at Lord and Taylor."

"Baby clothes?" Ma exclaimed at the same time that I said, "Lord and Taylor!"

"No baby clothes," Ma said in her halting English. "The bad luck."

"Oh, pish," Mrs. Klein said. "That's an old wives' tale."

"Why invite the evil eye?" Ma said.

"I thought you were freethinkers," Mr. Klein said. His voice was slightly teasing, but not in a kind way.

"Ma, it'll be fine. I'm going to need things for the baby. Might as well bring them with me." But even as I spoke, the fear in my chest solidified. No one bought baby things before the birth. Ma was right. It simply wasn't done. But what could I do?

Mrs. Klein rewarded me with a nod. "Practical thinking, my girl."

Silence returned. The sound of forks tapping against plates was deafening.

Tateh broached a new topic. "Ground has been broken on the new East River Drive."

"A huge project," Ma said, delicately moving pieces of food around her plate. I wondered if the meat was *kashered* properly. I was pretty sure Ma was wondering the same thing. Eventually, she ate a string bean.

"The WPA is funding part of the road," *Tateh* said. "Creating quite a few jobs, which will hopefully make a dent in the unemployment situation."

"Oh, that's nice," Mrs. Klein said.

"Nice?" Mr. Klein said with his mouth full of food. "More government money being spent on pointless projects?"

"Pointless projects?" *Tateh* said. "This is a much needed road and it's providing much needed relief."

"That's what that Commie in the White House would have you think—," Mr. Klein started before Mrs. Klein cut him off.

"Oh, let's not bother ourselves with politics," Mrs. Klein said. "It will give you indigestion."

I saw Ma angling for a battle, but *Tateh* placed a calming hand on her arm. Ma grimaced and returned to her plate.

"There are so many more interesting things than politics," I said, wanting to move to safer ground.

"I can't imagine what," Ma said.

"I couldn't agree with you more, Rose," Mr. Klein said. "Molly's head is so far into the society page, she wouldn't know a Nazi if he bit her on the behind. If I don't grab the paper before Molly, she'll have the maid using it to clean the kitchen floors."

"I glance at the front page, I'll thank you very much." Mrs. Klein looked at me. "Did you see that darling article about Bing Crosby's secretaries?"

"I must have missed that," I said.

"Anyway, that New Deal is what I would call a raw deal," Mr. Klein said, stabbing another piece of meat on his plate. "Handing out jobs as if they were penny candies. It's Communism, I say."

Willie and I exchanged panicked glances. We were trapped in the middle of a Noël Coward play. And not one of his more amusing ones.

"Communism?" Ma said. "What do you know of—"

"Seems to me we're about ready to retire for coffee," Willie interrupted. "Don't you think, Mother?"

Not a single one of us had finished our meal, and yet no one protested.

"Of course, dear," Mrs. Klein said. Picking up a small bell, Mrs. Klein rang for the maid. When the girl came to the door, Mrs. Klein said, "Fiona, bring coffee and dessert to the parlor, please." Turning back to the seated group, she said, "Shall we?"

Tateh looked longingly at his half-eaten supper, but Ma pulled him along. We would get through this evening, but it would be helpful if it ended sooner rather than later.

At coffee, Willie and I kept the topic on neutral subjects: the new Fred Astaire–Ginger Rogers picture, *Top Hat*; the hurricane that was approaching Florida; the races at Saratoga Springs. We were a vaudeville act, trying to speak quickly enough not to allow anyone else a word in edgewise.

"Well," Mrs. Klein finally said at the end of the evening, "who knew you had so much to say, Dottie?"

While I was abashed at monopolizing the conversation, I was sure it had been the safest way to manage the evening.

"It simply means she'll be a fine hostess when we entertain abroad." Willie put his arm around my shoulder.

"It's getting late," Ma said. "We should be leaving."

"Yes, I agree," I said. "Willie, shall we retire to the hotel?"

Willie looked down at his sleeves and straightened his cuffs. "I arranged to meet a few folks before I leave town. Writing colleagues. I will meet you later at the hotel."

"I can come with you," I said, standing to go.

"Aw, you'd be bored. I'll see you later."

Willie refused to look at me, and I understood that while this night had not gone badly, that we'd proved ourselves able to work together, we were not yet a twosome.

Ma, *Tateh*, and the Kleins were tactful enough to pretend they weren't listening. I was mortified that they were witness to my humiliation.

"Yes, all right."

Willie finally looked at me. "Don't be cross. I won't be out late."

"No, of course." I gave him a kiss on the cheek, the ever-submissive wife. "I'll see my parents out and meet you later."

After a round of polite good-byes, the three of us were on the street. Ma sighed and unbuttoned the top of her skirt. "We survived. I didn't think I would be able to breathe if we stayed there much longer." She sounded much more at ease speaking again in Yiddish. "Is Perle really that much smaller than me?" she said, revealing the secret of her new outfit.

"You are a perfect size," *Tateh* said, giving Ma a squeeze.

I looked at them with envy. Could I create that easy way with Willie? Would I be able to make this marriage work?

"Shall we take a streetcar or the subway from here?" *Tateh* asked.

Ma said, "You go ahead. I'd like to walk with Dottie a bit."

"Are you well enough to walk?" *Tateh* asked.

"Do I look unwell? Of course I am fine to walk."

"I will come with you," he said.

"No. A mother needs time with her daughter."

"Ah, of course." *Tateh* gave Ma a wink, and he scurried off to catch the subway.

Ma took my arm as we walked.

"I'll be all right, you know," I said.

"Of course you'll be all right. Who said anything about you not being all right?"

We walked silently for a block, and I was grateful for Ma's presence, grateful I could lean on her. How would I make it on the other side of the ocean?

Half a block more and Ma started, hesitatingly. "Do you— Is there anything—"

"What?"

"Is there anything still for you to know?"

I laughed. "A little late for that, don't you think?"

Ma chuckled. "Yes. But anything else?"

"I think I know what I need to know, Ma."

A window of hats beckoned my attention. I steered Ma to peer into the darkened store.

"Now, even I can tell that's a fetching little hat," Ma said, gazing at a velvety brown one with deep curves and delicate netting.

"Look at you noticing fashion," I said.

Ma turned to me. "You don't have to go, you know. You can stay with me and *Tateh*. Raise the baby with us. You don't have to go to Europe. You don't have to be with . . . him."

"If I stay here, do you really think Molly Klein will allow her grandchild to be raised on the lower East Side? And will I spend the rest of my days avoiding the Rabinowitzes and Avenue A? Who is going to be seen with the deserted wife?" I pulled Ma closer to me. "I have to go."

She looked back at the hats and nodded. "Maybe you should

get something like that? For your trip? Hats I can't sew. You will need some fine hats. You still have money, no?"

Money was no longer an issue for me. Not only did I still have the stash from Willie, safely nestled away, but he had given me a generous allowance to buy all we needed to take to Europe. And of course there were Mrs. Klein's store accounts. "I still have money, yes," I said.

"So you get a hat?"

I shook my head. As beautiful as the hat was, I could no longer spend money on frivolous things. "No," I said. "Someone once told me that a woman should always save a little something. Just in case."

Ma smiled. "A very wise someone, I think."

"Perhaps I'll find a little tin. Keep the money in it."

With genuine laughter, Ma and I left the window and continued our walk.

Rose

Wednesday, September 4

ZELDA, Linda, and Edith joined me and Dottie on our shopping trip, which was good because I could barely keep my eyes open. I didn't get a minute of sleep the night before, worrying about my poor Dottala after that dinner. What kind of man had she married?

"Look at this fabric," Zelda said, holding up a bolt of cotton dotted with tiny roses. The girls spoke Yiddish for my benefit.

"That pattern is too old-fashioned," Dottie said.

"What about this?" I asked, pointing to a pale cream chiffon covered with large orchids. I glanced at the *McCall's* in my hand. The pattern looked similar to the one in the pages.

"Yes, I like that."

I handed the bolt to Edith to take to the counter. Edith was hopeless when it came to choosing clothing and fabrics, but she was a horse of a girl, perfectly suited to hauling our finds.

We made our way through two more fabric stores plus J. W. Mays, Ohrbach's, and S. Klein. I showed Dottie how to look for quality: seams sewn in a single line, rather than the quicker double-needle stitch. Buttons applied with a cross-stitch. The pattern aligned where the bodice met the skirt.

The day should have been joyous, girls shopping for a friend's trousseau, but instead a pall hung over us; the laughs that day were forced. The way Linda fingered each fabric with such longing; the way Zelda eyed Dottie, already missing her; the way

Edith dragged her feet, out of place among the frilly dresses. The tone was more funereal than festive.

Zelda rubbed Dottie's back in a comforting way. "It *will* be an adventure. You'll see."

"But what am I going to *do*?" Dottie's voice was so plaintive, I could have cried.

Linda looked at her oddly. "What do you mean?"

"Willie will be writing." Dottie's fingers felt the material of a gabardine before she moved to the next. "I'll be home. Alone. No job."

"But you'll be busy keeping house." Linda's voice held bewilderment, and I wanted to hug that poor girl, too. "Keeping house" was all Linda wanted, and now Dottie—who had hoped for so much more—had that and didn't want it.

Dottie shook her head. "I know. It's just . . ." Her voice trailed off. She looked at Edith helplessly, then glanced at me. "I thought, after marriage, I'd be doing the accounts and keeping the books at . . ." Her voice trailed off. We all knew where she would have been keeping the books: at Abe's store.

"Being a wife and a mother is more important than working," Linda said, her voice almost scolding. She looked to me to agree, but I couldn't. Hadn't I wanted to be done with motherhood so I could get back to my own work?

"What if . . ." Edith leaned on a bolt of fabric, her elbow perched on the top and her hand on her chin. She disappeared a moment in thought.

We all looked at her expectantly.

"It's not bookkeeping," Edith said. "But the Joint Distribution Committee is desperate for volunteers in Europe to help with the refugees."

European refugees? What a worthy thing to do, but more importantly . . . Before I could even form the words in my mind, I said, "Yussel!"

The four looked at me, startled. More quietly, I said, "From

Europe, perhaps you could help Yussel. Or convince the JDC to help Yussel. Get him a visa. Or arrange for him to travel to the Baltics so he can leave for Palestine. Or . . . something."

"I don't know if that's something the JDC can do," Edith said. "Germany is the major concern at the moment." Seeing my face, though, she shrugged. "Though, maybe. Can't hurt to try."

Dottie nodded slowly, saying, "Yes, yes." A grin grew on her face. "I *could* help refugees. And maybe Yussel."

Linda's eyebrows drew together as she frowned. "That sounds dangerous."

But Dottie smiled at me. "No more dangerous than protesting the czar."

"You should be at home for Willie," Linda said.

"I can arrange for you to meet with my boss," Edith said. "He could give you a letter of introduction."

"I would appreciate that," Dottie said.

I looked at my baby. And proudly realized she was her mother's daughter.

I pulled a bolt of camel-colored wool. "This will make a lovely winter coat. Perfect for going to an office."

Dottie

WILLIE made the sounds that I'd learned indicated he was about to awaken. I thrust my book to the side table, and lay down, my back to him. He stirred and the next thing I felt were his fingers running up and down my side. They slipped to my front and cupped my breast. With a nibble on my neck, he rolled me over, and once again, we performed as husband and wife.

At least we had this.

TWO hours later, I was sitting with Ma in the apartment.

"You want the stitches to be even. What needle are you using?" Ma leaned over to peer at my work. "No, no. With the silk thread you should be using a sharp needle. That's a rounded one." She sorted through her basket till she found a different needle, which she handed to me.

I set down the dress. "This is hopeless. I'll never get it right."

"It's not hopeless. It just takes practice. In time, it will be second nature."

I looked around the front room, the room I'd wanted to change for so many years, and I tried to imprint it on my mind. I made note of every detail, every *tchotchke*, every book on the shelf. For so long, I'd yearned to escape this front room and now I wanted never to forget it.

"Stop dawdling and get back to work. You were right; I should have taught you years ago," Ma said. "Me and my foolish pride."

Picking up the dress, I worked on sewing in the strip of cloth that would allow it to expand. "Do you miss your home, Ma?"

Her eyes darted up, then quickly looked back to her work. She was doing the more delicate pieces that needed an expert hand.

"I miss my family. I miss *Shabbes* at home." She hesitated briefly, before saying, "I had a boy at home. Once in a blue moon, I miss him."

"A boy?" I continued with my sewing to disguise my surprise. Although later when I considered it, I didn't know why I'd been taken aback.

"Shmuel. He had fine blond hair and eyes like cornflowers. Went into the army. Never came back."

"Does *Tateh* know?"

She laughed. "Of course not. Secrets, remember?"

I laughed with her, but the sorrow that we were having these conversations now, right before I left, and wouldn't have them again, cut me with a new ache.

"Ma," I said, a fresh thought occurring. "What if I visited Bratsyana? See if Shmuel ever returned."

"Ow," she said, pulling her finger to her mouth. "Such a foolish idea, I stabbed myself."

She sucked on her finger for a moment, made sure she wasn't bleeding, and then went back to work. "Promise me you will never go there. That place is not fit for humans anymore, only dogs. I *don't* miss the pogroms and the hatred and the starvation. What the czar's army did to that place . . . Promise!"

"I promise, I promise."

"And besides, what if you did find Shmuel? That is over and done. You understand that?"

And I did. Someday, Abe would be my Shmuel, a memory. But for now, he was an open wound.

Softening, Ma put down her work, and looked me in the eye

with a mischievous twinkle. For the first time, I saw a glimpse of her not as she was at that moment, but as the girl she'd once been. I imagined she and I would have been great friends if we'd been young at the same time.

"I have another secret," she said.

I leaned into her. "What is it?" Both of our voices lowered to a hush.

She looked around, even though we were alone in the apartment. "You take this secret to your grave?"

"Cross my heart," I said.

"No crossing," she said, scolding like the ma I remembered. "That's *goyishe.*"

"Okay, I promise."

She leaned even closer until her mouth almost touched my ear. "I'm forty-two years old."

Now I *was* shocked. "I thought you were thirty-nine!"

She giggled as she *shhh*ed me.

"Pregnant at forty-two," I said.

Nodding her head, she said, "Let that be a lesson to you. The women of our family—my mother, my grandmother, may their memories be a blessing, me, *you*—the women of our family are made for childbearing."

We both returned to our stitches. She worked her way through her piece before I was even a third of the way through mine.

"So. Do you enjoy . . ." She searched for the words. "Being married? It is going all right?"

Blushing, I gathered her meaning. "That's the only part that's going all right."

She waited for me to continue.

I set aside my work. I couldn't concentrate on making even stitches. Ma had confided in me. It was time I confided in her. "He wants to give me a *get*. After I have the baby, he wants to divorce me."

Her silence, I assumed, came from horror.

"I'm going to make sure that doesn't happen." Desperation seeped from my voice, but I couldn't control it. "I promise, Ma. I'm going to do everything I can to make sure I don't disgrace you and *Tateh* any more than I have."

Ma looked at me oddly. My panic increased.

"I'm going to be the perfect wife. I'm going to sew and cook and make sure he never even hears the baby cry."

Slowly, Ma shook her head. "A *get*," she said. Her voice was soft. Thoughtful. She spoke again, more firmly. "A *get*. Why didn't I think of that?"

"What?" I spoke louder than I should have. I did not want to draw the attention of the neighbors.

"You go away. You have your baby. You get divorced. Is it ideal? No. But it is acceptable."

I must have heard her wrong. What mother thinks her child should get divorced? "I'd bring shame on the family! On myself! What would I do as a divorced woman with a child?" I worked hard to keep the screech out of my voice.

"People get divorced. It happens. It's not so bad. Remember Mrs. Cohen? *Oy*, that first husband of hers. A drunkard! And now she is happily married to Mr. Cohen and none the worse for wear. You get divorced. You come back home. We go to the matchmaker. She'll find you an older man. A widower, perhaps. Someone whose circumstances won't allow for a better match."

I stood up as if trying to escape that room, those ideas. "How in God's name is that better than being married to Willie?"

Ma grabbed me by the hands, pulling me closer to her, back into my seat. "Because then you will be home. You go to Europe now. You help the refugees. *Hashem* willing, you help Yussel. And then you come home. You will be off that continent, which is about to be consumed by war. You will be rid of that dummy who doesn't have enough sense to stay away from danger. You will be near me."

I began to cry. "Ma, I want to be near you. But I want my

marriage to work. I don't want to be divorced." Another failure. Another disgrace. "Ma, I'm going to stay married to Willie."

With a sigh, Ma picked her sewing back up. "If you say so. But at least you know: You have a way back home. With or without Willie, you can come home."

Rose

---❦---

Friday, September 6

MUCH needed to be done, but first things first. When I arose early on Friday morning, before I started the *challah*, before I began on Dottie's clothes, I sat at the kitchen table. With a piece of paper and a fountain pen I had taken from the credenza, I wrote a letter.

> *Dear Yussel,*
> *Dottie is coming.*

Dottie would get Yussel out of Europe. Of that I was sure. But that didn't mean Yussel couldn't watch out for Dottie in the meantime.

FOR the rest of the day, I sewed. All I could do was sew. I sewed her dresses, embroidered her collars, monogrammed her linens. Each stitch was an amulet, a bit of protection. It was all I could do for her now. Sew.

Sitting at the kitchen table, I had yardage of wool to make a coat for Dottie, one that would last through her pregnancy. If I were near to her, I'd simply let it out every month. If I were near, I'd do so many things.

A knock at the door startled me. I expected Dottie, but she

didn't knock. Perle too would simply bound in at this hour. Sweet Perle, who ran errands for me, jumping up for thread when I ran short, for needles the moment one broke.

Pushing the fabric to the side, I hauled myself up from the table. No leg twinges, no abdomen pain. I was back to my normal self.

The knock came again. A male voice called out something, but I couldn't understand him.

"Excuse me?" I said, opening the door.

A man in a uniform, holding a toolbox and odd equipment, stood there. In English, he said, "Bell Telephone, ma'am. I'm here to install your phone."

"My what?" I was dumbfounded, unsure of what he was doing.

He looked at his paper. "This the Krasinsky place? I got an order from a Ben Krasinsky for a phone."

A phone! With a laugh, I let him in. "A phone!"

Looking over the apartment with a critical eye, he asked, "Where do you want it?"

I pointed at the credenza. "Is good there."

The man went to work as I continued my sewing. Perhaps I wouldn't need the stitches as my amulets; I would have a phone. Didn't I read about transatlantic calls? They were possible. I was sure of it. If Dottie was truly in trouble, she could call her mama for help.

Though good stitches wouldn't hurt.

Dottie

Monday, September 9

IN our bed at the hotel we planned our day, as had become habit over the past week. Or rather, *I* planned the day. Willie's day consisted of going to his office and God-knows-what-else. He didn't keep me abreast of his schedule, just threw me tidbits here and there. I looked over the list I made.

"Your mother ordered monogrammed stationery for us. I'll pick that up this morning. And then I need to help my mother with my European wardrobe." Better to say "European" than "maternity." No need to remind Willie that I would soon be fat.

"Mm-hmm," Willie said, turning the page of the newspaper.

Glancing at the clock, I saw it was close to nine a.m., and I was antsy to start the day. "Willie." I put down my list and looked at my husband. *Husband.* The word still felt exotic. "Didn't you tell me you have a ten a.m. meeting with Mr. Ross?"

He glanced over the top of his *Tribune* toward the bedside clock. "Oh, good God, you're right." He leaped out of bed, downed the last of his room service coffee, and headed to the bathroom. I blushed as I watched him go; would I ever get used to seeing a naked man?

While he prepared for the day, I dressed in a skirt and blouse. Skirts were easier than dresses because I could leave the blouse untucked and the skirt unbuttoned. My belly wasn't that big yet, but I was bloated enough for dresses to be snug.

As I was brushing my hair, the hotel phone rang, startling me. Willie came out of the bathroom, wiping the remnants of shaving cream off his face, a towel around his waist, and he hurried to answer it. Who did he think it was? When he picked up the receiver, I watched his face change from concern to mirth. "Hey, Edie," he said. "Calling to gossip with the new Mrs. Klein? Hang on." He held the phone out to me.

I took the receiver. "Hello?"

"Hi, Dottie, it's Edie."

Hearing her voice on the tinny line was strange. Never, in all our years, had we ever spoken on the phone. "Edith, hi," I said, uncertainly.

"Listen, doll, can't talk, but you have an appointment to see my boss, Mr. Bechoff, at noon. Can you make it?"

"Yes!" I said, my eyes darting nervously to Willie. I hadn't mentioned my idea to him yet, didn't want to upset him when it wasn't a certainty. "I'll be there."

"Great," Edith said. "When you get here, ask for him. I put in a good word for you."

"I can't tell you how much I appreciate this. Thank you, Edith."

Hanging up the phone, I was aware of Willie's eyes on me. "That was too fast for any good gossip. What was she calling about?" he asked.

Smoothing my skirt, I turned to look at him, putting on what I hoped was a charming smile. "I had the idea I might volunteer with the Joint Distribution Committee when we're in Europe." Noting the look on his face, I hurriedly added, "I would of course make sure it doesn't interfere with my taking care of our home. But I thought it might be good for me to not be idle. Edith has made an appointment for me to meet with her supervisor today."

He pursed his lips. "The Joint Distribution Committee?" He nodded his head, agreeing with some unspoken thought. "The JDC. That would be . . ." He looked at me and smiled. "That would be aces!"

"What?" I said. This was not the response I had expected.

"If you work for the Joint, you'll have access to refugees and all kinds of information. You'll be an incredible source! This is a fantastic idea," he repeated. "What time is your appointment? I'd like to join you."

"Noon," I said hesitantly, unsure about this turn of events. Dared I be hopeful?

"I'll meet you in front of the JDC at five to noon."

"All right."

He threw on his suit and, within moments, looked the crisp, handsome professional man. Looking at him made me long to touch him, but I knew he had to leave. "You better hurry. You'll be late for your meeting."

Willie grabbed his briefcase and headed for the door, before turning back. "Thank you," he said. "You're a handy little schedule keeper." Taking me in his arms, he gave me a deep kiss that I felt in my stomach. It was the first time he'd kissed me like that when it wasn't for show or as a prelude to making love. This was a kiss of affection just because. "I'll see you close to noon." He rubbed his nose against mine before leaving.

As the door shut, I put my finger on my lips, trying to hold on to that kiss.

AT ten to noon, I stood in front of the JDC, nervous that Willie would be late. But at exactly five minutes to noon, he came bounding up the sidewalk.

"Are you ready?" he asked, placing an arm around my waist.

"Absolutely," I said, even though I was buckling-at-the-knees nervous. This simple interview now held the weight of my marriage.

Walking into the foyer, I gave my name and asked to see Mr. Bechoff. We were led into a cramped office, with wooden chairs and a desk covered in files.

"Mr. Bechoff is finishing another meeting and will be with you momentarily," the secretary said, before exiting.

Two chairs in front of the desk were piled high with papers. Willie had no compunction about picking up the folders, sliding them to the floor, and taking a seat. Unsure of what etiquette required, I remained standing. I walked around the small office, looking at the binders in bookcases and the loose papers scattered on the desk. One contained a sheet of numbers, seemingly a list of donations. My eye immediately flew down the page. The total was wrong.

The door burst open and in scurried a balding man, round about the waist, but containing the shadows of what must have been a handsome youth. Willie stood as he entered.

"Sit, sit," the man said, taking the papers from the second chair. "You're Edith's friend? Mrs. Klein?"

He slid around the desk and plopped in the seat.

"Yes, Mr. Bechoff. I appreciate your taking this meeting."

"Who's that?" he said, nodding toward Willie.

Willie proffered an outstretched hand. "William Klein, sir."

"Right, right. Mr. Klein. Okay, so what am I meeting you about?" His eyes were cast toward the sheet of numbers and he tapped a pencil on it repeatedly.

"My husband and I will be moving to Europe at the end of this week, and I was hoping to procure a position helping refugees with the JDC."

That got his attention. "You're moving *to* Europe?"

"Yes, sir," I said. I gripped my clutch tightly.

"You know we're trying to get people *out* of Europe. Going *to* Europe is the very definition of insanity."

I looked nervously at Willie, but he smiled and nodded at me. "My husband is a writer for *The New Yorker*, and he will be writing about the political situation in Europe. He wants to raise awareness of the threat of National Socialism, not only to Jews, but to all of Europe. I thought that while I was there, I'd make myself useful."

Mr. Bechoff tented his hands, placing his index fingers on his chin. He looked more closely at Willie. "Foreign correspondents are being expelled from Germany, you are aware?"

"I am," Willie said, "which is why we will begin in Paris and see where we are able to go from there."

Mr. Bechoff released his fingers and said, "Please make sure to stay in touch with the Joint. You might be of use to us as well."

"And what about volunteer work for me?" I asked, trying to keep the desperation from my voice. This was about my future, not Willie's.

"Yes, we are in grave need of help. People who can distribute food and clothing, provide minor medical treatment until nurses are available. Most definitely."

Out of the corner of my eye, I saw Willie grinning. This was better than I had hoped. "That sounds wonderful, Mr. Bechoff. I am delighted to serve the JDC until the baby comes."

Mr. Bechoff's eyes widened and he leaned back in his chair. "You're expecting?" His voice acquired a whining tone. "No, no. This is physical work. We cannot have an expectant woman working with the refugees."

I glanced at Willie and saw disappointment plain upon his face. Panic overtook me and my voice came out shrill. "I'm sure I can handle it! I'm quite fit."

Mr. Bechoff stood to show us out. "It's not proper. It wouldn't reflect well upon the JDC to have a—a woman such as that in the field."

Willie and I stood, and I fought back tears. My one hope for work. Gone.

"I apologize, Mr. Bechoff, for wasting your time. Thank you for meeting with me."

He walked us to the door, when I remembered the sheet on his desk. "Mr. Bechoff, if I may be so bold, before we go, I noticed an error on your tally sheet."

Mr. Bechoff halted his step. "What?"

I was sure he'd chastise me for prying, but I couldn't let it go unsaid. It was an affront to my numbers. "Here, look."

Mr. Bechoff returned to stand behind his desk, and I moved next to him. "This says you are forecasting a six percent increase in donations. Yet, here"—I pointed to a number in the middle of the page—"you've multiplied by point six, which is actually sixty percent." My finger slid down to the total. "Giving you the wrong projection."

"I thought the number was high," Mr. Bechoff said.

"You need to multiply by point zero six, so the actual total is . . ." I looked off so as to see the numbers more clearly in my mind. I mumbled to myself, "Let's see, $5,365 times point zero six is . . ." I realized my fingers were waving a bit in the air as I carried numbers from column to column. Looking back to Mr. Bechoff, I said, "It's $321.90. Plus $5,365 is . . . a total of $5,686.90 for next year."

Mr. Bechoff, working the calculation with pencil and paper, feverishly scribbled for a few minutes before looking up, astonished. "You're correct!" He looked at me carefully, as if I were hiding a tabulating machine somewhere on my body. "How did you do that?"

Willie stood at the door, evaluating me silently.

"I'm excellent with numbers, sir."

He waved his hand and said, "Sit back down, please. What do you mean by 'excellent'?"

Smoothing the back of my skirt, I returned to the other side of the desk and took my seat again. "Top of my class in mathematics in high school. Head bookkeeper at Dover Insurance." I hesitated, but thinking I had nothing to lose at this point, I said, "My plan is to study accounting."

No one asked *when*, to my great relief. Willie had his head cocked, and his eyes were penetrating. My hands shook.

"Can you type?" Mr. Bechoff asked.

"Forty words a minute," I said.

Mr. Bechoff switched to Yiddish. "Can you speak Yiddish reasonably well?"

Without missing a beat, I responded in Yiddish, "I am American born, but Yiddish was my first language. I speak it as comfortably as I speak English."

Willie looked between the two of us, confused.

Smiling, I added, still in Yiddish, "My husband, however, doesn't understand a word."

Mr. Bechoff raised his eyebrows. "And he is going to report on Jewish refugees?"

"I will help him."

Switching back to English, Mr. Bechoff said, "The Paris JDC office needs a secretary. It's not accounting, mind you. But they need someone who can speak to both the English-speaking donors and the incoming refugees. Typing and minor bookkeeping are part of the job. It doesn't pay much—twelve dollars a week—but it's necessary work, and something you can do while you're in the family way, especially as they are having a difficult time filling the position. Do you want the job?"

A quick glance at Willie's pleased smirk, and I said, "Yes, sir. Absolutely."

Mr. Bechoff stood again, but in a more kindly manner, and said, "You leave for Europe when?"

"This Thursday," I said.

"Time is of the essence, then. Can you return in an hour and pick up a letter of introduction from my secretary? I'll wire the Paris office and let them know of your imminent arrival."

"Thank you, Mr. Bechoff!" I didn't try to disguise the relief in my voice.

"Make me look good for recommending you," he said.

"Of course, sir," I said.

"And," he added, looking from me to Willie and back, "keep

your wits about you. It's a dangerous time for a Jew to be in Europe. Be safe."

"Of course," Willie said, as he led me from the office.

ON the sidewalk, I turned to face Willie straight on. He took me by the waist, lifted me, and spun me around. Despite my growing girth, I was light in his arms and I wanted him to spin me forever. But he set me down, laughing, and said, "That was marvelous!"

Giggling, I let myself be a happy newlywed.

"That couldn't have turned out better," he continued. "Look, there's a diner across the street. Let's get lunch before I have to hurry back to the office and you have to go back for your letter."

Opening the door to the tiny shop, I was relieved to see a KOSHER sign in the window. I knew once we were in Europe— once we were on the ship, in fact—*treif* would be unavoidable. But I'd deal with it when the time came.

We took a seat, and Willie ordered us both coffees and a corned beef sandwich for himself. I asked for the *kishkes*.

"So," Willie said, taking my hands in his. My first instinct was to pull them away, but then I remembered, *This is my husband.* Holding hands in public was permitted.

"So," I said back with a smile.

"I had no idea you were good with numbers."

Shrugging, I said, "Why would you? There's not much call for arithmetic at the Second Avenue café or at Camp Eden."

Chuckling, he said, "True, true."

When the coffee came, I was sorry, because it meant Willie had to pull his hands back to make room for the cups. His hands had felt nice on mine.

"This job will be a boon for us," Willie said. "You'll be privy to all sorts of information. You'll be my best source."

Pleased, I sipped the coffee. "I'm looking forward to it. I'll be doing charitable work and earning an income." As soon as the words left my mouth, I regretted them. "Not that we need my income, of course."

Willie laughed. "Do you think my masculinity depends on my wife not working? If the job works out, perhaps we'll use that money to hire a girl to watch the baby once he's born."

Startled, I sloshed my coffee.

"Are you opposed? I mean, of course you *can* quit when the baby is born, but it seems a shame to lose valuable contacts because of a child."

On the one hand, he saw the child as an impediment, and it was hard to envision someone else taking care of my baby. On the other hand, this was the first time he had alluded to us as a married couple after the baby was born. Divorce wasn't on his mind. As long as I remained a source of information for Willie, he'd want to keep me around. The work did sound exciting. And if the precedent was set of having a girl watch the baby, perhaps one could continue to do so when we returned to America and I *could* study accounting. Shaking my head slightly, I had to remember not to get ahead of myself. One step at a time.

"Why don't we see what happens when the baby comes?" I said. "Who knows what Europe will be like and where we'll be?" I tried to imply that if we weren't in Paris, perhaps we'd be in London or Amsterdam, when really I was hoping we'd be back in New York.

"Yes, of course." Willie added, "But a possibility?"

Setting my cup down, I placed my hand on Willie's. "A definite possibility."

Willie's tone took on a dreamy quality. "I'll write brilliant exposés with the inside dope you bring me." He paused for a moment, listening to the chatter at the next table. Leaning in, he whispered, "Listen. The Germans are everywhere. Do you hear that couple at the next table?"

I glanced over and saw a couple, not much older than us,

looking at the menu in seeming confusion. They sat stiffly, and it was clear from their movements that they were greenhorns.

"Do you think they're talking about Nazis?" Willie whispered.

I listened to the man and woman briefly and patted Willie's hand. "They're a real threat to democracy! Discussing whether they should just split a pastrami sandwich or splurge and also order chicken soup." I laughed, but stopped quickly as Willie sat back hard in his seat. What did I say to upset him?

The food arrived. Self-consciously, I cut my *kishke*. "Aren't you going to eat?" I asked Willie, who was still sitting back, staring at me. I nibbled at my food.

"You don't actually speak German, do you?" he said slowly. "You were guessing at what they said."

"You're right. I don't speak German." I took the napkin and dabbed the corners of my mouth.

Willie looked crestfallen.

"But," I said, taking another bite, "I understand a good deal of German."

He perked up again. "How do you mean?"

"You know that Yiddish and German are similar. I'm helpless if I have to *speak* German, but I can usually make out some—not all, mind you—of what's said."

"Can you read a German newspaper? Eavesdrop on conversations?"

"I won't get every word, but, yes, I can."

Willie looked as if he had won a prize. "Well, isn't that something? What an asset you're turning out to be."

Willie couldn't stop smiling, and it was contagious. Picking up his sandwich, he said, "I think bringing you to Europe is the best idea I've ever had!"

I prayed the feeling would keep.

Rose

---✟---

Wednesday, September 11

MY fingers were raw with all the sewing, but Dottie's wardrobe would be first-class.

"Ma," Dottie said, "you've done enough."

I ignored her. "Dottala, move that light closer to me." I strained to see the grain of the fabric.

Picking up the lamp, Dottie tried to angle it in such a way to shed more brightness, but it did little good. "Ma, I have plenty. Stop working."

"A little more won't hurt," I said. My voice was gruff, but it had to be. Nothing would be simpler than crawling into bed and mourning the loss of my baby girl. Nothing would be easier than succumbing to the ache that reminded me of losing Joey, of the miscarriages, of the dear soul that had departed only two weeks ago. Sewing required enough concentration that it kept the images from invading my head, images of my daughter, alone in Europe, becoming a mother without me. It was easier to stay up all night than to sleep, where nothing could keep the dreams away.

I nodded toward the credenza. "You will take Yussel's last letter? It has his address and his plans, so you can use it to assist him."

Dottie took the letter and placed it in her clutch. "I will keep this safe with me the entire time, Ma. I promise I will do whatever I can to get him out of Europe."

My daughter made me so proud. It was difficult to contain

my emotions, but I didn't want another evening to dissolve into tears. "I've taken the rest of the money from the tin," I told her, "and sewn it into the lining of your suitcase."

She started to protest. "But you could use that money for Izzy's schooling or save it for when Yussel comes—" I cut her off. "It's for your return trip. Promise me if anything goes wrong, you'll be on the next boat back. No hesitations. You and the baby. If Willie wants to come, fine. This isn't enough for a third-class ticket, but if you start to save right away, you'll soon have enough to get you back to New York."

"Money isn't going to be a problem for me. Willie's allowance may seem small to him, but it's enough for us to live in luxury."

"I know," I said. "But you know it doesn't hurt to have a stash on the side. Just for you and the baby. Enough for you to come home."

"I will keep it, just in case," Dottie said. "But understand, I don't want to come home. I am going to make my marriage work."

"Then you'll make it work." Considering a moment, I said, "In some ways, Willie reminds me of your *tateh*."

Dottie's eyes widened. "How?"

"Your *tateh* was a hothead. Passionate about that union work as your Willie is about reporting." I smiled, reminiscing. "But I convinced your father to be sensible. He still attends union meetings, works himself into a lather occasionally, but he's no longer putting himself in danger. Remember, women make the decisions. We just can't let the men know it."

Dottie chuckled.

"Oh," I said, remembering. "The phone! You remember our phone number?"

"Yes, Ma. Tompkins 64562." Her voice was soft enough to alarm me, to make me look up from my needle.

"Dottala, you will be fine. I know it."

Her voice broke as she asked, "Ma, how will I do this?"

I don't know, I wanted to say. *You shouldn't. You should stay*

*right here with your mama, where you'll be safe and I'll take care of
you and the baby.* But that wasn't the right thing to say. So I did
the best I could. "You just do it. You cannot think about it too
much. You just act." I returned to my sewing, my hand moving up
and down rhythmically. My motion was as smooth as any machine.
"It's like prayer," I said. "You say the words over and over whether
you feel the prayer or not. And then, in those rare quiet spaces,
suddenly the prayer embraces you, and you see the truth of it. We
do the actions and hope for the meaning. Sometimes it comes
sooner. Sometimes we have to wait for it. But we keep praying.
We keep doing." I looped the thread into a knot. "You go with
Willie. You raise your son or daughter. You will find the meaning."

Dottie slid her knees to her chest and wrapped her arms
around them. "What if I don't?"

I shrugged. "Then you don't. But still you must *live.*" I looked
my Dottala in the eyes, those big sad eyes. "You will always have
your mama and your *tateh* here. Remember that. Let it keep you
strong."

Picking up a collar I wanted to embroider, I squinted. "Ah,
my eyes are too old for such small work."

"Your work is as beautiful as ever, Ma."

"You should have seen what it was like twenty years ago." I
glanced at Dottie again, and she looked so forlorn. I thought
about the night before I'd left home, lying in my bed, holding
tight to Eta. My knowledge of the New World consisted of bits
and pieces from my brother Heshie's letters. I can still feel our
hard straw mattress, the warmth of the down comforter, the
sweet smell of Eta's skin; as terrified as I was, I also felt like my
real life was about to begin, and it was thrilling. Dottie must be
feeling the same way.

I set down the work and walked over to the credenza. Without hesitation, I picked up two of my four *Shabbes* candlesticks
and turned to my daughter. "Take these with you."

She startled. "How can I take your candlesticks?"

"I'm giving you two. I will keep the other two. You'll need them. To make *Shabbes* wherever you are. You will have a piece of me when you are gone. When you light the candles, you'll think of me lighting mine. And when you return to America, I will give you the rest of the candlesticks. Because when you come back to America, we will both be complete."

I saw Dottie begin to tear up. "I don't need anything to remind me of you. I will think of you every day."

"Of course you will. And I will hold you in my heart. But how nice to think of each other as we usher in *Shabbes*."

She hesitated. "Willie doesn't make *Shabbes*."

"So you'll do it after he's left for the evening. You'll do it for your child." I smiled at her. "At this point, what's one more secret?"

Taking the candlesticks in her hands as if they were gold, she smiled. "Another secret won't hurt."

Moving back to the couch, I said, "Hand me the green thread." When she brought it over, I glanced up, and caught sight of the clock. "*Ach!* Don't you need to meet your friends?" Her final night in New York, it was important she see all that she was leaving behind. It would give her all the more reason to come back.

"I should stay here with you," Dottie said.

"No." I stitched the leaves. "You go have a night of fun."

"I want to stay with you, Mama." Dottie's eyes started to tear up.

"Oh, *bubelah*," I said, putting aside my work. I didn't know if she meant tonight or always. I stood and gave her a kiss on her cheek, holding her arms in my hands. "Don't stay here with an old woman. Go out. Be with your friends." I looked her deeply in the eyes. "Remember, you must *live*."

And with that, I pushed her out the door, before she could protest anymore.

Dottie

—⚭—

IF I could have, I would have stayed with Ma. But as much as I didn't want to leave the house, I would have been devastated to get on that boat without saying a proper good-bye to my friends, without having one last night out with the girls. I met them at the café on Second Avenue, the place that in my previous life had been all about fun and romance and being with friends. But now, as a married woman, about to sail away from every person and every thing I ever knew and cared about, the café seemed as inviting as a slaughterhouse.

The solemnity of the occasion was proved by Zelda, making a rare appearance on a weeknight. With a forced smile, I fished for inanities about which to chatter. Was it really less than a month ago I'd sat here with Abe, caring only about my job at Dover Insurance and what fashions I could buy with my salary? Now at the same table, Edith and Linda gave me sidelong glances, unsure of what to say.

"Ah, baloney," Zelda said, breaking the silence. "This is a send-off. Where's the cheer? This is exciting!"

"Sure it is, sweetie," Edith said. Her smile was strained.

Linda was still sweet Linda, but now that Ralph was gone, she was already starting to develop a crust, an edge of bitterness that was unattractive. I knew of women who ended up alone, how hard they became, angry at the world. I hoped Linda would avoid that fate. After all, Edith didn't seem unhappy.

The door to the café opened, and I startled. But it was a group of high school girls out for a romp.

Zelda placed a hand on mine. "I checked. He'll be at the store all night."

"Of course," I said, both relieved and disappointed. I knew I'd crumble at the sight of Abe, but that didn't stop me from longing for a final glance of the man who I had thought was my *beshert*. But he wasn't, was he? My fate was different from what I expected. I needed to accept it.

"So what's your plan?" Edith asked.

Pray until I mean it, I thought. "We're going to Paris. From there, he may travel, but I'll be staying put so I can work at the JDC."

"At least Paris is safe," Edith said. "Haven't you read about the restrictions being placed on Jews in Germany? He wouldn't go there, would he?"

"He will go where the story is," I said, trying to show a confidence I didn't have.

"Aren't you worried?" Linda asked.

I looked from Linda to Edith to Zelda and back to Linda before admitting, "Terrified."

"Aw, sweetie," said Zelda. "Focus on the good. Like, how do you like married life?" Her tone and wagging eyebrows left no doubt about what she meant. I was grateful for the change of subject.

"Zelda!" Linda said. "That's private."

"Oh, why can't we talk about it?" Zelda said. "Don't be so old-fashioned!"

For the first time that night, my smile was genuine. "I had no idea it would be so . . ." How to describe the sensations? Words couldn't do justice. "So exhilarating."

"They don't teach you *that* in school, do they?" said Zelda.

"Really that good?" Edith asked.

"Divine. Truly divine. No matter what else happens, we have that."

Everyone nodded, trying not to think about what could happen in Europe.

"I still worry," Edith said.

"We are going to do amazing work in Europe," I said, feeling defiant, "and return as heroes."

Linda held up her beer. "To Dottie and Willie. May your 'for better or worse' be far better than worse. *L'chaim!*"

FOR my last night in New York, I decided to sleep at home, although it worried me to leave Willie by himself. Things had been going so well for us, and he hadn't brought up divorce since our wedding night, but I didn't know what he might get up to if left to his own devices. However, as of tomorrow, it would be just the two of us. For six months, we'd have only each other and then we'd have our child. My last night, I wanted to be with my family.

When I returned to the apartment, Ma was still sewing, sitting on the couch.

"Go to sleep," I said.

"I'm almost done," she said. "But you. You need your sleep. I will clear the sofa for you." She started to stand and move to the table.

"No, don't." I looked around the room, the room that had been my bedroom for so many years. Nothing about it resembled a proper bedroom—this was our living room, after all—but it had been mine. Tonight, though, I didn't want to be alone. "I'm going to sleep in the boys' room."

She sat back down.

I slid off my dress and slipped on the nightgown that Ma had pulled out of her room, so as not to disturb *Tateh*. It was old, one not worthy of a married woman, but was well-worn and smooth on my skin. I would miss this nightgown. I turned to go into the other room, but a thought occurred to me. "Ma?"

"Yes?"

"You'll take care of Eugene for me. Won't you?"

She was about to speak, perhaps reprimand me for my insolence, but instead she pursed her lips and nodded. "Of course.
Sweet dreams, my *bubelah*."

"Sweet dreams, Ma."

In the boys' room, I spied Izzy asleep on the mattress on the
floor, and Alfie and Eugene curled up in the bed. I slid between
the two. They stirred momentarily. I looked at them, wondering
when I would see them again. "I'm going to miss even you, Alfie,"
I whispered, tousling his hair.

"I guess I'll miss you, Dottie," he said sleepily.

I smiled and rolled over to my Eugene. Slipping my hand over
his body, I pulled him close to me. "I love you, Eugene, more
than anything in this world." He was fast asleep, but I hoped the
words would sink in, that he'd hear them inside, that he'd know
I wasn't abandoning him.

Staring at the rise and fall of his chest, I was certain I'd be
awake all night, but soon I was lost in a fitful sleep.

Rose

—⚷—

Thursday, September 12

WE were a somber group traveling to the harbor. Ben went first with the luggage in a truck borrowed from a neighbor who made deliveries. We piled in Dottie's trunks and suitcase, the same suitcase we'd given her when she was fifteen and started going to Camp Eden. Ben offered to buy her a new one, something to complement the fancy matched pieces I knew the Kleins would have. But she insisted on this beat-up case.

At breakfast we ate and stared at one another and started to speak but ended up talking over one another and then, ultimately, saying nothing. When the morning mail arrived, there was a letter from Yussel, but even that couldn't rouse me, and I set it aside to read that evening. I wanted nothing to distract me from my final moments with Dottie.

With time on our hands, we decided to walk to the harbor. Better than sitting and fretting. Besides, I wanted to stretch out our time together, be with Dottie for a bit longer. Not that there was much left to say; we just wanted to *be*. On the way down, she let me hold her hand.

And now, here we are at the ship, the SS *Manhattan*. These past weeks, with their ups and downs, have brought us here, to this moment, to this dock, staring down this hunk of metal that somehow manages to stay afloat. The pungent air, the behemoth vessel, the pandemonium of the ship crew: I close my eyes, and it's 1914 and I'm about to board for America. The trepidation overwhelms me, and I listen to the mishmash of voices. Even here in America, so many different languages trumpeting at once.

Dottie's voice interrupts my reverie. "There's Willie."

We move to the Kleins, but I feel as if I am floating. I know this is happening right now, but it doesn't seem possible, me saying good-bye to my baby girl. I speak as if through a cloth, my ears plugged with cotton. I greet the Kleins without any awareness of what I am saying. Molly dabs her eyes with a handkerchief. I wonder where my tears are.

That ship. Looming. It looks exactly the same as mine, although I know it is not. And Dottie is not the same as I was. Dottie is well fed, she's dressed fashionably, and she isn't destined for the bowels of the ship. First-class, my Dottala sails.

I try to focus on Willie, so stiff and regal. His clothes are stylish—what is the word Dottie likes to use? Snazzy? Next to Ben, who is in his work clothes so he can return to the garage, Willie looks like a movie star. No wonder Dottie was taken in.

Snippets of the conversation drift into my consciousness. "You promise you'll come back if things get worse," Molly says. My head feels as if it is full of ether, although I am not numb. I wish I were. *This* is the child I cannot lose. This is the child I *am* losing. *This* is the child I will mourn.

"Don't try to be a hero," Ira says. "And watch your wallet. Those Parisians are filthy crooks."

Ben has Dottie in an embrace. His words dance on the salt air. "Remember who you are. Remember what you are. We are Jews. We have made it through worse. And you can always come home. With or without Willie, you can always come home."

Alfie is asking for postcards, Eugene is whimpering, and I am bewildered, not sure how this is happening.

"We should board, Dottie," Willie says, glancing at his watch. She nods and then turns to us for a final time.

So much for me to say. But nothing for me to say. For perhaps the first time in my life, I stand mute. Dottie gives final hugs to the boys.

Izzy says, "Be safe."

Dottie says, "I will."

He leans into Dottie and I hear him whispering into her ear, "Be brave," before he pulls away. He wipes his eyes brusquely.

Alfie gives her a quick kiss on the cheek and a long squeeze. "Remember. Postcards of those French airplanes."

"I'll remember," Dottie says.

Eugene is next and he holds on for so long, I wonder if he plans on ever letting go. I should take him. I should pull him off. But part of me hopes if he holds on long enough, she will stay.

Dottie kisses his head and murmurs, "Now behave. I'll be back before you know it and I don't want to hear any reports." Finally, he releases her, his tears freely flowing, and Dottie is ready to take leave of her brothers.

At last, it is my turn. "Dottala," I say.

"Ma," she says.

I hug her. In that hug I put in everything I have, all my wishes for her, all my love, all my dreams. I try to press them into her as one final good-bye.

"You will do good," I whisper into her ear.

Her body trembles in my arms. She is on the verge, I can tell, and I hold my breath, hoping she will change her mind, hoping she will return to the apartment and raise her baby with me. But she pulls away and moves toward her husband.

"Good-bye," she says.

"God be with you, Dottala," I say. And now my tears are free. My body shakes, and Ben holds me, keeping me steady, keeping me from chasing after her.

Willie holds out an elbow for her to take. The porter has already carried up the luggage. They walk up the gangplank, the metal grates shaking beneath their feet. We are sobbing, all of us; even Alfie has tears streaming down his face.

They disappear into the metal monstrosity.

"We should go," Ben says gently, but I shake my head.

"I need to stay. Make sure she is safe." As if my gaze could protect her.

Ben and Alfie and Izzy leave, but Eugene stays behind with me. He curls into my side, as he used to with Dottie, and my arm goes around him. It feels natural. And right.

Eugene and I stand there for over an hour, waiting for our Dottie to change her mind, waiting for her to come running down the ramp and into our arms, waiting for her to come home with us.

With three blasts of the horn, the ship leaves port and sails out into the Atlantic.

Dottie

---❦---

Thursday, September 12

THE Statue of Liberty grows smaller and smaller as she shrinks from view. It occurs to me this is the opposite of what is supposed to happen; Lady Liberty was meant to welcome, to embrace, not to send off. I lean on the rail of the ship until she is completely gone from sight.

Four weeks ago I had my work, my family. Abe. Just four weeks. And here I am.

I am a married lady. Beginning my married life. With my married husband.

Our luggage awaits me in the cabin and needs to be unpacked. Before we left port, Willie decided he needed a drink and went off in search of the ship's bar. And being alone in that sardine can—even if it is a first-class sardine can—made my skin crawl, so I escaped to the deck to watch New York disappear from view. I didn't think it would go so quickly. I thought the city would linger on the horizon, but now there is only boundless water stretching on all sides.

I am a married lady.

We will arrive in Le Havre on September 18. Just seven days to travel 3,514 miles. That's 502 miles a day; 20.9 miles an hour. A third of a mile a minute.

I am a married lady.

The weight of my decision sits in my stomach. What have I

done? The water in front of me is not the blue of picture books. It is dark and roiling, nearly a black ink churning all around me. The sound of the ocean fills my ears and the salty air stings my eyes.

New York. It's all I know. I hadn't expected this longing, at least not this soon. The longing for my mother. For the boys. For Abe. Abe. Will he be the thought I hold on to in the middle of the night? I mourn for the political arguments, the squabbling over *pulkes* at the *Shabbes* table, the frustration at Abe's stubbornness. I mourn for nights at the café with Edith and Linda, for the Yiddish theater, for Ma's goose liver stew on a freezing winter night. I mourn for the afternoons gossiping with Zelda and the summer nights under the stars at Camp Eden. I mourn for Eugene's hot breath on my neck as he slept snugly next to me, for Alfie's clever mischief as he swindled coins from me, for Izzy's quiet determination.

But mourning is pointless. I have to remind myself, I am my mother's daughter. I will do what I need to do. Yes, I am married to a stranger. Yes, I am going to have a baby in a foreign land. Yes, I am about to embark on work that could risk my life as easily as it could save others. Yes, I am more afraid than I have ever been in my life. But I will do what I need to for this baby. It is what the women in my family do.

I am a mother.

Straining, I look for anything comforting, familiar, out over the ocean, but all I see is emptiness.

My hand brushes my head and I feel the mess my hair is becoming. With a last look, I turn to go back to the cabin. I had better unpack and fix my hair. It is time to join my husband.

ACKNOWLEDGMENTS

———— ⚜ ————

AS the saying goes, *Yedes vort oyf zayn ort*. Every word in its place. No two people did more to help each word fall into place than my agent, Laney Katz Becker, and my editor, Tracy Bernstein. Laney edited, critiqued, and read more rewrites than one would think possible, while cheering me on the whole way. Tracy is an editor extraordinaire, whose insightful ideas and deft edits brought greater depth to the world of Dottie and Rose. I am so grateful that I had both on my team.

I am also lucky to have my own *landsfroyen*, the fabulous women of my writing group who saw this story in its infancy and helped it grow into the fully formed novel it is today. Jennifer Davis-Kay, Sarah Endo, Sheryl Kaleo, Sarah Monsma, and Mary Rowen, you have my eternal thanks. Thank you to my other readers, Betsy Aoki, Estelle Berg, and Julia Schilling, who gave their thoughts and suggestions, correcting facts along the way (and any factual errors that remain are entirely my own).

A weekend seminar on historical fiction with Cam Terwilliger at Grub Street in Boston helped me germinate the idea. Thanks also to Katrin Schumann and Lynne Griffin of Grub Street's Launch Lab for helping me figure out what to do once the writing was done.

My friends have all proven to be incredible *menschen*. I owe a great deal to my morning running crew and our vaulted conversations.

And what would I have done without the women of Dallin, who provided me with laughs and lots of bourbon (and especially to Rosemarie Connell, who has plotted and planned even before the book was finished)? The Emunah gang, especially Linna Ettinger and Sharon Levin, have answered questions, planned my readings, and encouraged me the whole way. My fellow writers at the Debutante Ball—Aya de Leon, Abby Fabiaschi, Louise Miller, and Heather Young—have given me some of the best advice and support a writer could ask for.

And then there's my family. The words aren't there for the gratitude I have for my *mishpocheh*, my earliest of readers and my biggest of fans: my parents, Peter and Carol K. Brown, and my sister, Melissa Brown. I didn't always take their feedback happily, but I always took it, and the novel is the better for it. (And I didn't take any wooden pickles along the way.) With love, I thank you.

Finally, "thanks" isn't enough for Adam, Nathan, and Sadie Medros. This novel wouldn't exist without them. They encouraged me, supported me, and provided me with quiet writing time and gummy bears. This novel is as much theirs as it is mine. Adam, Nathan, and Sadie, *ikh hob aykh lib*!

Modern Girls

――――――❧――――――

JENNIFER S. BROWN

A CONVERSATION WITH
JENNIFER S. BROWN

Q. *What was the inspiration for* Modern Girls?

A. As the self-appointed family historian, I've begged relatives to tell me stories every time we gather. In days of yore, I'd whip out an old-fashioned cassette player to record what they had to say; these days I merely pull out my iPhone's voice recorder. A number of years ago, my father casually said, "Your great-grandmother had an unwanted pregnancy." I was shocked that not only did she have one, but that it was common knowledge in the family. Unfortunately, by this point my grandmother (her daughter) had died, so I needed to fill in the details with my imagination. Why would a married woman in those days not want a child? What were the options open to women? What if she'd been unmarried? All those "what ifs" led to Dottie and Rose.

Q. *What kind of research did you do?*

A. The first thing I did was return to those cassette tapes and try to understand how my family lived, how they behaved, what they believed. I wanted to get a sense of the time. Some details I shamelessly stole: the names Rose and Ben came from my own great-grandparents; another ancestor was trampled by a horse at a protest in Ukraine; many of my family members were Socialist. Yet the story itself is complete fiction.

The next step was to read about the time period, in both nonfiction and fiction. Many wonderful books helped shaped the world I was creating: *World of Our Fathers* by Irving Howe, *Bread Givers* by Anzia Yezierska, *A Bintel Brief: Sixty Years of Letters from the Lower East Side to the Jewish Daily Forward* by Isaac Metzker, *Call It Sleep* by Henry Roth, *The Rise of David Levinsky* by Abraham Cahan, and *In My Mother's House* by Kim Chernin, among others.

Finally, a trip to New York helped me solidify my facts. At the New York Public Library, I accessed *New Leader*, a Socialist newspaper, to understand the issues of the day. I also looked at transportation maps from the 1930s to learn how Dottie would have gotten around. A visit to the Tenement Museum helped me picture what Yetta's apartment would have looked like when Rose first arrived in America.

Q. *While the Lower East Side of New York is familiar territory for many people, Camp Eden is not. Was Camp Eden a real place?*

A. Socialist camps for Jewish adults were not uncommon in the 1930s, the most famous being Camp Tamiment in Pennsylvania. Camp Eden was another such camp, beginning in the late 1920s, although by the late 1940s, it was primarily a children's camp. I knew about Camp Eden because my grandparents met there, but I could find no information on it, so I made up details about what it was like based on family photos. I was thrilled when, later reading the Socialist paper *New Leader*, I found articles about the camp, and much of what I had written was not far off base (although some is complete fiction; that's what novelists do when we don't know something—we make it up). Wonderful ads appeared touting the benefits of the camp, and I loved the ones that read: "Where the Spirit of Comraderie [sic] Prevails" and "Special Rates for Party Members."

Q. *Do you have a set writing routine?*

A. My best writing days are the ones on which I've had a long morning run. I find a good run clears my mind and prepares me for the day. I can work just about anywhere, and I do. At home, I sit on the living room couch with the computer on my lap. I'm a regular at my local café when I need a change of scenery. My town's library has a gorgeous reading room built in 1892, which makes me feel like I'm in another time period.

I'm fortunate that I don't need silence to write. I've been known to write out ideas while sitting in a roomful of noisy kids while waiting for my daughter's dance class to end or on the sidelines of the soccer field. If I feel a need to tune out the noise, I have playlists of music popular in the time period I'm writing about to help give me a better feel for what my characters would be listening to.

Q. *What are you working on now?*

A. More historical fiction! It's a little early for too many details, but I'm knee-deep in research on Prohibition and the Hebrew Orphan Asylum, with a dash of World War II history (in particular about returning soldiers) thrown in.

QUESTIONS FOR
DISCUSSION

1. *Modern Girls* focuses on a Jewish immigrant family during the Depression. Do you think that Rose and Dottie could as easily have been Irish or Italian or another immigrant ethnicity? Why or why not? If the story were set today, with a modern-day immigrant family, might the story be different?

2. Dottie's friends have different ideas on what marriage should be. What did marriage mean in 1935? How has the definition of marriage changed?

3. Traditions—keeping kosher, lighting *Shabbes* candles, having a *chuppah* at her wedding—are important to Dottie, and she can't imagine her life without them. What traditions would you have a hard time breaking? Do you believe in the values behind those traditions or do you maintain them simply because that's what your family has always done?

4. Both Rose and Dottie have definitive ideas about what makes them modern women. Do you identify with their conceptions of modern? Does holding on to tradition and "old-world" ideas make them less modern in your eyes?

5. Rose thinks Willie is a fool for wanting to travel to Europe at such a dangerous time; Edith admires him for his commitment

to journalism and politics. What do you think of his decision? If you were Dottie, would you have gone with him?

6. Eugene spent a year and a half of his life with his aunt, and Rose feels that Eugene is a stranger to her. With Dottie gone, how do you think Rose and Eugene will fare? What do you see for Eugene's future?

7. Many themes are touched on in this novel: motherhood, family, assimilation, immigration, the rights of women and workers. Which most resonated with you?

8. Rose changed her name and her age as she shed her past life to become an American. If you could start anew, what would you change?

9. How much does the place where you live affect how you think of yourself? Are place and identity linked?

10. Dottie's future is uncertain when the story concludes. What do you think will come of her marriage? What will her future bring?

Photo by Jim Pogozelski

Jennifer S. Brown has published fiction and creative nonfiction in *Fiction Southeast, The Best Women's Travel Writing, The Southeast Review, The Sierra Nevada Review,* and *The Bellevue Literary Review,* among other places. Her essay "The Codeine of Jordan" was selected as a notable essay in *The Best American Travel Writing* in 2012. She holds an MFA in creative writing from the University of Washington.

CONNECT ONLINE

jennifersbrown.com
twitter.com/j_s_brown

APR 0 0 2016